"No man has ever dominated me, not even my father or my fiancé, so why should I change for you?"

Raveneau's eyes registered astonishment, irritation, and even a flicker of amusement. Then, they took on the narrowed canniness of a bird of prey preparing to capture a delicious prize, and Devon shivered in ecstatic anticipation.

His dark hands encircled her waist with practiced skill and Devon melted. The pleasure was too intensely glorious to be denied; it surpassed anything that she had ever felt in her life, save their first kiss in Nick's carriage. She revelled in his touch, molded herself to it . . .

Raveneau's mouth was firm against hers, demanding that her lips yield. He kissed her with deft tenderness, gauging her response intuitively so that she was moaning as he progressed from the first soft touch to a kiss of such depth that Devon went faint and limp . . .

Also by Cynthia Wright
Published by Ballantine Books:

CAROLINE

TOUCH THE SUN

SILVER STORM

Cynthia Challed Wright

BALLANTINE BOOKS • NEW YORK

For
STAR HELMER,
my laughing friend,
with love and appreciation

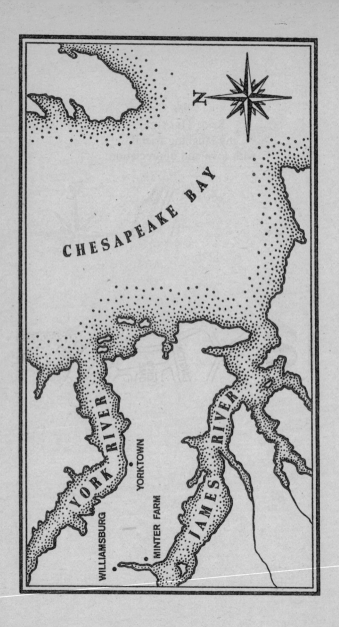

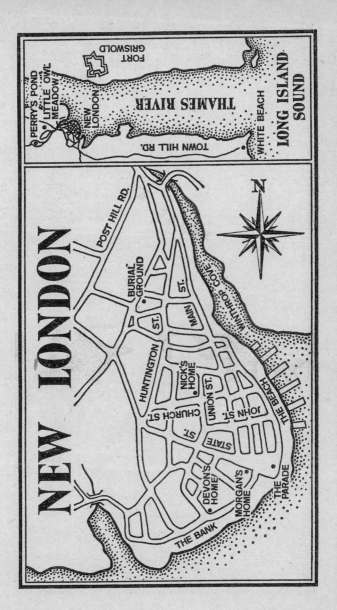

Chapter One

———◆———

April 20, 1775

THE afternoon sun hung high above the tiny Linen
and Pewter Shop, hinting at the summer to come,
while inside the narrow building the heat was exaggerated by quiet. There had been only two customers
all day.

Deborah Lindsay sat in a worn ladder-back chair
near the doorway in a wide beam of sunlight. Her
fingers, rough but still delicately shaped, worked
quickly at the large piece of white netting spread
across her lap. When completed, the embroidered
canopy would bring a fine price, but Deborah's face
was pinched with worry all the same; anxiety had
pressed tiny creases into her thin countenance. No
one would describe her as pretty now, though not so
long ago her blond loveliness had turned heads on
every street.

Her eyes burned. Blinking, she glanced up at
Devon, her twelve-year-old daughter. Typical! The
girl stood at the other end of the shop, polishing-cloth
and pewter bowl in her motionless hands, gazing out
the small window toward the Thames River.

Just like her father! Deborah seethed, blaming
Hugh more than Devon, though she felt guilty about

1

harboring such bitter feelings for a dead man. Had it been only sixteen years ago that Hugh Lindsay had turned her world upside down? Daughter of one of the wealthiest shopowners in Boston, Deborah could have married any man. Hugh, a successful young sea captain, had dined at her family's home and captivated her with tales of adventure and far-off places. They were married within a month, then he kissed her goodbye and sailed off to the West Indies.

It wasn't long before the stars in Deborah's eyes began to dim. Hugh was a handsome, magnetic man, but his first love was the sea and she could never hope to compete with it. They moved to New London, and within five years she gave birth to two beautiful children. Her son Jamie was her one delight, for he seemed to take after her. He was blond, sweet-tempered, considerate of her feelings, and comforted her during the lonely years when Hugh was only an occasional visitor in his own home.

Devon, the younger child, brought Deborah aggravation and little else. Her bright red-gold hair didn't quite match the red fire of Hugh's, but even as an infant her eyes had sparkled like his, and the girl was happiest when running free along the banks of the Thames.

Deborah's life had splintered one sunny day in 1772 when Jamie announced that he was going with Hugh on the next voyage to the West Indies as a cabin boy. He was only twelve years old, but Deborah's heart sank as she recognized the eager gleam in his eyes. For the first time her resentment toward Hugh flared into real hatred.

Three months later, Hugh and Jamie were killed in a hurricane off Trinidad.

Deborah became the bitterest sort of survivor. Hugh had been in debt, due partly to the import duties imposed on the West Indies trade by the Townshed Acts. The lovely house was sold, and she and Devon moved to the upper floor of the Linen and

Pewter Shop, owned by Zedidiah Nicholson. "Nick," though two decades older, had been Hugh's closest friend. After amassing a small fortune as a sea captain, he had become a merchant, eventually building several stores, a warehouse, a wharf, and sending out his own ships. Deborah worked feverishly in his Linen and Pewter Shop, hoping to amass enough money someday to buy the shop from the wages she was left after rent and food and from the handmade goods and bonnets she included in the stock. It was a dim prospect, but one that gave her life its only purpose.

"Mother?"

Deborah finished knotting the white net before looking up. She knew what Devon would say, and her face tightened.

"Mother?" Devon repeated hopefully. "I thought that since it is such a quiet day, I might go out and pick berries. I saw some lovely ones yesterday above Winthrop's Cove . . ."

Her eyes, so wide and blue, were pleasing. Just recently twelve years old, Devon was already a glowing promise of beauty. Her strawberry-blond hair shimmered in the square shaft of sunlight that slanted through the window, curling against her face and down her back. Spring had barely arrived, but already her skin was peach-gold, her small body lithe from exercise.

Deborah frowned. The girl was undisciplined, useless. It was impossible to get any work out of her. Mother and daughter stared at each other across bolts of linen.

"Go on," Deborah said, her voice brittle. "Go! You aren't worth anything to me here. I don't know why I put up with your laziness. I'd be better off alone." Devon was already running for her basket. "I expect you to return with that basket full. Do you hear me? No excuses! And stay away from Nick! I won't have him poisoning your mind with those sea tales of his!"

"Yes, Mother!" Devon sang as she dashed out the door.

Outside on Bank Street, which was commonly called "The Bank," the air was mild, fragrant with new flowers and grass. The Thames River lay before her to the east, flowing into Long Island Sound to the south of New London. Water was as familiar to Devon as land, for her town depended on its ideal harbor, one of the longest and deepest on the Atlantic coast.

Breaking into an exuberant run, she rounded the corner of State Street and peered through the window of Gadwin's Drug Shop. George Gadwin, framed by shelves of medicine bottles, spotted her impish face and grinned.

He opened the front door and said, "Morgan hasn't returned home from school yet, Devon. Shall I give him a message?"

"Yes, Mr. Gadwin! Tell Morgan I'll be at the cove. He knows where."

With a smile and a wave, she was off again, running straight toward the Thames, basket swinging and red-gold hair flying. She turned the corner of the waterfront street known as "the Beach" and collided with something, head-on. Her calico skirts billowed as she sat down hard on the cobblestones. Feminine laughter rang nearby, then lean, dark hands lifted Devon effortlessly, dusted her off. Shielding her eyes in the sunlight, she squinted up into a face that made her heart skip. She was used to hardy seamen—had grown up surrounded by them—but this man was in a different class altogether. Cool gray eyes met hers briefly before shifting to the chestnut-haired girl who held his arm so tightly. Devon had an impression of strength, magnetism, dangerous good looks that surpassed those of any man she had ever seen—his eyes were nearly silver-colored, his hair raven-black, a thin white scar traced his brown jaw.

"Ex . . . excuse me . . ." she stuttered.

"Excuse *me*," he replied in a low, wry voice. With a French accent, thought Devon. "You are not hurt? Good." A fleeting bow, then the man and his lushly beautiful companion passed Devon and continued around the corner. She followed, watching his broad shoulders and narrow hips in fascination.

A horse stopped beside her, but she did not notice.

"Devon? Devon!"

Finally she heard and looked up. A well-loved face smiled down from the open chaise. "Nick!" she exclaimed, immediately climbing up beside him.

"Where were you, child?" he inquired affectionately.

"I was looking at that man, Nick. Do you see him?" She leaned over the side, pointing at the distant shoulders.

Nick pulled her back in, bushy gray eyebrows raised in surprise. Was it already beginning for her? He sighed, remembering the girl of a year ago who had furiously wiped her mouth when kissed by a neighbor boy.

"Yes, yes, I know the man. Don't fall out of the carriage, Devon!" He snapped the reins and they clattered off down the street. "It's André Raveneau. He's a French sea captain and a good one at that; full owner of a newly built privateer called the *Black Eagle,* and quite famous for escaping at the crucial moment from the most impossible situations. Never lost a ship, they say, and not yet thirty years of age."

"Goodness!" Devon breathed. "What is he doing here?"

"He's just arrived with a ship full of European goods, but it is my opinion that there's more to it."

"What do you mean?"

"It's none of your affair, child. And you shouldn't be staring at men yet! You are not old enough."

Devon surprised him by blushing, and he asked quickly, "What did you learn at school this morning?"

Devon forgot André Raveneau as she recounted the

morning's lesson. She never missed a day at school, though the hours for girls were from five to seven in the morning, and she adored Nathan Hale, her young teacher. He was strict yet fair, idealistic and patient, and Devon drank in every word he spoke.

By the time she finished speaking, the chaise had passed the procession of handsome vessels anchored along the Thames, and Nick said, "Well, Devon, this is where I turn. I gather you are bound for the cove?"

"Yes!" she laughed. "I have to fill this basket with berries, or Mother won't let me out again in the afternoon."

"You're a scamp," he said fondly.

Hopping down to the grass, Devon turned back to ask, "Where are you going?"

"I've a meeting with Nathaniel Shaw and a few other men. It seems that a post rider's brought news of some sort to Shaw."

"Well, I hope it's exciting! Thank you for the ride, Nick."

Zedidiah Nicholson paused, the reins slack in his hands, watching her small figure scamper up the green hill. His face, still handsome after nearly sixty years, puckered in a sigh. Devon was leaving childhood behind, and he prayed she would learn caution as she matured.

Arms outstretched, Devon stood on the crest of the hill overlooking the wide blue river, taking deep breaths. Across the cove, on the finger of land known as Winthrop Neck, new ships were being built, while to the south, tall-masted vessels lined the bustling waterfront that was the hub of crescent-shaped New London. The Thames was a beautiful river, and trustworthy rather than treacherous. All manner of craft dotted it, including the ferry that was making its way across from Groton Bank. Devon shaded her eyes against the sun, counting the well-dressed men on board. Could they all be coming to Nathaniel Shaw's meeting?

A dull boom echoed from the hills below New London, followed by a puff of smoke outside Fort Trumbull. A cannon had been fired to herald the arrival of a large, cargo-laden brigantine, sailing up from the seemingly endless expanse of Long Island Sound. Devon watched it approach, white canvas sails billowing in the sunlight. She wondered where it had been and what tales of adventure would spill from its crew that night as they sat drinking rum or ale in the taverns.

Suddenly, damp hands covered her eyes. Startled, she tried to wriggle free. Her basket tangled in the other person's arms and she pushed it between them, sending her assailant sprawling in the grass.

"Morgan!" Devon exclaimed.

"Devon, do you have to be so violent? I was only having a joke." The boy got up, picking bits of grass from his coat.

"I'm sorry." An irrepressible giggle belied her words. "A girl can't be too careful, you know. You might have been some wild-eyed sailor after a lone female."

Morgan snorted. "Why would he be grabbing you, then? You're only twelve, just a child."

Devon frowned. The budding mounds concealed beneath her bodice were her dearest secret. Perhaps she wasn't grown up yet, but neither was she a child!

"You think you're so important since you had your thirteenth birthday, Morgan Gadwin," she said hotly. "There isn't one thing you can do better than I can, and until there is, you just watch your tongue!" Devon turned away, adding over one shoulder, "I have to pick berries today. You can help or not." With that, she zigzagged down the grassy slope toward the nearest thicket.

"Blast you, Devon!" Morgan yelled at her back.

"Don't go off mad! I don't know what I did, but whatever it was, I'm sorry!"

She skidded to a stop, turned with a grin, and put out her tongue. Typically, her irritation was over as quickly as it had begun; she and Morgan had a dozen minor tiffs each day.

Girls her age were too prim and well-behaved to suit Devon, but Morgan was the perfect comrade. A quiet, rather dull boy by nature, he was enchanted by Devon's tales of the Caribbean and Europe, of life aboard ships, which she had heard from her father and Nick. She spun vivid dreams of the adventures that lay in her future, always including Morgan in the scenarios. Until he had met Devon, he had supposed he would someday own his father's drug shop. Those plans seemed impossibly drab now that he knew he would grow up to explore the world with this bold, magical creature.

He followed her now, his own descent slower, more careful. He could never understand how she was able to charge through the tallest, most tangled grass without falling.

"Devon!" he called breathlessly. "Wait! I almost forgot! There is news—tremendous news!"

Morgan's frantic tone intrigued her and she paused near the trees, watching him stumble across the meadow. The sallowness of Morgan's narrow face emphasized his great brown eyes and dark, wavy hair, which was coming loose from its ribbon. His shoulders seemed so small, his body so weak and uncoordinated, and Devon remembered the splendidly made man she had crashed into on the Beach. Could Morgan grow up to be such a man?

"Devon!" he exclaimed, panting. "It's war! The British struck at Lexington, but we were prepared. We fought them to Concord. The word is that the Minutemen were one thousand strong! The redcoats were finally forced to retreat. Master Hale told us they lost three times more men than we—"

8

Devon stared, open-mouthed. "Morgan! Is it truly *war?* Where did you hear this?"

"Of course it's true!" he shouted, his voice cracking. "A post rider brought the news to the Shaw mansion, and soon afterward one of their stableboys came running to the schoolhouse. All the militiamen around Boston are being called. Everyone is going! By the time I started up here, the word was spreading all over town; I've never seen such excitement! Just think, Devon, America is going to be independent at last!"

"Come inside, child!" Deborah scolded from the doorway. "It's nearly dark."

Devon sat on the stoop, yearning to be at Miner's Tavern to hear her schoolmaster speak. She had watched the men of New London pass on their way to the town square and had called out questions to old friends of her father. The news was that Nathan Hale had closed the school and was joining a corps of Rangers who were bound for Boston.

The New London militia unit was also meeting tonight. In fact, it seemed that every male citizen was out in the gathering darkness, for the excitement was fiercely contagious. Important plans had to be made and each man wanted his voice to be heard. New London had suffered the heavy-handed authority of English law these past years, and the townspeople were eager to join in this real, potent revolution against the Crown. New London, with its superb harbor and sleek ships, could make a valuable contribution.

"Oh, Mother," Devon sighed, twisting her calico skirt. "I wish I were a boy—then I could go with Master Hale to Boston!"

"Don't be foolish," Deborah returned sharply. "You are full of silly dreams. You have no idea of the real world. This war will be a curse to New London. There will be privateers everywhere, the West

Indies trade will be smothered, we'll lose all our best men and ships, and Lord only knows how I'll keep this shop going—"

"Privateers!" Devon breathed, thinking again of the Frenchman, André Raveneau.

"Don't look so spellbound. They will be our own ships, manned by Connecticut boys who will be as full of romantic dreams as you are. Adventure!" Deborah said venomously. "More likely hardship—and death."

Devon barely heard her mother's words. The meeting Nick had gone to . . . it must have been to plan New London's sea strategy. She could scarcely wait to speak to him and learn all the details.

"I want you indoors," Deborah said tiredly. "I have tasks for you, left from this afternoon. We shall be forced to work harder than ever, Devon, now that the war is begun."

"Yes, Mother. I'll be along in a moment."

Devon listened to her mother's footsteps retreating to the rear of the shop before she stood up. Distant voices that grew clearer caused her to linger on the stoop. A shadowy quartet approached and Devon could soon distinguish Nathaniel Shaw, Jr., New London's most prominent citizen, flanked by his friends Gurdon Saltonstall and Zedidiah Nicholson. The fourth member of the group was the much younger Nathan Hale.

The men were engaged in a spirited discussion, but Nick glanced up as they neared the Linen and Pewter Shop and smiled at Devon's straight little form. Despite the darkness, he was not surprised to see her outside.

She needed no further encouragement. Dashing into the street, she blurted, "Gentlemen, please excuse me! I only wish to say farewell to Master Hale."

She looked up at her clear-eyed teacher, piercingly conscious of the impact he had had on her life. Plainly dressed, he wore no wig, and his hair was drawn back into a simple queue under a tricorn hat.

"Thank you, Miss Lindsay," he said. "I hope you will continue to study. You have an excellent mind, and I expect you to have made great progress by the time I return to New London."

"Oh, I will, I will. I promise! And, sir . . . I wish you good fortune in Boston."

"I am grateful for your concern," said Hale, smiling slightly at her fervent face.

"Devon!" Deborah called impatiently from an upstairs window.

The four men murmured, "Good evening," and Devon backed away until she had reached the doorstep. Her hand found the latch, but she continued to gaze after the group until Nathan Hale's shape was swallowed by the night.

Chapter Two

———◆———

October 20, 1780

NEW London glowed with autumn's deepest colors. Leaves of crimson, gold, rust, and saffron blanketed the stone walls that bordered every road; pumpkins lay fat and orange on their vines; bright red apples dripped from orchard branches.

Devon, at seventeen, seemed an additional gift of the season. Her cloud of strawberry-blond curls and her soft golden skin were more beautiful than ever against the fiery leaves, and the sight of her on the street lightened the hearts of the war-weary citizens.

On this October afternoon she strolled toward the Beach, a faded hatbox swinging on her arm. Deborah had labored for hours over the bonnet that Nick had ordered for his wife's birthday, a perfect copy of a European original. Devon had stern instructions to deliver it directly to the Nicholson home, yet she could not resist the urge to make a detour along the waterfront. Pausing in the shadow of a Shaw warehouse, she surveyed the activity on the docks. True to her mother's prediction, war had changed New London. The past five years seemed like a dark eternity.

The town itself harbored nearly sixty incredibly successful privateers, and the anchorage was used by vessels from all over America, even Europe. Many New London men had chosen to join the army, and ships had been built for the State and Continental navies, but privateering was supreme. Privately owned vessels had been armed and fitted out at their owners' expense for the purpose of capturing enemy craft, and everyone—owners, crew, and the government—divided the booty. Five years ago it had all seemed a great romantic adventure.

Devon thought sadly of the night she had said goodbye to Nathan Hale. Eighteen months later the young captain she had so admired had disguised himself as a Dutch schoolmaster to spy on the British who occupied Long Island. He was discovered and hanged on September 22, 1776. Too many men, men she had known since birth, were now dead like Mr. Hale, or imprisoned.

New London lived under a cloud of fear; even now Devon could see a great British ship anchored to the south in Long Island Sound. The townspeople expected to be attacked at any moment and there had been countless false alarms, leading to the evacuation of all women, children, the ill, and the elderly. Devon's heart tightened at the remembered nightmares—screaming, sobbing, praying all around her as wagons rumbled out of town in the middle of the night.

Less than a month ago General Benedict Arnold had conspired to surrender West Point to the British. Though his plot had been discovered, he had escaped, and New London continued to reel under the shocking blow, for Arnold had grown up just ten miles north, in Norwich. Until now, his exploits had been a source of deep pride to everyone from the area. Disillusionment and mistrust abounded. Neighbors and lifelong friends suspected one another of being Tories; several had actually admitted their loyalties and left for British-occupied New York town, including the local Anglican minister.

Despite the dark days and harsh realities that had

been thrust on Devon, she still passionately wished that she were a boy so that she might sail off to fight for America's independence. No one cheered more loudly than Devon when Fort Griswold's cannon fired the three-shot signal to greet the latest privateer returning with its prize. Her heart would race with joy and pride at the sight of the racy craft sailing up the Thames, laden with cargo from British ships. Devon knew that New London was truly hurting the British, and she was convinced that the hardships of the past five years had not been suffered in vain.

A chilly breeze swept off the Thames and Devon stepped into the sunlight. Approaching the docks, she scanned the sleek, lightweight vessels at anchor and strove to seem nonchalant in her search for the *Black Eagle*.

She saw *him* first, shouting orders on the deck of his ship.

Many of the captains and officers who sailed privateers had achieved glamorous reputations, but none could match André Raveneau, who at thirty-four had become a legend. Men thought him the most daring, successful, and charmed of captains; women knew only that they went weak in his devastatingly handsome presence. Raveneau had given his time, his expertise, and his beautiful privateer *Black Eagle* to the American cause for reasons he chose not to discuss. Of course, averaging a dozen prizes a year, he had become abundantly wealthy, but there were plenty of less hazardous ways to pursue riches. Because of Raveneau's fearlessness and his ability to succeed in the face of seemingly impossible odds, townspeople whispered that he was allied with the devil.

Devon watched as he jumped lightly to the wharf, her heart racing and palms icy. Raveneau had fascinated her for five years, though he was dangerous-looking, his dark face chiseled and unsmiling. He strode past Devon, but she might as well have been a barrel of molasses for all the notice he paid her.

As he disappeared around the corner, Devon wondered why he didn't look at her the way other men did. In the past two years strangers had begun to gape openly at her blossoming figure and exquisite face. Most of these admirers were either old men or twelve-year-old boys; nearly every healthy male between the ages of six and sixty had gone to war, except for the inevitable rowdy seamen.

"Good day to you, miss!" a husky voice called. Startled, Devon spun around to face a stocky, genial-looking young man whose sandy hair was queued neatly at his neck. "Have you business on the *Black Eagle*? Perhaps I might help?" A square hand reached out, but Devon eluded it. She was beginning to regret coming down here, for no decent girl would wander the docks alone.

"No . . . I—"

"Devon!"

She gasped with relief at the sound of Morgan's voice, and took his arm enthusiastically. "I'm so glad to see you! You can walk me to Nick's. I have this hat to deliver to Temperance, and Mother will thrash me if I'm not back soon." As they started off, she nodded to the sandy-haired privateersman, who shrugged good-naturedly.

Morgan was delighted by Devon's attention. At eighteen, he still adored her and felt awkward in her presence. The years had added a few inches to his height, but he fell far short of six feet, and his shoulders remained narrow. To his chagrin, Devon continued to treat him as an affectionate friend.

"I heard today that we won a great victory at King's Mountain," Morgan said, conscious of her arm linked through his.

"That's splendid news," Devon said awkwardly.

Morgan's face burned, for he knew what was on her mind. For two years she had been urging him to sign on with a privateer or even join the army and had been confused and disappointed by his refusal. His excuse was that his father needed him, for both his brothers were gone, one at sea, the other a soldier. Morgan could never admit that he was simply afraid. The thought of battle made him nauseous; he even had nightmares about it.

"My brother Tyler's company may have been engaged in the battle." he said hastily, thinking to absorb a bit of family glory. "Last we heard, they were nearby."

"I am certain he was the hero of the hour." Devon couldn't help the accusing note that crept into her voice.

They walked in silence for several minutes. Morgan wished that he could calm the fever in his body. It seemed to intensify each time he was near Devon, and he feared that only she could cure it. Other boys his age—the few who remained in town—had found relief with the easy women who haunted the docks. One evening, after spending hours lying innocently in the grass with Devon, he had taken his aching groin down to the Beach and had stood and watched the painted harlots. One had actually approached him, but her brazen manner had scared him to death.

I want Devon and only Devon, he thought now, and the words seemed to sear his brain. She still talked of their future together . . . surely she would not reject the advances of her husband-to-be? If not for the chaos of the war, they probably would have been married by now! Impulsively, he put an arm around her slender waist. She glanced up in surprise, then smiled. Morgan's heart began to pound.

Devon was feeling sorry that she had spoken to him so impatiently. She must not press him to do her will, she thought. Morgan was Morgan, and she of all people should be able to accept the fact that he was not a warrior at heart. Still . . .

Unbidden, the dark image of André Raveneau filled

Devon's mind and a chill ran down her spine. She could not understand the madness that swept her at the mere thought of that Frenchman! Still painfully innocent, Devon was curious, yet fearful, about these feelings she had. The fact that they were confined to a rakish privateersman who did not know she existed was bewildering.

Feeling her shiver, Morgan tightened his hold. Devon, guilty, leaned against him. Her face flushed self-consciously. Morgan took that as a good sign. She's shy but willing! he thought. His fingers fanned out from her waist to touch the soft curving hip. He felt a hot pressure spread down his belly.

"Devon . . ." he gulped. "Look at those apple trees! I am famished—missed my last meal. Do you have time to stop?"

"Well . . ." she murmured doubtfully.

"Come on!"

Morgan led her past dozens of beckoning branches to the tree farthest from the road. Plucking an apple for each of them, he persuaded her to sit down.

"Captain Clark made it back safely from the West Indies today," Devon commented. "I heard him telling stories about Jamaica in the shop today, and I simply ached to see what he has seen. Such adventures! When we sail, Morgan, the West Indies must be our first stop. I want to run barefoot on the white beaches, and—"

"Devon!" Morgan rasped. He suddenly lunged forward and enfolded her in a clumsy embrace. Shocked at first, Devon soon allowed her curiosity to take hold. So this was to be her first kiss! Rather excited, she relaxed and waited for Morgan to proceed.

Briefly he froze, but instinct led to an immediate recovery. Devon felt hot, wet, trembling lips press against hers. Revolted, she started to pull away, but Morgan shoved her backward into the grass and fell on top of her. His slippery tongue invaded her mouth; he rubbed his body against hers, flattening her breasts. A bulge beneath Morgan's breeches pressed into her belly, edged lower. Devon reacted violently. She pushed at him with all her considerable might and yanked the hair fastened at his neck until he screeched and rolled away from her.

"Morgan Gadwin, have you gone mad? Are you possessed? What lunacy was that?" Devon stood up, trying to rearrange her faded blue gown, eyes blazing at the mortified Morgan. "You scared me half to death!"

He sat with knees drawn up to hide his shame. "I thought you loved me, Devon!" he mumbled at last, looking up with stricken brown eyes. "I'm . . . sorry. I didn't mean to . . . I just *need* you so much!"

Softening, she knelt on the grass and reached to smooth his hair. "I *do* love you, Morgan, but that *attack* scared the wits out of me!"

"I'm sorry," he repeated woefully, encouraged when her hand moved to pat his shoulder. "I won't be so rough—next time. I love you, Devon!"

"I love you, too." She kissed his brow with bittersweet affection.

"Wasn't it even a *little* exciting for you?" Morgan demanded anxiously, watching her face.

Forcing a smile, Devon managed, "Well, yes . . . of course. It was my first kiss, after all."

They stood up, brushing brittle leaves off their clothing.

"Morgan. I really must go. No, I'll go alone. I have to hurry, or Mother will be furious."

He started to reach for her, but Devon slipped away and ran out onto the road. Tears of disillusionment blurred her eyes as she turned west toward Nick's house.

The Nicholson home was located on Union Street, not far from the schoolhouse, and its cobalt-blue exterior was a symbol of warm, happy times to Devon.

She loved to visit here, having shamelessly invented excuses over the years, and now, as she lifted the brass knocker, Morgan's kisses began to fade from her thoughts.

Mary, the buxom, white-haired housekeeper, opened the door. She smelled of cinnamon, tea, and freshly baked bread.

"Miss Devon! It's good to see you! You get prettier every day."

"Thank you, Mary. I'm glad to see you, too! I brought this for your mistress—a birthday gift Nick ordered."

"Shhh! It's supposed to be a surprise. Miss Temperance is abed again today, but you know that she has a great skill for hearing! Why don't you just take that into the library? Oh, no! Wait—there's a visitor. Let me ask the master."

Mary lumbered off, leaving Devon to gaze around the cozy, cream-colored stairhall. Temperance Nicholson, though sweet and gentle, was forever imagining herself stricken by some terrible illness. Devon was of the opinion that she simply enjoyed a life of leisure, tucked into bed with a novel and a tray of imported sweetmeats. Somehow she always managed a recovery in time for Sunday church, only to develop a new malady on Monday.

Mary returned, and said, "You can go in, lass. You're just in time for tea."

Devon grinned, picked up the hatbox, and sauntered down the hall to the library, only to stand paralyzed on the threshold. Two men stood up, and Nick came forward to take her hand, which had gone cold as ice.

"Devon! Do get hold of yourself," he whispered, chuckling. With a flourish, he turned back to his guest and pulled Devon to the center of the room. "My dear, I would like you to meet Captain André Raveneau. André, this is Devon Lindsay, my goddaughter. She is

20

fascinated by the sea, so I knew she would enjoy a chance to converse with you!"

"How do you do, mademoiselle?" Raveneau said, his voice deep, charmingly accented, and faintly amused.

When Nick pinched her, Devon blurted, "Oh, I am fine! And you?"

"I am also . . . fine." A fleeting grin revealed teeth which seemed startlingly white against his tanned face.

Mary arrived with the "tea" tray, which held three glasses, a decanter of brandy, and a small goblet of red wine. Devon always had wine at Nick's, one delightfully forbidden glassful. The distraction enabled her to find a chair and sit down. Nick returned to his desk, Raveneau to the red leather wing chair, and the tray was passed.

"How is your mother?" Nick inquired, adding to the visitor, "Devon's father, my closest friend, was lost at sea some years ago. Tragically, her brother was on board as well."

Raveneau turned steel-gray eyes on Devon and she felt her heart thud alarmingly. "I am sorry," he said.

"Oh . . . I appreciate . . ." Flustered, she looked at Nick. "Mother is worse than ever, I think. She's totally absorbed in the shop, working every minute. There must be two dozen quilts and as many net canopies, all unsold, and still she makes more. She never mentions Papa or Jamie any more and hardly speaks to me. Doesn't even bother to nag about my behavior . . ." Devon broke off, blushing.

Raveneau had been watching her with detached interest. She was the prettiest girl he had seen in months, though sadly in need of grooming. Her cloud of burnished-rose hair was loose and windblown, boasting a dried leaf on one side. The plain blue dress she wore was too small, though it did outline the high curve of her breasts well. But her face was simply enchanting. It had been a while since he had observed such fresh beauty: sparkling blue eyes, dusky cheeks, and a mouth that enjoyed laughter. Ah, innocence! he thought, and allowed himself a lazy, cynical grin.

His expression deepened Devon's blush. She retreated into the safety of her wing chair, listening to the conversation. Apparently, whatever business was between the two men had already been discussed, for now they only exchanged news of the war.

Raveneau had been at sea until two days ago, and was interested in the details of Benedict Arnold's treason and the execution of the British officer who had acted as go-between. Devon found the Frenchman's cool attitude toward Arnold quite surprising. It had been nearly a month since General Arnold had scurried down the Hudson to New York town, leaving the popular British Major André to be hanged as a spy, but everyone in the area continued to talk of the traitor daily. Anger, shame, and bewilderment were emotions that ran high, yet here sat this nonchalant Frenchman, asking questions as though he were discussing the price of rum.

"I understand that Major André requested a military execution by firing squad," he remarked.

"Yes. General Washington wished to grant him that much, but since André was found guilty of spying, Washington was forced to have him hanged."

"He was a brave man, unlike that toad Arnold!" Devon exclaimed. "He put the rope around his own neck, and do you know what his last words were?"

"No, but I trust you will enlighten me," Raveneau murmured, amused.

"He said, 'My only wish is that you all bear witness that I die like a soldier and a brave man.' "

Nick coughed with embarrassment. In desperation, he drew out his watch and examined it at length, at which point André Raveneau stood up. Devon gazed at his tall, hard physique until she heard Nick cough once more. Both men were watching her, and she was conscious of the deep flush that spread over her face.

Nick rushed around his desk. "Devon, child, what's this box you have?"

"Oh, I nearly forgot. It's the bonnet you ordered for Temperance's birthday. Mother did lovely work on it. It hardly seems fair that you should buy it, since you own the shop, but times being what they are—"

"Hush, minx! I may own the shop, but I don't have a talent for making bonnets! Leave me the bill, now. Stay awake in church this week and perhaps you'll see the thing modeled." His eyes sparkled mischievously.

"Nick, you are too bad."

"And you, miss, are an authority on that subject! Which reminds me—Shaw mentioned today that he's seen you wandering about the docks! That's got to stop, Devon. You'll find yourself with more trouble than even you can handle." He looked at the Frenchman. "Isn't that so?"

"Unquestionably," Raveneau confirmed dryly.

"You'd better be off as well, Devon. Your mother will give me the devil for keeping you all afternoon. Knowing you, you took the longest route getting here." Nick put an arm around her shoulders and pressed a kiss to her tumbled hair. "Can't you find a comb in that shop?"

"Oh, stop it! You are a worse nag than Mother! I can see that this is not the place to come for a good laugh any longer!"

Nick chuckled and gave her an affectionate wink. "Say, I've an idea! Perhaps Captain Raveneau would see you home. What do you say?"

"Sir, you have read my mind," he said. Devon doubted it but was thrilled all the same, until he added, "The only drawback is that I came on foot."

He's laughing at us! Devon thought, humiliated. The man is a cad!

"Oh, that's no problem," said Nick. "It is getting dark; no time of day to be wandering the streets. I insist that you take my carriage. I'll have a boy drive you."

Raveneau lifted a dark brow, but his only reply was, "You are too kind, M'sieur Nicholson."

"Nonsense! Wouldn't want anything to happen to America's most valued privateersman!"

"What about *me?*" Devon demanded, feigning outrage.

"Well, now, that's another story!" Nick laughed, ducking her ill-aimed slap. They left the library and were walking toward the door when Nick inquired conversationally, "Still reading *Gulliver's Travels,* Devon?"

She giggled. "You underestimate me! That was last week! I've finished *Candide* and that tiresome *Vicar of Wakefield* since then."

"And now?"

"I don't think I should tell you."

Raveneau looked on with interest as Nick's bristling gray eyebrows came together. "Devon—"

"*Tom Jones!*" was her cheerful reply.

"Good Lord! Where on earth did you get a copy of that?"

Mary opened the front door and Devon scampered outside before calling back, "From your library, of course!"

Nick clapped a hand to his head and was shaking it hopelessly from side to side as André Raveneau bade him farewell. "An interesting visit!" he commented, unable to repress a smile. "I will see you in a few weeks, M'sieur Nicholson."

Nick recovered enough to grasp the Frenchman's hand and wish him luck with the voyage he would undertake on the morrow.

A handsome carriage was brought around, the horses tossing their heads at the sight of Devon, who greeted them and the young driver by name. A bemused André Raveneau helped her up, and after a last wave at Nick they started off down Union Street.

Suddenly Devon felt a choking shyness close in on her. Gazing at her lap, she was able to view

Raveneau's legs as well, only a few inches from her own. The long muscles of his thighs were outlined against the fawn breeches he wore; she yearned to touch him, to find out if his leg could actually be as hard as it looked.

Raveneau could feel her eyes on him. It was unsettling. What was the child looking at? "I was quite impressed to hear of all the books you have read this week," he said at last, hoping to halt her gaze before it continued any farther up his legs.

Startled, Devon looked up. Outside, dusk was deepening into a blue-gray mist, and she had the impression that this entire experience was not real, but one of her recurring dreams.

"Were you really?" she asked. Perhaps he was laughing at her again.

"Of course! I do not know many literary females—especially of your age."

"I am not so young!" Devon retorted hotly.

Raveneau could not help glancing at the soft curves displayed by her too-small dress. "No, of course not, mademoiselle. Not a child, by any means!"

Devon thought she detected a glint of silver in his penetrating gray eyes. Oh, he was so handsome! Even in her dreams he had not looked so devastatingly attractive. Her eyes moved over him in the dimming twilight, memorizing the gleam of his jet-black hair, the hard lines of his scarred jaw, mouth, cheekbones, the tendons in his neck, the width of his shoulders . . .

Raveneau managed to meet her dreamy eyes. "Mademoiselle, you seem to be greatly preoccupied with my looks! Would you like a closer view?"

He brought a tanned hand up to her chin. Devon shivered at his touch. Her heart pounded in her ears and he moved nearer, then slowly lowered his head until their lips brushed. Raveneau meant to kiss her briefly, to give her something to dream about, but her lips were so soft, as sweet and moist as crushed berries. Hesitantly, they moved against his harder mouth, and he slid his fingers around her neck, into the cloud of titian hair. Devon was sailing through a sea of stars; she tingled from head to toe. Tentatively, remembering the way Morgan had kissed her, she parted her lips. Raveneau was lost. His tongue touched even white teeth, then the soft, sweet tip of her tongue, and he was shot through with the fierce sort of desire he hadn't experienced in years.

Abruptly he broke away, forcing himself to remember that he was kissing an innocent girl who looked to be half his age. He slid his hand from her hair reluctantly, saw huge blue eyes staring up in confusion. He stared back, astounded.

"Nom de Dieu!" was all he could say, and each word was like a gunshot.

Devon's entire body blushed crimson with shame. As the carriage drew to a halt before the Linen and Pewter Shop, she rallied and delivered a stinging slap to Raveneau's dark, harshly cut cheek.

Chapter Three

———◆———

October 21, 1780

DEVON tossed in her narrow bed, her mind spinning. For the first time she regretted that she had no close girlfriends to turn to for advice. This was certainly not a matter she could take to Morgan or to her forbidding mother, and there was no doubt in Devon's mind that nearly every other girl her age in New London must know more about men than she did.

She thought that the sheer wonder of Raveneau's kiss might have been enough to combat shame, were it not for Morgan. What was wrong with her? How could she claim to love Morgan, plan to marry him, yet be so utterly repulsed by his kisses, his touch? As if that were not bad enough, she had allowed another man to kiss her the very same day! And André Raveneau had lit a fire in her. All night long her breasts seemed swollen, her nipples taut against the cotton bedgown she wore. And the hidden place between her legs ached frighteningly. She wondered if it were some physical punishment for the terrible thing she had done. Yet it was not really pain, but more of a throb that seemed to reach for something. During the long, dark hours she spent restlessly in bed, Devon wondered if perhaps Raveneau really *was* an agent of the devil and had put some curse on her.

When dawn broke at last, Devon rose, pulled off her bedgown, and paused to glance furtively at her body, which was beginning to seem quite foreign. Hesitantly she touched her breasts and was shocked when they tingled in response. Her hand moved to the red-gold triangle, toward the source of that pain which had nearly disappeared by now. When her forefinger brushed the hidden bud of desire, Devon gasped as the ache returned in a burst of fire.

Sick at heart, she pulled on her clothes, anxious to cover herself.

I must be ill! she thought wildly.

Deborah slept on in the next room; it would not be long before she would also awaken. Desperate for some air, Devon crept downstairs and headed for the shop door. At this hour it would be possible to run for as long as she pleased and feel alone in the world. Perhaps the cold chill of dawn would cure her affliction.

The sun had barely begun its ascent, and New London was bathed in an ash-rose light that softened the bright hues of autumn. Once on the Bank, Devon ran until her throat burned and her legs buckled. Finally she was forced to stop. She leaned, panting, against a building.

She was on the waterfront, directly across from the privateer with a figurehead of a magnificent black and silver eagle. There was little activity on the rest of the ships, but the decks and the masts of the *Black Eagle* were crowded with men. Devon remembered that it was leaving today. What am I doing here? she demanded of her traitorous legs. The sound of a familiar, French-accented voice brought her up sharply.

"Damn you, Carson, I told you to secure that line!"

Devon spotted Raveneau standing on the quarterdeck and shouting at one of the men in the rigging. Other voices drowned his out, but the sight of him was mesmerizing. After admiring the sheen of his black hair in the sunlight and the black hair covering his chest, revealed by his open white shirt, Devon noticed a girl standing on deck. Although she wore a dark pelisse with the hood up, Devon could see a few blond curls surrounding a pretty face. After a few moments the girl walked over and caught Raveneau's loose white sleeve. They embraced. A sour lump formed in Devon's throat.

When it became clear that the girl was leaving the *Black Eagle,* Devon stumbled back between the warehouses and kept on going. Humiliation, guilt, and undefined jealousy tortured her as she ran back to the Bank. It seemed that the whole of her simple existence had been turned inside out.

The Gadwins' home was located on Bank Street, just around the corner from their drug shop. Morgan had not slept well that night, either, and he was in the dining room when Devon went dashing by. By the time he reached the front door and shouted to her, she was halfway home, but she stopped and waited for him. Morgan ran to meet her.

Devon burned with guilt as she watched him approach, looking so young, his warm brown eyes so earnest. Remembering the things she had thought and said under the apple tree, she resolved to make it up to him. Perhaps that would cleanse her conscience all around.

"Devon, I am so glad to see you! I've been wondering when we would get a chance to talk. There's time yet before the shops open. Will you come with me?"

"Of course I'll come with you," she told him hastily. "I want to apologize for the way I behaved yesterday. I was quite callous . . . you didn't deserve it."

Morgan's drawn face relaxed as he looked down at her in surprise. Leading the way back to his house, he could feel his pulse quicken. They walked hand in hand through the yard to the little summerhouse where they had played as children. Devon perched on the edge of the built-in bench, facing the glorious sunrise. Morgan joined her. He felt awkward and nervous, yet encouraged by her unexpected apology.

"Devon . . . I'm so sorry about yesterday. I behaved like an animal. I never meant to frighten you!"

She turned to him anxiously, her china-blue eyes wide. "Don't be sorry. You love me and I love you. I know you couldn't help it. I should have been more understanding."

"Oh, Devon!" Morgan choked, throwing his arms around her. She endured a wet, smothering kiss and willed herself to think only of their childhood friendship and lifelong love. If a French privateersman could awaken her, then surely dear Morgan could, too. It just might take more time . . .

"I couldn't sleep last night," he whispered against Devon's ear. His hot breath bothered her.

"Neither could I. I was simply miserable."

"Devon! Sweetheart!" His damp hands caressed her neck, then moved to her shoulders and removed the shawl she wore. Frantically, he touched her bare forearms and lifted her hands to kiss each finger. Devon fought the nausea that twisted her stomach and managed to smile when Morgan raised his eyes.

"I have something to tell you," he said. "I've been waiting for hours. I almost came to the shop and woke you. Devon, we received word last night that Tyler was killed at King's Mountain. I have decided to fill his place in his militia."

Devon's mouth dropped. She could scarcely remember Morgan's brother, for he had been nineteen when he left New London five years ago, but the news of his death came as a blow. It didn't make sense, any more than her father's and Jamie's deaths, or Nathan Hale's. For a moment she wanted to beg Morgan to stay. What if he were killed? The thought left an acid taste in her mouth, and she selfishly realized that she would lose her best friend.

"Oh . . . Morgan. Your poor parents!" she cried, thinking of those quiet, kindly people.

"It is hard on them, of course, but I think they expected it. The odds were against both Tyler and Joshua surviving, I suppose."

"But how can they let you go? I don't think it is a good idea, Morgan. They will need you now more than ever!"

"No. Father agrees it is the right thing to do. I imagine he thinks I should have joined before now. I'm eighteen, after all, and healthy." He looked at her in surprise. "Just a minute, Devon! You of all people should be proud of me! You have badgered me for two years to fight for America's independence."

"Don't you see? Tyler's death changes all that! I never thought anything would happen to you. But now you seem so vulnerable."

"Please, I wish you wouldn't remind me."

He looked so sad and frightened that Devon threw her arms around his neck. Burying his face in her fragrant hair, Morgan choked, "I have to go! If I don't, people will think me a coward and laugh behind my back—and my father's. I cannot humiliate him. Tyler may be dead, but my parents are proud of him. Do you think I can go on any longer hiding behind the counter in the drug shop? I may not be the bravest person, but I do have some pride!"

Devon was swept by a warm tide of affection. Her arms tightened around him and her breasts pushed against his chest. "Oh, Morgan, what will I do when you are gone?"

"Sweetheart, please don't cry. I'll be back. The fighting will be over soon, everyone says so."

"Will you be careful?"

"I promise."

Devon's lips were only a few inches away and Morgan found them easily. Desperately she fought to remain still as his tongue thrust into her mouth. If only

I hadn't kissed that Frenchman, I wouldn't realize how horrid this is! she thought wildly.

Morgan's hands fumbled at her bodice. Devon realized that any eager lover would show him the way, but she could not. In desperation he forced his fingers down the neck of her low-cut gown. He gasped when his hand closed over her breast, but she was only conscious of a chafing discomfort. After poking her two or three times, Morgan pulled the offending hand free.

"Oh, Devon! You are so beautiful!" he breathed. "You will never know how much I love you. I would face a thousand redcoats by myself just to—"

Devon felt a stab of panic when he bunched up her skirt and caressed her leg. Her mind and heart were a jumble of warring emotions: guilt, affection, revulsion, forbidden desire for another man. Reminding herself that Morgan loved her and was going to war, she managed to endure his fumbling. Labored breathing was loud in her ear, and she could see the drops of perspiration beading on his forehead. She felt so sorry for him, but as his fingers groped upward, her control began to dissolve. Morgan pushed her back against the bench, panting and clutching at her until it seemed that she was covered by wet lips and hands.

She had to free herself, or go mad. "Morgan, Morgan, please, let me up," she cried. "Morgan!" She pushed his face away with all her might.

Clutching at thin air, he toppled sideways to the wooden floor and Devon jumped to her feet. "I am truly sorry, but I just cannot. I am frightened. Please, don't look at me that way."

Thoroughly humiliated, Morgan crawled back onto the bench and crouched there, afraid to meet her eyes. It was bad enough to lose all control with a female, but to do it so clumsily and then be rejected . . . The shame was too great to be borne.

Devon's heart was torn with pity. Feeling safe now, she hurried to comfort him.

"I don't understand!" he cried, blinking back tears. "Why don't you feel what I feel? When I am with you, I can't think clearly. I can only think of you, your scent and softness . . . how much I want you! Why isn't it the same for you?"

They were sitting side by side, Devon holding tight to Morgan's hand. He stared at the summerhouse wall as he spoke, which was a great relief to her, since she was blushing profusely at his words. Morgan was describing exactly her feelings of less than a day before, when André Raveneau had kissed her.

"I don't know what to say, Morgan," she blurted. "I'm *sorry!* I wish— Maybe it just takes time. I have heard that it's different for boys . . ."

"Do you think that could be the answer?"

"Oh, yes! It's not your fault! It's me, I am sure of it. Listen, Morgan, by the time you come home, I will be older. More prepared."

Morgan brightened considerably. "Will you wait for me, Devon? Truly?"

"Of course I will!" They hugged, Devon overflowing with love. "We'll be married the day you return. Then we'll save for our ship, unless we can somehow get the money while you are away! We'll sail to the West Indies and run on the beaches and swim in the ocean!"

Morgan cut off her bright dreams with eager lips that sent chills of revulsion rather than passion down her back. When the kiss ended at last, he moved to nuzzle one of her ears, and she struggled to ignore the awful sensation of his steamy breath.

"I love you, Morgan," Devon said loudly, as if to convince herself. "I promise you!"

Chapter Four

———◆———

September 6, 1781

DEVON awoke before dawn, opening her eyes to darkness. Rolling onto one hip in her narrow rope bed, she scrutinized the stripe of sky that was visible where the curtains parted. Five o'clock, at least. It wouldn't be long until her mother called her.

Time had passed slowly, and this new autumn found Devon restless and uncharacteristically unhappy. It had been only ten months since Morgan's departure to fight in Tyler's militia. Devon had clung to her guilt and her promise, reinforced by each glimpse of the feared Captain Raveneau. Whenever she heard that the *Black Eagle* was in port, she wandered the twisting lanes helplessly until she caught heart-stopping sight of the man who seemed to be her weakness. Yet she always stepped into an alley or doorway rather than face him. Each time, she returned to the shop more determined than ever to be true to her vow to Morgan. Raveneau was dangerous. Hadn't he kissed her and then never sought her out to apologize or even say good day? But Morgan was real and honest, and through the long, dull days working beside her mother, she forced herself to think of security and sincerity.

Curiously tense, Devon pulled back her quilts and

swung her feet onto the wide-planked floor. There was water in her pitcher, left from yesterday, so she poured it into the ewer and splashed her face.

"Devon? Are you awake?" Deborah called from the next room.

Devon made a face. There would be no chance to read the next scene of *The Taming of the Shrew* this morning.

"Yes, Mother."

"I think I heard a noise a few minutes ago. Did you hear it?"

"No, but perhaps that's what woke me."

"We will get an early start," Deborah decided. "You can churn the butter before we open the shop."

Devon was pulling a new yellow cotton dress over her head and was glad that her reply would be muffled in the material. "I can scarcely wait."

"What's that?"

"Nothing." Quickly she fastened up the front and reached for her hairbrush. Deborah was stirring in her room, and they emerged into the kitchen almost simultaneously. Devon started a fire and greased the griddle while Deborah stirred the batter for buckwheat cakes that had been rising during the night. Devon put the teakettle on over the fire and Deborah produced a small amount of butter along with a pitcher of maple syrup, payment from one of their customers for a bolt of linen.

"I wonder where Morgan is today?" Devon mused aloud while they were eating. "I'll wager he has had some wonderful adventures this past year."

"*I'll* wager he wishes he were back in Gadwin's Drug Shop where he belongs!" Deborah replied sarcastically. "When will you learn that that boy doesn't have your wild nature? I wish that *he* were my daughter and you were Gadwin's son!"

"If that means I would be off fighting for independence in his place, then thank you very much!"

Deborah stared at her coldly, and Devon felt a

twinge of sadness to see how dark her mother's blue eyes had become. She could still be pretty! she thought, taking in the pale hair drawn severely back from Deborah's face. If she would only *smile* now and then!

"Get on with your breakfast. There's butter to be churned."

Less than a half hour later, Devon began the tedious job, having first moved the churn to the window so that she might watch the street below and the river beyond. The sunrise was spellbinding, and she lost herself in the growing beauty of the eastern sky and thought idly about her life.

In normal times, there was little doubt that she would have been married by now. Was it possible that she was eighteen years old? Devon sighed, wondering where the future would take her. She had received a letter from Morgan a few days ago—the third communication since his departure. His regiment was preparing to march to Virginia. "It seems that everyone is going to Yorktown," he wrote. "Something big is in the air, but no one is quite sure what it is." He went on at length about the weather and his passion for Devon. She yearned to hear stories of the war, tales of Morgan's hair-raising adventures and narrow escapes. Still, it was wonderful to read his thoughts and to know he was well. Perhaps the war would toughen him.

Devon sorely missed Morgan, yet this last solitary year had changed her. Their daydreams in the meadow and Morgan's urgent kisses seemed part of a long-ago past. She was anxious for him to return to New London so that they might renew their bonds before time dissolved them entirely. The future she had planned with Morgan was the only ray of hope that she could cling to during the long days in the shop. It was increasingly more difficult to escape Deborah's watchful eye.

Cannon shots suddenly echoed from Fort Griswold. Devon listened—three shots, the signal for a returning privateer. A few minutes later there were three more shots, which was curious, especially since no vessels could be seen approaching. Her stomach tightened in alarm. She had noticed men riding south along the Bank, and now another group went galloping past the shop.

Devon raced downstairs, nearly colliding with her mother.

"You can't be finished yet!" Deborah accused.

"Something is wrong. I can feel it! I knew it when I woke up this morning!" With that, Devon ran outside, just as Nick came thundering down Bank Street on his best horse. She could read his face even before he dismounted.

"It's the British, isn't it?"

"Yes, child, it is. There's a whole fleet—two dozen vessels or more—at the mouth of the harbor."

"But the signal—"

"They must have added the third shot to fool us, though God only knows how they learned our signals. It may only be a plundering party, after stock, but I doubt it."

"Nick, where are you going?"

"To Fort Trumbull, of course! To meet those damned lobsterbacks head-on!"

He gave her a hug, then was off. Devon lifted her skirts and raced to the river to get a better view. A cold chill ran down her spine at the sight of the imposing British ships bearing down on New London, and she immediately returned to the shop to warn her mother.

"I am not going anywhere," Deborah stated flatly.

Minutes stretched into hours as New London frantically tried to evacuate. All around the Linen and Pewter Shop townspeople harnessed horses and hurriedly loaded valuables into wagons. Devon, unable to reason with her mother, retreated to the top floor to watch the chaos on the Beach as the privateers hoisted sail in a wild effort to escape before the British fleet could trap them. Devon was not surprised to see the *Black Eagle* sailing upriver first.

Several neighbors took a moment to run to the Linen and Pewter Shop to make certain that the Widow Lindsay intended to leave. Devon watched hopefully as Dr. Wolcott, Jonathan Starr, and Titus Hurlbutt each entered the door, but she expected no miracle. Deborah had been pulled along during the false-alarm evacuations, but now, as the enemy landed only a few miles away, she had no intention of turning her back on her shop. She seemed to feel that a cold stare would chase any intruders away.

News spread rapidly. By nine o'clock Devon had heard that half the British had landed at White Beach, just below the lighthouse, while the rest had reached Groton Point, south of Fort Griswold. She could see the shots coming from the Groton fort, aimed at the enemy vessels. Was there a chance that they might be frightened off?

Then she spotted the boatloads of men from Fort Trumbull crossing the Thames to join forces with the soldiers at Fort Griswold. So quickly! They must have been hopelessly outnumbered, Devon thought, feeling ill. She ran downstairs to relay these facts to her mother but was immediately distracted by a familiar figure on horseback. It was Jonathan Brooks, a boy from nearby Bradley Street whom she knew and liked well. Devon dashed outside, shouting, "Wait!"

"Devon! I can't stop any longer. Father has ordered me to hurry home and put the horse in the barn."

"Jonathan, you must tell me what you know. Mother won't leave! Did you see them? How many are there?"

"Yes, I saw them. Jenny here got caught in a mire while I was trying for the heights. A shot passed right over my head as I got down to free her! There are *hundreds* of redcoats, Devon, and they've split up. Half of those landing at White Beach made for the fort, but the rest are on their way to town. Father and about a hundred others have hidden along Town Hill Road and have managed to hit a few of them, but it looks bad. I've really got to be off now. I'm to wait for word from Father at home. You should get away! The redcoats will be in New London soon!"

"Thank you, Jonathan. Good luck!"

Jenny galloped off in a cloud of dust, leaving Devon standing on a nearly deserted Bank Street.

Back in the shop, Deborah stood firm. "I cannot leave my life's work to be plundered by those mad British. Let them ransack the other shops, but I will stay here to protect what is mine."

Devon wanted to wail, What about me? Does my life mean less to you than this pitiful shop?

At that moment they both heard a loud commotion outside. Devon ran to the window just in time to see a few dozen redcoats round the turn. They were laughing, several carrying bottles and drinking from them.

As she watched, the group split up, kicking in locked doors. Crashing glass and heavy thumps sounded from the invaded houses. Devon went sick with panic as two of the soldiers, each carrying a bottle of gin, started toward the Linen and Pewter Shop. She turned to her mother with wild fear in her eyes.

"They are coming, Mother! Two drunken redcoats with guns! Let us go out the back. There's still time!"

"No." Deborah stood next to a neat display of her handmade canopies, her hands spread protectively over the white net.

"Well, we can hide, then! Hurry!"

Devon was looking around frantically when the door flew open and the two British soldiers staggered across the threshold.

"Blimey, what a surprise! Looks like we picked the right address, Smythe!" one of them shouted, giving his companion an elbow in the ribs. Smythe seemed not to hear; he stared at Devon. Her red-gold hair haloed a face flushed and wide-eyed with fear, and her body was tensely frozen but for the agitated heaving of her lovely bosom.

"I want that one, Dobbs," he declared, pointing.

Dobbs stuck out his chin. "Hardly fair, old boy. Didn't give me a chance to discuss it!" Smythe was a surly sort, however, and Dobbs had no wish to provoke him. The other female was older, but rather good-looking and clean enough, he thought.

"I'll thank you gentlemen to leave my shop," Deborah told them icily.

Dobbs laughed heartily at this and took another swig of gin as he crossed the room. "I'll thank *you* to come upstairs with me, darling!" His fingers touched the pistol he wore. "Wouldn't want to have to persuade you."

He was a tall, thin man with sinewy muscles and easily pulled her off toward the stairway. Devon watched in horror, feeling as though her world were going up in flames of terror.

"Mama!" she cried, tears streaming down her cheeks. "Oh, Mama, no!"

The last glimpse she had of her mother would be scorched permanently in her memory. Deborah's perpetually bitter expression vanished. Devon had never called her Mama—only Jamie had—but in that moment all the lost years and love flowed back between mother and daughter.

"Devon, baby—" Deborah's voice was tender, surprised, sad. Dobbs yanked her around the corner and there was a long clattering noise as he forced her upstairs.

Smythe caught Devon's shoulder and she turned to face him. Wearing a white wig and a well-tailored red, black, and white uniform, Smythe gave a passable appearance, yet his bloodshot eyes were narrowed in a way that made Devon shudder. Seeing her reaction, his full mouth twisted in a mirthless smile.

41

Grasping each shoulder, Smythe pulled her against his body and kissed her brutally. Devon could taste the gin on his thick tongue and was horrified to feel something swelling against her belly.

When he began to pull at her bodice, Devon pleaded, "Please! The dress is new—"

Smythe grinned. Grasping the froth of lace trimming the neckline, he ripped the gown to her waist. Devon sobbed as he pushed her backward across the table, atop the net canopies, and pinned her wrists. His mouth sought the sweet young breasts. He sucked greedily until her nipples tightened instinctively, then he bit each one in turn, smiling when Devon cried out.

Her senses began to dull. She prayed she would faint soon. There was no sound from upstairs. Naturally, her mother would not allow herself to scream, Devon thought. She closed her eyes, streaming tears, as Smythe pulled up her skirts, fumbling until he found the tender, secret place no other man had seen. He was breathing heavily. Devon thought she would die when he touched her and his finger twisted up inside her. Oh, merciful God . . . please . . .

It was not God who delivered her, but the enemy. Suddenly there were voices and a step in the doorway.

"Smythe, damn you, what are you up to? Leave this play for later. Come on, then—"

"You can't expect me to stop now!" Smythe whined. "Have a turn yourself, Lieutenant. I won't tell anyone. Just let me have my own!"

"No! Let the girl up. If you stay here another minute, you'll be burned to death for your pleasure. We're putting the torch to every building on this street, and Captain Stapleton is waiting."

Smythe was furious; Devon dazed. The lieutenant departed and Smythe left her bent across the table. He stamped over to the stairway, calling, "Dobbs! They're burning the town. We've got to get out!"

He returned to Devon and tried to pull her across the room to the door.

"My mother!" she shrieked. "You must make certain they are coming! Mama! Hurry!" Her voice grew shrill, hysterical, until Smythe slapped her roughly across her mouth. When Devon began struggling in earnest, he cuffed her again with enough force to make her neck snap back, dazing her.

She was in such shock as he dragged her outside that she forgot her gaping bodice and bruised, exposed breasts. Acrid smoke burned her eyes. Flames danced through houses, shops, warehouses, and barns all along the Bank, spreading as she watched. Soldiers were carrying torches on their way to the Beach, laughing over the prospect of plundering the warehouses there. A young boy in uniform ran to Smythe to offer his torch.

"The lieutenant said to wait 'til you came out," he piped, ogling Devon.

Smythe grabbed the torch and tossed it inside the Linen and Pewter Shop onto Deborah's handmade canopies. The fire roared up as Devon began to cry out again, choking back tears. "Mama! Please, hurry, hurry!" Helplessly, she crumpled against her captor. "My mama!"

"Come on, then, wench. I'll have you yet," Smythe growled. The boy ran along beside them as they followed Bank Street northward. Devon stumbled and wept craning her neck to see the shop, her home, hoping to see her mother and Dobbs emerge. The entire front of the building was engulfed in tangerine flames before they had turned a corner.

A raw, angry survival instinct soon replaced her trembling numbness, but Devon went on pretending that she was in shock. Real hatred, unknown to her until today, filled her with clever courage. As they drew near to the rendezvous spot where Captain Stapleton and the other men waited, she could sense Smythe's carelessness. His grip on her arm loosened as he gulped gin and conversed vulgarly with the boy who accompanied them. Through the flames and smoke the battle at Fort Griswold was progressing, and after Smythe assessed Devon's zombielike stare and shuffling walk, he turned to peer across the Thames.

At that instant Devon snapped her arm free, raised her skirts, and started running.

Black smoke scorched her lungs as she ran on and on through the curving, blazing streets. Unable to look back for fear of seeing Smythe, she just kept running, turning random corners.

Three redcoats approached from the south, so Devon ran in the opposite direction. She knew, without consciously deciding, just where she might find refuge. The British soldiers had begun chasing her, but one by one they gave up, dulled by alcohol and fatigue. Devon clambered up a stone-reinforced bank and disappeared into a thick stand of trees. Quickly she chose a sturdy sycamore and ascended with the agility of a cat. Below and to the north lay the Burial Ground, where some of New London's earliest inhabitants rested. Devon relaxed for a moment, but then spied a man on horseback beside the Winthrop tomb. She leaned forward for a closer look. A redcoat! An officer, too, immaculately bewigged and uniformed. The man was watching the last moments of the battle at Fort Griswold, across the Thames. Devon pulled herself forward along the branch in an effort to see the face of this enemy who so coolly supervised the battle. The commanding officer? she wondered. The man responsible for her mother's death, her degradation? And Nick, over at the fort, was he dead, too?

A twig snapped against her knee and the British officer turned automatically. Devon held her breath, felt it burn her lungs. It was the most infamous traitor of all—Benedict Arnold!

She longed to jump to the ground and claw his face. He had betrayed not only his country but now his town as well. Only Arnold could have known the Thames so well, could have been so familiar with the habits of the harbor towns. No wonder the alarm from Fort Griswold had been botched! The traitor had to be certain the cards were dealt in his favor before the match began.

He sat astride his horse, watching the action at Groton Heights through narrowed eyes. Elegant, arrogantly handsome. Devon seethed with repressed fury, knowing that she must remain silent.

She lost all sense of time. The early foliage protected her from the sun. The fires in New London died down; the Parade was destroyed, its charred remains smoking dismally. Devon could see all the storehouses along the Beach and the Bank standing open while redcoats and Hessians carried off what remained of the contents. The store that had held the goods from the *Hannah,* the prize ship which had been captured just two months ago, stood deserted, its doors gaping open.

Her eyes burned and watered from the smoke; her limbs ached. It hurt too much to think about her mother or Nick or anyone else who might be dead, so she forced herself to stare at Arnold until hatred overcame grief.

Messengers came and went, whispering in the general's ear. Arnold began to look rather fatigued himself; several times he mopped the sweat from his brow.

Three British officers rowed across the Thames and landed at New London. A green-clad Hessian pointed toward the Burial Ground, and the men ran up Hill Street toward their commander. There was a great deal of gesturing when they reached Arnold. He appeared to be furious, but Devon could not discern his words. Then, quieted, he led them back to the stretch of shadow near his horse, stopping only a few yards from her perch.

"You've killed them all?" the general hissed incredulously. "I thought they surrendered the fort!"

"Yes. They did surrender," the tallest officer muttered.

"Hmm. I see." Arnold closed his eyes for a moment, pressing white fingers to his brow. "Well, it's done now. Have you made a count?"

"Yes, sir. Eighty-five dead, sixty wounded," said a plump and eager lieutenant. "They fought like tigers, sir! Even after they were run through, they kept on. One of their Negroes killed Major Montgomery, but we saw to it that he never lived to tell the tale."

Arnold's next words were muffled, but Devon wasn't listening. Eighty-five dead! Eighty-five of her lifelong friends and neighbors. It was a massacre! Devon shut her eyes and clenched her teeth until her jaw ached. Every muscle and nerve in her body longed to lash out and destroy these verminous redcoats.

When she finally opened her eyes, Arnold and his men were gone. For a moment Devon wondered if he had been some mad apparition. Perhaps her mind had snapped . . .

Looking toward New London, she saw that it was no dream. Most of the fires were out and the British were getting ready to leave. Satan's brigade! Devon thought bitterly. A fleeting memory of Smythe raced across her brain before she banished it. Struggling to sit up, she leaned back against the tree trunk, sore and cold. She watched the town empty as the British returned to their ships. Before long, the hill below Fort Griswold was bare as well, but many of the buildings along the east riverbank were now in flames.

The fiends! Devon seethed. Unable to bear another moment in the tree, she dropped to the ground. It was a long fall, but physical pain seemed a proper distraction. She was heedless of danger from the enemy; the split bodice was her only worry. Pausing barely a moment, she tore the ruffle from her petticoat, and wrapped it around the bodice of her gown, concealing her breasts. Well enough, she thought. The dress was ruined anyway.

Devon left the Burial Ground and started down Huntington Street. She wasn't sure where to go, nor could she think properly. Turning toward the water, she walked to Main Street. There was not a sign of life. The Parade was still engulfed in smoke.

Haltingly, Devon started south and promptly stumbled over a body. Red cloth was all she could see as she fell. Her heart pounded in panic as she imagined crimson arms grasping her, lifting her skirts . . . Shaking with terror and confusion, she crawled to one side of the road. It *was* a British soldier, but one so intoxicated that he was incapable of attacking even the road on which he lay. The air all around reeked of gin. Devon felt ill.

A horse was approaching! Devon commanded her head to turn and saw, with relief, that the rider was garbed in neither red nor dark green. He was not one of her neighbors, however. There was no chance of escape; the man had already seen her, waved, and was slowing down.

Devon could not find her voice. She watched dumbly as the stocky, sandy-haired young man dismounted and promptly searched the drunken redcoat. Smiling, he picked up the bayoneted gun which lay at the soldier's side, then unwound the cartridge box and bayonet sheath from the man's slack neck. Finally the stranger turned to face Devon.

"Were you eyeing these?" he inquired, showing no inclination to hand them over.

She shook her head vigorously.

"Say!" The man gave a shout. "I remember you! Little Miss Hatbox! You used to hang about on the docks."

He grinned with a cheerfulness that seemed macabre in the middle of a burned and looted town. Devon remembered him then. The seaman from the *Black*

Eagle who had spoken to her last year. It had been the day she'd been kissed . . . She froze against the memories and merely stared back at the genial privateersman.

"Do you remember me?" he coaxed. "I think you do! Say, are you all right? Why don't you say something?" His green eyes fell on her ruffle-bound bodice and widened quizzically.

"The Bank—" Devon croaked. "You saw? Take me there. My mama—"

"Miss, you can't go down there! The Parade's still burning. And as for the Bank, it's gone. The Shaw mansion was saved, but not much else. That was the first street to go, I think."

"Mama," Devon choked, her throat thick with tears.

"Aw, sweetheart." He put a muscular arm around her. "What've they done to you? Your mama died?"

Devon nodded, trying to staunch the flow of tears with her forearm. The stranger pried it away from her face.

"My name is Noah Jackson, and I'm going to help you. Looks like you need some!" He set the redcoat's gun down before wrapping his other arm around Devon. "Where's your papa?"

"Dead," she sobbed.

"You're all alone?"

She nodded convulsively.

"Shh, now. Don't worry! It'll be all right. I'll take care of you. Tell me your name, sweetheart."

Devon was ashamed of her tears and whimpering and incoherence, yet she clung to Noah Jackson desperately. "I'm . . . Devon," she whispered.

Noah grinned again, even more cheerfully. "That's the prettiest name I ever heard," he declared. "Just like you. Devon, you come with me. I'll see that no harm comes to you."

There was an openness about his grinning face that Devon trusted. She looked back just once at the ugly black smoke to the south before letting him help her mount his horse. They started off and were deep into the woods above New London before Devon realized she had not even asked where they were going.

Chapter Five

———◆———

The Evening of September 6, 1781

NORWICH, Connecticut, lay on the west bank of the Thames, ten miles north of New London. Near the town was a secluded cove where the *Black Eagle* swayed peacefully at anchor. André Raveneau had sent all but three of his crew below so that the privateer might remain as inconspicuous as possible, while he stood silently on the quarter-deck and sipped his evening's inch of cognac.

Part of him wished that he had stayed to fight the British in New London, but he knew the *Black Eagle* wouldn't have stood a chance against twenty-four well-armed ships. Two or three he could handle, but . . .

The Thames was like ebony glass tonight, under a lavishly star-strewn sky. It was so quiet. Raveneau guessed that Norwich must be holding its breath in fear that the enemy would strike here next.

The underbrush was dry and brittle this late in the year, making stealth on shore next to impossible. Raveneau discerned the first crunch of leaves and twigs, realized that it was not a small animal, and lost no time in crossing the upper deck, one hand on the pistol hooked over his belt.

"Come forward and be seen!"

The bushes rustled. Voices? Raveneau narrowed steel-gray eyes, unhooked his pistol. A man emerged into the open, a horse close behind.

"Jackson!" Raveneau hissed. *"Dieu!* What do you think you are doing?"

When the captain was upset, his English became almost unintelligible. He frequently abandoned it completely to curse at an offender in French. Noah understood his name, but little of what followed. This time he didn't need a translation.

"Captain, may I board?"

"No! Knowing you, you've British money in one pocket and a knife with my name on it in the other. Explain yourself now."

Noah was embarrassed to realize that Devon, who crouched behind him in the bushes, was listening to this unfavorable description of his character. Until now, he'd had her believing he was an knight errant who specialized in rescuing females in peril.

"Unfair, Captain! It happens that I have a very acceptable explanation for my absence this morning. Won't you allow me to give it privately?"

"Is your mother eavesdropping? For God's sake, Jackson, this *is* private! You waste my time. Get on with it."

"All right." Noah thrust out his chin like a stubborn child. "I was with . . . a woman last night. I fell asleep. By the time I awoke, the *Black Eagle* was only a speck upriver."

Raveneau continued to glare at him. Noah couldn't understand why the captain disliked him so, even after three years. Granted, he had moments of unreliability, but that was no reason to be treated so harshly.

André Raveneau wanted to tell Jackson to slink back to his whore, but common sense won out. The man was an accomplished sailmaker; his contribution was important. Still . . . there were so many qualities of Jackson's that Raveneau detested. He was lazy, never pulling his weight, and was the sort of man who would smile angelically while betraying his best friend. Anyone who smiled as much as Jackson automatically dropped to the bottom of Raveneau's list.

"This time I will let it pass, but not another. Is that clear? You know my rules, and you are the last man who deserves to bend them."

Noah splashed into the water and swam to the rope ladder that Raveneau tossed over the side.

Crouched behind a tangle of branches, Devon shivered with excitement as André Raveneau turned again to scan the dark shoreline. What if he saw her? Would he come and capture her?

During their ride to Norwich, Devon had quizzed Noah about his captain. Ever amiable, he had stiffened slightly at Raveneau's name. Yes, of course, the captain was truly a man of legendary qualities. Brave and lucky beyond human limits. Brilliant without a doubt.

But, Noah had told Devon, there was more. Raveneau was reckless to a fault, overconfident of his ability to outwit his adversaries. The man was unbending. He demanded more from his crew than normal men could give, stringent standards that were never relaxed. Madness! The men were certain to revolt one day.

Devon pondered Noah's words. So, Raveneau was flawed after all. Or could it be a simple case of the perfect man demanding excellence from his subordinates?

Noah began to think that Captain Raveneau was watching him. The stocky seaman had waited three hours for a chance to slip the girl on board, but Raveneau kept appearing. Now, Noah lay in his hammock in the midst of his seventy-odd smelly, snoring shipmates, waiting and listening to the watch walking the deck overhead. Noah was certain he would have no problem bribing them to ignore Devon. A female on board was just what they *all* needed, and Noah fully intended to be the prime beneficiary. Raveneau would be furious, but even he was known for his rakish streak. The girl would charm him. The worst that could happen would be Devon's being put ashore along the way. At least she wouldn't be able to say it was Noah's fault, and in the meantime, they would all have some fun.

Noah eased out of his hammock and stepped into the gangway, listening. The captain had retired to his cabin, and there was no law against walking around, after all, so Noah tried to relax. A bundle of clothes wadded under one arm, he climbed to the gun deck, then the quarter-deck. The two bored young sailors standing the night watch were delighted by the news Noah brought them. One of them stood by the ladder, listening for the captain, while the other helped Noah over the side.

Devon watched the action through a veil of leaves. She was cold and tired, but seeing the bundle that Noah held aloft while wading in, she knew she would soon be able to go aboard.

"Hello, Devon!" he exclaimed, wearing the same casually cheerful smile as ever.

"Have you really come for me? Are you certain it is all right? Captain Raveneau doesn't mind?"

"Of course it's all right, sweetheart. As for Captain Raveneau, what he doesn't know won't hurt him. Now, hurry up and put these on." His grin widened, but he turned away.

Devon peeled off her torn yellow gown and ragged chemise, then put on the clothing Noah had brought. From time to time she glanced hesitantly in his direction, but he did not turn back until she was dressed. There had been only the pair of loose, wide-legged sailor's breeches, a rough, light-colored shirt, and a smelly red knit cap, which Noah helped her pull over her mass of strawberry-blond curls.

"I will hunt up some shoes and a jacket for you later tonight," he assured her. "You look adorable!"

"I don't know if this is a good idea," Devon moaned, feeling foolish.

"Maybe it's not, but seems to me it's the only idea we've got! Don't worry. Nobody on this ship would hurt you, Devon."

He gallantly carried her through the water, back to the privateer. She got almost as wet as he did, but appreciated the gesture.

A leering teen-aged sailor helped her over the side and Devon found herself standing on the gun-deck of the *Black Eagle*. In the moonlight, she could see the glow of rubbed mahogany and teak, the gleam of polished brass. The canvas sails were starkly white against the black sky.

"Hurry!" the sailor urged Noah. "The captain could be up any minute!"

Noah was beginning to feel a bit panicky himself, especially at the thought of Raveneau appearing, but his smile barely faltered. Devon saw this with relief.

"Forward?" she asked.

"Yes. Greenbriar is right. We must hurry."

They climbed down the ladder and entered lantern-lit darkness. Devon expected the usual suffocating odors of bilge water, pitch, and unwashed bodies, but what she smelled was only a fraction as strong as that in most ships. The berth deck was lined with lanterns, all spotless and burning brightly. As Noah guided her urgently toward the crew's quarters, she could not resist whispering, "Your captain keeps a clean ship!"

Noah shrugged. "It is a simple thing to make rules for others to do the work."

Devon glanced at him curiously.

"Here we are. Shh! They're asleep!"

A lantern flickered on the far wall, offering the barest illumination. Devon peered at the rank, snoring sailors who lay head to toe in their hammocks like six dozen sardines. A few stirred when Noah led her into the cabin, but none troubled to wake up.

Guiding her to his own hammock, he whispered, "You sleep here. I'll find another." He took off his jacket and held it out. "Put this on for now. Cover your chest and don't let it show. Lie down, get some rest, while I think of a plan for tomorrow."

Devon climbed into the hammock without a word, drained of energy and anxious for an hour or two of deep sleep. It seemed years since she had awakened in her bed above the Linen and Pewter Shop.

At that moment yellow light flared in the doorway. Startled, Devon turned her head and saw a candle, held by a dark, masculine hand. Her eyes widened, shifting to broad shoulders, then meeting the steely gaze of Captain André Raveneau.

Devon automatically looked down to make certain her jacket was closed, then returned her eyes to the shadow-shrouded figure across the cabin, praying that the gloom would hide her burning flush.

Raveneau wore his usual loose white shirt, carelessly buttoned only halfway up his chest, fawn breeches, and black knee boots. Devon thought him stunningly handsome, yet terrifying. Did he know who she was? Could he see? Her heart raced anxiously.

"Jackson, who the hell is this?" he demanded abruptly.

Noah could be heard clambering over hammocks, then he was standing at Devon's shoulder. "I'm not certain, Captain, but I think I heard Mr. Lane say he's a new . . . ah . . . surgeon's mate. Came on yesterday while you were ashore."

Raveneau lifted an interested brow at these words as Devon turned to Noah, staring incredulously.

"I can scarcely believe anyone would sign him on without my knowledge, but they must have known I'd welcome a surgeon's mate." Raveneau looked at

Devon. "Christ, but you look young! Is your father a physician?"

"Yes, sir," Devon agreed, trying to speak in a deeper, boyish voice.

"What's your name?"

"James, sir." Her brother's name.

"All of it, sailor." Raveneau was looking skeptical.

"Uh . . . Hugh James."

"All right, James, I'll give you a try. Whatever skills you possess may be greatly appreciated in the weeks to come. For now, though, I have other tasks to occupy you until a bit of surgery comes along. Come with me." As Devon left her hammock, he said, "Jackson, you're excused. I'll let you sleep tonight so that we may preserve your eyes for the sails awaiting your attention tomorrow. They have missed you!"

Noah winced at the sarcasm, but also at the sight of Devon following André Raveneau out the door. It would take a miracle to carry her undetected through a private encounter with that man. Noah had planned to keep her so well hidden among the seamen that Raveneau would never have noticed her. He groaned aloud and muttered, "Perhaps my luck will hold until we're at sea. I can't afford to be tossed off the ship for that child!"

Devon felt paralyzed, yet her legs were moving. How should she act as Hugh James, surgeon's mate? she wondered. And what could Raveneau need at this hour?

She scrambled along behind the captain, who moved down the narrow gangway with practiced ease. She watched the back of his head, noting the texture of his clean black hair, and remembered with poignant clarity the kiss they had shared almost a year ago. A rush of excitement swept through her. After all, this *was* the *Black Eagle* and she was traversing the berth deck alone with the legendary André Raveneau. The possibilities were staggering! Wasn't this the very situation she had dreamed of for years? She was going to sea, aboard the most notorious privateer of them all!

The captain's cabin was the farthest aft. They passed the officers' quarters and the wardroom before reaching it, and Devon was conscious of a progressive improvement in the accommodations. In this self-contained world where a man could never be alone, even when he went to bed, only the captain possessed a haven of privacy. Raveneau's was singularly comforting.

There was a real bed of polished mahogany, sturdily built but inviting, a matching drop-front desk, and a simple table. A wing chair, upholstered in glove-soft red leather, stood near the desk. A collection of charts, instruments, and almanacs lay on the table, flanked by a brandy snifter and a bottle of French cognac. Candles burned in lanterns and wrought-iron holders, lending a cozy glow to the cabin. The scents of tobacco, fine leather, and Raveneau himself mingled in the air.

He poured some cognac for himself, then turned to look her up and down. Devon pretended shyness, hunching her shoulders and surveying her stockinged feet.

"Shoes?" Raveneau asked, as though wishing he could ignore their absence.

"I forgot." Devon strove for a masculine voice.

"In the future, I think you should remember."

"Yes, sir."

"Now then, James, let me explain what I require of you. My steward is ill—tonight's cooking, I fear—and to avoid utter chaos in my cabin, I would like to employ you until he is well. I do not foresee any sea battles or injuries for a few days, so it would seem that you are the perfect choice."

Devon rubbed her toes restlessly against the buffed floor.

"You behave like a bashful child!" Raveneau exclaimed sharply. Devon noticed that his accent became more pronounced. "I have no patience for men who can neither speak nor move without instructions. I suggest that you straighten your back and attempt to convince me you are a worthy addition to my crew."

Shakily Devon raised her head, but knew better than to throw back her shoulders. "Yes, sir. I'm sorry. I want to be a part of the *Black Eagle* more than I can say."

Raveneau gazed long and hard at his new surgeon's mate and substitute steward. There was an alarming softness in his husky voice, and his body and face were fragile-looking. Such large, luminous eyes!

"How old are you, James?"

"Uh . . . fifteen, sir."

"I have a feeling that sea life may be exactly what you need!"

Devon's face grew warm. "I am afraid that I spent too much time in my father's office, watching him and reading medical books." What am I saying? she thought hysterically.

"I suppose that will be our gain, James. But, for the present, there are other matters on my mind. We will be at sea before dawn and there are things I want done before then. Minter was boiling water for my bath when he became ill. I want you to finish that task, prepare my bath, then see to it that the stores of fresh water are replenished before we weigh anchor. It may be a long while before we've access to fresh water again, and I don't like to ration my men."

"Pardon me, sir, but I'd always heard that was necessary."

"James, you will find that I have some rather unorthodox policies." Raveneau smiled slightly, but his eyes remained flinty, tired-looking. "I wish there was time to chat about all of them, but unfortunately—"

Devon blushed, all too aware of his sarcasm.

"Sir, where will I find this water for your bath?" She looked around. "Also, is there a tub here?"

"The water is heated in the galley, the tub is in the wardroom." He smiled. "All the officers share it, though few have time for real baths. Luckily, I don't need much sleep, so I am able to indulge in some luxuries."

Devon longed to banter with him, to flirt and enjoy his company, but she realized that until they were at sea, her position was extremely precarious.

"I'll go, then, sir," she declared, backing away. He made no reply but continued to watch her, so she offered a clumsy salute, backing into the doorjamb at the same time.

Raveneau's grin was blinding, his teeth as white as a tiger's, eyes sparkling silver. "Fortunately, that gesture is not required on board the *Black Eagle*," he told her, highly amused. Devon's face was burning. She stared at her stockinged feet as he added irrepressibly, "James, I hope you won't be offended if I say that it is my ardent hope never to lie under your knife!"

Devon found the wooden tub, dragged it out of the darkened wardroom and back through the open cabin door. Raveneau's good humor had vanished. He now sat at his desk, poring over papers and making notations. Devon shrugged and set off for the galley, which was located just aft of the crew's quarters. The wooden buckets held at least five gallons of the steaming water, she discovered, which splashed over the sides and onto her feet as she staggered along. It was a mystery to her why any man as intelligent as the captain would choose a little weakling to fill his bath! Didn't he realize how difficult it would be? Or was he just so preoccupied with his own comfort and worries that he had no time to think of anyone else?

Perspiring, she upended the fourth bucket and watched with relief as the water level rose. One or two more would be enough. Devon almost growled at the wide shoulders bent over the desk, their owner totally oblivious to her suffering as he labored over a chart, aided by a handsome brass protractor.

I'll fill just one more, she decided angrily. Let him get more if he wants it!

Arms quivering, she lugged the fifth bucketful along the starboard gangway. Her breeches and shoeless feet were soaked by the time she staggered into the cabin, close to tears. She glanced up and found the tub occupied by Captain Raveneau.

He was completely naked, his tanned, muscular back wet and gleaming in the candlelight. Absorbed in the task of washing, he didn't bother to look up and missed the sight of Devon weaving sideways into the wall, her eyes round with alarmed surprise.

"Will you get over here with that water, James? I'd begun to think you were ladling it into the bucket with a teaspoon! *Depêchez-vous!*" he shouted, looking over his shoulder with steely eyes. "I am freezing!"

Devon's knees were wobbly, but she commanded them to move and reached the tub. It took all her remaining strength to lift the bucket high enough to pour. Raveneau sighed with pleasure as the steamy water encircled his body; then he frowned and re-soaped his sponge.

"You are as slow as an old woman. I'm not certain that there is a place for you in my crew."

Devon came to life. "Oh, sir, no, please! I will work hard, I promise you! Don't put me off—I have no place to go!"

"James, if I took on every homeless boy roaming this coast, I would not have much of a privateer."

"Please, give me a chance!"

Her earnest expression deepened his scowl. "You even plead like a female," he muttered. "Make yourself useful, then, and wash my back."

Aghast, Devon felt the soapy sponge drop into her hand. He had propped a large map and another chart in the chair nearby and now turned his attention to these, while Devon found herself staring at the brown expanse of back that tapered into narrow hips and hard buttocks below the waterline. Never in her life had she seen, much less touched, a man's unclothed body, but before the captain could reprimand her again, she reached out to rub the sponge over his skin.

Fleetingly, the face of the soldier who had tried to rape her jumped into her mind, yet Devon could make no connection between him and Captain Raveneau. Of course, she would not want *any* man to touch her as Smythe had, but there seemed little danger now that she was dressed as a boy! She rubbed the sponge from side to side, watching the soapy rivulets trickle over the lean ridges of Raveneau's back. A splendidly made man, she mused, then chided herself for such an audacious thought. He turned to retrieve the sponge and Devon scrambled to her feet, standing awkwardly to one side as he ducked his head under the water. He rubbed soap into his hair; dark hands were lost in the suds. Devon saw that his eyes were closed and she let herself stare at him, memorizing every chiseled line. She glanced down briefly at the dark blur in the water below his waist, then blushed so profusely that she had to press her cheek against the cool, damp bulkhead.

Raveneau finished rinsing his hair. Devon looked around for towels and found expensive linen ones folded on top of his trunk, elegantly monogrammed. He stood up in the wooden tub, and she glimpsed a lean, tanned, and powerful body with a great deal of black hair on it.

Taking the towels, Raveneau said in a voice both tired and abrupt, "Go to bed. We will weigh anchor in a few hours."

"Yes, sir. Good night, sir."

"Report to me after we are at sea. I'm afraid Minter won't have recovered by tomorrow."

"Yes, sir." Devon was feeling more relaxed since he had wrapped a towel around his waist. "Good night. And thank you."

"Don't thank me," he admonished, vigorously rubbing a towel over his gleaming black hair. "Just prove to me that you can work like any other man on board the *Black Eagle*."

Making her way back to the crew's quarters, Devon became aware of the full extent of her exhaustion. Every muscle ached, along with her head, eyes, and heart.

She glanced into the dark galley in passing and saw a shadowy body. Long arms, groping hands, surrounded her, but she managed to let out a healthy scream before a palm closed over her mouth and she was dragged into the darkness. Devon had never felt so tired and weak; her struggles were ridiculously ineffectual. The stranger pressed her into a corner and began to pull wildly at her clothing. One knee jabbed the intimate places that had already been abused once that day, while fingers squeezed and rubbed her breasts. Devon heard her shirt tear. She felt warm tears sliding down her cheeks onto the hand that covered her mouth.

"Mon Dieu! What is going on here?"

There was light. Devon could see Captain Raveneau through a mist of tears, then she saw her attacker. It was the boy who had been standing watch and had helped her over the rail. Stunned and frightened, he released Devon. Raveneau caught her as she fell. The last thing Devon remembered was his arm under her breasts and a startled, enraged shout.

"It's a girl! Damnation! Who is responsible for this?"

The cabin was spinning, then dipping gently, and Devon opened her eyes. Cool linen caressed her cheek. She could smell . . . what, whom? She smiled, closing her eyes again. Raveneau. From far away voices came to her.

"This time you've gone too far, Jackson. You've cut your own throat. I don't know why I let you get by with so many things in the past, but never again. York-town will be your last stop."

"Captain Raveneau, you must try to understand!" It was Noah's voice, ingratiating yet edged with panic. "The poor child. Her parents are both dead now, her home destroyed. You wouldn't have wanted me to leave her there for the redcoats?"

"I wanted you on board today, where you were *supposed* to be!" Raveneau's voice was dangerously low. "God's life, Jackson, I cannot run this ship like a mother hen! You knew my rules when you signed on, yet you've flouted them time and time again."

"I promise, Captain—"

"Spare me," Raveneau interrupted in a venomous tone. "I hope you read the Articles of Agreement well before signing on? They specifically state that any man behaving indecently toward a woman shall lose his shares *and* receive whatever punishment I see fit to administer. However, since you placed the temptation before him, I shall let Greenbriar keep his one meager share. He'll stand on deck with you tomorrow and take five lashes, though."

There was a long, tension-laden pause. Devon struggled to clear her mind and make sense of this conversation.

"What of me, sir? How many lashes will I receive?" Noah was asking.

"Five. You will lose your shares as well, Jackson, and leave the ship when we reach Yorktown. If you cause trouble in the meantime, I'll put you adrift at sea. Understood?"

"Yes, sir," Noah said acidly.

"That's all. Tell Mr. Lane I want to see him."

Devon listened to the receding footsteps and tried to ascertain whether or not the *Black Eagle* was under-way yet. Was it morning? Were they at sea? Or had only a short while passed? Did Raveneau intend to put her ashore? She kept her eyes closed and listened. The cabin swayed to and fro, but Devon was certain the privateer was not moving forward. She cautiously opened one eye a fraction and peeked through a haze of lashes. The cabin was dark, except for the lantern which hung over Raveneau's desk. So it was still night. He was sitting in the leather wing chair, garbed in a gray, soft-looking dressing gown, the kind that men usually wore over clothing during leisure hours. Devon strained her eye; it appeared that Raveneau wore nothing beneath his robe. He was holding a fresh snifter of cognac, his tan, handsome legs stretched out and crossed at the ankles. Abruptly he turned his head and stared hard at Devon; she squeezed the eye closed.

"Eh bien. Are you awake?" Raveneau crossed the cabin and leaned over her. "Damn, what did Jackson say her name is?" he muttered. "Wake up, *petite chatte."*

Across the cabin, someone coughed. "Excuse me, Captain."

"Come in, Mr. Lane. Have you heard what has happened?"

"Bits and pieces, sir."

Devon heard Raveneau walk toward the other voice, and reopened her eye a fraction. Mr. Lane must be the first officer, she guessed. Raveneau had paused to light a slender cigar, and now he paced back and forth across the cabin, glancing her way so frequently that Devon decided to be safe and close her eyes completely.

"That damned Jackson reappeared a few hours ago and, like a fool, I let him come aboard. After I returned to my cabin, he apparently sneaked this *female* on—had her in the crew's quarters, no less, wearing pants and a red cap! Told me she was a surgeon's mate!" His voice grew more harsh with each sentence. "Minter is ill, so I went over to the crew's quarters' to recruit someone to take his place. This little hooligan prepared my bath! No wonder it took so long!"

Devon swallowed a bubble of laughter.

"Jackson tells me he had confided this plot only

to the men on watch, so that they would help him get her on board. That drooling pup Greenbriar came below and waylaid the girl as she passed the galley."

"Was that the scream I heard?" Lane inquired expressionlessly, as though they were discussing wind directions.

"Yes. She had just left here. I had been suspicious about her . . . but I'll admit I didn't guess she was actually a girl. When I saw the new 'surgeon's mate' with Greenbriar, I thought we had a different sort of problem."

Raveneau stopped next to Lane, and now they lowered their voices so that Devon could only make out snatches of their conversation.

After a minute or two Mr. Lane said in a clear, stiff voice, "As you wish, sir."

Devon heard him leave. The silence that followed made her uncomfortable. There was not a sigh or a scrape or a step. Had they both gone? She counted to one hundred. Nothing but the sound of water sloshing against the *Black Eagle*'s hull. Cautiously, Devon opened one eye a fraction. There was no sign of him. She decided to shift positions. With a dramatic moan, she stretched and rolled slowly onto her side. Another peek from this new angle. He was not in the leather chair or at the desk or table. He must have gone out with Lane, his bare feet making no sound.

The corner of her mouth had been itching torturously for minutes, and now she lifted a hand to scratch it. Lean fingers appeared out of nowhere to grasp her own.

"How long have you been awake?" Raveneau demanded.

Devon craned her neck and found him towering over her head, his gray eyes steely. She scrambled to her knees, ready to do verbal battle, and was horrified to see her torn shirt come open, exposing impudent breasts. Blushing, she pulled it together and retorted, "I was only hoping to avoid being put ashore!"

"I suppose you never fainted at all."

"That is not so!"

"Sit down. You look ridiculous."

"How dare you say that? You look quite ridiculous yourself with your legs showing!"

Raveneau blinked as though unable to believe his ears; then the barest suggestion of a smile bent one side of his mouth. "You are the first female who has ever mocked my legs. In fact—"

"Oh, yes, Sir Privateer, no doubt all women praise you endlessly, but not, I hope, after you have described them as ridiculous!"

He perched on the edge of his table, handsome calves dangling, and smoked for a moment in silence. Devon sat, and drew the linen sheet and silk comforter up to cover as much of her body as possible. Her strawberry-blond curls had been freed, but she was beginning to suspect that André Raveneau didn't recognize her. He seemed to have no memory of their earlier meeting, or of the enchanting kiss they had shared in Nick's carriage. This realization hurt her more than she could admit, even to herself. Those few minutes they had spent alone together, when he had awakened her deepest passions with one kiss, had filled her dreams and fantasies for a year.

She glowered at him. Raveneau's own anger was being replaced by puzzled curiosity. He had expected the girl to weep and plead, perhaps pretend to faint again or even offer him her body in an effort to persuade him to let her stay. Instead, she glared at him with what appeared to be undisguised hatred!

"I find I am confused; perhaps you can enlighten me. Didn't you want to remain on the *Black Eagle?*"

"Yes!" she spat.

"Then why are you insulting me and looking as though you would like to murder me?" His tone was conversational.

"I dislike your intimidating manner . . . sir." Desperately Devon tried to stifle some of her rage. He was right; she would find herself in Norwich if she didn't change her tactics.

"I am the captain, mademoiselle. It is my prerogative to be intimidating." He was half amused by now.

Devon sighed loudly. It helped. "I am sorry. I do have an excuse, of sorts. You see, I've been attacked *twice* today, and I am not feeling very charitable toward men in general."

Raveneau's eyes narrowed. "This happened in New London?"

"Yes." She stared down at her hands, which were twisted tightly together. "Two . . . two redcoats came. One took my mother upstairs, the other kept me on the first floor. He . . . tore my gown. The army wanted to burn our store. A lieutenant stopped the soldier before he could . . . finish with me."

"Your mother?" Raveneau asked softly.

"They never came out."

"And it was after that that Jackson found you?"

"I got away from the redcoat and then hid in a tree for hours. The British had gone when I encountered Noah." She looked up angrily. "Do you know who I saw when I was in the tree? The man who was behind the whole thing! Benedict Arnold! If I could, I would kill that man!"

Raveneau seemed unsurprised by this information. He dropped lightly to the floor and walked over to sit near Devon on the bed. "Don't brood about Arnold now; you've got to think of yourself. Haven't you anyone to whom you might go?"

"I . . . I had a friend who was like a father to me, but he was killed in the battle." Bitter tears came to Devon's eyes for all the death and destruction of that day. She sobbed and shook, unaware of André Raveneau's strong arms enfolding her, pulling her onto his lap, cradling her head against the gray velvet robe and his warm, tanned chest. At last, when her tears were spent, she felt a numbness spread where the agony had been.

Awareness returned. To Devon's horror, a tingle ran down her spine at the realization that she was in his arms. He smelled clean, intoxicating; a wild urge possessed her to nuzzle the soft black hair covering his chest. But her mind stubbornly reminded her that this was the conceited beast who had kissed her and forgotten. Reluctantly she lifted her head from his shoulder.

"I am fine now. You may release me." Her voice sounded cold and distant. When his arms fell away, she wanted to beg for his embrace again. Instead, she shifted herself back onto the bed and hoped her face did not look as hot as it felt.

"Do you feel better?" he inquired, reaching for the cigar which burned in a bedside dish. "You have been through a great deal . . . but I cannot believe that coming on the *Black Eagle* will help you. There is no reason—"

"But there is! You asked if I had someone to go to. There is one person. You are going to Yorktown, and I am certain that Morgan will be there as well. He is my fiancé, and we have been apart for nearly a year. We love and need each other so very much. Only he can help me now. Please, say that you will take me to Morgan!"

e sunny and cool.

Chapter Six

———◆———

September 7, 1781

THE *Black Eagle* was slicing rapidly through Fisher Island Sound by daybreak. All was well. A healthy wind filled the snow-white sails, speeding the privateer toward the open sea, while the morning promised to be sunny and cool.

André Raveneau stood on the quarter-deck beside Mr. Lane, his first lieutenant. The crewmen appeared topside, having stowed their hammocks and eaten breakfast. Wheaton, the old, crusty boatswain, piped various orders, and the crew rushed to carry them out. The captain had spent the night awake on the quarter-deck and was exhausted. Now, seeing how smoothly things were going, he decided to go below and get some sleep.

"Mr. Lane?" he asked.

"Yes, sir. I will have you roused if we spot any likely-looking sails."

Raveneau smiled. Personally, he could barely tolerate Lawrence Lane, but professionally, the man was indispensable. He would never leave him in command, but Lane's tireless attention to detail, discipline, and duty was a tremendous help.

As Raveneau turned toward the ladder, Lane mur-

71

mured, "May I ask, sir . . . is it true that you have kept the, ah, young lady on board?"

"Yes!" Raveneau ground out. "And if anyone mentions her, I want it understood that she is *not* available to the men. Is that clear?"

Despite Lane's serious expression, his eyes leered. "Oh, yes, sir!"

Below deck, Raveneau found himself hurrying toward his cabin. Now that the *Black Eagle* was safely out of the Thames River and on her way, he had a moment to think of the girl, and suddenly found himself worried that she might be attacked again.

He threw open the cabin door and looked around. Devon was sprawled across the bed on her back, arms outstretched like a trusting child. He had given her a fresh shirt to wear, and it seemed to float over the outline of her firm, delicate body, framing the perfection of her face and the abundant cloud of titian hair.

She was appealing. But she was also a girl on a mission—to be reunited with a fiancé who sounded as though he had been created in heaven. André Raveneau would be the last man on earth to take someone else's woman. He would never be that desperate!

Nor was he about to let this girl disrupt his life. An act of gallantry was one thing, undue sacrifice quite another. In the light of day he had trouble believing that he had actually agreed to take her to this Morgan. Yet how could he have put her ashore at Norwich? Damn Jackson for beginning this mess! The devil of it was that he could not allow the girl to sleep anywhere but in his cabin, for her own safety. She had insisted that she would cheerfully sleep on the floor to get to Morgan. The way Raveneau felt at the moment, she might have to.

Without hesitation, he stripped off his clothes. The hell with her! Let her look if she pleased! The education would do her good. However, he did pull on his robe to sleep in, for the time being at least.

"Hey!" Raveneau stood beside the bed and realized again that he didn't know her name. It seemed to him, however, that she had occupied the bed long enough. It was his turn. "Mademoiselle. Wake up! I need this space."

Obligingly, Devon rolled over to one side and burrowed her head into the pillow. Raveneau debated momentarily, then shrugged. Off went the dressing gown as he slid beneath the silk comforter. She looked so soft and vulnerable beside him that he relented and reached out to trace her fragile jawline with one dark finger.

"Sleep well, *petite.*"

Devon slept past nine o'clock and awoke to the sight of André Raveneau's chiseled, handsome face beside her. Even in repose it was harshly masculine, the mouth firm above the rakishly scarred jaw, the nose aquiline and noble. The thought of his naked, warm flesh so close to her own made her blush and shiver all at once.

Sunlight poured through the transom; the sight of it drew Devon out of bed. She used Raveneau's fresh water to wash and wished his breeches would fit her half as well as those Noah had donated. She would simply have to acquire another pair for washing days.

After locating the captain's comb, Devon used it on her own hair until the golden-rose curls crackled.

She didn't think twice about leaving the cabin. Actually, she was glad that the captain had discovered her identity, since he had grudgingly agreed to deliver her to Yorktown and now she could walk about undisguised. Further, she would not be forced to endure a crew member's hard existence. Raveneau had declared that it would be impossible for her to sleep anywhere else but in his cabin.

Emerging on the gun deck, Devon hung back and observed the spectacle around her. The *Black Eagle* glided across the water like a great white-winged bird. Loving ships as she did, Devon recognized a truly beautiful, efficiently designed vessel. There were at least sixteen cannon lined up behind their gun ports. There were special sails for speed: a ringtail on the driver, spritsails, studdingsails, and royals on the very tops of the masts. Most warships had red or brown bulwarks, but the *Black Eagle*'s were painted the same cool gray as the stripe which bisected the black hull. All around her, privateersmen cleaned and polished the decks, rails, and brass fittings. They wore the seaman's usual assortment of clothing: a flat-brimmed hat or knit cap, neckerchief, peacoat, and loose, bell-bottomed trousers.

The privateer sailed with amazing speed and style, and the men worked with disciplined efficiency. What statement did this make about the captain? Devon wondered. Was he a tyrannical, unfeeling slave driver as Noah had suggested?

She could feel someone staring at her. The seamen had glanced only briefly at her, for they guessed she must belong to the captain. Devon sought her observer and found him standing on the quarter-deck, his brass telescope caught between arm and body at a smart angle. The sun was in Devon's eyes, but the man's silk stockings betrayed his identity as well as a clear view of his face would have. It was Mr. Lane.

Despite the sun, Devon returned his stare for a long minute until at last he averted his face to display a haughty profile. She longed to make a rude gesture in return.

Someone touched her arm and she spun around, panicked.

"Hello, Devon!" Noah's easygoing smile made her laugh with relief. She reacted to him the way she once had to Morgan. It was wonderful to know that there was one safe person, like an amiable brother, to whom she could turn in the rocky moments of confusion. Suddenly Devon remembered what Noah's good nature had cost him. Five lashes, his shares lost, and dismissal from the crew, all because he had be-

friended her at her worst moment. Impulsively she
gave him a hug. "Good morning! It's good to see you!"

"Beautiful lady, you are just the medicine I need.
A kind word and pretty smile mean more than I can
say."

Devon perceived the melancholy in Noah's green
eyes, though he grinned as usual. "Noah, I . . . I
heard what happened. I am so sorry to be the cause
of such misfortune for you! It doesn't seem fair—"

His smile vanished abruptly. "That's true. It is *not*
fair, but typical of our dear captain."

"I believe you are right!" she exclaimed. "Why
should it be such a terrible offense to help a lady in
distress? Why, you'd think that fraternizing with me
was as bad as spying for the British or sabotaging the
ship!"

There was a step on the hatch behind her. "On the
contrary, dear child . . . either of those crimes would
be punishable by death."

Devon froze and Noah paled. Hesitantly, Devon
looked over her shoulder, into the slate-colored eyes
of André Raveneau.

"I . . . thought you were asleep . . ." she stam-
mered.

His grin flashed white in the sunshine. "The devil
never sleeps. Remember that." The next moment his
expression was harsh and forbidding. "Return to my
cabin and do not leave."

Devon's mouth fell open. "How dare you? Of all
the—"

"You dislike my attitude? The way I stand or smile
or swear, perhaps? Do feel free to leave the ship at
any time. I would be the last person to insist that you
remain where your sensibilities are offended."

Devon had never heard such caustic sarcasm in her
life. Momentarily, she expected Noah to come to her
rescue, but he had shrunk back against the mainmast
while Raveneau's eyes pierced them like splintered
silver. Devon could not speak, but she presented a

haughty profile, as she had seen Mr. Lane do, then swept away toward the hatch. This last gesture was difficult to carry off, since she was wearing breeches, but she did her best.

On the ladder which led to the berth deck, Devon paused and heard Raveneau speaking to Noah, his voice dangerously cold. A strange chill ran down Devon's spine. She had known evil men in her lifetime—had encountered many of them yesterday—but this captain was of a breed she did not recognize. He frightened her, yet fascinated her. She found she could not despise him.

She wondered why Raveneau had awakened. Had Mr. Lane called him? Devon dropped into the captain's wing chair and noticed that the cabin was neater and that the clutter of charts and instruments had disappeared into a handsome mahogany "bittacle," or cupboardlike box. Who had put it all away so quickly?

Then the answer to her questions walked in, in the form of a young red-haired steward carrying a fresh supply of monogrammed towels. He smiled at Devon with no noticeable surprise. "Hello! You must be the cat!" he greeted her. "My name is Minter. I'm the captain's steward."

Devon's answering smile faded. "The cat? Why do you call me that? My name is Devon Lindsay!"

"Captain Raveneau doesn't know your name, or he's forgotten it. He calls you *petite chatte,* but not, I must admit, in the most complimentary tone of voice!"

"I can imagine!" Devon smiled wryly. "Are you feeling better, Minter?"

"Much, thank you." Picking up the pitcher, he started off for fresh water but paused long enough to murmur conspiratorially, "I appreciate your taking over for me last night! That is one scene I would have enjoyed witnessing!"

Devon blushed, but laughed. She liked Minter. He passed Raveneau in the cabin doorway, silently, but they exchanged smiles and Devon was pleased to know that Raveneau did not growl at every crew member.

"I hope that you have prepared a good explanation for your conduct this morning!" Raveneau stood over Devon, his harsh, handsome face as hard as a statue's. Devon scrambled up and stood on the seat of her chair to put them nearly eye to eye. Embarrassed but angry, she thrust her chin at him. "Well?" Raveneau demanded.

"I don't know what you mean, *sir.* I went up for some air. And I wanted to see the *Black Eagle* in full sail."

"Ah, yes. Air . . ." His eyes narrowed. "A promenade on deck! Charming group up there today, *n'est-ce pas?* I'm surprised they aren't lined up outside my door with their tongues hanging out!"

Devon half wanted to sit down again. He was only inches away; their eyes were locked. Her heart thundered. He grasped her arm, and she thought her knees would buckle.

"You didn't tell me to remain here," she finally said.

"You little lunatic! I assumed, after last night, that you would have the normal good sense—"

"Listen, M'sieur Captain!" Devon heard herself shout. "It just so happens that I grew up on the Beach in New London. I am used to ships, and I am used to their crews. Those men on deck didn't frighten me! There is a great difference between an abduction in a dark galley and being seen by a few dozen seamen in broad daylight!"

His long, dark fingers tightened on her arm. "I realize that this may be a difficult concept for you to grasp, but do make an effort. There is a very real possibility that any one of those men could be hiding in a deserted corner tonight, or tomorrow night, or several days from now. Even Greenbriar had more sense than to toss you to the deck when he first saw you, didn't he?"

"Are all your men barbarians?"

"As long as they do their jobs on board, I haven't the slightest interest in their lives ashore. But many a normal man can turn barbaric if he's deprived of a woman long enough. You may be quite . . . *résistable,* but there is no accounting for some people's tastes. Particularly when their need is great enough . . . if you take my meaning."

This speech was delivered in a tone of voice that reminded Devon of a knife being inserted repeatedly, each time deeper and more painfully. For a long moment she gaped at him in shock, then hissed, "You are utterly hateful!"

"True enough, but I've made my point, I trust."

The spirited wind died away that afternoon. The stillness intensified the foreboding atmosphere. Raveneau had not returned to bed and was in a vile temper. He worked on his charts, conferred at intervals with Mr. Lane, and cursed the ebbing wind.

Devon lay on the bed, alternately watching Raveneau and the ceiling. She had decided that she truly despised the man and berated herself for wasting so many thoughts and dreams on him. She felt hemmed in, and ached with the need to run. Every time Raveneau got up to pace and curse, her own nerves grew more taut. She wished she had stayed in New London . . . yet she longed for Morgan, her touchstone of sanity.

During the afternoon Minter brought food. It smelled wonderful, but she remained stubbornly on the bed, silent. Raveneau divided the portions and sat down to eat, a thick book open beside his plate. When Devon finally realized that he was not going to beseech her to join him, she rose and did so. There was boiled beef, gravy, biscuits, an apple. Raveneau poured red wine into her cup and watched with detached amusement as she drank it thirstily.

The wine smoothed Devon's frazzled nerves. She

ate slowly, stealing an occasional glance at her companion, helplessly admiring the rugged lines of his profile. His forehead was perfect, she decided, and his black hair grew away from it with casual elegance. He probably just ran a hand through it; other men labored long before their mirrors to achieve that smooth sweep of hair. Studying him, Devon bit into her apple and wondered why one man should possess every masculine trait while others—like Morgan—merely fumbled and groped after manhood.

She sighed, and felt her face heat up at such traitorous thoughts of Morgan. I do love him! she reminded herself, remembering the blissful, uncomplicated days they had spent together on the banks of the Thames. She had been safe, cheerful, in control . . .

"Was that sigh for your absent lover, or are you hinting for more wine?" Raveneau inquired.

Devon looked at him triumphantly. "As a matter of fact, I *was* daydreaming about Morgan."

Raveneau shrugged.

"But that does not mean I won't have more wine." She poured it herself, watching him challengingly. "By the way, Captain, Morgan is not my *lover*. We are *betrothed*."

"*Petite chatte,* frequently the two terms are interchangeable."

"That may be true among the girls *you* know, but I assure you it is not true for me."

"A pity for what's-his-name. I hope there was no problem."

Devon saw the silver sparkle in his eyes, but rose to the bait all the same. "*Morgan* is the name of my fiancé, Morgan Gadwin. And I resent your implication, sir! Morgan exercised discipline for my sake, because he loves me!"

Raveneau listened and smiled. He thought that Devon looked quite ravishing and passionate. Either Morgan was a fool, or the girl was a convincing liar. "*Mon Dieu,* I am glad that I decided to deliver you to Yorktown, so that I may have a look at this paragon of self-restraint!"

There was a sharp knock at the door then and Mr. Lane appeared. "It is time, Captain."

Raveneau's devilish grin vanished, replaced by the more familiar expression of tense fatigue. Above them, the boatswain's pipe shrilled the call for all hands on deck.

Devon paled, an icy chill rippling from her scalp to the small of her back. "Please, please reconsider!" she begged. "Noah doesn't deserve to be punished! I'm at fault if anyone is! He only tried to help me—"

"Silence!" Raveneau thundered. "I will not tolerate interference from anyone on my ship, least of all *you,* who are here simply on my sufferance. If you attempt to meddle again, it will be the last time!"

Devon glared at him as he started for the door. "Wait! I am going—"

"No!" He turned back only briefly, his harsh face satanically angry. "Do not dare to leave this cabin until I have returned, or you'll find yourself under the lash as well. *Comprenez?"*

He was gone. Devon clenched her fists. She longed to throw something; to break his dishes, destroy his charts, smash his furniture. But she was too much of a coward to face his anger, and that realization only enraged her further. Defiantly she gulped her wine, and his, too.

The *Black Eagle* was eerily quiet, but when she pushed the door ajar, she could hear each lash stroke clearly. Her heart burned as she imagined Noah's quivering back under the knotted cat-o'-nine-tails. It seemed an eternity before she heard the captain's command to halt, followed by the sound of scattering footsteps. She wanted to rush up to Noah and could not have felt more responsible for his wounds had she wielded the cat herself.

Recognizing Raveneau's step in the gangway, Devon let the door close and moved away. The first thing he saw upon entering was her trim, rigid back, partially hidden under the mass of apricot-gold hair that curled past her shoulders. She stood in the middle of the cabin, still and ominously silent.

Raveneau headed for the table and reached for his glass. "You drank my wine?" he inquired coldly.

"Yes." She turned her head slowly, gazing at him from under the fringe of her lashes. Her arms were crossed tightly over her breasts; her stockinged feet were spread defiantly.

"Do not do so again. The supply of wine is limited; it belongs to me personally. God only knows why I shared it with you at all."

"In that case, I could not be persuaded at gunpoint to taste your wine again."

"That is reassuring. Since you have consumed three large portions in less than an hour, I was beginning to worry that my entire stock might be gone before sunset."

Devon fought a wild urge to attack him like a wildcat and claw his cynical face. Instead, she merely turned her head away, wondering what to do next. Raveneau poured the remaining wine from the bottle into his glass, then sat down and crossed his booted feet atop the table.

Devon realized that her own consumption of spirits had emboldened her, but suddenly she didn't care.

"So you have finished your afternoon's entertainment?" she asked. "The whipping of defenseless men is over?"

"Your tongue is dangerously sharp," Raveneau said in a low, even tone. "It needs blunting."

"It is not as sharp as your cat-o'-nine-tails, Captain."

"I hope that you are a proficient swimmer, mademoiselle, because I am sorely tempted to test your skills."

"Ah, so your appetite for sadistic amusement has not been satisfied!" As she spoke, Devon could see his jaw tightening with real anger, but the words continued to pour out. "Have you keelhauled anyone lately?"

His dark hand moved with the speed of a striking snake. He caught and twisted her hair until she fell to her knees before his chair, her neck arched and mouth open.

"You are a nasty little bitch, do you know that? No wonder your chaste fiancé hasn't managed to bed you. You probably destroy his passion with your malicious tongue."

Devon thought about putting up a fight, but a portion of her brain was tantalized by the notion that he might cover her open mouth with his hard, warm lips. Her back was arched, her breasts pushing against the linen shirt she wore, and she could feel his eyes upon her. He released her hair abruptly and Devon fell backward, hitting her head on the floor. She felt like a fool. Face burning, she scrambled up and hissed, "I hate you. I truly do. You are the most uncivilized beast I have ever encountered."

"*Vraiment?*" Raveneau pretended surprise.

"Yes, *vraiment,*" she mimicked.

"But Jackson . . . *he* is the soul of goodness and respectability. True?"

"True!" If André Raveneau thought otherwise, then it *must* be true.

"*Petite chatte,* you have a great deal to learn about men."

"Don't take that superior tone with me, Captain! And my name is Devon!"

"*Devon?*" He made a face of mild distaste. "What sort of name is that?"

"I am named for the English birthplace of my father!"

"Devon," Raveneau repeated experimentally. Pronounced with a French accent, it sounded beautiful.

"Now that you have changed my name to suit yourself, I wish you would tell me how Noah is. Is he conscious?"

The concern in her blue eyes irritated him. "Unfortunately, yes. You needn't worry. The surgeon is tending to him."

Devon glared at him, but her features softened in relief. "You're certain that he is all right?"

"Yes, damn it! What reason have you for such concern?"

"Noah has been very kind to me. He has lost everything because of me. Did you expect me not to care?"

She was pacing the cabin, and now Raveneau stared into his wine. There were a dozen things he could say at this point concerning Jackson's personality and the nature of discipline aboard a ship. But why should I explain myself? he thought. "If you care so much for dear *Noah*," he said, "then why bother to seek out Mandrake—"

"Morgan!"

"—at all? I would be excessively happy to put you and Jackson out in a small boat and be well rid of the two sharpest thorns in my side." He nonchalantly drained his glass, then looked around for a cigar.

"Beast! Cad! Base, uncivilized—" If she had searched deep inside herself, Devon might have realized that she hoped Raveneau would react to her with a passion equal to her own.

Slowly, deliberately, he stood up; only a few inches separated their bodies. Devon was breathing hard, breasts quivering beneath her linen shirt, but Raveneau was maddeningly still. "In America, your behavior would be called 'biting the hand that feeds you,'" he said. "Don't you agree? I think that you must have acquired your manners in a farmyard, except that I do not know any animals whose language would match yours."

"I am not some mush-brained female to blush and tremble in your presence, Captain!"

"It seems to me that you are doing both at this

moment," he observed dryly. "As to your right to argue with my orders, I think you know my feelings. Each insult that escapes from your lovely mouth could be the last. I am captain here. No man on board the *Black Eagle* would dare to raise his voice to me, no matter how justified he might be. What makes you think that you are an exception to the rules?"

Watching Raveneau exit, Devon, trembling at his nearness, realized that her behavior truly mystified him. A dozen biting rejoinders jumped into her mind, but she rejected them all. She was speechless, blushing, gazing up into silver-gray eyes that drew her helplessly.

When Raveneau finally touched her, his hands were rough, gripping her shoulders and sliding over her arms. "You behave like a spoiled brat, Devon. If you do not curb your vixen's tongue, I fear that you will not last as far as Yorktown. I have enough problems without you adding to them."

Devon returned his gaze, wanting to submit to his strength and to promise to behave herself. However, this was easier thought than spoken. "Captain, I am not spoiled, but I am used to doing and saying what I please," she said. "No man has ever dominated me, not even my father or my fiancé, so why should I change for you? Perhaps it's time someone spoke up to you!"

Raveneau's eyes registered astonishment, irritation, even a flicker of amusement. Then they narrowed like the eyes of a bird of prey preparing to capture a delicious prize. Devon shivered in anticipation. "Mademoiselle," he said, "perhaps it is time that *you* were silenced! Now that you are venturing into the world, you must learn that frank and outspoken females are not widely tolerated. I shall be pleased to instruct you in the fine art of submission."

His dark hands encircled her waist with practiced skill, and Devon melted like butter. The pleasure was too intensely glorious to be denied; it surpassed everything, save their first kiss in Nick's carriage. She reveled in his touch, molded herself to it, and suspended all thoughts and feelings that threatened to interfere.

Raveneau's mouth was firm against hers, demanding that her lips yield. He kissed her deftly, tenderly, gauging her response intuitively. She moaned as he progressed from the first soft touch to a deep kiss, then she went faint and limp. Her arms embraced his wide shoulders, her fingers touching his sleek hair, his smooth neck and collarbone. She pressed him closer.

In a distant corner of his mind Raveneau realized with a twinge of alarm that he was losing control. His detachment was vaporizing, but he found, oddly, that he was enjoying the sensations of pure passion and desire. The question was, why should this little hoyden affect him so? He had intended to teach her a lesson, but it seemed that she was in control after all. The fire rose in his loins and an ache spread over his body as he held her and kissed the sweetness of her mouth. He slid his hands inside her shirt, felt her satiny skin quiver where he touched it, and knew that the girl was caught in the same web of pleasure.

Devon felt as if she were falling slowly through a delicious cloud. She was so hungry for this man; his body was a powerful magnet drawing her to him. He eased her shirt off and lay her down on the bed, kissing her neck, shoulders, then, tentatively, her eager breasts. Devon was on fire. She clung to him, clenching her teeth, caressing his powerful neck. Raveneau moved so that she could feel the hard length of his maleness against her leg. Oddly, she recalled her total revulsion when Morgan had lain atop her, also rigid with desire. Now, with Raveneau, she yearned to touch him intimately.

He was kissing her again. Their tongues touched and danced, teasingly, then eagerly. Devon ran her fingertips under his shirt to trace his broad chest, the texture of hair that covered it, and the ridges of muscle that skipped down his belly to the wild, mysterious staff hidden under snug breeches.

Her touch sent a spear of reality into his brain. Reluctantly, he remembered that the girl was supposed to be betrothed to another. He usually kept his distance from females who expected him to behave like a gentleman, but there was a chance that this Devon was a virgin, in which case he was out of line.

Her tiny fingers brushed the fastenings on his breeches; her mouth searched hungrily for his. Raveneau put his hand between her legs and felt the heat of her desire. *"Petite chatte,"* he whispered with husky regret, "I do not deflower innocents. I will ask you this only once. Have you saved yourself for your flawless fiancé?"

Devon dropped out of her cloud and fell with terrifying speed the rest of the way to earth. The irony in his voice humiliated her. Pulling away from him, she crossed both arms over her naked breasts. "What do you care?" she retorted.

Raveneau looked at her flashing eyes and burning cheeks, then sat up. "I do not care. I thought that you might—or perhaps Merlin might," he said sarcastically. The ache in his groin did little to cheer him.

"His name is Morgan!" Devon screamed. She reached for her shirt and whipped it on.

"My dear, you must at least give me credit for remembering the fellow when you could not. Or perhaps you forgot his existence by choice?"

"No!" She was furious. "It was all your fault!"

Raveneau stood. His brown face was a mask of cynicism, one brow arched over flinty eyes. "Mademoiselle, I think we both know better. However, I have no wish to tempt you beyond your power to resist. After all, I know how much you love Malcolm. So if you can restrain yourself in my presence, I shall do likewise." He started to walk away, then turned back, a devilish smile playing about his mouth. "By the way, I trust that our argument about domination has been settled? You would do well not to press the issue."

Devon thought that she might explode. Fastening

her clothing, she left the cabin. Damn him! The man was utterly unbearable. Devon clenched her fists and gritted her teeth, hesitating in the gangway. Noah! That was it. She would find him and tend the wounds inflicted by order of the devil-captain. Noah was a fellow victim of his cruelty; only he could help her now.

As a sea captain's daughter, Devon could guess where she might find the surgeon. Heedless of her stockinged feet, she descended into the hold, where the cockpit was located. A series of pitiful moans pinpointed the curtained cubicle. In spite of its meager size and depressing location, the surgeon's space was as unusually clean as the rest of the *Black Eagle*. Ordinarily, one could retch from the stench in a ship's hold, but here the air was only mildly disagreeable.

"Excuse me!" Devon called, stopping outside the canvas hangings. Immediately a thin, angular face appeared.

"Hello! I'm Treasel, the surgeon! You must be the chit who caused all this trouble! And for a moment there, I hoped I was going to have an assistant. Instead, you turn out to be a girl and have only brought me more work. Well, come on in! Maybe you can calm these two down."

Devon stared at Treasel. He looked like a human greyhound, and she expected him to race off in a blur of speed at any moment. Pewter-haired and blue-eyed, the surgeon spoke so quickly and emphatically that Devon wearied just listening to him. Even his gestures were like exclamation points.

"Ohh!" came a dramatic moan from a few feet away. Devon looked around to find Noah lying across a table, while Greenbriar was sprawled on the floor, groaning with each roll of the ship. Noah smiled wanly.

"Oh, thank God you are all right!" Devon exclaimed, rushing to his side. She stared at his back, which had been badly slashed. The wounds were not deep, however, and had been cleaned and carefully daubed with salve to ease the sting; they would be healed soon. Noah would not be disfigured by his harsh punishment. "Oh, Noah," Devon cried, mustering up the full strength of her temper, "just look what that monster has done to you! Is the pain unbearable?"

"No. I try not to think of it." His boyish grin twisted her heart with guilt. She smoothed his damp, straw-colored hair and returned his smile.

"Now, Devon, don't you feel bad about this," admonished Noah, pleased by her tender gesture.

"How can I help it? It is my fault, isn't it? Yes, it is! Though I'll lay a share of blame on that villainous captain."

Devon's tone was so venomous that Noah pricked his ears with interest. If she had come to hate the captain, he, Noah, might have a chance with her. He mustn't let it slip away. Clenching his teeth, he managed to sit up. Treasel had said that his wounds looked worse than they were. Noah experimented by moving his solid, freckled arms, watching the muscles flex. He glanced craftily at Devon and was delighted to find her enchanting face puckered with concern.

"I don't think you should be moving, Noah!" She looked back at Treasel for confirmation. "Should he be moving? Tell him to lie down, Doctor!"

Treasel crossed quickly to his patient, raised and lowered his brows a few times, then shrugged. "He'll be fine! Hope he's got sense enough to move only as much as comfort allows. Right, Jackson?"

Noah flashed a brave grin. "Devon, you could cure anyone. The sight of you helped me more than all of Treasel's potions."

"Well, I'd do anything to ease your pain, you know that. I feel so responsible! I swear, I could *kick* that devil-pirate!"

Watching her, Noah suddenly understood the nature of her flushed energy. There was more to this than anger or guilt . . . the energy was sexual; lush, glowing, frustrated.

Noah was flooded with desire. He forgot his wounded back, forgot everything but Devon with her golden-flushed skin, passion-luxuriant hair, sapphire eyes that sparkled with needs that he would be happy to satisfy. "Do you know what I would like best?" he asked softly. Treasel took his cue, lifted the canvas, and stepped out into the gangway. Only the moaning Greenbriar was left with them in the cubicle.

"What?" Devon asked.

"I would like to get out of here. Will you help me? Nothing would please me more than a few private moments with you, to rest and talk. If you don't mind my saying so, you look as if you could use someone to confide in."

"All of that sounds like heaven except the last part. I don't have anything to confide, and I'll talk only of you. Right now my problems cry to be forgotten."

"A splendid notion!" Noah approved. He was ecstatic. The situation was ideal; he would gain revenge on the Frenchman and a huge measure of physical pleasure for himself at the same time. He would take her to the empty brig.

Shakily, Noah wobbled to his feet. Devon did not disappoint him, insisting on putting an arm around his waist; the soft, red-gold hair that touched his cheek smelled of Raveneau. Noah's grin hardened with cold resolve.

The brig was located just forward of the cockpit, heavily grated like a gloomy cage. It would eventually be filled by unlucky British seamen, but for now it stood empty. Noah headed for one of the benches that lined the walls. Sitting down beside him, Devon wrinkled her nose. The entire brig had been scrubbed recently with strong-smelling soap, but it could not disguise the foul stench left by the prisoners who had been enclosed here for weeks on end. She shivered a little.

"I don't like this place."

"Ah, Devon, don't think about it. Think about me.

89

Enjoy your freedom from Captain Raveneau's heavy hand."

"Yes . . . I do. That beast. He is a tyrant!"

"So you have actually decided you do not like him?"

"Definitely!" Her voice echoed in the dismal brig, though she could not meet his eyes.

"Are you certain?" Noah pressed. "The man is notorious for his effect on women, you know. I have worried that you also might fall under his spell."

"Me? Ha! Never!" Her cheeks flamed. Agitatedly, she twisted a button on her shirt. "I'll have you know that I have a mind of my own."

"You certainly do." Noah grinned. "May I ask your opinion of me?"

"I think you are wonderful! You have done so much to help me, Noah, and I deeply appreciate that. You've been so brave."

"Do I deserve a reward?"

Devon looked at him. His square face with its open grin seemed so boyish and carefree. If Raveneau was the enemy, then Noah must be her champion. "Yes, of course you do."

"Would you give me a kiss?"

Kisses had proved dangerous so far, Devon thought. Morgan, Smythe, Greenbriar, André Raveneau . . . Yet it sounded so simple when Noah said it. A kiss. It was the least she could do. Smiling, she put a hand on his cheek and leaned forward.

Noah moved quickly. His arms caught her, pressed her to his chest. He saw the panic that flared in her eyes before he kissed her. So sweet! Her mouth was soft and moist; he crushed it, forced his tongue inside. Devon was fighting him now and he loved it. It seemed years, rather than one day, since he had had a woman, and he could not remember the last time he had held one as lovely as Devon. He fumbled inside her shirt and cupped a firm breast.

Devon felt smothered. His arms were like iron. How

could she escape? What about his back? How could he—

"Excuse me. I *do* hate to interrupt, but this sort of behavior is not permitted." It was Raveneau. Dark and sardonic, he watched them from the doorway. "I would have sworn you knew the rules by now, Jackson."

Noah's face was expressionless. He released Devon and stared back at the captain. Devon instantly jumped to her feet, burning with shame. How had he found them? She didn't know what to do. Raveneau's cynical mouth told her that he thought her a willing participant. Was she to run to him and blurt the truth, tell him that he was right about Noah and she had behaved like a fool? Would he even believe her?

I will not give him the satisfaction, she thought crazily. Let the conceited beast think what he will. Let him think that I left his arms to seek out Noah— it might teach him humility!

"Devon, unless you would prefer to remain locked in the brig with Jackson, I suggest you come with me."

Noah said nothing, but narrowed his eyes icily. Devon wavered. If Noah had not behaved so badly, she would have stayed with him just to spite Raveneau, but she knew what would happen to her if they were locked in together. No amount of pride could bring her to suffer that. Lifting her chin, she walked haughtily across the planked floor. When she was only a few steps from Raveneau, the *Black Eagle* suddenly lurched to one side and Devon lost her balance. She fell against him and he caught her arm with painful force. Looking into his angry gray eyes, Devon forgot her frosty pose. "I suppose one prison is very like another," she choked.

Raveneau arched an eyebrow, but there was no humor in his smile. Thrusting her out into the gangway, he stepped outside and locked the brig. As they walked away, Devon could feel Noah's eyes burning through the grating, staring at her and Raveneau.

Chapter Seven

September 8, 1781

DEVON stood on the Bank, facing the wall of fire that had been the Linen and Pewter Shop only moments before. There were British soldiers standing all around, leering as they slowly tore off her yellow dress. She was screaming and crying "Mama!" over and over.

Deborah appeared at the upstairs window, naked, haloed by orange flames. She screamed, "Devon, he's raped me! I'm going to die! Die!"

Behind Devon, the redcoats had begun to point across to Fort Griswold, which had magically moved toward New London. The Thames had shrunk to a narrow ribbon of water, and the battle that was in progress could be viewed easily. The gates to the fort were open. Devon could see the redcoats that swarmed inside, could watch them murder the captured patriots. Suddenly Nick appeared at the gates. He killed two men with his sword before he was stabbed in the back. He staggered to the crest of the hill, sobbing, "Devon, take care!"

She tried to break through the lines of men behind her, but they only caught her in their arms, pawing her, ripping away her clothing.

"Mama! Nick! Mama!" Over and over she screamed their names.

Hard, bare arms enfolded her, cradling her head against a muscular shoulder. She opened her eyes to inky darkness and clung to the warm body, weeping hysterically. A low voice whispered beautiful French words in her ear while a hand stroked her back and hair. Finally, like a child, she quieted, lulled into forgetfulness. Nestled against a furry chest, she rocked gently with her comforter.

"Petite chatte?"

Devon heard the whispered words, felt his breath on her ear. She resisted reality, knowing only that she felt more content than at any moment in her life.

"Devon, if you are listening, I have something to say. I wish that you had presented your plight more sympathetically to me in the beginning. You were so hostile that I scarcely listened when I heard what you had suffered in New London. I apologize if I have been callous."

Devon couldn't believe her ears. Was this André Raveneau speaking? "It is as much my fault," she whispered.

"Pardon?" He gave it the French pronunciation.

Reluctantly, Devon lifted her head from his chest and looked up. His handsome face was etched as a black silhouette against the indigo darkness. She could see his lips and yearned to be kissed. "I said, I am as much to blame as you are."

"That is true," he agreed. "You have behaved this past day like a foolish child."

A spark of outrage flared in Devon. These were the first words they had exchanged since that afternoon. In fact, it was the first she had seen of him since he had locked her in his cabin. A wary-looking Minter had brought her supper, explaining that the captain would be busy above deck. It had been a miserably restless evening, and Devon had retired early.

Now she met his silver gaze in the early morning

darkness until her anger subsided. He was right, but she would die before admitting it.

"I would not put it quite so strongly, sir. And while we are on the subject, let me say that your behavior has been less than ideal."

"I did not ask your opinion." His tone was dry, amused.

"I did not ask *yours!* And I don't care if you *are* the captain!"

"You would be wiser if you did care, mademoiselle."

Devon put out her tongue, thinking he would not see it in the darkness, but a long finger appeared to push it back into her mouth.

"Childish," he admonished.

"Oh, be quiet!"

"Marcus will have his hands full with you!"

Devon didn't bother to correct him. "It so happens that Morgan and I get along perfectly. We have never quarrelled."

"Oh, no," Raveneau groaned. "A henpecked fiancé. I was afraid of that."

"He is not henpecked!"

"If you never quarrel, it must be because you are leading him around by the nose."

"That's not true!" Her guilty flush was, mercifully, unobserved. "He is very manly! He's at war, isn't he?"

Raveneau chuckled. "You probably pushed him into the army, poor boy. Besides, how strong can your attachment be, when you turn to the first man who comes along?"

"What do you mean?" she shrilled.

"Shh. You'll wake the crew. I mean Noah Jackson, of course. Your new love."

She bit her tongue. "I don't want to talk about that. You misunderstood."

Raveneau stiffened. "Are you saying that he was forcing you?" When she did not reply immediately, he prompted, "I demand an answer!"

"You may demand all night, sir, but I needn't give

you one," said Devon, nettled. "What happened is none of your affair. I can handle Noah."

A cold silence fell between them. Unaccountably, Devon felt like crying again. Raveneau softened. "I should not press you now. Again, you have pushed me to forget what you have so recently suffered."

"I am so tired," she whispered. "So tired of quarreling. I am not used to this. I never know what anyone will say or do."

His arms tightened around her. She settled back into the warmth of his chest, pressing her ear against his heartbeat. "Please hold me," she said. "I don't want to fall asleep alone . . ."

When Devon awoke the next morning, she felt warm and happy. Raveneau had already risen. Rolling onto her stomach, she propped up her chin with both pillows and watched him eat breakfast.

Several minutes passed before he noticed her. As usual, he was reading, and the book seemed to take priority over the eggs and muffins on his plate. Devon looked him over, critically eyeing the cut of his breeches, the shine of his boots, and the whiteness of the linen shirt he wore. All were as flawless as Raveneau himself.

To get his attention, Devon finally gave in and coughed. Absently, he glanced over his shoulder and discovered her grinning happily.

"Good morning!" she greeted.

"I must say I'm surprised to find you awake. It is barely six o'clock! I'm sorry if I disturbed you. You had better go back to sleep now." Raveneau turned back to his book.

"No, wait! I went to bed early last night, so I am quite rested." Wasn't he going to mention the closeness they had shared so early that morning? Hadn't she slept in his arms?

"That's fine, but I don't know what you will do all morning." He drank the last of his coffee, then stood up. "I've got to go above now. I will tell Minter to bring you some hot water and breakfast."

"Wait, Captain . . ." That title sounded too formal now, but he didn't protest. Devon swung the covers back, revealing bare legs beneath her loose shirt. "Please, I wanted to ask you . . ."

Raveneau was removing his compass and quadrant from the bittacle. "Yes? What is it?" Vaguely irritated, he looked up expectantly and felt an unfamiliar twinge at the sight of her. In spite of her bare legs and drowsy appeal, this was not simple desire. A strange current of warmth possessed him.

"Please . . . would it be all right if I came up today? I would love to see the ocean and taste the salt air, and since you will be there . . ."

"I am flattered that you ask my permission for once. Dare I hope that you are tamed?"

Devon could not ignore so ironic a challenge. "That is not quite the way I would word it. Let us say that I am wiser today, but not vanquished by any means!"

"Well, I am heartened to find you making progress. Yes, you may come above today, if you give me your word that you will behave. And no stops or detours on the way up, particularly in the brig!"

"Believe me, that is the last place I would go. However, I will say that I think it was bad of you to confine Noah. You've only compounded your error."

"Mademoiselle, your outlook is highly biased. Nor am I interested in any opinion you might offer on the subject of Noah Jackson, or on any other matter relating to the *Black Eagle*. Do you understand?"

"Yes." Her pout was half playful, just as she could sense that his sternness was, in part, an act. There was a visible crack in the icy wall that surrounded him; it was almost wide enough for Devon to reach inside and touch the real man that was kept so carefully protected. Was it possible that she might come to know the gentle, sympathetic person who had cradled her in the middle of the night?

Devon grinned deliciously. Raveneau's mouth twitched in response. "You are looking very pleased," he said. "Why so meek and sweet-tempered today, Devon?"

"Because you are not yelling at me. Because I will be in the sunlight and wind today. Or maybe because I am too drowsy to be disagreeable."

"That sounds more like it," Raveneau muttered. "Enjoy your breakfast. I will see you later, and remember your promise!"

Minter brought Devon a huge, steaming breakfast of eggs, muffins, sweet butter, and coffee. She wondered skeptically what the crew ate, then scolded herself. André Raveneau was not the sort of man who would run a beautiful, clean ship and then feed his men like animals, no matter what Noah said. It would be interesting to talk to some of the other men on board. Were they all as bitter as Noah?

Between bites of breakfast, she peeked at the book Raveneau had left on the table. To her dismay, she discovered that it was Voltaire's *Mérope* in French. She had been on the verge of asking permission to use his library, which was displayed along the far wall behind iron-braced shelves. Were all the books in French? Devon knew enough to get by in a pinch, but could read nothing difficult. Just as she was ready to examine the bookshelves, Minter knocked. At her call, he entered bearing a sea-green frock, white stockings, and feminine, silk slippers.

"Minter!" Devon exclaimed. "Where on earth—"

"That is my secret, Miss Lindsay." He flushed and glanced instinctively toward the captain's bed. Devon's stomach hurt. So she had not been the first female in this cabin. She eyed the green dress critically, comparing the waist to her own, the length of the skirt to her height. It would fit, she thought.

"It was wonderful of you to hunt these up for me," she gulped. "I really do appreciate it."

"I only wanted to help. I did take in the waist a bit."

Devon took the gown, then turned back on a wild impulse. "Who was she? Please tell me, Minter!"

He grinned. "Just someone from the past, Miss Lindsay. It was never serious for the captain."

Devon was delighted by his soft accent and his candor. "Minter, where are you from?"

"Virginia. A few miles south of Williamsburg. Maybe I'll get to see my mama in a few days."

"Why do you say that?"

"Oh, no reason!" Flustered again, he backed up toward the doorway. "I hope the slippers fit. Here!" He thrust them toward her, then disappeared.

Devon wished that she could have pumped him some more. Obviously, Minter knew everything worth knowing!

By the time she went on deck, Devon was in high spirits. The stab of jealousy she had suffered at the first sight of the frock was soothed when she tried it on. Thanks to Minter's alteration, it fit as though it had been made for her, and it was still in excellent condition. Her breasts swelled above the frothy cream-colored lace edging the square neckline, while the snug bodice set off her waist to its best advantage. Even the slippers were a perfect fit. As she was leaving the cabin, Minter appeared with a lace shawl and draped it around her shoulders.

On the gun deck, the men worked with quiet efficiency, and this time they barely glanced at Devon. Not one of them forgot Captain Raveneau's presence on the quarter-deck. He and Mr. Lane stood side by side, a striking study of opposites. The *Black Eagle*'s captain was dressed in casual garb: boots, snug tan breeches, a loose, frilled shirt. His raven hair was unpowdered, and the only signs of his rank were the brass quadrant in his hand and his presence on the quarter-deck. Mr. Lane was far more the man of fashion in his silk stockings and carefully curled white wig. He tilted his nose when he spied Devon crossing the gun deck.

She ignored him. Lifting her skirts, she ascended to the quarter-deck and walked forward to stand beside Raveneau. He was staring at the sky, which was slightly overcast. Devon watched him, waiting to be acknowledged. Raveneau was poised like a wild animal, all his senses alert, and Devon could see him listening, smelling, scrutinizing the air and the sea. She thought him beautiful, like a sculpture, and longed to touch him.

He noticed her finally. "Good morning, again."

"Good morning. Is something wrong?"

"I hope not." Glancing back at her, his gray eyes finally registered the change in her clothing. "Where did you get those things?"

Was he angry? "Why, Minter gave them to me. I was as surprised as you seem to be."

A long moment passed, then his expression softened. "You look lovely, Devon. Minter is talented with a needle and thread."

A crisp, salty breeze caught her titian curls. One wrapped itself around her neck and Raveneau unwound it, his long, dark fingers heating her bare flesh.

"Thank you. I hope you don't mind . . . the clothes, I mean. They feel wonderful."

He returned his attention to the sky. "No. I don't mind."

Ill at ease, Devon turned to survey the quarter-deck. Above the stern flew the American and French flags, both of which would be lowered and replaced by a Dutch flag if enemy sails were sighted. The sailing master and his mate were at the wheel, with Mr. Lane hovering officiously nearby. Devon was certain that he smirked at her. She frowned at him, then turned back to Raveneau.

"Captain, excuse me—"

"Hmm?"

"If it's not too much trouble, I was hoping you might tell me about the *Black Eagle*. You see, my father was a sea captain, and I've wondered how this ship would compare to his."

She already knew much of what he told her, but she reveled in his attention. "A privateer is a very special ship," he explained, "designed for great speed and for an appearance of military strength. The *Black Eagle* is light—just strong enough for the heavy pieces of sail and the recoil of our battery. We don't carry cargo, or anything else that will add unnecessary weight, though we do have a large crew, since we must man and sail any prize that is captured. You may think that we have sixteen guns, but that is only an illusion of strength; the weight would slow us too much. Half of those cannon are 'quakers'—fakes made of light wood. We rarely engage in battle because we avoid British naval vessels. Their holds are empty, but their guns are all too real. The merchantmen are our targets, with their small crews and valuable cargoes. They are easily frightened by our speed and 'guns'." Raveneau grinned wickedly. "You Americans would call them pieces of cake."

Devon shivered with excitement. The numerous, billowing sails were spread before them, carrying the *Black Eagle* through the churning, slate-colored ocean with piercing grace. She could smell the canvas, the damp wood, the hemp, and feel the deck swell then dip beneath her slippered feet.

Raveneau's grin had faded. He was staring at the sky again, his jaw set in concentration. Devon could not understand his gloomy preoccupation.

"Captain . . . please tell me what is wrong."

"There's a storm ahead. I can smell it. The question is—do we raise sail and hope to outrun the storm, or lower the sails and hope to ride it out?"

Devon knew that the question was purely academic, considering André Raveneau's personality. The *Black Eagle* was as bold as its captain. They would sail, meeting head-on whatever weather lay waiting for them.

Minutes grew to an hour. Raveneau scarcely spoke, and the rest of the crew carefully ignored Devon. She was reluctant to return to the cabin, although it was obvious that Raveneau expected her to do so. Mr. Lane's disapproving gaze seemed to burn holes in her back.

The seamen grew quieter as the sky darkened. Every now and then the captain would shout an order through his speaking trumpet and there would be a general scramble up and down the ratlines to reef the sails one by one as the wind increased. At last Raveneau seemed to remember Devon. When he turned to address her, she felt a twinge of alarm at the sight of his furrowed brow. She hadn't imagined that he was subject to such a frail emotion as worry or fright.

"You'd better go below."

Devon sighed, pushing windblown curls out of her eyes. She was cold and more than a little scared; this was not the time to argue with Captain Raveneau. "All right, but I want to be kept informed. Don't you dare leave me below to sink with the ship!"

Raveneau's grin was involuntary. "Devon, I do not think we shall sink. But, to put your mind at ease, you may tell Minter I want to see him. I shall have him bring news to you for the next few hours."

"Thank you." The *Black Eagle* had begun to rock violently. Devon put a tiny hand on Raveneau's arm. "Do take care. I shall have Minter bring up your peacoat."

"Fine."

With that, he walked over to converse with the sailing master and Devon turned to leave. A voice from high on the mast stopped her.

"Sail ho!"

The strange ship bobbed on the far horizon; if the *Black Eagle*'s sails were spread, she could reach it easily. Devon was unable to turn her back on such excitement.

"We will not give chase," Raveneau said quietly, and the boatswain passed the order.

Without pausing to think, Devon ran back to Raveneau's side and pulled at his sleeve. "Why aren't we going after it? Perhaps it's one of those merchantmen you spoke of! You can't just let it sail away like this!"

"Young lady!" Lane attempted to step between them, but Devon angrily bumped him aside.

"Devon, there is a reason why I have made this choice. As captain, I may or may not choose to explain it to you later." Raveneau's eyes were as forbidding and stormy as the skies overhead. "I have asked you to return to my cabin. Do so now!"

A dozen tart rejoinders hovered on Devon's tongue, but the look on his face made her think twice. There was no telling what this Frenchman might do if truly provoked, and this would not be the first time she had tested his patience. So, instead of shouting, she merely scowled angrily and stamped off across the quarter-deck. Before climbing through the hatch, she looked back at Raveneau. He was huddled with the boatswain and the sailing master, his back to her. How maddening to be ignored! The only person watching her was a red-faced Mr. Lane.

Still, she sent Minter up with the peacoat. The steward soon returned to report that the weather was worsening and the *Black Eagle* was swinging to the starboard side in an effort to avoid the heart of the storm. "It's a squall left over from that hurricane that's been plaguing the islands," Minter explained. "We should be able to maneuver through it, but on the other hand . . ."

He left her alone then, promising to return every quarter hour with a report. When he had gone, Devon sat on the bed, clutching the sides, and let her imagination run wild. The *Black Eagle* swayed and dipped more and more erratically. Waves pounded the hull with increasing violence, until it seemed that the ocean would smash the privateer like a paper toy. Footsteps thundered down the gangway, though they didn't come as far aft as the captain's cabin. In the distance the boatswain's pipe sounded a series of shrill, urgent calls. Devon was chilled with terror as she realized that the pumps were being manned at a frenetic pace.

Shrouded in an eerie green haze, the cabin pitched chaotically as the pounding of the waves grew louder and louder. Devon found herself thinking of André Raveneau. What was it like up on deck? Could anyone be left alive in such a storm? Her heart thudded painfully at the thought that Raveneau might be dead, swallowed by the greedy, rampaging sea.

More than an hour had passed since Minter's last visit. Was he dead, too? In desperation, Devon threw open the cabin door and started into the gangway just as the *Black Eagle* fell sideways. She lurched, crashing into a bulkhead. When she opened her eyes, Minter's face was above her, pale and young.

"What—" Devon managed.

"It's bad, but the captain will see us through. He is charmed, and so is this privateer." Minter spoke as much for his own comfort as for Devon's.

"He's not hurt, then . . . ?"

Minter imitated Raveneau's sarcastic snort. "Don't be silly. He is indestructible!"

Devon smiled weakly and Minter helped her struggle to her feet. She was weak with relief to hear that André Raveneau was alive and working to save his ship and crew, but there was no chance to examine her feelings now.

"Minter, don't you think Noah Jackson should be let out of the brig? I've been worried in case anything should happen."

Minter nodded and hurried toward the hatch. Devon thought, He has them all well trained. They can't make a move without his approval, even during a crisis!

Minutes later, a wet and bedraggled Minter was on his way down to the brig, and Devon watched as Noah followed him back to the gun deck and the chaos of the storm. She wondered if she had done Noah a favor, after all.

For what seemed like hours, Devon stood in the gangway and fell back and forth with the savage motion of the *Black Eagle*. When she couldn't stand another moment of waiting, she worked her way over to the main hatch. It was open, and wet spray blasted Devon's face as she started up the ladder. No sooner had her head appeared above the deck than she heard a loud, splintering crack.

One of the middle yardarms had broken off and Devon watched, horrified, as a man fell helplessly through the storm-swept air into the sea. It was Noah.

Without a second thought, she climbed onto the gun deck, hair whipping across her face, and staggered toward André Raveneau at the rail. Black hair sleek and unbound, he pulled off his knee boots and peacoat and dove into the angry green and white sea. The wind pushed Devon back with the force of two men, but she crawled forward toward the rail with panic-derived strength. Almost immediately, she spotted Raveneau's black head bobbing among the choppy waves. One arm was hooked around Noah's neck.

Devon looked wildly about the deck. Mr. Lane was clutching the foremast, oblivious to all except his own survival, and everyone else was in the rigging. She found a line that had been secured with a deadeye, the excess looped around the bottom. She unwound it rapidly and flung it over the side toward Raveneau. But before she could see if the line had reached him, a mighty blast of wind knocked her backward. For one moment she felt a consuming panic, then her head struck the deck and there was nothing but wet, salty blackness.

It was the strangest of sensations, to feel a man's head on her breast. Devon knew what it was even before she opened her eyes to look. She felt the contours of the brow, cheekbones, and jaw. Her own head hurt badly, and opening her eyes required a huge effort.

Curiosity won. A warm glow settled in her belly when she opened her eyes to find Raveneau sitting on the floor with his head resting back on the bed. She was his pillow.

It all came back to Devon then. The storm, the raging seas, Noah falling when the yardarm broke . . . and André Raveneau's suicidal rescue attempt. She could remember tossing the line out, then falling, but nothing more. Was it possible that her action had saved them? Or was it true that Raveneau was simply charmed and indestructible? Dreamily, she admired him as he slept. He wore a clean, heavy shirt that emphasized his swarthy tan. His hair was still damp, curling slightly against his neck as it dried.

As though sensing the change in Devon's breathing, he opened his eyes and turned his face against her breast. Devon's heart beat a wild tattoo. Raveneau's smile lit the room.

"You are awake!" he murmured, obviously pleased. "How do you feel?"

"My head . . ." she whispered. Her mouth was like sandpaper. Raveneau was up in one movement, lifting the bottle of cognac and one snifter from their special, padded case.

He splashed some cognac in the snifter and held it to her lips. Devon felt the warm strength of his fingers bracing her neck; it was astonishing that she should be so poignantly conscious of the man's touch!

The cognac helped, wetting her mouth and spreading its heat through her stiff body. "Thank you. I seem to be all right, except for my head. It hurts."

"We shall keep you quiet for the next day, to be safe."

"Please tell me . . ."

"I caught the line you threw." He grinned, white teeth flashing. "So, you see, I owe you my life!"

Devon was skeptical. "I think you could have managed without me, but I'm glad I could help. Is the storm over?" She realized that the cabin wasn't pitching as before.

"We've run out the worst of it. This craft is tenuous."

"I was terrified. I thought we'd all be killed!"

"Petite chatte, if you had been that afraid, you'd have been cowering under this table rather than sliding across the gun deck!"

"Where is Noah?"

Raveneau's sharp eyes monitored her expression. "He fell a long way and apparently swallowed a good deal of water. When I got him onto the deck, I thought he was dead, but Mr. Lane managed to revive him. He's in the surgeon's cubicle now."

"Mr. Lane?" Devon queried, perplexed.

"I was looking after you."

Their eyes locked for a long moment. Devon was seeing a new side to the man. She would have thought Noah's death would be a relief to him, yet he had risked his own life to save a man he despised. And he had been concerned about her . . .

As though reading her mind, Raveneau said laconically, "I haven't put up with all this bother to see you killed. I've promised to reunite you and Maxwell, and so I shall. I consider the trials of Devon Lindsay to be my one great contribution to the cause of true love."

Chapter Eight

———◆———

September 9, 1781

DEVON lay awake all night. Raveneau's sarcastic references to Devon and Morgan's engagement had rebuilt the wall of tension between them. To make matters worse, they had visited Noah in the surgeon's cubicle and Raveneau had scrutinized her face whenever the injured man moaned, his eyes letting her know that he was fully aware of her affection for Noah. Finally, Devon had called him on it, demanding that he stop leering, insisting that he was all wrong about Noah, that they were just friends. Raveneau's only response had been a sharply raised black eyebrow.

A moonbeam slanted in through the transom, pouring silver over the bed and its occupants. Devon turned on her side, toward Raveneau. The harsh, lean beauty of the Frenchman was mesmerizing, but more fascinating was the puzzle of his personality, principles, emotions, if he possessed such mortal qualities. He lay with one arm thrown over his head, the other resting on his chest, so strangely peaceful that Devon found herself smiling languidly.

She awoke to late morning sunlight and the sound of Minter's voice.

"Miss Lindsay? Can you hear me?" He smiled with delight when she opened her eyes. "I've brought your breakfast!"

Gingerly, Devon propped herself on an elbow. Her headache had diminished. "I don't know if I am hungry."

"Don't try to get up! You'll eat right there. The captain doesn't want you to move about. He was very upset when you insisted on seeing Mr. Jackson last night, feared you might make your own injury worse."

Devon mulled over this news as she watched Minter assemble her meal. She could see that it had been carefully prepared; the dishes were fit for an elderly invalid.

"You seem in fine spirits today, Minter."

"We all are! We're thankful to be alive and dry this morning. It is a blessing! And from the sound of it, Captain Raveneau should be most grateful. If not for you, he'd have been drowned!"

"I doubt that. Didn't you tell me he leads a charmed life?"

Minter laughed, his red hair agleam in the sunlight. "So far, that seems to be true!" Spreading a linen towel over Devon's lap, he presented her with a warm dish of custard, then stood and watched until she had taken the first bite.

"How's Jackson doing?" he asked.

"I don't know. He certainly looked ill last night. I do wish Captain Raveneau would let me out of this bed!"

"Eat that custard!" Minter scolded. "As for you and this bed, it's my opinion that the captain believes you fancy Jackson. He seems to think you want to be near him."

"Rubbish! Where would he get such an idea?"

"That I don't know. I will say that he thinks it was Jackson you were out to rescue yesterday. And once he decides something, there's no changing his mind."

Devon fell back against the pillows, wide-eyed with disbelief. Then she became angry, and, deciding that she couldn't just lie in bed knowing nothing, she begged Minter to ask the surgeon about Noah's condition and report back to her.

"Well, what did Treasel say?" Devon demanded impatiently when Minter returned.

"Miss Lindsay, he's not really what you would call a physician. He just matches up medicines and cures from his books. He can take off arms or legs, remove bullets, and do a fair job of healing festering wounds, but this sort of thing . . ."

"You mean there is nothing he can do?"

Minter squirmed. "It's really just one of those things. Men drown at sea. Jackson had a second chance . . . You don't know that he won't make it yet! Please, you haven't eaten your breakfast—"

"Take this food away!" Devon shrilled. The dagger had renewed its attack on the back of her head. "You are as coldblooded as your captain! Doesn't anyone care that Noah is dying?"

A maddeningly familiar voice answered from the doorway. "Perhaps we all realized that you are concerned enough for at least ten men, so we don't worry that Jackson is deprived in that respect." Raveneau crossed to the bed and stood looking down at Devon, the coldness of his expression belying his light tone.

"You appear better, mademoiselle," he commented. "How is your head?"

"Worse, since you came in!" Devon shot back. She could have bitten off her tongue, but the beast deserved it. Her eyes misted in frustration and she failed to see Raveneau's jaw tighten.

"How inconsiderate of me to enter my own cabin. Perhaps you would rather be in the surgeon's cubicle, where you and your sweetheart could nurse each other!"

Devon had finally had enough of his sarcasm. "Sir, I will thank you to stop twisting everything I do or

say. Do you believe that I give my heart to every
man I meet?"

Raveneau had started to turn away, but froze at
her words, looking back with a small, wicked smile.
"Perhaps not your *heart*, Mademoiselle Lindsay . . ."

After Raveneau left, Devon settled in for a day of
rest. She was oppressively tired. Treasel paid a noon-
time call and assured her that such fatigue was normal after a head injury, but he had no hopeful news
to give her about Noah Jackson.

Minter brought food, but she pretended to be
asleep. It was André Raveneau's step that Devon listened for all day but never heard. Finally, at sun-
down, she came fully awake. A dinner tray rested
nearby on the floor; the small pitcher of cream had
toppled over with the motion of the *Black Eagle*,
soaking the beefsteak, roll, and squash on her plate.

Where was Raveneau? Would his contempt for her
keep him from taking the evening meal in his own
cabin? Devon felt cold, nauseous, and miserable. She
wrapped herself into a protective ball. Bitter pain
built inside, burning her heart.

Out on deck, Minter urged his captain to go below
and share a warm meal with Devon, but Raveneau
could not be distracted until all the storm's damage
had been seen to.

"Miss Lindsay is a human being!" Minter cried,
following him across the gun deck. "This can wait!
She needs you!"

"You talk as if there were a romance between us!"
Raveneau thundered as he surveyed the progress being made on the broken yardarm.

"Captain, I know you won't like this, but I happen
to like this girl and I think it is unfair for you to
judge her as you judge all other females. Simply because you have been disillusioned . . ."

"Minter! I am at least a dozen years older than
you and I have observed enough women to know
that they mean deceit and trouble!" He saw the

stricken expression on Minter's face. "I don't intend to toss the girl overboard, but please remember that she is here because of my charity! I am not the villain!"

It was dark when she heard Raveneau approach. Devon hurt inside. Her stomach ached with loneliness as she thought of her mother, Nick, Benedict Arnold, Noah . . .

And then Raveneau opened the door. His wonderful male scent wafted over her; the pain ebbed. Somehow the mere sight of him made the black gloom worthwhile.

Raveneau returned her smile. *"Bon soir, petite chatte,"* he whispered.

"Bon soir." Why was he smiling? Wasn't he supposed to be angry?

"I am famished." He sat beside her on the bed. "I could eat a whale!"

Devon raised her head. "You haven't had supper?"

"No! I've been busy as hell all day. The yardarm had to be repaired, plus all the other more trivial damage, and matters were complicated by the number of injured men. Most will be good as new tomorrow, but there were several sprains and bruises."

Devon felt a dizzying elation: he had been busy! "That's terrible!"

He peered sideways in the darkness, quirking a brow at the cheerful tone of her voice. "Your concern is commendable."

Blushing, Devon dropped back into the bed and grinned into the moonlit transom. "I suppose I am pleased to find you in such good humor."

"Well, there's a reason. In spite of the havoc wrought by that squall, it could have been worse. We might have been blown days off course, but as luck would have it, the storm sent us in the right direction."

"Oh, really? How close to Yorktown are we, then?" Inexplicably, Devon's chest tightened.

"A day away. With the right wind, we might arrive tomorrow night."

"Oh . . . that's wonderful."

Raveneau stood up and stretched, his powerful body silhouetted against the moonlight. "I thought you would be pleased. I know how you burn to be reunited with Milton."

Minter arrived with the captain's supper and lit the candles, while Devon hesitantly reflected on Morgan, her supposed reason for this perilous voyage. His existence seemed so remote that she experienced a twinge of panic.

"Worrying about Jackson?" Raveneau inquired abruptly.

Devon looked up to find him seated at the table, cutting into a fragrant beefsteak.

"Someone has to," she replied.

"Devon, come over here."

She wore only one of Raveneau's linen shirts. When she stood up the lace-edged cuffs fell past her fingers, but the hem barely touched her knees.

"I should . . . put my breeches on . . ."

"What a horrifying thought! Please, do not cover such enchanting legs."

Delighted by this flattery, Devon joined Raveneau at the table. He casually offered her a bit of this or that dish, until she had consumed as much food as he. It was obvious that he wanted to smooth things over between them; Devon thought that he was probably too exhausted to quarrel. She could see signs of fatigue in his lean face.

They spoke little, yet the silence was not strained. Devon felt peaceful.

After Minter had removed the dishes, the two of them leaned back and sipped cognac. The *Black Eagle* cut smoothly through the dark sea, rocking gently, and Devon persuaded Raveneau to tell her about some of his more famous captures. They were tales she had heard a dozen times from Nick and the men of New London; they were threads in the fabric of Raveneau's legend. Yet when he spoke of his exploits, he rarely mentioned himself, detailing instead the maneuvers of the ship, the daring of his crew. Pride softened the hard lines of his face.

"Captain?" she inquired hesitantly.

"Devon, I think that you should call me André." His grin was teasing.

"Fine. Thank you . . . André." Devon blushed. "I was wondering if you might explain to me now why we didn't chase that ship yesterday."

There was a slight flicker of irritation in his eyes before he answered. "You may assume that any decision I make is the correct one. I ought to leave it at that, but this time I'll explain. This is no ordinary cruise we are making, no circle from New London to Yorktown and back again. We will stay in Yorktown for an indefinite period, and I cannot spare even one man to take a captured ship back to Connecticut."

"Do you mean that you'll be fighting in Yorktown? Will there be a battle?"

"I dearly hope so, *petite chatte*. If all goes well, there will be a battle that will never be forgotten."

Something was wrong. Devon awoke, chilled, opening her eyes to moonlight. Next to her, Raveneau slept deeply, his brown chest rising and falling. The *Black Eagle* swayed like a cradle; the night was still.

What was wrong? Devon wondered. Something clutched her heart with icy claws. Noah? She wanted to bury her face in the pillow and be covered by sleep, but her legs carried her up out of the cabin, and all the way to the surgeon's cubicle.

Noah looked worse. He could have been a ghost, staring up at Devon with glassy, unseeing eyes that made her want to scream. His mouth was open between hollow, ghoulish cheeks. She would never have recognized him. This was not the Noah she had allowed to charm her.

Helplessly, Devon knelt and laid her ear against his chest. There was no heartbeat. She was paralyzed, staring at this unfamiliar face as images of a different Noah flickered crazily through her mind. There had been a time when she believed him to be fine, boyishly charming, and unselfish, when she had defended him to Raveneau and agonized over his torn back. Perhaps those qualities had been real, coexisting with irresponsibility, impulsiveness, and the cancer of his hatred for André Raveneau.

If not for Noah, she might have gone quietly insane beside the British soldier in New London. Whatever his motives, he had given her a second chance at life, and Devon would always be grateful. Tears burned her eyes, trickling down to drop onto Noah's ghostly face. She wept and rocked back and forth on her heels until she felt sick. Then Raveneau was beside her, lifting her up into his arms, carrying her back to his cabin, where he sat in the leather wing chair with Devon huddled on his lap. She sobbed uncontrollably, clutching his warm chest and shoulders. Gently he caressed her hair and whispered softly against her wet cheek until she began to quiet. Eventually she retreated into the safe haven of dreamless sleep, but Raveneau remained awake, watching Devon's tear-streaked face, his eyes like splintered steel.

Chapter Nine

September 10, 1781

DEVON awoke at dawn, alone in the bed. Raveneau was shaving. "Feeling better?" he asked coldly.

"I feel terrible. As though I'm dying myself. Please, may I come above with you today?" To her dismay, Devon heard her voice crack.

Raveneau glanced at her in a way that drove her insane—cynical, cold, knowing. "You may do whatever you like as long as it does not interfere with the *Black Eagle*'s speedy passage to Chesapeake Bay." He paused while buttoning a fresh shirt over his hard, tanned chest. "However, if you are planning to weep and moan all day, stay down here. I can't have the entire crew comforting you."

He pulled on his boots and walked out the door. Devon wanted to throw something at him, but instead, she ran behind, calling out the door, "Arrogant French beast! Coldblooded pirate! I hate you!"

Raveneau paused at the hatch. "Do you expect me to care?" he inquired emotionlessly, then disappeared from view.

Devon was wounded, but only momentarily. She was angry at herself for being hurt by anything he said or did, and stamped across the cabin, muttering between clenched teeth, "I hate him!" over and over.

Yet even as she dressed, she found herself going back over all their conversations, remembering the various expressions on his face, the few real smiles. He was a true enigma. Deciding that she would never be able to dissect the man, Devon left the cabin, telling herself that she despised him all the same.

It was a strange day. The *Black Eagle* strained to reach Chesapeake Bay before nightfall, but it soon became obvious that the wind would not cooperate. Raveneau's mood was one of tightly strung irritability; soon the crew began to snap at one another as well.

Devon stayed close to Treasel, who had come above to get a bit of sun. When Noah's body was committed to the sea, it was Treasel who held Devon's hand. The crew gathered, heads bowed, while Mr. Lane said a few trivial words. Raveneau had disappeared below. Someone said he was eating lunch, adding the hope that food would improve his temper.

After Noah's body, wrapped and weighted, had disappeared between the waves, the surgeon chatted on briskly, hoping to clear the dazed look in Devon's sapphire-blue eyes. The crew scattered and they were left alone at the rail.

"Did you care so much for Jackson?" asked Treasel.

"No . . . and I feel worse for that—guilty. It was so awful to see him dead."

"That's odd! The rumor is that you two were sweethearts—that you risked your life on deck during the storm to save him!"

Devon stared at him, her forehead puckering as he spoke. "Why would anyone leap to such conclusions?" she gasped.

"Because Jackson said as much the day your presence was made known! Everyone said you had followed him to the *Black Eagle* and begged him to hide you. As far as I know, he never denied it." Treasel vigorously scratched his pewter hair, remembering.

"The men thought it was wrong of the captain, locking you in his cabin and refusing to let you see Jackson! But then, there are the rules . . . and, of course, the two of them never did get along."

"I don't understand!" Devon exclaimed. "This is ludicrous. It was nothing like that!"

"No? Why, Jackson even complained to me when I was dressing his wounds, about how mad he was! Said it would be just like Captain Raveneau to soil his woman for him, just for spite. So, then, it was no surprise to me when you turned up down in the cockpit, all tears and worry." He gave her a sharp sidelong glance. "How do you explain that, if you didn't care?"

"I felt responsible!" she shrilled. She wondered if Noah had spread such stories in order to turn the crew against Raveneau. Her head began to pound. "I do not want to talk about this anymore," she groaned. "Oh, Treasel, how I wish we were in Yorktown!"

Just then André Raveneau appeared at her side, and Devon realized with a pang that the end of this voyage would mean the end of their association. Looking up into his flinty, smoldering eyes, she tried to imagine life without him.

"I trust you have recovered your composure, Mademoiselle Lindsay?" he inquired coolly.

"Why, I never lost it, Captain," Devon replied.

"What? Do you mean to say that you have not been washing down the deck with tears and yanking out clumps of hair in your hysteria?"

"You are insufferable." She averted her face.

"I am devastated to hear you say so, mademoiselle. Allow me to remove myself from your sight." Smiling ironically, he went on to the quarter-deck, while Devon seethed.

"Sail ho!" came the shout from high on the mainmast. The seaman paused for only a moment before scurrying down the ratlines and racing toward the quarter-deck. Captain Raveneau met him halfway.

"There's a whole fleet due south, Cap'n!" the man cried breathlessly. "Damned if they aren't British! Over a dozen ships!"

Raveneau's eyes lit up. He smiled briefly to himself, then gave the order for the flags to be changed.

"We'll stay on course," he announced. "I have to find out what has happened!"

Before long, the fleet loomed ahead on their starboard side. The huge frigates dwarfed the *Black Eagle,* but their sails were torn and powder-stained, their bulwarks splintered. One ship had lost its mainmast.

Devon edged her way toward the quarter-deck, consumed by curiosity. The captain and his first lieutenant stood side by side at the rail, which Raveneau was gripping with tense delight.

"Mon Dieu!" he hissed. "It is the combined forces of Admirals Hood and Graves! *Regardez!* Just look at the condition of those ships! I'm afraid we have missed the battle, but if this was the outcome, then I am sufficently pleased. Oh, to have been there! De Grasse must be ecstatic!"

Devon stared at Raveneau, hypnotized by his energy. He was the embodiment of lean, carefully leashed power; he shone in the sunlight.

The battered British fleet sailed past, barely acknowledging the presence of the *Black Eagle*. The nearest ship saluted halfheartedly when it came alongside. It seemed to Devon that the crew looked weary and downcast.

When they were long clear and the flags had been replaced, the wind suddenly improved as though prompted by Raveneau's good spirits. Snowy sails billowed above the sharp-hulled privateer, sending it slicing effortlessly through the aquamarine waves.

Treasel had gone below to change the dressings of some of the men injured during the storm, and Devon decided to approach the captain. She boldly ascended to the hallowed area of the quarter-deck, ignoring Mr. Lane's icy stare.

"Excuse me."

Raveneau held his brass quadrant in his left hand and a complicated chart in his right, which he studied with narrowed eyes. Without looking up, he murmured dryly, "You wish a word with this insufferable, beastly, arrogant, coldblooded French pirate?"

Devon blushed from the roots of her hair to the bodice of the sea-green gown. "Captain, it is your own fault that I say such horrid things," she countered lamely.

"Oh, really?" Raveneau raised his head, eyes sparkling silver, teeth gleaming in a wicked smile. "I cannot wait to hear the reasoning behind *that* statement."

"You provoke me."

"But, *petite chatte,* you provoke me as well, and I have yet to speak aloud all the names I have called you in my mind."

Anger deepened Devon's blush. Raveneau felt his heart soften as he gazed at her. He thought that it was a crime for such loveliness to go untasted. But, of course, her perfect Morgan would have that pleasure soon enough.

She was a vision. The sun struck sparks on her strawberry-blond curls, which blew softly around the oval of her face. Such luminous, deep blue eyes, tempting lips, and soft, peach-gold skin. The chit had no idea how intensely he desired her, and Raveneau couldn't let her know as long as she was betrothed to another man. If he could not have her, admitting his weakness would be fatal.

"I did not come up here to trade insults with you, Captain," Devon said slowly. She wished she could hit him squarely on the jaw. "I was hoping you might tell me about the British fleet we just passed."

Raveneau looked out to sea or at his chart as he spoke; anywhere but at Devon. "I am not certain, but I think that I know what happened. Admiral de Grasse, who is one of my countrymen, took a fleet into Chesapeake Bay to fight the British navy and prevent any ships from coming to the rescue of General Cornwallis and his army on the mainland. I had hoped to do what I could to help the blockade, but from the looks of those British warships, it would seem that the confrontation is over."

"And the British were the losers?" Devon prompted.

"I think that is a safe deduction." Raveneau smiled. "I am anxious to reach the bay and learn all the details!"

Mr. Lane cleared his throat to capture the captain's attention. Devon slipped away, retreating to the cabin for a light meal and some rest. She still felt very weak.

Minter brought a delicious-smelling tray and was so meticulously cheerful that Devon wondered if he believed the story that she had been in love with Noah. Part of her wanted to discuss it with him again, but she was just too tired.

Returning in midafternoon to retrieve the tray and dishes, Minter found Devon lying on her back on the bed. Her sapphire eyes were open, staring at a point in space.

"Miss Lindsay?"

"Hmm? Oh, Minter, hello. How is everything?"

"Fine. And you?"

"Tired. Apprehensive."

"I'll wager you are happy to know you'll be with your fiancé soon."

"Oh, of course. If he is in Virginia, if I can find him . . . and if he's still alive."

"I'm certain things will work out for you. You deserve it." He smiled with real affection. "Do you suppose you might miss the *Black Eagle* a bit?"

Devon's eyes clouded. "This is the finest craft I have ever seen. Of course I shall miss it—and you, too!"

Minter crouched beside the bed. "The crew hoped you'd feel that way, Miss Lindsay. They asked me to invite you to share some grog with us tonight. It's a custom to have a party on the last night before we reach port. Captain Raveneau gives every man a double ration."

"But why would they want me there?"

"The men feel sorry for you. They think you've had a rough time of it, and they just want to cheer you up and let you know they care."

"In that case, Minter, I would love to go. Will you escort me?"

Raveneau returned to the cabin that evening to find Devon sitting at his desk, peering into the mirror from his shaving stand while brushing her red-gold hair.

"Hello," she greeted him absently.

"Hello." He was curious, but tried not to let it show. She still wore the sea-green gown, which looked as if it had been ironed. Her skin was pink and gold and satiny in the lantern light; her lips were moist and lush.

No sooner had Raveneau poured himself a portion of cognac than Minter arrived with his supper.

"That was quick," he commented suspiciously. "Where is Devon's plate?"

"I've already eaten," she explained.

Minter wore clean clothes and had combed his bright red hair. "Are you ready, Miss Lindsay?"

"I certainly am! I don't mind saying that I'm excited!" She stood up, smoothing her skirts. "Thank you for asking me, Minter."

He flushed happily, but Raveneau's face was stormy. "Will someone tell me what the hell is going on around here?" he asked.

"Why, Captain, your crew has invited me to share a cup of grog with them to celebrate the last night at sea. Isn't that nice?"

"Oh, yes! They are a thoughtful group," he said caustically.

"I hope you don't mind, Captain," Minter interjected anxiously.

"As a matter of fact—"

"Of course he doesn't mind." Devon was standing beside Minter, but her eyes were locked with Raveneau's. "Your captain has assured me that I may do whatever I like until we reach Yorktown. Isn't that right, Captain Raveneau?"

"That wicked tongue will get you in trouble one day," he warned, his voice deadly even. "Minter, you are responsible for this little witch. See to it that she stays out of mischief and is treated with respect by those brutes."

"Oh, yes, sir, I will!"

Devon had a fine time in the crew's quarters. The hammocks were stowed out of sight, replaced by the hinged tables which were secured against the walls at night.

The men were freshly shaved, hair plastered down flat and wet, with clean kerchiefs tied around their necks. All the still-damp, musty-smelling clothing left from the storm had been hung to dry elsewhere, and the hatch was wide open to let in the cool evening air.

Every man wanted Devon at his table, yet for all the enthusiasm displayed, she was treated with deference and courtesy. After a half cup of grog, she joined in the festive spirit, moving from table to table with each new toast. Minter was careful to stay by her side. He glared at any man who ogled Devon, but couldn't help feeling that his expression could never match Captain Raveneau's for sheer menace.

Devon regaled the sailing master and the boatswain with stories of her father and his exploits at sea. Wheaton, the boatswain, professed to remember Hugh Lindsay, which won Devon's heart. The crusty old man recounted their last meeting, his wording suspiciously ambiguous, while Devon helpfully supplied details.

"Aye, there's no doubt that Hugh Lindsay was as

fine a sea captain as any," Wheaton declared at last. "Exceptin' Captain Raveneau, o' course."

Devon's face fell, while every man raised his mug and shouted, "Hear, hear!"

"You can't mean that!" she cried to the old man. "I know that he puts on a good show, but I thought that you would have been perceptive enough to realize—"

Wheaton's eyes were like blue ice in his leathery face. "Miss Lindsay, Raveneau is the finest captain I have ever known, and that's plain truth. I don't happen to believe in lucky ships. Such luck is the captain's doing, and for my money, Captain Raveneau makes bloody miracles happen!"

Glancing around the quiet room, Devon found every man's eyes fastened on her. It galled her to give in, but she realized that these men were stubbornly, blindly, loyal to their captain. "You are right, of course," she said. "I cannot imagine what came over me."

Minter held Devon's arm on the way back to the captain's cabin, for she could barely stand.

"Oh, Minter, I ruined it all!" she wailed. "The men hate me now, don't they!"

"For goodness' sake, Miss Lindsay, don't cry. They don't hate you. They like you a great deal, but everyone is fiercely loyal to Captain Raveneau."

"I thought Noah had turned them against him."

Minter understood what she meant. "The men knew Jackson for what he was, and they worship Captain Raveneau. They trust him. Even if he did do something morally wrong keeping you from Jackson, it would seem permissible since *he* did it. To tell you the truth, we all rather hoped for a romance between you and the captain. Certainly none of us wanted Jackson to have you!"

Devon blushed and giggled, pausing to hug Minter right there. "You are adorable, do you know that?"

"Thank you." He ducked his head. "Miss Lindsay, I'm afraid you've had too much grog. Try not to fall over a chair, all right? The captain will have my head!"

The cabin was dark, except for one lone candle that flickered on Raveneau's desk. He was in bed sleeping, his chest and arms nut-brown against the snowy sheets.

Devon put out the candle and stripped to her chemise. She lay her gown over the wing chair and padded softly to the bed. Her heart jumped into her throat as she looked down at André and contemplated sliding between the sheets, her body touching his. Even in sleep he appeared incredibly strong and magnificent, but above all, appealing.

It is like an enchantment, Devon thought helplessly. She lifted the sheet and lay down. She inched closer to him and brushed her fingertips over the mat of black hair on his chest, trailing them across his collarbone and down a lean, muscular shoulder.

Raveneau stirred and rolled onto his side, toward Devon. One long arm hooked her waist, drawing her against the warm, hard length of his body. Then his mouth closed over hers. "You reek of rum," he murmured huskily, then recaptured her lips.

Devon was swept by a dizzying tide of desire. She responded wildly to his kiss, while her hands traced the planes of his broad back and narrow hips. He was naked, but that didn't shock or surprise her; she boldly pressed herself closer to him. Raveneau's kisses were slow, sleepy, and tantalizing. Tingling currents of pleasure ran over Devon as he brushed his lips over her throat and the soft curve of her shoulder. He drew the sheet away, then deftly unfastened and removed her chemise. Moonlight silvered her trim, eager body as he explored and teased every inch with skillful fingers and mouth.

Despite the last shreds of Devon's pride, she writhed in ecstasy and longing. Her hips sought his, driven by primitive instinct. Raveneau's mouth was on hers again, one hard-muscled arm clasping her back as his passion mounted, his other hand cupping her buttocks, pressing her to his flat, hard belly and his maleness. It felt warm, smooth, and immense against Devon's soft skin. There was a sweet, wild throb in her hidden female place; it did not pass, but grew ever more intense.

"Oh!" she gasped. "I want . . . I want . . ."

Raveneau sighed into her hyacinth-scented hair. "Ah, *petite chatte,* it is bad of me to do this, to take advantage of you when you have had too much rum."

"I *want* you to!" Devon implored. "I demand it!"

Raveneau chuckled softly. "I've warned you that your willfulness would get you into trouble."

"Yes! Yes!" she groaned, touching him anxiously. "Oh, I cannot bear another moment!"

"It is your own fault, for getting so tipsy. Remember that."

Then he moved over her, kissing her lips, neck, sucking her tender breasts with tantalizing skill. Every nerve seemed exposed and Devon shivered in exquisite torment, caressing her lover as he worked his magic on her. At last, gently, Raveneau's fingers touched her aching desire. He stroked her leisurely, again and again, until she opened slim legs to him. After one last, searing kiss, Raveneau knelt to enter her. Devon, feeling tiny and fragile beneath him, panicked momentarily, but the instant he touched her she was lost. Now she knew what she had yearned for since the first time this dangerously irresistible Frenchman had kissed her in Nick's carriage. Clinging to him, her nails digging into his back, she let him take her. The one stab of pain was meaningless; it seemed an intrinsic part of the ecstasy. Devon wrapped her legs around André's body, as they fused and teasingly drew back, over and over, Raveneau's breath harsh against her ear.

They shuddered together and Devon wondered at the tremors that shook her. She floated, searched Raveneau's face with her lips and kissed him, wanting never to let him go. They lay entwined, blissfully spent.

Chapter Ten

———◆———

September 11 and 12, 1781

THE sheets were soft and warm, André's scent mingling with her own. Devon burrowed into her pillow, luxuriating in the sensation of smooth linen against bare skin. Half awake, she put out a hand and was startled into alertness when her fingers failed to encounter Raveneau.

He was gone. Frantic, Devon sat up, eyes open wide. Her head hurt and she felt ill. The cabin was empty.

The grog. Devon was flooded with sickening memories of all she had said and done the night before. And André . . . was that a dream, or had it truly happened? The ache between her legs confirmed her worst fears, and she heard his voice again, warning, "It is your own fault, for getting so tipsy. Remember that."

Falling back against the pillow, she pressed her palms to her throbbing head. She could close her eyes and see him again and remember every touch, each word he had spoken. And a voice in the farthest corner of her heart whispered, It was wonderful, it was worth it, even if you never see him again!

See him! Devon opened her eyes, stricken. How

could she ever face Raveneau again? She had insisted that he make love to her, had reached out to touch his erect organ with no word of encouragement, and had responded wildly to his every kiss and touch. She had behaved brazenly, shamelessly. But the very scent of him in the bed ignited her desire: even in her shame, she craved him helplessly.

I will never drink another drop of that evil grog again! Devon vowed. She tried to sit up on the edge of the bed but felt strangely disembodied and off balance. Her shirt and breeches were neatly folded on Raveneau's trunk, so she put them on, pulled up the sheets to cover the smudges of dried blood, and gratefully lay down again.

There was a familiar knock at the door.

"Come in, Minter." The words sounded garbled to her own ears, but apparently they were clear enough, for the door opened and Minter entered the cabin.

"Miss Lindsay? Are you feeling the aftereffects of the grog?"

"I'm afraid so. It must be that, for I've never been sick like this before."

"Yes. I knew you shouldn't have drunk so much!"

"I wish you could have convinced me last night, Minter." Gingerly, she sat up again and accepted the mug of coffee he had brought.

"Well, I tried, but you kept shouting that you were a sea captain's daughter and born to drink grog. The crew was cheering you on—they thought you were wonderful!"

"Certainly. I was the most entertainment they've had for weeks, I'll wager."

Minter smiled ruefully. "You know, Miss Lindsay, we've reached Chesapeake Bay. We're anchored beside the French fleet."

"Oh?" Devon's stomach knotted with apprehension.

"The captain wants me to take you ashore in case we have to fight."

"Oh." She swallowed a lump of misery. "And where is the captain now?"

"He was rowed over to the *Ville de Paris* more than two hours ago. That's Admiral de Grasse's ship. Did you know that it's the biggest in the world?"

"No, I didn't."

"At any rate, the captain has known the admiral since he was a boy. His father was the admiral's friend."

"It must have been a very moving reunion." Devon had never felt worse.

"No doubt. Captain Raveneau hopes to be of some help. You see, the French fleet is here to blockade Chesapeake Bay and prevent General Cornwallis from escaping General Washington and Rochambeau, who are marching to Yorktown with their armies. So the big battle is yet to come. And although the British navy has been beaten off for now, Captain Raveneau says that another fleet could be sent down from New York at any time to rescue Cornwallis. He wants you removed to a safe place before it is too late."

Minter sat down in the leather wing chair, oblivious to the torment Devon was suffering. "I see," she said flatly. "Am I to be put off on a raft and left to my own devices?"

"Oh, no!" Minter laughed. "I'm to take you to a small farm up the James River. It's on the other side of the Yorktown peninsula, not far from Williamsburg." He flushed self-consciously. "As a matter of fact, it's my home. You'll stay with my parents and sister. Then when the fighting is over, you can look for your fiancé."

Who? Devon almost blurted. Then she asked softly, "Are we to go now?"

"Yes. Captain Raveneau asked me to bid you farewell for him. He said to wish you much happiness with your future husband."

Devon's insides cramped. She could just imagine the

expression on André's face when he uttered *those* sentiments!

The Yorktown peninsula was shaped like a thumb, pointing downward into Chesapeake Bay. Yorktown itself perched near the tip of the peninsula and Williamsburg stood at the junction of the peninsula with mainland Virginia, on the opposite coast from Yorktown. Two rivers flowed down the peninsula into Chesapeake Bay; the York River ran through Yorktown, while the James ran through Williamsburg.

Minter and Devon set out from the *Black Eagle* that morning in a neat thirty-foot cutter with lugsails. It took them a full day to sail up the James and reach the Minter farm. They encountered dozens of other boats with passengers who frequently recognized Minter and shouted greetings to him but he concentrated on sailing the cutter while Devon sat glumly in the bow, staring at the water before them.

They reached their destination shortly after dawn the next day. Devon had tried to sleep, with little success. As Minter navigated their cutter up the narrow inlet that led to his farm, she was overcome by anxiety. Why did I ever leave New London? she asked herself. I could have lived with Temperance and Mary, or even with the Gadwins, until Morgan returned. Instead, I am in the middle of a swamp on my way to stay with a family I don't even know! Suppose Morgan is dead or I cannot find him? What will become of me?

She put a hand up to her tangled curls. A nasty film coated the inside of her mouth and she felt dirty all over.

Minter held out his canvas ditty bag. "There's a comb inside," he offered, "and a bit of cloth you might wet to wipe your face."

Devon smiled her thanks and opened it eagerly, rummaging through the razor, wooden shaving dish and brush, jackknife, scissors, and wooden ditty box, which contained Minter's sewing gear. At the bottom were the comb and square of flannel. She did what she could to improve her appearance and was particularly refreshed by the cool, wet cloth on her face.

"Feel better?" Minter asked gently.

"Yes. Thank you. And, Minter, I'm sorry if I've been a terrible shrew."

"I've been worried, is all. I'm used to seeing you a good deal more lively." He brought the cutter alongside a small dock and furled the sails. "If you are worried about living here," he said, "you needn't be. My family will love you, and I have an older sister who is only twenty-three. Her fiancé is fighting, too, and she's been waiting for him for five years, so she will welcome your company."

"Thank you for telling me. That does help."

Minter tied the cutter up, scrambled onto the narrow, makeshift dock, and put a hand out to help Devon. They walked through a thick grove of hickory and chestnut trees and came upon a small frame house with a catslide roof. In the distance Devon could see fields, a tobacco barn, and two other buildings.

"It's not very much," Minter apologized, "but my people have lived here for over a century, so it *is* home. After this war ends, we have many plans . . ."

The farmhouse door swung open and a tiny, thin woman stepped onto the walk. "Halsey?" she called. "Is that really you?"

"Mama, you know it is!" He trotted forward and embraced his mother. Devon thought that the woman looked more like his grandmother. Lank gray hair was twisted into a severe coil at her neck, accentuating her haggard face.

"Mama, this is Devon Lindsay. She came from New London, Connecticut, to look for her man, and I know you'll be glad to share our home with her 'til the fighting is over at Yorktown. Her own family is dead."

"Good morning." Mrs. Minter put out a wizened hand, which Devon stepped forward to shake. "My name's Constance Minter. Welcome."

"I don't want to impose . . ."

"Nonsense. Perhaps the day will come when you can do us a good turn." The words were kind, yet she didn't smile.

"It was Captain Raveneau's idea that she come here, Mama," Minter explained. "He brought her south on the *Black Eagle* after there was a battle in New London. The British burned the town and her mama died."

Raveneau's name seemed to set Mrs. Minter's mind at ease. "You poor child . . . I expect you've been through a lot of suffering," she said. "Come on inside. After you two have eaten, I'll have Azalea heat up some washing water."

Devon found the main room cozy and surprisingly well furnished. The cherry drop-leaf table and matching chairs were as fine as she had ever seen, while the oak cupboard boasted rows of hand-painted china. The windows were glass, and a large Oriental rug covered the brick floor. There was a long sofa, upholstered in green brocade, and two threadbare wing chairs.

"Why, this is lovely!" Devon exclaimed.

"Captain Raveneau brought us every piece of furniture you see in this room, except for the wing chairs," Mrs. Minter replied. "He's the finest man . . ."

"Where's Pa?" her son broke in. "And Azalea?"

"Your pa's outside, having a look at the tobacco curing in the barn. Azalea's getting dressed." She turned to Devon. "You'll sleep upstairs with her."

"Fine. I would like that."

"I think I'll go and greet Pa," Minter said. "Do you mind, Devon?"

"No, please go ahead. I'll be fine."

Mrs. Minter crossed to the huge brick fireplace which formed the east wall. There was a baking oven on one side, and a kettle of water boiled over the low flames in the hearth. "I was just about to make some tea. Would you like a cup?" she asked.

"Yes. That would be very nice." Devon was so tired that her own voice sounded flat and unfamiliar.

Footsteps tapped down the narrow stairway and Devon looked up to see an attractive, deep-rose gown appear, and finally a face. Azalea Minter was a lush, beautiful girl with curves in all the right places. Her thick chestnut hair, dark doe eyes, and pink cheeks shone with good health. "Hello! I must confess that I've been listening to this conversation!" she said, reaching the bottom step and hurrying over to clasp Devon's hands. "I am so happy to meet you! My name's Azalea Minter and I just know you and I will be good friends!"

Devon admired the straight, pearl-like teeth that showed behind Azalea's smiling ruby lips. "I am Devon Lindsay," she said, "and I would like nothing better than to be your friend. I'm so glad you don't mind my intrusion—"

"Good heavens, no! Why, we all have to help each other during this war. Besides, I've been aching for a friend!" She looked around to find her mother pouring the hot water into a Queensware teapot. "Mama, please do keep our tea hot. I'll take Devon upstairs so she can start to get settled."

Devon picked up the tiny cowhide trunk Minter had packed for her and cheerfully followed Azalea upstairs.

The roof came to a point over the long, slanted bedroom. It was cheerfully furnished with an unmade low-post bed, a slant-top desk, an armoire, and two Windsor chairs. A worn Turkish rug covered the floor, and the bedspread and curtains were made of the same blue and white fabric. There was a small washstand next to the bed, with a miniature painting of a young man balanced on its far corner.

"This must be your fiancé!" Devon exclaimed.

"Yes. It is." Azalea smiled adoringly at the likeness of a blond, rather heavy set man with a florid complexion.

Devon noticed a sword hanging on the wall. It was a rakish-looking weapon, highly polished, with a length of pearl-gray satin tied around the handle. "I suppose this is his?" she asked. "I'm sorry, but Minter—that is, Halsey—didn't mention his name."

"It is Isaac. Isaac Smith. But, to answer your other question, the sword isn't his. It was a gift from André."

Devon choked. "André?"

"Yes. André Raveneau. You've met him, haven't you? I assumed that he must have told Halsey to bring you here."

"Why, yes . . . I know him. I came here from Connecticut on the *Black Eagle* after the British attacked my town and my mother died."

"Oh, I'm so sorry. But if one must escape, I can't imagine a more exciting way!" Azalea turned away to lift Devon's small trunk onto the bed. "Are you André's mistress?"

Stunned, Devon put a hand on the washstand for balance. "Of course not! No!"

Azalea looked back, smiling archly. "That's a shame. I'm so sorry."

Blushing furiously, Devon opened the trunk. She pulled out an extra shirt and pair of breeches, and as she reached for the folded sea-green dress, Azalea exclaimed, "For goodness' sakes! That's my gown! I'll own I never thought I'd lay eyes on *it* again!"

Chapter Eleven

---◆---

Late September, 1781

DEVON adapted quickly to life on the farm after Halsey Minter returned to the *Black Eagle.*

Jud Minter was tall and lanky like his son, but his skin was brown and weather-beaten. Unlike Constance Minter, who complained of every ache, her husband never talked about himself, yet his fatigue and pain showed in his eyes and every labored movement.

Azalea was as young and vital as her parents were old and bitter. She worked on the farm with the endurance of a man, and Devon was caught up in her whirlwind of energy. At night, when the younger girl lay utterly exhausted on her side of the bed, Azalea would talk on in the darkness.

Azalea's connection with André Raveneau had been explained the first night. Over six years ago, she had said, before her betrothal to Isaac, she had been restless and quarrelsome during the long, dull winter of 1775. Just before the war erupted, she had run away from home, searching for adventure.

"I know it was foolish, but many good things came from that escapade," she said, smiling. "I was kidnapped by a horrible British seaman who used me

137

badly and took me aboard his ship. Once we were at sea, the *Black Eagle* swooped in like a bird of prey, captured the British ship, and André stole me away. What an adventure! I lived and breathed for that man all that spring."

Remembering the first time she had seen Raveneau —in April of 1775—and the female companion who had clutched his arm while they strolled along the beach, Devon smiled feebly. "Were you in New London?"

"Goodness, I think so! I paid little mind to anything but André. We were *very* close, if you take my meaning."

Devon, sick at heart, imagined Azalea's wink in the darkness. "What happened?" she asked. "Did you quarrel? Was this before you knew Isaac?"

"Oh, I knew Isaac and I was quite certain I'd marry him one day! As for André, there was no quarrel. He simply brought me home when the war began in earnest and he was ready to sail south." Azalea managed a stiff laugh. "I was prepared. I'm no fool! Opportunities like André come as often as falling stars, and they are as impossible to grasp. I knew he would never marry me, but I couldn't refuse him. I have always loved Isaac—I've waited years for him! But André is special. He's magic." There was a heavy pause. "Didn't you feel it? Didn't it make you hot just being near him?"

"No! And it's not a subject we should be discussing."

"Hmmm. You say no so loudly, I think you might mean yes." Azalea rushed to soothe Devon's temper by finishing the story. It seemed that Raveneau had met her brother, Halsey, when he brought Azalea home. The boy had signed on as the captain's steward and had been there ever since. The Frenchman's friendship with the entire Minter family had endured.

Days passed. Devon helped Mrs. Minter in the house and listened patiently to her complaints. She also went with Azalea to the tobacco barn, where the meager crop had been hung to cure, watching as the older girl inspected its progress. Then they would walk through the fields and trees or ride the two aging horses.

Their friendship prospered. Eventually Devon told Azalea about the British attack on New London and Groton Bank, shakily describing the soldiers who had burst into the Linen and Pewter Shop and the nightmarish events which had followed. Azalea listened in horrified fascination, but in the end she threw her arms around Devon and hugged her until it hurt. Devon wept to the point of feeling sick, then laughed nervously and drew away. They smiled into each other's eyes and their friendship was sealed.

Azalea never tired of discussing Isaac, her thirst for romance, or the men in her past. She had no qualms about telling all, but Devon, though she spoke freely about Morgan, never mentioned any aspect of their physical relationship, and she froze whenever Azalea mentioned André Raveneau.

One evening Azalea left the house for a walk. Devon watched her through the window as she headed toward the dock, and thought she seemed oddly furtive.

Constance Minter came up behind Devon, smelling of herbs and potatoes.

"She's up to something," she declared, and crossed the room to poke her husband, who was dozing on the sofa. "Azalea's up to something!" she shouted in his ear.

Jud Minter made an unsuccessful attempt to revive himself, then propped his chin on the opposite shoulder and began to snore.

"Do you see?" Mrs. Minter asked Devon harshly. "I'm as helpless as a kitten! My husband cannot help me deal with that child. She's always been headstrong, uncontrollable. You follow her, Devon, make sure she stays out of trouble."

"Oh, I wouldn't worry," soothed a somewhat confused Devon. "What sort of trouble could she get into around here? Aren't all the eligible young men at war?"

"Azalea can always find a man when she wants to. You follow her."

It was easy to follow Azalea, for she had left a wide ribbon of broken, crushed grass along the water. Devon unsuccessfully fought feelings of anger and resentment. She was tired, and here she was plowing through a swamp. Her feet and skirt were wet, she was perspiring, and there was no sign of Azalea. What if she were simply out for a walk? What if she *was* breaking the monotony of her existence by meeting a neighboring farm boy? What was Devon supposed to do about it?

Then Devon heard a stealthy rustle in the grass. A snake? It would be the perfect end to a terrible afternoon if a snake were to bite me, she thought. She took a few more cautious steps, then froze as a groan broke the quiet. It reminded her of the sound Azalea often made in her sleep, but it couldn't be . . .

"Azalea?" Devon kept her voice low, just in case.

There was another, louder groan. Devon went toward the sound and discovered her friend lying in the tall, heavy grass.

"Oh, Devon," Azalea gasped, her face contorted with pain. "I must have stepped into a hole . . . Oh, my ankle!"

Devon dropped to her knees, lifted Azalea's head, and rested it on her lap. "What on earth were you doing?"

"You will have to go now. It's so important! Please . . . you must take the message in my place. Worry about me later. There will be hell to pay if someone is not there when he arrives—"

"Who? Where? What are you talking about?"

"Just a little way . . . where the water forks. He'll be there at sunset. Any minute! He will give you a message. If he doesn't trust you, tell him that you have come in my place to get the Blue Jay's message. Don't forget! Afterward, you have to come back this way, the way you came from the farm. You'll find a giant oak . . ." Azalea paused, wincing in pain, and licked her lips. "It has yellow leaves and a foot-tall A carved in the trunk. Wait there as long as you have to. A man wearing a cape and a black silk mask over his eyes will come in a boat from the James. Give him the message."

"The Blue Jay?" Devon inquired skeptically.

Azalea managed a weak smile. "Jay. He calls himself Jay. The redcoats call him Blue Jay because he appears and disappears the way the blue jay dives and then swoops back up to the trees to laugh."

"But what about you? How shall we get you home? I feel terrible leaving you here this way! It is cruel, Azalea! Besides, how important can this message be?"

"Very important," Azalea said urgently. "There isn't much time. All I can tell you is that the first man is from the American armies marching on Yorktown. The Blue Jay is from the French fleet anchored in Chesapeake Bay. This farm is where communications are exchanged between the army and the navy."

"This farm?" Devon repeated doubtfully.

"Both men have traveled with great speed to meet here tonight. They know I can be trusted." Azalea put her head back, and Devon could see how pale her usually blooming cheeks were.

"I suppose that Captain Raveneau vouched for your character. I'm not certain that he would do the same for me!" Her friend narrowed her eyes warningly. "All right, I'll go, but I hope this doesn't take long. I am so worried about you!"

"Devon, I'll be fine. But do hurry. If he has to wait, he may grow suspicious and leave."

Devon kissed Azalea's cheek and spread her shawl over the injured girl before starting off.

It took less than a half hour to reach the fork in the

creek, but by that time the twilight was deep and rosy. Devon waited, wondering and worrying. The entire situation was beyond belief. To think that two weeks ago she was safely living in New London.

A sharp, scolding bird cry pierced the quiet dusk and Devon looked around nervously. Should she say something? Was that some sort of question from the messenger? "I've come in Azalea's place," she offered quietly. "She's been hurt."

A man stepped out of the trees, only a few feet away. He was small, swarthy, and sharp-eyed. His uniform was a far cry from the neat garb of New London's militia—soiled buff breeches, a blue coat which looked much-mended, and a sword.

"Why have you come?" His eyes were like daggers.

"I have come to receive a message."

"For whom?"

They stared at each other suspiciously.

"How do I know that you are the right person?" Devon demanded.

"How do I know that *you* are?"

"Where are you bound? If you tell me that," she said, "I will tell you the name of the recipient of the message."

The swarthy little man considered this. He studied Devon's earnest, innocent face and decided to trust her. "My eventual destination is Yorktown."

She grinned. "Do you have a message for the Blue Jay?"

"Yes." His smile was almost imperceptible. Extracting an envelope from his inner pocket, the man held it out to Devon. "Do you know where to find Jay?"

"Yes. Azalea told me."

"Hurry, then. I will be here again in three days." With that, the man turned and disappeared into the trees. Devon found herself following, but when she reached the edge of the woods, he was nowhere to be seen.

It was dark by the time Devon reached Azalea

again. She paused there only long enough to be certain her friend was able to endure the wait; then, at Azalea's urging, she set off for the giant oak.

Luckily, the moon shone brightly and Devon had quite a clear view of the trees. She thought she saw the oak several times, but closer inspection failed to reveal the A she sought.

Finally, there it was. The tree was immense, and even in the moonlight Devon could see the yellow tint of the leaves and the large A carved into the trunk. Standing beside it, she wondered idly what the letter stood for. Had Isaac carved it for the A that began his sweetheart's name? Or was it Azalea's work? Could it stand for André—the pirate she had loved but couldn't keep?

Devon heard a soft splash and glanced toward the water, her heart beating with fearful excitement. She saw the boat a short distance downstream, then a man walking toward her in the darkness.

He was very tall, possibly as tall as Raveneau, Devon thought, with wide shoulders covered by a midnight-blue cape. He wore a tricorn hat tilted forward, a black silk mask over his eyes and nose, and knee boots. Doeskin gloves covered his hands, while a short, bristly beard concealed the lower half of his face.

"What are you doing here?" Blue Jay asked in a husky, French-accented voice.

"Azalea hurt her ankle. I discovered her, so she asked me to do her—errand."

"What is your name?" His eyes glittered as he loomed over her.

"Devon."

"You are very beautiful, Devon." One side of his mouth curved upward.

She blushed for the first time in a week. "Me?"

"Do you wish me to insist?"

"You must think I am a poor replacement for

Azalea." What am I saying? she thought. How can I flirt with this stranger out here alone in the dark?

"On the contrary. I find you refreshing and delightful. Azalea is an entirely different type."

"I think this is a ludicrous conversation. I don't even know you!"

"Do you wish to?" The other side of his mouth went up in a wicked smile.

"No, I mean— Oh! You are insolent, sir, and I must ask you to stop!"

"And if I do not?" He stepped nearer. He smelled of tobacco and brandy . . . and man.

"Please—"

"I could never hurt you intentionally, my lady," he whispered. "I shall do as you ask. The message?"

Devon colored again as she realized she had put it into her bodice for safekeeping. Jay grinned when she produced it.

"I shall treasure this," he murmured. One gloved hand reached out to clasp her own lightly. His eyes were on her face as he lifted her fingers to his mouth. A tingling warmth coursed up Devon's arm when he kissed her palm, his beard tickling her soft skin.

"*Adieu,* Devon," he said huskily. "Until—"

"Three nights from now," she replied, somewhat stunned by her response to so simple a gesture.

He began to turn away, then said, "I am ashamed of myself. Your lovely presence has caused me to forget poor Azalea. Has she found a way to return home?"

"No! Could you help her? She has been lying in the grass for more than an hour and I have truly wondered how I would be able to get her back in the dark."

Without another word, Jay gestured for Devon to lead the way. He took her arm in a hard grasp as they walked, keeping her from stumbling when her skirts became tangled.

Before long they reached Azalea's side. She had fallen asleep, so the spy lifted her into his arms as though she were a child. "Come on," he said over one shoulder, "let us get her home."

Devon felt uneasily envious of Azalea. She wondered how it would feel to be held in that man's arms. As she was thinking this, Azalea awoke, purring adorably. She registered no surprise at finding herself in Jay's arms, but nestled against him and cooed, "Well, I am glad I got to see you after all!" She put a creamy hand up to his beard and tugged. "I like this. *Very* mysterious!"

"For a young lady who has hurt her ankle, you seem remarkably cheerful," he remarked sardonically.

Devon, tripping along behind them, was beset by an unaccountable urge to break Azalea's other ankle.

Jay left Azalea and Devon outside the front door, and with a wave of his gloved hand, disappeared into the trees. That left Mrs. Minter to contend with. It was bad enough that they had missed the supper she had labored over for hours, but her suspicions about Azalea's activities and her alarm over her daughter's ankle caused a deluge of questions, nagging, and scolding. Devon got her share as well, for she declined to confide in the old woman, supporting Azalea's tale of a simple walk and stepping into a simple hole. Eventually, the girls were grudgingly served portions of reheated stew and cold corn bread, which they dutifully praised.

At last Devon assisted a pale Azalea up the narrow stairway. Alone in their bedroom, they undressed and Devon helped the other girl get into a bedgown. Both were silent, mulling over their separate thoughts, but once in bed with the candle out, Azalea asked conversationally, "How do you like being a spy?"

"I hate to admit it, but I found it rather fun!"

"Oh, really? And Jay—how did you find him?"

Devon froze. "I liked him."

"He reminds *me* of André."

"I suppose," Devon mused. "But Jay is much less sarcastic and more charming."

Azalea peered through the darkness. "Are you looking forward to your next meeting?"

"Azalea! You ought to know better than to ask me questions like that!"

"You can't blame a girl for trying! You sound angry—that must be a sign of something." She yawned extravagantly. "You know, I'm fearfully tired . . . think I'll just close my eyes . . ."

She fell asleep almost immediately, leaving Devon to stare up at the shadow patterns on the slanted ceiling. There was no doubt about it . . . she certainly had felt something for the mysterious Jay! Part of her was elated and relieved to know that André Raveneau was not the only man who could send hot and cold chills down her spine. Yet another part of her wondered if she found Jay so attractive only because he reminded her so poignantly of Raveneau.

When the girls awoke the next morning, they found that Azalea's ankle was still swollen. When she moved it experimentally, she let out a squeal of pain.

Her infirmity left Devon free to run over the farm as she pleased. She divided her time between helping Mrs. Minter, conversing with a bored and restless Azalea, and slipping outdoors for an hour or two of solitude. Devon thought about Raveneau and Morgan and the spy, Jay, a great deal. She wondered what her future would hold, and whether she could ever regain the old relationship with Morgan if she found him.

On the third day after Azalea's injury, Devon felt nervous from the moment she awoke. She found herself constantly picturing the events of the evening to come, making up dialogue for herself and Jay and visualizing him in her mind. When four o'clock arrived, she put on her breeches and set off to meet him, having memorized at least a dozen witty rejoinders.

Devon's heart raced with excitement all the way to the fork in the inlet. She couldn't remember the last time she had felt such delicious anticipation. The same small, swarthy man came out of the trees to meet her, smiling.

"I am glad to see you here—"

"Devon," she supplied, returning his smile. "Will you tell me your name?"

"I cannot. I am sorry. How is Miss Minter?"

"Except for her ankle, she is fine. She's had to stay inside, and that makes her cross."

"I can imagine. You may tell her that I have news of her fiancé and he is well."

"She will be cheered to hear that." Devon paused. "It is probably silly for me to ask, but have you heard of a young man named Morgan Gadwin? He is part of a Connecticut regiment—"

"No, I am sorry. Your brother?"

"Actually, he is *my* fiancé." It didn't sound true even to her own ears.

"You have come to Virginia to look for him?"

"Yes."

"Then I wish you good fortune, Devon." He fished inside his coat for the envelope and handed it to her. "By the way, you look very well in breeches." He flashed a startling, impish smile. "I hope to see either you or Miss Minter one week from tonight," he said, and turned to leave.

Devon tucked the envelope into a pocket and started back toward the yellow-leaved oak. Darkness was gathering quickly now. Crickets chirped, owls hooted, and from time to time Devon heard a strange animal noise.

The moon was hidden behind a blanket of clouds, but Devon found her way to the giant oak as if by instinct. It was chilly; a breeze off the water ruffled her red-gold curls and she crossed her arms to ward off the cold. She was lost in thought by the time Jay arrived. This time Devon saw no boat. He came from behind, soundlessly, and put his hands on her shoulders, causing her to jump with fright.

"My God!" she gasped, her blue eyes sparkling. "You scared me half to death!"

"May I feel your heartbeat?" Jay inquired, trying to repress a smile.

Devon almost agreed until she realized that her heart lay behind her breasts. "Men! You think only of one thing."

"I think that you enjoy my interest," he murmured huskily. "And if all men think alike around you, you have only yourself to blame for being so tempting and lovely."

"You say these things to amuse yourself," she accused. "You flirt with every female you meet. I saw the way you looked at Azalea and I heard you cooing at her."

Jay's mouth was bent in a half-smile. "You may believe whatever you need to in order to be content."

"Fine." Devon glared at him, wishing she had the courage to pull off his mask. "I am curious . . . why do you affect this disguise?"

"Affect?" Jay repeated, obviously amused. "Devon, your choice of words hurts me deeply. Are you not impressed by the fact that I am important enough to keep my identity a secret?"

"No!" she lied.

"That is a pity. But it will not persuade me to unmask."

"Do you want this message, or have you come only to tease me?"

"Of course I want the message . . . but I would like you as well."

"I am not available at this time, *sir*. Here is your letter. I must say, I cannot understand why you two men don't just meet together and avoid all this confusion. You certainly take yourselves seriously!"

"That's true; we do. And so would the British if they caught us together." Jay read the letter quickly, then tucked it beneath his cape, a smile flickering at the corners of his mouth. "You look charming in those breeches, Devon. Where did you get them?"

"I—oh, never mind! It's none of your affair."

"You are very rude, do you know that?"

"Your insolence invites rudeness!"

"That is not what I meant to invite." His smile flashed in the darkness and Devon went weak. "Now, I am giving you this letter to keep until the next time you meet my comrade. When will that be?"

"Not for a week."

"So be it. Protect this well. I am counting on you to see that it reaches his hands."

"Do you trust me so much?"

"Should I not?" Jay smiled. "Devon, dear, you are the picture of integrity."

She eyed him warily while putting his letter in her pocket.

"I must go now," he whispered. "I know that you would not accept this for yourself, so let us call it a get-well message for Azalea."

To Devon's total astonishment, his gloved hands reached out and pulled her against the length of his body. Warm, determined lips came down over her own, forcing a response that she could not conceal. Her hands fluttered, then caressed the hard strength of his arms until he shifted to hold her nearer. She spun in a dizzying whirlpool, her body hot and tingling against his. She wished his kiss would never end, but of course it did. She stared at him as though mesmerized, one hand reaching up to touch his close-cropped beard.

"I can see you are a true friend to Azalea," Jay murmured ironically. "You knew exactly what she would need to aid in her recovery."

Azalea breathed softly in the darkness, while Devon rolled from side to side, trying to find a comfortable position. It must be the middle of the night, she thought despairingly. This is awful, terrible. I must get to sleep!

Endlessly, her mind replayed the few moments when Jay had kissed her and she had been trapped in a web of magic not unlike Raveneau's own. Part of her was shocked that she should be so undone by physical desire, particularly for a man whom she barely knew.

Yet Devon found herself mulling over the inescapable conclusion that she could respond to a man other than André. She had believed that he alone had the power to make her hungry for a man's touch, kiss, and even that total union. Knowing that a future with him was impossible, Devon had feared that she would go through life deprived, remembering the fire he had lit in her body. But now, after Jay, she hoped that she might find that magic a third time. Morgan might hold the key to her future after all.

"I think that I will be able to go tomorrow night," Azalea decided.

Startled, Devon looked up from her sewing. The two girls had been sitting quietly all morning on the sofa. Azalea was reading a romantic novel, while Devon worked on one of the two dresses for which her friend had given her material.

"Well, Devon, you needn't look so shocked! My ankle is fine. I scarcely limp at all. Besides, why should you have all the fun? This will probably be the last message. The battle is bound to begin soon, and when it's over, winter will have set in and I'll be bored, bored, bored. You'll have gone off with that fiancé of yours, and I'll be left with Mama and Pa. I just can't miss tomorrow night!"

Devon's heart dropped. If Azalea went, she would probably never see Jay again. She would have nothing to look forward to, nothing to dream about.

But what of Azalea? Didn't she deserve a taste of adventure as well? Devon had discovered so many hints of her own selfishness lately that she was beginning to feel like a stranger to herself. Maybe the time had come to make a decision, rather than allowing life to just sweep her helplessly along.

"If you are certain that your ankle is strong enough, then I agree that you should go. You and this Jay seem to be such *close* friends after all."

Azalea's eyes were twinkling with mischievous curiosity. "Why, Devon, are you jealous? For all your declarations of faithful love for your Morgan, I'll wager you're not immune to a man like Jay." She leaned closer, whispering suggestively, "Tell the truth. Don't you think he's delicious?"

Devon found herself blushing. Hastily she threw up a barrier of outrage. "You are truly terrible! I think it's a mistake for you to marry at all, Azalea. What will happen when you have to live every day with one man? Does Isaac know how fickle you are?"

Azalea laughed, running a creamy hand through her gleaming curls. "Isaac is a quieter sort. I suppose we complement each other. He'd never admit it, but the wild streak in me excites him. Besides, I have to think of the years ahead. I want children and I love this land and the challenge of rebuilding the farm. There won't be many men like Jay roaming about . . . he'll be gone forever once the war's over. And André, too." She sighed, her doe eyes wistful. "Besides, Isaac worships me, and I need that from a man if it's going to last. Men like Jay and André could never give me that. They live only for the moment, then it's on to the next breathless female. Why should they marry? They've got the whole world at their feet."

Devon pricked herself with the needle. She watched a crimson drop of blood form at the tip of her finger and nodded. "You're right . . . of course." Her blue eyes lifted to meet Azalea's brown gaze. "I'm glad I didn't get involved. I couldn't take it all in the same spirit you do. It would be hard to go to Morgan after a man like Jay, or Raveneau . . . I'm afraid I'd never stop comparing."

Azalea shrugged. "I don't have that problem. I hoard my memories. They'll keep me warm when I'm old like Mama."

Nights on the farm were friendly and peaceful. The darkness draped the house like a velvet cover and night birds called from the woods.

Devon lay alone in the attic bed, dreaming of old age with Morgan. He was pale and thin and feeble, with tears in his eyes. In her dream he sat alone in the drug shop, too frail to clear away the dust and cobwebs that filled the room and discouraged customers. Devon saw herself, solitary and shriveled, in a room upstairs, identical to the living quarters above the Linen and Pewter Shop. Portraits of cold-looking children and grandchildren lined the walls; she was sitting by the window, watching the people pass below.

Devon awoke repeatedly, but the loathsome dream returned whenever she dozed off again. It filled her with sickening dread. Finally she got out of bed and crossed the floor to look outside, hoping to see Azalea. Part of her was worried; the same evening errand had brought *her* back to the house at least an hour earlier. Could Azalea have hurt herself again?

Devon's instincts suggested that the delay was not due to any accident. The odds were that Azalea was out there hoarding memories with the Blue Jay . . .

A scolding cry pierced the night and Devon straightened her back, alert. It couldn't be! she told herself in an effort to still her racing pulse. She tried to remember if she had ever heard a blue jay call at night. Perhaps it was some other bird. Then she spotted Azalea creeping out of the trees, clad in her brother's breeches. She hadn't wanted to wear them, but Devon, worried about her ankle, had insisted.

There was a trellis that reached to their bedroom window. Devon watched anxiously as her friend climbed up, then crawled over to Devon's outstretched arms.

"Are you all right? Where have you been? I've been worried sick!"

Azalea's face was radiant. "That was wonderful. I'd forgotten what such excitement is like!"

"I'm so glad it was worthwhile for you!" Devon heard the brittle tone of her voice and flushed when Azalea stared at her in surprise. "It's fortunate that you didn't reinjure your ankle. I certainly wouldn't have wanted to nurse you back to health a second time!"

"Then we are both happy," Azalea remarked coolly. "If you are done being mean-spirited, I think you should get out of that bedgown and into some clothes. Jay brought me back to the farm to be sure I didn't fall again. He wants to see you."

"He does? Me?" A wave of elation washed over Devon, sweeping away all the lonely, bad feelings. "I wonder what he wants."

Jay stood in shadow, surrounded by hickory trees. As Devon approached, she could see that his disguise was intact, from tricorn hat and mask to his gloved hands and midnight-blue cape. Only the gleam of white teeth betrayed his mood.

"I am glad you could make it," he murmured in the husky voice she had tried to re-create in her daydreams. "I like the gown. I wish I could have helped you down from the roof."

"You are a wicked person." Devon smiled. She wanted to laugh out loud, to dance and clap her hands.

"That doesn't seem to bother you."

"I can see why you are so pleased with yourself, with both Azalea and me sneaking off into the woods to see you."

"Well, Azalea was serving her country." His grin was irreverent.

"And what am I doing?"

"Saying goodbye." One gloved hand caught hers, and Devon swayed as his fingers tightened. "I wanted to express my gratitude. You took risks for an important cause."

Devon flushed guiltily, knowing that she had only craved adventure. "Well . . ."

"Is there anything I can do for you? I won't be back again, but I will be going to Yorktown. Can I carry a message for *you* this time?"

Devon thought of André Raveneau, and hated herself for it. It was Morgan she was supposed to want! In the inky darkness she tried to read Jay's shadowed eyes. What was he thinking? "No," she said. "When the battle is over, I shall have to carry my own messages. But if you should happen to meet . . ."

"Yes?" His voice chilled.

"Never mind."

Slowly he drew her closer, looking down at her delicate, expressive face. His other hand reached out to smooth her shining curls. "You are an enchanting girl, Devon." Gently, he lifted her off the ground, kissing her mouth, tasting its hesitant, quavering response. Her arms went around his neck and she could feel the heavy wool of his cape through her thin bodice. It seemed that her heart would shatter, so frenzied was its pounding. Jay's steely arms held her prisoner, and she trembled with a thousand conflicting emotions, both physical and mental.

"I want you," he whispered, his breath harsh against her ear. "Can you give yourself to me? Or . . . is your heart with another man?"

His words broke the spell. Like a specter, Raveneau's chiseled, sardonic face filled her vision, and it seemed that his arms held her, rather than Jay's. It would be wrong, she thought. I cannot complicate things any further. I am betrothed to a boy and haunted by a man who has left my life forever. If I'd face up to it, I would admit that Jay is only a substitute for Raveneau.

Tears sparkled in her sapphire eyes. "I sometimes feel that I don't know myself any more," she whispered apologetically.

Jay inclined his dark head, waiting.

"I won't be able to face myself in the morning if I go with you. Please . . . I'm sorry, but you're right. My heart is with someone else."

"That is all I wanted to know." Jay's voice was strangely bitter. He released her and stepped back. "Good fortune to you, Devon. I hope your young man appreciates you." His gloved hand lifted hers and firm lips burned her soft palm. *"Adieu, chérie."*

Devon stood frozen amidst the hickory trees, watching as the Blue Jay's dark, broad-shouldered figure melted into the night. I'll never see him again, she thought, and felt tears sting her eyelids. Is it possible that he could have cared for me a little, or was that some act he has performed for dozens of girls before me? And why would he refer to my young man?

She mulled that over on her way back to the farmhouse, and even awoke Azalea to discuss the matter with her. The older girl scanned her face sleepily for a long, tense moment. "You've read too many novels, Devon," she said at last, her voice jaunty. "There's a simple explanation. I told Jay about Morgan, but I suppose he figured you were worth a try, anyway."

"Oh. I see."

"Jay never could resist a challenge." Azalea rolled over and pulled up the covers again.

"You make it sound as though you have known him so long! Do you know who Jay really is?"

"Perhaps," Azalea teased. "But I'd never tell you even if I did know. Let me go back to sleep. You just put him out of your mind, Devon. The Blue Jay is gone, and I don't think he will *ever* be back."

Chapter Twelve

◆

Mid-October, 1781

A fortnight passed with agonizing slowness. Azalea and Devon found themselves starting at every noise, wondering how events were progressing at Yorktown. The town was only fifteen miles across the peninsula, and sometimes the two of them lay awake at night and made detailed plans to travel there on horseback, just to find out for themselves what was happening. They both knew this was an idle dream—neither wished to *die* for adventure's sake. There was no sign of either the first messenger or the Blue Jay. Devon hadn't expected a reappearance, but continued to hope for one during the long, tedious October days.

One morning in mid-October, Devon rose early and crept out for a solitary ride. After saddling the aging mare, she set off across the farm. It was cold and clear; the trees created bouquets of rust and gold, and the sight of them made Devon homesick for the brilliant autumns of Connecticut. The wind put roses in her cheeks and tangles in her curls, and she began to feel briefly like her old self again: free, impetuous, and confident.

As she approached the uncleared oak and chestnut trees on the farm's border, Devon made ready to turn the mare back. Suddenly she spied another horse emerging from the woods, the rider half slumped on its back. Devon called out and urged the mare forward. As they drew near, the man raised his head and she saw that it was Halsey Minter. "Minter! What has happened to you?"

He was pale and haggard, his lips dry and cracked. "I was . . . wounded." He gestured weakly to the bandages under his coat. "I'll be fine—but the captain thought it best for me to come home."

"You look terrible. Come on, let's get you into bed." Devon desperately wanted to ask about Raveneau, but she swallowed her questions and led Halsey's horse back to the house.

The rest of the Minters were awake and eating breakfast, but even Jud interrupted his meal at the sight of Halsey, leaning against Devon in the doorway. The old man was on his feet before his wife could move. He almost carried Halsey upstairs to the large four-poster, where he quickly removed his boots and coat. When the boy was lying back against the pillow, Mrs. Minter undid his bandaged shoulder to inspect the wound.

"Nothing serious," Halsey protested. "It only needs to heal."

"Hmm. I'll admit it's been well cared for. 'Tis clean."

"Captain Raveneau did it. When our ship's surgeon saw the wound, he said he couldn't have done neater work himself."

"A wonder of a man!" declared Jud, and his wife nodded agreement.

" 'Tis not the first time he has come to our aid," she said.

Devon asked, "Where were you wounded—at Yorktown?"

"Yes. Damn, I'm thirsty."

His mother frowned at the vulgarity but brought him water, and after a few greedy swallows, Halsey continued. "The captain decided that we could do more fighting on land, since the sea battle was over. He left a skeleton crew on the *Black Eagle* to maintain the blockade, but the rest of us sailed for Yorktown in that same cutter you and I used, Devon."

"André, what about André?" Devon asked breathlessly.

But Halsey's eyes were drooping and Mrs. Minter shook her head, saying there was plenty of time to hear the rest of the story. He slept instantly.

Azalea and Devon, consumed by curiosity, spent the day pacing the floor, waiting for him to awaken. The aroma of glazed ham and corn bread filled the air by the time Halsey's brown eyes fluttered open. The girls rushed to his side.

"Mama's fixing your favorite supper," Azalea told him. "We've all helped. There's even apple pie."

Halsey smiled. Devon watched him, full of real affection for this boy who had befriended her when she had felt so alone.

"It's so good to be home," he murmured. "Devon, how have you been getting along? Has it been a tedious month?"

"No, of course not. Everyone has been wonderful to me, and there's been a bit of excitement as well."

"Oh?"

"The Blue Jay has kept us busy," Azalea explained, raising first one eyebrow and then the other.

"You don't say!" Halsey exclaimed. "Was Devon involved, then?"

"I fell the first night out—stepped in a rut and twisted my ankle. Devon found me and carried on in my place."

"Well! How did you like playing spy, Devon?"

She had watched the brother-sister exchange with interest. There was something odd about the tone of their voices. "I rather enjoyed it. It was diverting," she replied carefully.

"And Jay?"

159

"So you know him, too?"

"By reputation," Halsey said hastily. "How did you find him?"

"Diverting," Devon repeated, striving to keep her voice disinterested. A traitorous blush crept up her cheeks, prompting her to turn away and mumble something about helping Mrs. Minter with supper.

Halsey alternated between eating and sleeping through the evening, while revealing, piece by piece, the story of Yorktown. It seemed that the siege was progressing well; there was no doubt of the outcome. The first shots had been fired on October ninth. The Americans and the French had bombarded the British works around Yorktown, working their way closer day by day, trench by trench. The night of October tenth, French gunners had sent red-hot balls into the harbor, firing the British ships, and during the next day nearly four thousand shots had fallen on the town and harbor.

The next two days had been spent storming two large British redoubts near Yorktown. Halsey fought with Alexander Hamilton and his detachment of four hundred Americans. Raveneau fought with the French, he said. He told Devon and his family how General Washington had delivered a simple speech of encouragement before the battle.

"It was dusk when we all gathered to hear him speak. I don't mind saying that I was frightened, particularly when they began passing out axes and bayonets. I thought that I'd grown used to fighting after so many sea battles, but this was different. The waiting was horrible. I looked around me while General Washington was urging us to be brave and wondered how many of those faces would be gone the next sunset.

"Nine of us died," he continued, "and I was one of the two dozen or so wounded. Those redcoats made it easy on us. They acted brave for only a moment or two, to save face, then ran like rabbits or gave themselves up. The entire conflict lasted a bare quarter-hour, and the French were nearly as quick with their mission."

Devon wanted to ask again about Raveneau, but Mrs. Minter, presenting Halsey with a piece of warm pie, saved her from that.

"And André? You say he fought with the French?"

"Yes." Halsey paused to savor his first bite of pie. "This is better than I remember, Mama. Let's see . . . Oh, yes, Captain Raveneau. Well, as I said earlier, he took care of my little bayonet wound. You all should know better than to ask after him. That man has more lives than a cat and more luck than any human. The longer I know him, the more tempted I am to believe that legend about him being the devil's son—"

"Halsey!" Mrs. Minter gasped. "That is a terrible thing to say, even if you meant it in jest!"

Raveneau's steward grinned, his mouth full of pie, and his mother was hard put to retain her scowl.

As Halsey told his tale in the farmhouse on the peninsula's south side just before midnight, Cornwallis attempted to escape across the York River. The first division ferried safely across, but no sooner had the second wave of troops set out in the boats than a severe storm swept over them.

"It was an act of God," beamed Washington several hours later. The storm had scattered the British boats and foiled any plans of escape. A joyful messenger had brought the general the news: Cornwallis himself was still trapped in Yorktown.

Unable to sleep, the principal officers gathered at Washington's headquarters to share a cask of wine and discuss this newest development. Washington himself sat at the small desk, his tired face softened by the golden light of two candles burning on either side of him. The field tent was even more crowded than usual, with Rochambeau, Lafayette, and Lincoln occupying the chairs, and other officers, including Captain André

Raveneau, seated on the ground wherever they could find room. The front of the spacious, square tent was open, letting in the cold, misty night breeze and allowing the weary soldiers a view of the luminous moon.

Raveneau sipped his wine and listened to Washington and Rochambeau outline the plans for the next flurry of fighting; a series of blows designed to bring Cornwallis to his knees once and for all. Soon he found his mind wandering. How strange and unlikely this autumn had become, he thought. He was not used to fighting with an organized army, and while he believed in the American cause and was glad to help in any way he could, he yearned to stand on the quarter-deck of the *Black Eagle,* breathing salt air and sailing into the expansive Atlantic. He was a man of the sea and had chosen the sea for his home because it offered the ultimate freedom. Aboard his ship, he was the master of all he could see and never had to bend to another man's rules.

Devon.

As the chorus of voices rose around him, Raveneau tasted her name in his mind and on his tongue. He thought of her often since he had sent her away. It was a sweet, addictive habit, and one he longed to break.

Devon sat beside the four-poster bed, reading aloud from *Poor Richard's Almanac* and being rewarded by an occasional chuckle from Halsey Minter. The selection of books at the farmhouse was limited; there were none of the latest novels that Devon longed to sample, nor even a volume of Voltaire or Shakespeare to improve her mind. *Poor Richard* was the best of the lot.

"I do not intend to offend your reading, Devon." Halsey yawned. "But I do feel in need of a nap."

"I must confess I understand," she laughed. "And I did promise to start your mother's stew!" Mr. and

Mrs. Minter and Azalea were paying a visit to a newly widowed cousin of Jud's.

"Will they be back in time for supper, then?"

"They expect to be home by sunset," Devon replied, closing the book and standing up. "That leaves at least two hours. Perhaps if I hurry with the stew, I might be able to take a nap myself." The silence from the bed made her look around. Minter was sound asleep, his mouth open.

Smiling to herself, Devon went down to the kitchen. The vegetables were laid out neatly in a row on the worktable, while a tough piece of beef bubbled in a pot over the fire. She tied a voluminous apron over her dress. The gown was newly made from fabric donated by Azalea, and Devon knew the reason for her friend's generosity. The heavy wool made her skin itch, and the color, a dark taupe, was singularly unattractive. Sitting down to work, Devon looked at her hands against the drab sleeves and thought that her peach-toned skin seemed a trifle yellow in contrast.

No sooner had she begun to slice the carrots than the front door opened, letting in a flurry of autumn leaves and sunshine. "So you're back early," Devon said. When there was no response from the Minters, she lifted her head.

Her heart lurched. There, leaning indolently against the doorframe, was André Raveneau. Clad in an elegant white uniform with red facings, he looked indecently handsome and his gray eyes sparkled wickedly. Devon's bones seemed to melt.

"*Bonjour, petite chatte.* I am glad to be early if that means we shall be alone together."

"Oh, I didn't mean— That is, I thought you were the Minters. They are in Williamsburg today."

"Really?" White teeth gleamed against his tanned face.

Devon blushed maddeningly. "Stop this, now," she

declared, striving to sound firm and controlled. "Please sit down and tell me why you are here."

Raveneau arched an amused eyebrow but did as she asked, taking the chair beside her own. Why is he here? she wondered frantically, trying to contain the wild excitement that coursed through her body. She could see the fine lines in his face and each shining black hair on his head. Dropping her eyes, she stared at his familiar hands with their long, deft fingers and square-cut nails.

"Can I get you some refreshment?" she asked abruptly, jumping to her feet with such haste that Raveneau had to catch her chair to save it from toppling over.

"If you insist." He laughed softly. "I must say, your attire is very becoming. I have always admired that . . . color."

"It is bad of you to tease me. I made this dress myself. It is better than wearing breeches!"

"I might take issue with that. I rather like you in breeches." He watched as she shakily poured wine into a glass, and held up his hand. "That will be fine. Perhaps you should have a glass, too? You appear to be rather overwrought."

"I am not!" she cried.

"Whatever you say, Devon. Why don't you bring me a knife and I'll help with these vegetables. In your state, you might take off a finger or two."

By now she was thoroughly unstrung. She put the wine and a knife beside him, then seated herself and silently attacked the vegetables.

"Aren't you going to ask me how the battle went?" Raveneau inquired casually.

"Why, yes. Obviously, I want to know."

"Obviously." His mouth bent in a rakish smile. "We have won. Cornwallis surrendered this morning and only the discussion of terms remains."

"Oh, André, that is splendid news!" Elated, Devon

automatically moved to embrace him but froze, one hand holding her knife, the other a potato.

Raveneau pretended not to notice. "Yes, it is splendid. The war isn't over by any means, but I would say the enemy has sustained a mortal wound. Cornwallis's army made up a quarter of the British forces in America, so it seems unlikely that the fighting will go on much longer."

"Oh, *heaven*," Devon said happily.

Raveneau gazed at her, thinking that she had never looked more radiant and bewitching. Her apricot-gold hair was illuminated by the dusky light, baby-soft tendrils framing her face from brow to chin. Was she thinking of Morgan? he wondered. It seemed likely, but why was she so tongue-tied around him? Perhaps she was plagued by embarrassing memories of the night they had spent together on the *Black Eagle*.

Another in a long line of guilt pangs visited itself on Raveneau. Guilt! he thought despairingly. At my age!

Deliberately, he cut himself with the knife—nothing too deep, just enough to draw a sufficient amount of blood. He cursed.

"Oh, dear! What happened?" Devon rushed to wash and bandage the injured finger, her sapphire eyes full of concern until she looked up to find Raveneau watching her, his expression both tender and amused.

"Are you angry with me?" he asked.

"Why would I be angry?"

"Because I made love to you."

"Why . . . I . . ." Flushing, Devon looked away, but Raveneau caught her chin and turned it back.

"I shall be very uncomfortable if you continue to blush and stammer and fall over chairs while I am here. The Minters will think it very strange! Can you not forgive me? I should like to resume our friendship."

Breathing unevenly, Devon stared at his lean, tanned face, wanting to say that she was to blame for that entire episode. But of course he knew that. He had told her so that night.

"Well, I suppose if Azalea can be so casual about *her* past with you, I should be able to follow her example."

Raveneau, lips twitching, was not about to mention the fact that Devon and Azalea were total emotional opposites. "I think that is a very healthy attitude, *petite chatte*. After all, these things do happen, and considering my legendary good looks, your weakness is understandable."

On cue, Devon tensed angrily. "What? I cannot believe my ears! Legendary *conceit* would be a more accurate description!" She assaulted a huge onion with vigor.

"Careful, careful," Raveneau admonished. Smothering laughter and a fierce desire to take her in his arms and kiss her until she fainted, he finished slicing up the vegetables at a leisurely pace.

When Azalea opened the door, the scene that met her eyes was one of cozy domestic bliss. A pot of stew bubbled fragrantly over a perfect fire. Halsey lay on the sofa, where he had insisted on moving, looking happy and warm under a pile of blankets. A dreamy-eyed Devon occupied one wing chair, while André reclined in the other, more tanned and magnificent than ever.

"Azalea!" her brother exclaimed. "Look who is here!"

"I see," she murmured.

Raveneau got up, smiling, and came forward to embrace her affectionately. "It's good to see you. I trust you are well?"

"Y—yes!" She felt the shock wearing off and took advantage of the opportunity to throw her arms about his neck. Nothing had ever made her feel so good as the sensation of André's hard body against her own. "This is a wonderful surprise! Just what we needed. Isn't that so, Devon?"

"Well . . . " Devon allowed carefully.

Jud and Constance Minter came in then and lit up at the sight of Raveneau. Obviously he was a hero in this house, but Devon couldn't help rebelling against the prevailing mood of adoration. All the Minters hung on the Frenchman's every word and smile, so Devon took it upon herself to keep him humble.

Still, there was an odd ache in her breast whenever he paid attention to Azalea. Her friend had no qualms about following him around, sitting beside him, and touching him whenever she could. Raveneau seemed to enjoy this, which rankled Devon. Further, she believed that he was actually amused by her irritation.

The next morning Devon couldn't decide what was more important—looking her best or getting downstairs as quickly as possible. Azalea and Mrs. Minter had risen at dawn, anxious to prepare a sumptuous breakfast for their honored guest.

What could she wear? Devon worried. The sea-green gown that Minter had given her was the most attractive, but it had once belonged to Azalea. The taupe dress was out of the question. That left the one other gown that she had made. The fabric Azalea had donated was white muslin, which was more suited to midsummer. Devon had made a simple gown, embellishing it with eyelet lace salvaged from the ripped yellow dress. She donned it now and surveyed her reflection in the small mirror, moving up, down, and sideways in an effort to see the full effect.

I look like a child, she thought in exasperation. Even though the bodice was cut low enough to display her breasts, they could not compete with Azalea's lush curves. With a sigh, she brushed her hair until the fiery highlights gleamed in the sun. It was the best she could do.

So absorbed had Devon been in her appearance, she had failed to notice the splashing noises coming from downstairs. She paused on the top step and listened curiously. Hurrying below, she discovered a giggling Azalea in the kitchen.

"Look! Here's André in the bath!"

"What?" Devon wondered incredulously. A few more steps and she saw a bathtub set up before the huge fireplace. Raveneau reclined against the curved back, leisurely smoking a thin cigar. At the sight of Devon's startled face, he smiled with wry amusement.

"Good morning! Why so shocked, mademoiselle? This is not the first time you have seen me in my bath."

"What does that mean?" Azalea demanded.

"Never you mind," said Halsey from the sofa. "It's none of your affair."

Devon felt herself turning pink all the way down to her breasts. "I for one would like to know what is going on. Azalea, where are your parents?"

"Milking the cow. They believe that André won't seduce me." She smiled coyly, then shrugged. "Unfortunately, they are right."

"I fear Devon has a point," Raveneau remarked, reaching for his sponge. "You two had better find me some towels before they walk in and see you ogling me."

His gray eyes danced as they looked up at Devon. Almost against her will, she had been staring at him, mesmerized. The bronzed skin, the width of his shoulders over well-muscled arms, and a chest covered with just the right amount of soft black hair. She bit her lip. The mere sight of him heated her blood.

That afternoon the quartet assembled around the bed. Azalea sat beside Halsey's legs, Raveneau and Devon took chairs, and a lively round of card games began.

Devon's spirits began to plummet, however, when she realized that Azalea and Raveneau had passed the time together this way on many other occasions.

In the middle of a game of whist, while waiting for her turn, Devon imagined them in the cabin on board the *Black Eagle,* sitting on the bed where *she* had slept. In her fantasy, he reached for Azalea, laughing.

"Devon? Devon! It's your turn!" Azalea cried irritably.

Flustered, she glanced over to find Raveneau watching her, his eyes gleaming in a way that made her angry. She picked a card at random and tossed it on the bed. Everyone stared in surprise.

"Well, I am already losing, so what does it matter?" she said.

Raveneau's face was inscrutable as he sat forward in the chair and gathered the cards already played into a neat pile. "I think that is enough," he said evenly, then slanted a smile at Azalea. "I'm going for a walk. Would you care to join me?"

Eyes alight, she was on her feet. "That's the best invitation I've had in ages!"

Devon felt ill.

Raveneau and Azalea wandered through the fields, pausing in the tobacco barn to inspect the crop of curing leaves. Afterward, they headed toward the water and sat under a dogwood tree that would be pink the next May.

"I wanted to talk to you," Raveneau said.

"Oh?" Azalea's heart leaped, but she could sense that his mind was not on her. For all her giddy pleasure in his company, he continued to treat her like an irrepressible sister. It was as if they had never been lovers at all.

He caught her hand and held it absently. "How would you like to go to Yorktown with me? The ceremony of surrender will likely be tomorrow, and I thought we might be able to locate your fiancé."

"Oh, André! I would adore it!" Suddenly her thoughts were full of Isaac.

"Good. I was planning to take Devon along as well. Do you think she would agree?"

Azalea peered at Raveneau's chiseled face, searching for a clue to his feelings. "Well, certainly she would agree. I don't know why not. What did you have in mind for *her* in Yorktown?"

Raveneau glanced at her sharply. "I have not forgotten that she has a fiancé in Virginia. Has *she?*"

"Forgotten? Her darling Morgan? Heavens, no."

"Good. I would not want to have brought her all this way for nothing."

"I may be mad, but I have this suspicion that you may care for her yourself."

"You're right. You are mad." His eyes were stormy. "I feel a certain responsibility, that's all. I promised to bring her to Virginia and help her find this paragon of manhood."

"You're jealous! Listen to you!" Azalea stared for a moment in shock, then began to laugh.

"Jealous? Why in God's name should I be? It's not as if I couldn't have her if I wanted her. Devon's not like you, though. She takes everything too seriously."

Azalea heard the anger in his voice, but went on, anyway. "I think you are upset because she doesn't care for you. You cannot conceive of any girl not falling all over you the way I do."

"That is not so! You're beginning to irritate me, Azalea! Besides, what makes you so certain she *doesn't* care for me?"

She smiled slyly. "Oh, André, you can't fool me!"

"Just answer the question, wench!"

"Well, I only know what she says to me, and we are very close. She almost never mentions your name. As far as I can tell, she isn't interested in the least. Perhaps you're not her type."

Raveneau narrowed his flinty eyes at her. "I ought to strangle you. You are doing this purposely."

Azalea giggled. "Let's go home and tell Devon the

news. The sooner she and I reach Yorktown, the sooner we will be reunited with our true loves. And *you*, sir, will be able to return to your single great passion—that privateer!"

Chapter Thirteen

———————◆———————

October 19, 1781

SHORTLY after dawn, Devon said her goodbyes to the Minters. Halsey would be remaining behind, though he hoped to join the *Black Eagle* before its departure. Devon wept as she kissed his cheek in parting, thinking that they would never meet again. It was just as unlikely that she would ever see Mr. and Mrs. Minter after today, and in their final moments together she realized how fond she had become of them, despite their failings.

"My parents are both gone," she whispered to Mrs. Minter, "and I couldn't have come to your home at a better time. I needed you. I haven't felt alone . . ."

Constance Minter blinked back tears of her own and told Devon that she hoped she would find happiness with her fiancé. Jud got up to give her a hug, and the old couple stood in the doorway, watching the carriage until Devon lost sight of them.

The Minters had insisted that the trio use the team and buggy, and Raveneau tied his saddle horse to run along behind. Azalea sat beside André, and Devon felt silly perched all alone on the other seat, as though she were a little sister or chaperone.

Azalea could never have dreamed what thoughts

173

were whirling in Devon's mind. Ever since Raveneau had taken Azalea out for the solitary walk the day before, Devon had been convinced that they had resumed their affair—even if it would last only until Isaac was found. Considering Azalea's frivolous views on love and adventure, no behavior seemed too outrageous for her.

So Devon sat behind them, feeling ill and blue, while they chatted about old times on the *Black Eagle* and Cornwallis's surrender.

The landscape was pretty enough, but the closer the buggy drew to Yorktown, the more desolate the farms and houses appeared. The roads and yards were thick with grass, fences were broken, and most of the fields were overgrown and neglected. Many homes had been abandoned, their windows shattered and doors swinging in the autumn breeze.

After an hour, Raveneau gave the reins over to Azalea and fell asleep. Both girls watched him, while pretending not to. Devon was angry with herself for the tender response he drew from her heart. She longed to nestle against him, to be wrapped in his warm, hard embrace and listen to his heart beat.

They reached the tent headquarters of Comte de Rochambeau about noon, where a few stragglers reported that the ceremony was scheduled to begin at two o'clock and most of the troops had already left for the field.

Raveneau seemed unsurprised to learn how perfectly he had timed their arrival. Descending from the carriage, he slipped into his white coat and put a hand up to check his unpowdered hair. Then he untied his horse and called to Azalea and Devon to alight.

"There is bound to be a huge crowd," he informed them, "so I think it would be best for you ladies to walk."

"Are you going off without us?" Azalea demanded.

"I must join my regiment. Don't worry, the field is not far—just follow this street to the town outskirts.

174

I'll be on horseback and easy to spot. Find a place near me, and I will come to you when the ceremony is over."

With a last jaunty smile, Raveneau bent to graze first Azalea's lips, then Devon's. He mounted his gray stallion in one graceful movement.

"*A bientôt!*" he called, then galloped off.

Azalea and Devon looked at each other.

"I feel as though we've been jilted," Azalea declared, and the younger girl nodded agreement.

"That man is insufferable. He thinks he can get away with anything."

"Devon, I hate to say it, but he probably can."

Thousands of people from the countryside thronged the field where the allied armies had formed columns to await the British. Raveneau had been right; a carriage wouldn't have brought Azalea and Devon within a quarter mile of the ceremony, but on foot they were able to make their way to the front of the crowd. All around were men on horseback, carriages that held the families of wealthy planters, and brimming farm wagons of children with their parents. Overhead, small boys perched on tree branches.

The French and American armies were a study in contrasts. The French were immaculate in white linen and pastel regimental silks, while their allies had no uniforms and were dressed in ragged, soiled homespun. Many of the men were barefoot, but their bearing was proud and defiant.

Devon spotted Raveneau almost immediately. He had joined a group of French officers, all on horseback, and although he wore no powdered wig or elaborate decorations, she thought him by far the most handsome of all.

When General Washington appeared, walking his horse between the seemingly endless allied files, a deafening cheer went up from the crowd. Devon joined in, impressed by the sight of the tall, somber man who was leading America toward freedom. Washington joined Rochambeau, and the two leaders waited expectantly for the redcoats to appear. A band played.

Before long, the British and Hessians emerged from the ravaged village. Their band was playing a melancholy march that Devon recognized as "The World Turned Upside Down." The enemy columns were splendidly garbed, their swords and muskets polished to a high gleam, though nearly half the original six thousand soldiers lay dead, ill, or wounded behind the shattered walls of Yorktown.

Cornwallis was not to be found. A handsome, ruddy-faced brigadier general led the British column. He sat erect on his horse and smiled cheerfully at the French as he passed, ignoring the Americans. The British leader introduced himself to General Rochambeau as Charles O'Hara. Washington's face darkened. The Frenchman shook his head and pointed across the road, announcing, "We are allied with the Americans. General Washington will accept your surrender."

Thoroughly incensed, Washington refused to deal with O'Hara. Since Cornwallis had sent his second in command, he would do the same. Introducing the redcoat to Benjamin Lincoln, his field commander, he declared that Lincoln would direct the surrender. Shrugging, O'Hara gamely turned over his sword to Lincoln.

A regiment of French Hussars surrounded a nearby field, where the British were instructed to march and lay down their arms. They did not surrender gracefully. Bitter and grieving, many of the men wept and tried to break their muskets as they hurled them down.

The ceremony ended, the crowd began to disperse, and suddenly Isaac Smith appeared and seized Azalea in a crushing hug. Devon would have recognized him anywhere, for he looked exactly like his miniature.

Even his face was as ruddy as it had been painted. He obviously adored Azalea, listened to every word she uttered, yet managed to voice his own thoughts. It soon became evident that he possessed a talent for making her believe she was getting her own way while coaxing her into cheerful compromise. After an hour with the couple, Devon knew they would be happy together.

A short time later, she attempted to leave them together. They had meandered over to a tree and leaned against the trunk, embracing and whispering. As the crowd thinned, Devon wandered to and fro on the road, looking for Morgan. He had to be here today—if he hadn't been wounded or killed. That thought was horrifying, even though she hadn't the faintest notion what she felt for him any longer.

Even the soldiers were heading back to their separate camps. There was no sign of Raveneau, but it seemed certain that he would return for her. Now that the excitement was over, Devon felt slivers of panic. What if she *didn't* find Morgan? What then? She could wander through the camps and inquire, but what if he were long dead? Azalea would be going home, Isaac in tow, for he had already announced that he was finished with the war. Raveneau would surely be anxious to return to the *Black Eagle* as soon as possible. What would she do?

"You look anxious, mademoiselle," a familiar French-accented voice observed. Devon whirled to find Raveneau behind her, still astride the gray stallion. He swung easily to the ground. "I take it you have been denied the tearful reunion you have dreamed of for so long."

While pacing the road, Devon saw two men on horseback riding unhurriedly in her direction. They each wore the dark-blue and buff uniforms of officers in the Continental Army and, as the pair drew near, Devon could see that they were splendid representatives of the male species. Their flashing smiles were wickedly reminiscent of Raveneau's own.

The first man, who appeared to be about thirty, wore a cockaded hat over his jet-black hair, and even from a distance, Devon could see that his eyes were a vivid shade of turquoise.

"Fair and sweet young lady, my friend and I have been wondering if you are in need of our assistance? You appear to be rather distraught."

"I don't believe I am acquainted with you gentlemen," Devon replied frostily, only to be greeted by soft laughter as the two men exchanged ironic glances.

"We beg your pardon, *chérie!*" the dark-haired officer exclaimed. "My name is Major Alexandre Beauvisage."

"And I am Captain Lion Hampshire," supplied the younger man. He had removed his hat to display molten-gold hair that gleamed in the sunlight, and his handsome face was as deeply tanned as that of his companion.

"We were on our way back to the house of a friend, and it happens that I have a bottle of excellent brandy," Major Beauvisage explained smoothly. "Perhaps you might consent to join us for a much-deserved celebration."

"Absolutely not!" Devon burst out in astonishment.

"I hope you do not imagine that we are less than trustworthy!" Hampshire interjected.

"That is precisely what she ought to imagine," a fourth voice said sarcastically.

Devon whirled around. Of course, it was Raveneau, astride the gray stallion, one dark brow arched high over flinty eyes.

"*Bonjour,* Major Beauvisage," he said coolly. "I thought you were with Francis Marion in South Carolina these days."

Beauvisage grinned lazily. "I wanted to be on hand for the surrender."

Raveneau glanced inquiringly at Lion Hampshire,

and Major Beauvisage made the introduction. Then
Raveneau fastened a wintry, gray stare on the two of
them and said, "I gather that you lechers thought to
amuse yourselves with this defenseless girl?"

"Raveneau!" cried Beauvisage. "You needn't get
angry. How were we to know she belonged to you?"

"She does not. This is Mademoiselle Devon Lindsay
and she is here to seek out her fiancé."

"And *you* are assisting her?" The major could not
repress a snort of doubtful laughter.

"Perhaps you know of him?" Devon interjected.
"Private Morgan Gadwin?"

Lion Hampshire seemed amused. "No, Miss Lindsay, I fear not."

Raveneau and Beauvisage conversed briefly concerning the latter's family-owned fleet of privateers
and the latest exploits of the *Black Eagle;* then the
Frenchman slanted a look in Hampshire's direction
and said, "We do not want to keep you two gentleman
from your celebration. Mademoiselle Lindsay is desperately sorry that she is unable to attend, however . . . "

The handsome officers laughed, offered Raveneau
and Devon mock bows, and bid them farewell. As they
rode off, Raveneau observed, "Back to the matters at
hand—I take it that you have been denied the tearful
reunion you have dreamt of for so long."

Devon turned around in time to see him pull off his
white gloves and swing easily to the ground. "I can't
understand it," she said. "Why isn't Morgan here?"

"He may have been. Perhaps he was so far away
that he simply didn't see you. There are a number of
alternate explanations. Many things can happen to a
soldier, you know."

Devon's eyes brimmed with tears, and she saw his
cool expression harden to ice. She couldn't tell him
that her tears were not those of a lover, but of a girl
who seemed to be blundering into progressively deeper
predicaments.

"I was a fool for ever allowing you to remain on the *Black Eagle*," Raveneau said, his voice angry and cold. "I must have lost my reason. However, now that I am involved this deeply in your tangled affairs, I suppose I must see this through. You shall stay with me. Tonight I will search the camps for your precious Morgan. I'll wager that if he is not to be found, some-one will have news of him."

"And then?" Devon whispered, hating herself for needing him.

"We will follow and find him. No one will be more pleased than I when you are reunited with that cursed phantom!"

Chapter Fourteen

———◆———

October 20, 1781

RAVENEAU and Devon rode into Williamsburg the following afternoon. There had been no sign of Morgan in any of the American camps, but Raveneau did hear that he had contracted a mild case of camp fever during the march south and was likely to be found in the hospital in Williamsburg.

During the twelve-mile journey from Yorktown, André had filled Devon in on Williamsburg's recent history. Williamsburg had been the colonial capital and the social hub of the Tidewater region not so long ago, he said. The town was small and elegantly designed, memorable for its gardens, its charming white houses, and a reckless air of merriment.

Three years ago, Governor Thomas Jefferson had decided to move the capital to Richmond, nearer his own Monticello. Williamsburg had yet to recover from the blow. Many of her most prominent citizens followed the governor, including a number of physicians and attorneys, as well as the printers of the *Virginia Gazette*. Cornwallis's ten-day occupation the previous June had further ruined the town.

Devon had listened with one ear. So much had happened that it was difficult to absorb all these details after the quiet month on the Minter farm. She had waved goodbye to Isaac and Azalea that morning as they set off in the buggy to return to her parents' farm. Raveneau had kept his stallion and managed to buy a chestnut gelding for Devon to ride from a farm near Yorktown.

Now, slowing her horse to a walk, Devon glanced over at a pensive Raveneau, whose eyes examined every person as they turned from the York Road onto the broad Duke of Gloucester Street. There was no escaping the fact that she was glad to be here with Raveneau, glad that he hadn't located Morgan yet. It was too good to last, but for now she would take a page from Azalea's book and hoard her memories of these hours.

Williamsburg proved to be an enchanting town, despite its recent decline. The public buildings were stately and built of brick, each one surrounded by sweeping grounds and abundant gardens. The private houses were generally constructed of wood, one and one half stories tall with numerous dormer windows. Devon had never seen so many gardens. Every home seemed charmed by patterned brick walkways and geometric boxwood-edged flowerbeds.

"Williamsburg must be heavenly in the spring," Devon sighed.

"Yes," Raveneau agreed, walking his horse to the left to avoid a lone cow that stood motionless in the road. "You'll find it a far cry from Connecticut. The English influence has been strong here."

They passed rows of shops with distinctive signs shaped like sheep, boots, teapots, or a wild boar. The windows were like pictures with their displays of imported hats and fruit, baskets, pewter, and elaborate wigs. Other shops stood empty and forlorn, their goods now enticing the people of Richmond. Soldiers were everywhere.

Anthony Hay, proprietor of the Raleigh Tavern, barked that he had no rooms, until turning to find

Raveneau standing there. The two men laughed about things Devon didn't understand as they climbed the stairs, and she found herself wondering about all his adult years before they had met. Obviously Raveneau had spent a portion of his time since 1776 in New London, but where else had he been? She stole a glance at his dark, laughing face and wondered if he had ever been in love. Dozens of women must have been in love with him. And how many women had he kissed?

All these thoughts served to make her feel more insignificant than ever. Raveneau left her at her room to wash and rest and went on to his own with Hay. The chamber was pretty, with a canopy bed and wing chair covered in matching rose and cream cotton, several other cheerful and useful pieces of furniture, and two gleaming dormer windows that offered a view of the garden below. A serving girl knocked, then brought fresh water for the pitcher and a neat stack of snowy linens.

No sooner had Devon washed her face and slipped out of her dusty gown than her eyes began to droop. The feather tick was deep and cool; she sank into it and fell instantly into a dreamless sleep.

She woke with a start to the sound of a throat being cleared. Alarm squeezed her heart as she remembered the soldiers in the street, many of whom had been laughing and shouting drunkenly. Still half-asleep, Devon struggled to sit up.

There was Raveneau, standing at the foot of the bed, leaning against one of the posts.

"How did you get in here?" she demanded.

"The usual way."

"You might have knocked! I'm not dressed!" She put one hand over the bodice of her thin chemise.

"I don't mind." He grinned. "And, for the record, I did knock. Several times."

Devon dropped back onto the pillows and yawned. "I must have been too tired to hear."

"You should be glad that I came in, otherwise you might have slept right through the night and missed the festivities."

"What festivities?"

Raveneau brought a tray over from the bureau and set it on her lap. "You must be hungry. It is past six o'clock."

"Six!" she exclaimed, then noticed the indigo darkness outside and the candle he had lit beside her bed. The tray looked and smelled wonderful, containing hot spiced shrimp, tender rolls, strawberry jam, and green beans in a cream sauce. Between bites, Devon repeated her question. "What festivities?"

"Well, a friend of mine has a new home here that he hasn't been able to enjoy because of the war. The victory at Yorktown seemed a perfect excuse for a party, so he has planned a ball of sorts for tonight. I know that you are anxious to look for Morgan, but—"

"A ball!" Devon echoed rapturously. "But what would I wear?"

A sardonic smile flickered over Raveneau's face. Crossing to the wardrobe, he opened one door and withdrew an exquisite gown. Devon choked on her shrimp. The dress was fashioned of ivory satin embroidered with slender, blood-red flowers on swirling green stems. The square bodice, sleeves, and petticoats were lavishly trimmed with ivory lace.

"Do you like it?" he inquired.

"It is the most beautiful gown I have ever seen! But—"

"I have many friends in town, *petite chatte*. I simply queried a few dressmakers until I discovered one who had the right gown of the right size." He brought it to the bed so that she might feel the heavy fabric. "You understand that it is just for tonight. It was made for the mistress of a nearby plantation."

Devon was radiant. "I don't mind. One night will be more than sufficient!" She reached out to touch one of his strong hands. "Thank you."

Raveneau returned the gown to the wardrobe, then seated himself at the foot of her bed. This reminded her of many occasions past on the *Black Eagle*.

"You don't mind postponing your search for Morgan until tomorrow?" he asked.

Devon could feel her cheeks heat guiltily. "Well, after all, it is already dark."

"I could have gone. If he is in one of the hospitals, I would have known within a few hours."

The Governor's Palace had been converted into a hospital for wounded Americans. The capitol building and the College of William and Mary served as hospitals for the French.

She didn't know what to say. It seemed terribly impolite for him to put her in such a position. She really ought to forgo the ball and send him straight after Morgan.

Unable to meet his steely gaze, Devon stared down at her food, crumbling a roll. Closing her eyes, she imagined herself in that gown, dancing in Raveneau's arms. "No," she whispered. "Morgan may not be at the first hospital, and then the entire evening would be wasted. You deserve a party, and—" She looked up defiantly. "So do I!"

Raveneau bit back a smile and an urge to toss aside that tray and hold her. Just when he would begin to convince himself that she was not special in the least, there would be a moment like this one when she absolutely bewitched him. She possessed none of the glamour of his past lovers, yet right now, with her tousled strawberry-blond curls, vivid blue eyes, and flushed cheeks, he found her breathtaking. Worse, the memory of the night they had made love remained with him, tormented him. He was convinced that he felt guilt for taking her virginity, and that by reuniting her with Morgan he would be able to erase the stains on his conscience.

Still, he thought, it isn't guilt that makes me want to touch her now . . .

*   *   *

Devon could not break away from the mirror, so fascinated was she by her appearance. It was difficult to believe that she was truly the same girl who had run full tilt down the winding streets of New London and had stowed away on a privateer, disguised as a surgeon's mate.

At Raveneau's request, she had left her hair unpowdered, though she entertained a secret wish to see what the effect would have been. A girl had appeared to help her dress, and she arranged Devon's golden-rose hair with skilled hands. It had been pulled up from her face, but wispy tendrils had been left to curl across her brow and temples. The rest of her gleaming ringlets were pinned in expert disarray on top of her head.

There was no need for cosmetics. Excitement made her beautiful, eyes sparkling and skin glowing. The gown fit as though it had been designed just for her. The bodice hugged her breasts, flattering them, and Devon thought even the lush Azalea might cast an envious eye her way. Her tiny waist was accentuated by the panniers that held her satin and lace skirts out on either side.

Though she had no jewelry to wear, the gown seemed enough. She stood before the mirror as she waited for Raveneau, fingering the heavy satin and frothy lace and turning her head this way and that, studying the contours of her face and neck. What a night this will be! she thought, and grinned, closing her eyes in an effort to contain her joy.

"You are a vision, Devon," a voice said from the doorway.

She opened her eyes and saw his reflection in the mirror. "Oh, my God!" she gasped. "You look beautiful!"

Raveneau's eyes widened, then he burst out laughing. Devon turned around and stared at him. She had never imagined a man could look so magnificent. He wore his raven hair unpowdered. His shirt and cravat were white as snow against his dark jaw. His coat of rich forest-green velvet fit like a glove, outlining broad shoulders and lean hips. Finally, there were white breeches and stockings and buckled shoes. Devon thought illogically that she hadn't seen his calves since the day on the *Black Eagle* when he had sat on the table in his dressing gown.

"Beautiful, eh?" Raveneau repeated cynically.

"I didn't mean it that way!"

"I know." His harshly cut face softened and he walked over to her and gave her a gentle, grazing kiss. "Every man shall envy me tonight."

A sweet current of warmth swept over Devon at his words, but she knew that, in truth, she would be the envied one.

The evening passed quickly, but Devon was so happy she wished to stop time.

The magnificent new home of the Marquis de Benet was huge, built of red brick, and recently furnished with thick imported rugs and Chippendale pieces upholstered in rich brocades. Candles blazed in crystal or silver chandeliers. Punch bowls sat on every table and there was every sort of meat, pastry, and sweetmeat, as well as a variety of shellfish.

The guests ate and drank and laughed and danced, their jewels and brilliant clothing reflecting the candlelight. Raveneau kept Devon at his side, and she found that she had been right; every female present had her eyes trained on André, even the elderly ladies. Raveneau remained slightly amused by the entire affair. His eyes gleamed with cynical mischief as he played the part of heroic privateer captain. It was evident to Devon that no one impressed him in the least, no matter what their title or the size of their fortune. And it seemed to her that he was impressed least of all by his own notoriety.

In the ballroom, velvet-garbed musicians played

harpsichord, violins, and harp as the guests moved through the motions of the minuet. Devon hung back. "I have danced before, but never like this," she confessed.

Raveneau grinned. "I will teach you."

Her heart sped with happiness as he led her out the French doors into the moonlit garden, where the music sounded faintly.

"Don't be nervous," he chided. "It is but a comical dance, *petite chatte,* and worthy only of your laughter."

He took her hands in his and she shivered. Slowly, he showed her the steps, letting her practice while watching the couples in the ballroom. When she began to move with more confidence, they danced an entire minuet without stopping. Devon loved the feeling of their bodies moving in harmony, back and forth, touching, releasing, turning, bowing. Raveneau's grace was effortless, though he surely couldn't have had much opportunity to practice.

After a while the musicians went to have a glass of punch, while the other guests could be seen returning to the tables for more refreshment.

"Are you cold?" Raveneau asked.

"No, I'm fine."

"Good. Let us remain here for now."

He led her along a brick walkway, into the mazelike garden. The breeze was chilly, but Devon didn't notice. "You don't seem to like those people very well," she remarked.

"I wouldn't put it quite that mildly. Most of them are totally obscured by artificial layers of social grace and contrived behavior. I have no patience for it or them."

"Then why did you come tonight?"

"Because Benet is an old friend who, momentarily mad, seems to aspire to this life." He stopped and looked down at her. "And I came for you. I thought you might enjoy it."

Their eyes met and Devon was suddenly seized by a chill. Her palms grew moist as Raveneau reached out to trace the line of her throat with a finger. She could feel her breasts trembling and wondered crazily if he noticed.

"Devon, I—"

"*Là!* Raveneau!" came a shout from the ballroom. They looked back to see the marquis outlined against the light from the French doors. He hastened down the path.

"Where have you been? The women are badgering me mercilessly, demanding a dance with you. For my sake, André—"

Raveneau sighed sharply. "I hate this, Jacques. Do you know that? These people have the manners of frogs."

With that, he strode away, leaving Devon with the marquis, who clucked his tongue and shook his head. "*Zut!* There is not a man alive who would not love to be André. It is as though the women are bees and he is the honey, yet he behaves as though that were a curse."

Devon smiled, happy to think that Raveneau might prefer her company to that of the elegant women inside.

"I understand that you have come to Virginia to find your fiancé!" Benet remarked as they started back to the ballroom.

"Well, yes."

"A fortunate man. Such devotion as yours is rare. And I am pleased to find André in the role of cavalier. It is encouraging to discover that he has a—how shall I say it?—a fatherly, protective side to his character."

Devon froze.

"Mademoiselle Lindsay, you look positively ill! Are you faint?"

"No, no, I am fine. Just a bit lightheaded for a moment."

The music had resumed, and through the French doors Devon spied Raveneau dancing with a tall, stunning young lady who wore a gown of gold cloth encrusted with jewels. He was smiling, his eyes gleaming with silvery lights.

"Would you care to dance, mademoiselle?" Benet inquired cheerfully.

"I don't know. I haven't had much practice."

"Then it is fortunate that I am here to help. I am a veritable master of the minuet."

Without another word, he led her inside and they took their places. At first Devon was too distraught to concentrate, but after Raveneau glanced in their direction, she determined to enjoy herself. Her body moved of its own volition. Benet smiled and she smiled in return, brilliantly.

By midnight, Devon was confused. She was piercingly jealous of every woman who danced in André's arms. Women followed him like puppies, but he appeared to be enjoying himself. After a while Devon's pride came to the fore. She ignored him, flirting with the men who begged a dance and fetched her pastries and punch, and enjoying the flattery they lavished upon her.

She was standing in the dining room with a pompous college official when Raveneau suddenly materialized. "I trust you are enjoying yourself?" he inquired bitingly.

Devon lifted her chin. "Yes, thank you. Captain Raveneau, may I introduce Mr. Peabody? He is a member of the board at William and Mary."

The two men exchanged curt nods.

"I think we should be going," Raveneau announced. "I *know* you will want to be up at first light."

Devon shrugged a delicate shoulder and averted her eyes.

"Miss Lindsay, might I presume to inquire if you

would receive me tomorrow?" Peabody interjected. "I would be pleased to share tea with you."

Raveneau's jaw tightened. "Miss Lindsay is unavailable. She is getting married in a few days. Good evening, sir."

With that, one brown hand gripped Devon's arm, pulling her along before she could say another word to Mr. Peabody. Outrage swelled in her throat, but in this sea of curious, smiling faces all she could do was smile tensely in return. The marquis tried to discover their reason for leaving so early, but after the briefest goodnight, Raveneau propelled Devon outdoors.

She watched him stalk along in the moonlight, the picture of tremendous power straining to be unleashed. His face looked positively frightening. Although simmering with anger herself, Devon had no wish to provoke him into losing control. They walked the short quarter mile to the Raleigh Tavern, her courage building all the while.

"Excuse me, Captain Raveneau," Devon said at last, her tone both frosty and quavering. "I think you owe me an explanation!"

He stopped and turned to glare down at her, his eyes blazing like silver stars. "Sweet Devon, I am confused myself. Just exactly what sort of girl are you?"

Her mouth dropped. "What do you mean?"

"I mean that over a month ago I met an innocent child who begged me with pathetic sincerity to take her to Yorktown so that she might be reunited with her one true love. I have seen little of that true love since then. It might have been a stranger whom I watched tonight at Benet's. *Dieu!* If not for your hair, I wouldn't have been able to discern you from every other simpering coquette of marriageable age!"

"You are the most ill-mannered—"

"And you are avoiding the issue. I think that I have a right to some answers after wasting so much time on you." Every word he uttered was like a stinging slap to her face.

"You have not been exactly a model of propriety yourself!" she cried. "If you desired me to remain pure of mind and purpose, you should never have robbed me of my innocence!"

Passersby slowed to stare at them until Raveneau bent a dangerous look on the eavesdroppers. When he turned back to Devon, there was a glint of amusement in his expression. "Women! You all possess the most amazing facility for reshaping the past. We both know what happened that night. I will not be painted as the villain!"

Her face flaming, Devon turned and started up the walkway to the Raleigh. "I do not wish to continue this discussion."

Behind her, Raveneau arched a black eyebrow and smiled slightly. He followed Devon inside and up the stairs.

"Good night," she murmured tensely.

"*You* may not wish to continue this discussion, Devon, dear, but I do."

She tried to ignore him when he followed her inside and dropped into the rose and cream print chair. Standing before the mirror, she pulled the pins from her hair, one by one, and deposited them in a Staffordshire bowl.

"Tell me about your Merlin," Raveneau said at length.

Devon felt as though he had been putting needles in her all day, but this one struck a major nerve. The person who was most confused about her relationship with Morgan was Devon herself. "You are trying to annoy me!" she nearly shouted. "And furthermore, I resent your attitude. That ball was *your* idea, not mine, and I didn't notice you flying into a rage when I was dancing and laughing with *you*."

This came nearer to the truth than Raveneau was willing to admit. "You are skirting the issue once again, mademoiselle," he rejoined coolly. "There is a monumental difference between me and the rest of the men at Benet's. I know your situation; you are safe in my company."

Devon seized on this with glee. "Oh, please! I wish you might be on hand on my wedding night to explain to Morgan just how safe I have been in your company!"

He narrowed his eyes. "Are we going to go through that again? I would be happy to discuss it at length, if that is your wish."

Devon began to comb her lavish curls furiously. "No. I am tired. I wish you would leave."

He propped his legs on the bedframe. "I will do so just as soon as you tell me about Morgan. I am curious, especially since I may meet him at last tomorrow."

Devon glared at him but sat down on the edge of the bed. "There are times when I wish I had never met you," she hissed.

"Oh, really? You will be relieved to learn that I harbor that same wish—continually. Now, about Morgan?"

She wondered if that were true. Did André despise her? Inexplicably, tears stung her eyes and a painful lump swelled in her throat. "Fine. If that is what it will take to get you to leave my room, then I shall be happy to oblige."

Raveneau smiled like a cat, waiting.

"Morgan and I were inseparable friends almost since the day we were born. He is sweet and idealistic and always loved me better than anything in the world. He would have done whatever I asked—"

"Sounds like a man after my own heart," Raveneau murmured sardonically.

"If you are going to take that attitude—"

"No, please. I apologize. Do go on."

"Well, there is not much to tell. We led a quiet life, but we made wonderful plans for our future! We are going to sail all over the world someday. I want to see everything—"

"Ah! Morgan owns a ship, I take it?"

"Well, no, but——" His mocking expression made her nervous. "We are going to get our own ship after we are married."

"Really? How?"

"That is none of your affair!"

"Ah, *je comprends*. A secret plan. Hmmm . . . well, I wish you luck with this swashbuckling husband. Perhaps one day our ships will meet at sea."

"I hope not! Pirate that you are, you would doubtless attack us."

Raveneau laughed, but his gray eyes were watchful as he stood up. "I have just one last question. Won't Morgan mind your association with me? And what of tonight? How would he have felt if he had seen you fluttering your lovely lashes at all those men?"

Devon knew the answer but could never admit to Raveneau that Morgan was far too tractable to become angry over her behavior.

"Morgan trusts me. He knows that he is the one I love," she declared.

"An amazing man," Raveneau reflected, ". . . or a fool."

Chapter Fifteen

———◆———

October 21-23, 1781

Now a hospital, the Governors Palace had been home to seven royal governors between 1710 and 1775, and Devon stared in awe as Raveneau guided her under the brick archway, past neglected, lozenge-shaped flower beds and the brick buildings which flanked the forecourt.

"This is where Mr. Jefferson lived as well?" Devon asked softly.

"Yes."

A soldier appeared at the door, shading his eyes against the morning sun. "Do you need help? There is camp fever inside, so we don't encourage visitors."

Raveneau and Devon walked up the steps. "We are looking for a young man named Morgan—"

"Gadwin," Devon supplied, her heart racing with suspense. "He is from New London, Connecticut, and we were told that he could be found here."

The soldier smiled. "Oh, yes, I know Private Gadwin. You'll be happy to learn that he came through his illness in fine shape. He was discharged from here two days ago, but I have heard since that he is staying at the Market Square Tavern." He grinned at Raveneau. "Recuperating, you know."

After thanking the soldier for his help, they walked back toward the brick archway.

"Well!" Devon exclaimed. "The news couldn't have been better. Morgan is healthy and here in Williamsburg."

Raveneau grunted testily.

They started across the vast, autumn-tinted Palace Green that would bring them back to Duke of Gloucester Street. Since the tense discussion of the night before, she and Raveneau had remained cool and distant. His gray eyes were flinty when they met hers, and Devon's emotions were in a state of turmoil. It was impossible for her to understand her feelings about anything, Morgan or Raveneau, the present or the future. She wished she could turn back time to September fifth and find herself tucked safely into her bed above the Linen and Pewter Shop.

I was so confident and outspoken then, she thought. I didn't know when I was well off!

Duke of Gloucester Street was crowded with soldiers, slaves, servants, pigs, dogs, horses, cows and a sprinkling of the well-dressed gentry. Market Square was located at the street's midpoint, between the capitol and the College of William and Mary.

The Market Square Tavern was not as fine a building as the Raleigh, where Devon and André had rooms, but inviting all the same. It was surrounded by a stable, a Saddlery and Harness Making Shop, a charming garden, and a large smokehouse. The tavern itself was two rooms deep and one and a half stories tall, like most of its Williamsburg neighbors.

As they approached the door, Devon's knees weakened, accompanied by an apprehensive tightening in her breast.

Raveneau intensified his grip on her arm and lifted a dark eyebrow. "Why aren't you charging in like a runaway horse?"

She gave him a cold, disdainful look and reached out to open the door. The tavernkeeper appeared almost instantly, beaming. "Captain Raveneau! It is a great pleasure to see you! Can I offer you a room?"

"Bonjour, M'sieur Maupin." André reached out to shake his hand. "May I present Mademoiselle Lindsay?" Maupin and Devon exchanged greetings and Raveneau continued. "It is not lodging I seek, but this young lady's fiancé. We have reason to believe he may have taken a room here."

"Ah! A reunion of young lovers! I hope that I can help. What is this man's name?"

"Morgan Gadwin," Devon replied, flinching inwardly.

"Happy news!" Maupin boomed. "He is in the parlor at this very moment. Come along!"

Devon swallowed the lump in her throat and followed the tavernkeeper. Raveneau continued to hold her elbow, bending and whispering in her ear, "How long we have both waited for this moment, *petite chatte!"*

She made a face at him and tried to pull her arm away just as Maupin slowed and stood to one side. Flustered, Devon looked up, feeling Raveneau's hand drop away, and immediately saw Morgan.

The room was spacious, wainscoted in natural pine, with a large Queen Anne table at its center. Around the table, a dozen bow-back Windsor chairs were occupied by high-spirited young men, more than half of them clad in uniforms. The air smelled of smoke and ale.

Morgan seemed like a stranger. She had never seen him with an ale mug in his hand, let alone slack-jawed and blurry-eyed. His hair was raggedly queued, his shirt soiled and unbuttoned to reveal a thin, pale chest.

"D—Devon?" he quavered. His voice sounded high. She could sense the expression on Raveneau's face.

"Yes, Morgan." Even she could scarcely hear her voice. Morgan's drinking companions were leering at her, laughing and reaching over to hit Morgan on the arms and back. After a long moment he struggled to his feet and came toward her.

"Oh, God, Devon!" Tears filled his eyes, but the effect was spoiled by an ill-timed belch. "How—"

He grabbed her clumsily, and Devon was nauseated by the smell of ale. When his arms relaxed and he drew back, her eyes were also sparkling with tears.

Gabriel Maupin saw to it that the parlor was quickly emptied of its occupants so that the young lovers might have a few moments alone. As the men filed out, Raveneau made a move to follow them, but Devon frantically reached for his coat sleeve.

"No! Please stay! I mean—I want Morgan to meet you. After all . . ."

Morgan blinked, glancing from Devon to the tall, black-haired, dangerous-looking stranger. The man smiled, as though amused, and replied in a deep, French-accented voice, "As you wish, *petite chatte.*"

Little cat? thought Morgan foggily. "Who are you?" he asked aloud.

"My name is André Raveneau," the Frenchman said, showing a flash of white teeth when he smiled.

Devon walked toward the table, explaining nervously, "You remember, Morgan! He is captain of the *Black Eagle,* the most notorious privateer that ever sailed up the Thames."

The men took chairs on either side of Devon, and Morgan replied dully, "Yes, I remember. I am honored to meet you, captain. But I don't understand."

"Please!" Raveneau protested. "André. I feel as if we are old friends. Devon has talked of nothing but you these past weeks."

"Weeks?" echoed Morgan.

"André brought me from New London!" Devon exclaimed. "Actually, I sneaked on board, but he was kind enough to allow me to stay."

"I am very soft-hearted about true love," Raveneau explained gently.

Morgan's head began to hurt. He looked around for his mug. It was empty, so he picked up the next one and took several long swallows. "I still don't understand." He wished the Frenchman would go away so that he might lay his hands on Devon. How delicious she looked, her strawberry-blond curls tumbling about her face, her breasts peeping teasingly above the bodice of a sea-green gown!

Maupin appeared with glasses and a decanter of claret, then made a hasty retreat. As Raveneau poured the wine, Devon told Morgan what had happened in New London the month before, from the cannon shots before dawn to her recognition of Benedict Arnold. It was the first time Raveneau had heard the entire tale, and it seemed to Devon that his eyes were more intense than Morgan's.

"I don't know what became of your parents," she said at length, "but I am certain they were sensible enough to flee." She didn't mention that Mr. Gadwin might have been at the massacre at Fort Griswold.

"I have seen so much death and destruction," Morgan said brokenly, "so many battles, that it is hard to absorb this."

Raveneau wanted to say that perhaps he had absorbed too much ale of late, but managed to hold his tongue. He already loathed the boy, and he fought protective instincts toward Devon. How did I know he would turn out to be such a toad? he wondered. Of course, he had sensed it long ago, perhaps because it was she who took the risks to find Morgan and not the other way around. If the boy had been a man, would she have responded so intensely to the "pirate" whom she professed to despise?

"At least you were spared Yorktown," Raveneau said tightly.

"Unhappily, I became ill during the march south."

"It is fortunate that you made such a miraculous recovery." Devon looked at him sharply, but Raveneau gave her an innocent smile.

Morgan coughed dramatically. "I am not *quite* well yet, but I feared that someone might need my bed at the hospital. But please, enough about me. I am waiting to hear the rest of your story, darling."

"Well, to spare you tedious details, I was able to get away from New London, and André was kind enough to allow me on board the *Black Eagle*. After we reached Chesapeake Bay, I went on to stay with the family of André's steward until two days ago, when André returned to take me in search of you. It hasn't been easy—but here we are at last!"

"Yes, here we are," Raveneau echoed ironically.

Morgan, sharp-shouldered and glassy-eyed, looked back and forth in confusion. "It is rather a miracle, then, isn't it?"

This was Devon's cue to throw her arms around him and sob, "Yes, yes!" but instead, she only managed to smile and nod.

"We owe you a large debt of gratitude," Morgan went on, looking uneasily into Raveneau's steely eyes.

"Pas du tout!" Raveneau protested. "I am pleased to see two people in love reunited. The war has been hard on all of us."

"Yes." Morgan nodded gravely.

"I know Williamsburg as well as Paris, and I cannot leave matters as they stand now. Please, let me arrange your wedding. I know a wonderful parson. Unless you are Catholic—?"

Stunned into silence, Devon shook her head.

"No? Good. You will both like Parson Hume enormously. I know that you must be in dire financial straits, Morgan, so I insist that you allow me to pay for a proper wedding." He glanced at Devon, smiling wickedly. "Let us call it a dowry."

Devon thought that perhaps she was going mad. Raveneau finished his wine and rose to leave, and she wanted fiercely to throw herself into his arms.

She and Morgan alone? She remembered the last time they had been alone, when his clammy hands had fumbled inside her bodice to squeeze her breasts, then traveled up her legs ...

Pride won out. After all, Raveneau wanted only to be rid of her so that he might return to his privateer. She couldn't scream, "I was wrong!" after all she had forced him to do on her behalf. And Morgan was the boy she had loved for years. They had been happy once, not long ago, and now Devon must adjust herself to that state of mind again.

So she smiled sweetly, extending her hand, and said all the proper things. Raveneau managed to shatter her composure, though, by leaning over and pressing his mouth to her hand, scorching the soft skin and sending a tingling heat up her arm. Both nipples tightened against her chemise.

When they were alone, Morgan squirmed uneasily. "Well. He certainly lives up to his reputation!"

Devon blushed. "I don't know. He has his share of flaws."

"Do you think so?" Morgan was inching his chair closer to hers. "I am glad to know you weren't swept off your feet. Only a girl like you could stand firm and search for me with a rogue like that by your side."

His arms snaked around her waist and he stared greedily at her rosy lips. "I have missed you so, Devon. I was afraid that you might have stopped caring."

Devon closed her eyes as his face drew near. Lips flattened over hers, a tongue pushed between her teeth, and she remembered Raveneau's long-ago, magic kisses, and the fiery one she had shared with the spy, Jay. Why couldn't Morgan kiss like they did? Why did she shiver with passion at their embraces, when his inspired only revulsion?

She suffered the kiss obediently. Then his lips nibbled her ear, neck, the exposed curves of her breasts. However, when he moved to unfasten her bodice, Devon drew back abruptly. "No! I mean—Please,

someone could walk in. We will be married soon.
There is time enough—"

Morgan's chin quivered. "Oh, Devon, if only you
knew how much I *want* you! To think that in a few
short days we will be man and wife . . . oh, Lord, I
wish the wedding could be tomorrow!"

Two excruciating days passed. Devon remained in
her room at the Raleigh Tavern, for propriety's sake,
but Raveneau seemed to take diabolical pleasure in
depositing her with Morgan each morning. He made
a great show of leaving to make wedding arrange-
ments and deflected all of Devon's questions by insisting that it was to be a surprise.

So she and Morgan passed the time together, but
her intense experiences of the past weeks had changed
Devon. She felt much older, and less a prisoner of her
dreams now that she had tasted their reality.

Morgan had changed, too, but for the worse. Hardship had exposed his weaknesses, rather than unearth-
ing hidden strengths. He drank far too much and held
his spirits poorly, but what really worried Devon was
his apparent *need* for his ale. Whenever Raveneau
was near, Morgan began to perspire and look for his
mug, and the same held true for any situation that
required forcefulness or quickness of wit. After two
days Devon was horrified to realize that she could
scarcely bear to be near him. Even her old maternal,
protective instincts toward Morgan had evaporated.

The afternoon of the second day, Devon persuaded
Morgan to take her for a walk on Duke of Gloucester
Street, to the College of William and Mary and back
again. She was trying to separate him from his ale,
but their solitude only seemed to emphasize the distance between them. New London was a painful subject, Devon was uncomfortable discussing her time at
sea with André, and Morgan was equally nervous
when she questioned him about his year in the army.
So they talked about Williamsburg, the surrender, and

the likely future of the war. In the past, Devon had endlessly daydreamed out loud about *their* future, but now she avoided his every attempt to discuss it. The plans to sail around the world in their own ship seemed, at best, a cruel joke. She began to feel half alive, trapped into a fate that she dreaded.

And then there was Raveneau. She might have crazily abandoned the proposed wedding to Morgan if not for Raveneau's involvement. His smile mocked her each time they met; his supposed concern for the wedding plans grated on her nerves. Yet in the face of all he had done to get her to Morgan, it seemed unthinkable that she change her mind.

Now, Morgan held tightly to her arm as they strolled down Williamsburg's wide thoroughfare, past a colorful parade of shops, houses, and taverns. The fire-colored trees stood like torches against the vivid blue sky.

"It's pretty here," Morgan remarked, "but I've never been to a place that could match autumn in Connecticut. Gardens or no gardens."

Devon nodded sadly.

"Well, what do you know!" Morgan exclaimed. "There's Captain Raveneau now. Shall we hail him?"

"No!" Devon commanded, freezing in her tracks, her nails digging into Morgan's arm.

Raveneau was across the street, emerging from a shop which boasted a sign in the shape of a large pink bonnet above its door. He was not alone. Clinging to his arm and gazing into his eyes was a beautiful black-haired girl with a pale magnolia-blossom complexion. She carried a fancy hatbox, and to Devon's dismay, Raveneau held one as well. He looked dark and dashing as he laughed at some sally made by his companion.

Jealousy ate at Devon's already tortured heart, and she fought back tears as she begged Morgan to take her back to her room.

He complied, and they walked in silence to the

Raleigh Tavern, each alone with private thoughts. When they arrived, Devon went upstairs and Morgan headed for the taproom. He drank two large cups of rum punch, his mind whirling madly. He wanted Devon. His desire kept him up at night and made him sweat whenever she was near. The fact that the wedding would take place so soon only heated him further.

Wiping his mouth, Morgan put down a coin to pay for the rum punch, then stood up. He felt confident and strong. Unsteadily, he mounted the stairs and by a stroke of luck found the door open to her chamber. Devon had just set out her water from that morning and gone back to separate her soiled towels when she heard footsteps stop in her doorway.

"Morgan! Is something amiss?"

He drank in the sight of her, outlined by the soft afternoon sunlight that poured through the dormer windows. Golden lights gleamed in her curls, and her blue eyes were wide with—was it apprehension?

"No, no, my darling. I simply could not bear to be away from you." To his own ears he sounded irresistibly roguish. He slammed the door shut. "It has occurred to me that I haven't been forceful enough in our relationhip. I know that women often enjoy that."

Devon, sick at heart, watched him approach and repressed a wild urge to scream her frustration. Morgan, pale and sharp-chinned, looked ludicrous as he attempted to swagger toward her. His eyes glowed in a way that made her flesh crawl.

"Morgan . . . you are being silly. I like you just as you have always been, and you should know me well enough by now to realize that I don't want to be forced! Please, I am tired—"

Devon recoiled as a gust of rum-drenched breath assailed her nostrils. Abruptly, Morgan wrapped his arms around her, pressing her near, so that she could feel the revolting hardness—like a sausage—in his breeches. Devon twisted her head wildly. "Let me go! I mean it! If you do not release me, I shall scream!"

Morgan's arms went limp and he stepped back, staring in confusion. "I . . . but . . ."

"I'm sorry, Morgan, but I simply will not stand for that. If you love me, you will respect my wishes and keep your distance!"

Raveneau strode down the paneled hallway, candle-lit in the evening darkness. He started to open his own door but turned instead toward Devon's. It was unlikely that she had already returned from the Market Square Tavern and her supper with that sallow-faced pup, yet there was always a chance. It seemed an eternity since he had been alone with her in this chamber.

He knocked. Sensing a presence behind the door, he knocked again. "Devon? Are you there?"

Raveneau opened the door and peered inside. Someone lay on the bed, and for one terrible moment he imagined that it might be Devon and Morgan. Reaching into the hallway, he pulled a candle from its holder and held it aloft, its flickering light revealing only one figure on the bed. It was Devon, fully dressed.

"What is it?" he queried. "Are you ill?"

Crossing the room, he inserted the candle into a brass holder beside the bed, where it danced eerily over Devon's tear-stained face.

"I am fine," she choked. "You should not have come in."

"But why are you here, *petite chatte?* It is barely seven o'clock. Have you quarreled with Morgan?"

"No." She turned away and lay stiffly, her face shrouded by darkness.

Raveneau stood beside the bed for a minute or two, staring down at her pensively. Finally he spoke, his voice harsh. "I have some news that should help to cheer you up. The wedding is arranged. It will take place here, in the Apollo Room, tomorrow at two o'clock."

Devon sat up. In the candlelight her face looked

stricken, almost fearful. Blue eyes locked with gray, then Devon whispered, "Fine."

Raveneau changed his clothes before leaving the tavern again. He had arranged to dine with Helena, a girl with whom he had been involved off and on during the past year, but now he had second thoughts. He wanted to talk to Morgan.

Arriving at the Market Square Tavern, he gave a stableboy a shilling to take his regrets to Helena, then went inside. It was a rowdy establishment, especially since the surrender at Yorktown, ablaze with light and filled with noisy, hard-drinking soldiers. Raveneau paused in the taproom, his slate-colored eyes flicking over the crowd. Smoke hung in the air. Gabriel Maupin approached with a pewter mug of cold ale, but Raveneau shook his head.

"You've got your share of women here tonight," he remarked.

Maupin smiled and winked. "They attract the soldiers from other taverns. There are one or two real beauties, if you're of a mind."

"*Dieu, non!*"

"I thought only to ask! No offense, Captain, but it seems that even a man like you could have an occasional unlucky night."

One of Raveneau's black brows slashed down at an angle, but he said nothing.

"Is there something else you wanted, then?"

"As a matter of fact, yes. I crave a word with M'sieur Gadwin. Is he in?"

"Yes, but . . ."

"*Merci.*"

In a few seconds Raveneau had reached Morgan's door. He lifted his hand to knock but stopped short. Someone was laughing softly inside. A female. A surge of pure rage swept over his body and he whispered a string of French epithets.

Behind the door, Morgan was saying, "Dolly, you

are beautiful! You'll never know how much I need you. Oh . . . yes . . ."

Raveneau knocked sharply. "Gadwin, I would like a word with you!"

"Who is it?"

"André Raveneau." It was all he could do to refrain from shouting.

"Oh! Wait! I will be right out."

There was a mad scuffling, then the door opened a few inches to reveal Morgan's chalky face. "A friend of mine—wounded—is sleeping here tonight. I don't want to disturb him." He squeezed himself through the opening and into the hall.

"Perish the thought," Raveneau said. His eyes traveled over Morgan's half-buttoned breeches and inside-out shirt.

"I was just—ah—preparing myself for bed."

"I can imagine. However, I have not come here to discuss your sleeping habits. The wedding plans are firm. The happy event will take place tomorrow at the Raleigh Tavern, in the Apollo Room at two o'clock. I will obtain a suit of clothes for you to wear and will bring it by in the morning. Shall we say nine o'clock? Perhaps you might spare a moment to take tea with me." His face darkened dangerously. "There is a matter that I wish to discuss, but I would not keep you from your bed now."

"Of course," Morgan replied, open-mouthed with surprise. "Yes. Tea."

"Good evening, then. I am certain you are anxious to return to your dreams of Devon."

Chapter Sixteen

———◆———

October 24, 1781

DEVON had never undressed the night before. Sitting wide-eyed in the darkness, she had made her first real decision in what seemed like years. Some other girl might be too cowardly to strike out for herself, she thought repeatedly, *but I have never been a coward. How could I have tortured myself for so long? There is a simple solution. I will leave this place, and, with luck, I'll never see Morgan or André again.*

Watching the moon out her dormer window, she waited for the dawn to come. Her clothes were assembled, rolled into a bundle and tied with a strip of lace from an old chemise. The plan was simple, but it would separate her from Williamsburg and this horrible coil, and tomorrow's problems of survival seemed trivial.

Her conscience stung at the thought of taking the horse Raveneau had purchased in Yorktown, but there was no other solution. Doubtless he would be furious. And Morgan . . . Morgan would be crushed.

There is no other way! her heart cried out, and, as always, she would follow where it led.

I will go to a new town, she thought, *a new colony, and begin life all over again. I can sew, or work in a shop, or perhaps I could teach.*

Lulled by the comfort of her dreams, she tilted her head back against the wing chair and allowed her eyes to close for a moment. When they opened next, the sun had begun to rise.

Devon jumped up, but soon realized that only a miracle would find Raveneau awake at this hour. The past three mornings had not seen him emerge from his chamber until eight o'clock. Wearing breeches under her gown so that she might ride astride if necessary, Devon gathered her lace-bound bundle, slipped into her pelisse, and propped her farewell letter on the bed.

The hall was cool and still, fragrant with aromas of the breakfasts being prepared in the huge kitchen. Devon paused at Raveneau's door only long enough to assure herself that he was not astir, then tiptoed toward the stairway. From the landing she could see that the taproom was deserted except for a flock of servants. Feeling like a criminal, Devon stole down the stairs, smiling stiffly at the young girls who looked up in surprise from their cleaning chores.

Just a few more steps, she assured herself. Holding her bundle under her pelisse, she passed the doorway that led to the dining room when a French-accented voice called out and paralyzed her legs.

"Well, well! It's Devon! Ah, you young brides are all alike. Couldn't sleep, eh?"

Sick at heart, she turned her head to find Raveneau smiling casually at her from a table in the otherwise empty dining room. He sat with a cup of coffee and the *Virginia Gazette,* totally at ease, as though it were his custom to take breakfast at five-thirty in the morning.

"*Eh bien,* come and sit down. We will share the muffins that I smell baking in the kitchen."

Mesmerized by his silvery eyes, she crossed the room and sat down in the chair that he held out for her. When she extracted the bundle of clothing, he set it aside as though it were a loaf of bread, and conversed about her wedding that would take place that afternoon.

Devon felt nauseous, her senses blunted, yet when Raveneau put out a bronzed hand to smooth her uncombed curls, the usual crazy fire shot sparks across her brow.

By one o'clock, the Apollo Room had been cleared. Servants bustled about, cleaning the oak and cherry tables, sweeping the floor, and filling the two huge bowls with Anthony Hay's tastiest punch. Tantalizing aromas suffused the entire building as the food which Raveneau himself had chosen was prepared for the wedding supper.

Clad in a chemise and petticoats, Devon sat upstairs on the edge of her bed, feeling like a rabbit in a trap. She was doomed to endure the torturous day that lay ahead. As for tomorrow . . . that was too much to contemplate.

The same serving girl who had dressed her hair the night of the ball arrived, brandishing the white muslin gown that made Devon look so young. The girl brushed her flame-gold hair while she sat motionless, pale and tense. Step by step, her toilette was effected, until the young girl moved back and let out a pleased sigh.

"Ma'am, you are truly beautiful!"

Devon turned mechanically toward the mirror. Her reflection was lovely. Curls gleamed traitorously against soft and creamy skin. The gown was appropriately simple. Virginal, Devon thought bitterly.

As the servant opened the door to leave, Raveneau stepped in. Devon's heart twisted sharply at the sight of him. He wore a coat of indigo-blue over a white and blue patterned waistcoat and a spotless white shirt and cravat. The devil himself could not have possessed a swarthier complexion or eyes that glinted quite as wickedly.

"Ravissante!" he proclaimed after a brief, critical appraisal. "As pure as winter's first snow."

Devon's nostrils flared as her apathy gave way to burning hatred. "Don't be so smug about what you've done to me." She was thinking of many crimes . . . the foremost of which was this dreaded wedding.

"Smug? I? The truth is, I am extremely penitent about our brief liaison."

"Truth! You wouldn't know truth if it assaulted you!"

Raveneau put a hand to his brow in mock hurt. "You have the tongue of a viper, *petite chatte*. It is a relief to turn you over to the care of a man who is obviously better able to cope with you than I. No, no, save your expressions of gratitude for this." He reached inside his coat to produce a small box which he put into her reluctant hands.

Devon lifted the lid suspiciously. There, nestled in a bed of white velvet, was a wide, sparkling collarette of sapphires and tiny diamonds. It was the most beautiful piece of jewelry she had ever seen.

"I . . . I—" She raised wide, shocked eyes but couldn't coordinate her mouth.

"You approve? *Bon*. Do you know that your eyes are exactly the color of the sapphires? Here, let me fasten it for you."

His warm fingers sent chills down Devon's back as he worked the clasp; then his hands dropped to her shoulders and steered her over to the mirror. She gasped at her reflection. The simple gown had become a backdrop for the beautiful sapphires that encircled her slender neck, emphasizing the color of her eyes and the unique rose fire of her upswept curls.

"I don't know what to say," she whispered.

"Say that you are pleased."

"Of course I am. But I don't see how I can accept this . . ." She wanted to cry. Why had he done this now, just when she was learning to hate him?

"Think of it as a souvenir from your days as the

only woman on the *Black Eagle*. It may comfort you to know that it was purchased with ill-gotten gains."

Morgan was paler than Devon and refused to meet her eyes from the moment she entered the Apollo Room. In the brief space of time before the ceremony commenced, Devon looked at his stricken, averted face and remembered their shared childhood with a pang. That is what we were, she thought . . . children. Those dreams and plans we made were too innocent to be taken seriously. So much has happened to both of us since then . . . too much.

Only Raveneau's cool gray eyes kept her from calling a halt to the entire charade. His determination to see her married was a stronger consideration in Devon's mind than any fear of hurting Morgan. What on earth could *that* mean? Guiltily, she surveyed her nervous-looking husband-to-be, searching her heart for the lost glow of love.

Only Raveneau, Anthony Hay, and Morgan's three favorite drinking companions were present during the ceremony. The parson, who seemed ill at ease and smelled faintly of liquor, read the service in a booming voice, never looking up and barely pausing long enough for Devon and Morgan to make their responses.

Devon didn't care. Somehow the lack of emotion displayed by everyone present helped sustain her. No sooner had the parson intoned, "I now pronounce you husband and wife," than he seemed to disappear into thin air, not even bothering to say goodbye or wish them a happy life.

Well enough, Devon decided, and turned her attention to the steaming, fragrant foods that were assembled on the center table. Morgan stood tensely at her side as Raveneau uncorked a frothy bottle of champagne and filled the crystal goblets provided by Mr. Hay.

"To Devon and Morgan, and their futures." Raveneau smiled.

Devon lifted her glass along with the others and gulped the champagne.

The wedding supper was a meal to remember. There were four kinds of fish, from scalloped oysters to baked halibut topped with tomato slices. A delicious Virginia ham was the centerpiece, surrounded by corn bread, potato rolls, Jerusalem artichokes, bourbon sweet potatoes, greens, and rice. Devon ate with the fervor of someone condemned to hang at dawn, chatting sociably with her new husband and meeting Raveneau's laughing gaze with fiery, challenging eyes. Now that the deed was done, it seemed best to adapt with all the good spirits she could muster. The champagne was an enormous help.

Morgan was spending more time talking to his friends than hovering over her, but after all, there would be more than enough time for hovering later. Devon held out her glass to be refilled twice before the last bite of cheesecake was devoured. While the serving girls were clearing away the dishes, Raveneau stood up, lit a cigar against one long candle, and walked over to a window.

One of Morgan's friends pulled a bundle of cards from his pocket and dealt them. Devon stared in surprise. Morgan hitched his chair closer, smiling nervously at her, then began to assemble the cards that dropped before him.

Devon rose from the table, carrying her glass. "Where is the champagne?" she asked Raveneau.

He obliged by pouring a small amount into her glass, which she drank in one long swallow. She gave him a bright, flirtatious smile. "I've never tasted this before today. I like it immensely!"

"So I've noticed," he replied dryly, then stepped over to speak to Morgan. "There has been a grave omission from these festivities. The bride has not been kissed! May I do the honors?"

Morgan flushed guiltily and nodded. "By all means."

"But—" gulped Devon. Still, she had no desire to deny Raveneau's insolent request.

Smiling, he slipped lean, familiar arms around her and drew her slight body nearer until it was pressed to his. One hand came up her back to hold her head, curls and all, tipping it to the proper angle.

Devon stared into flinty eyes until her heartbeat betrayed her excitement. Slowly his face moved downward until warm lips touched her own, gently at first, then more demandingly. Lightheaded and tingly with champagne, Devon let her mouth part and gave herself to the splendor of his kiss. Just as her arms fluttered at his shoulders, she remembered Morgan and his friends and stiffened. Raveneau lifted his head and released her from his arms.

Devon's face flamed. She wanted to cry, to give herself to mindless sobbing. Unable to look at Morgan, she looked instead at the floor. Raveneau said softly, from far away, "You must be tired. It has been a long day, of course. I have arranged for you and Morgan to use my chamber since it is larger, so why don't you go on to bed? I'll order a bath brought to you."

Devon bathed with nervous haste, certain that Morgan would decide to burst in at any moment. Raveneau's spacious bedchamber was candlelit. The silk sheets and quilts had been neatly turned back on the bed, which loomed ominously in front of Devon's narrow bathtub.

Climbing hurriedly out onto the hooked rug, she rubbed her body with a soft towel and reached for the gown that lay across a chair. Devon had never seen it before. Fashioned of filmy, lace-trimmed peach batiste, it floated sensuously against her naked body.

After blowing out the candles, Devon sat on the edge of the bed and pulled the pins from her hair. She

set them in a pile on the night table, then ran a brush
through her curls, anxious to be safely ensconced between the sheets.

In the silent darkness, Devon grew cold with dread,
while a hard knot of nausea formed in her belly. It
was impossible to think of anything but Morgan; her
mind grew dizzy with a kaleidoscope of memories,
lingering torturously over past kisses and caresses.
She remembered the time in the summerhouse when
Morgan's hand had found its way under her skirt
and up her thigh. She had thrown him off onto the
floor . . . but that would be impossible tonight. This
time, thought Devon, I must welcome his touch and
allow him to do—all the things that Raveneau had
done that night on board the *Black Eagle*.

She shivered with revulsion. The warm glow from
the champagne was gone, replaced by a dull ache in
her head and joints.

Nearly an hour passed as Devon waited. After sitting up most of the night before, she found herself
growing heavy-lidded with fatigue and gratefully let
sleep overtake her. Perhaps, she thought drowsily, he
won't have the nerve to wake me.

Sometime later, Devon opened her eyes in the darkness. The door had clicked shut. Someone had come
into the room. She heard boots drop like gunshots to
the floor; panic flooded her heart. She could dimly see
a shadowy figure disrobing. As soft footsteps approached the bed, Devon lay rigid, her eyes squeezed
shut.

The soft feather tick sagged beside her. She could
feel his eyes on her; then a hand slid beneath the covers to touch her hip. It was a whisper-soft caress; the
silky fabric of her bedgown moved sensuously under
Morgan's fingers. The hand drew the quilts away and
returned to explore her batiste-covered breasts leisurely until the nipples tingled. This was a far cry
from Morgan's clumsy, overeager technique of the

past. Devon could scarcely believe that a hot glow had begun to spread through her loins.

As if sensing this, the astonishingly skillful hand slipped downward, across her belly, blazing a fiery trail over her thigh. The hem located, Devon felt her bedgown lifted and gently removed. She could hear her own labored breathing which seemed to fill the room, but she couldn't bring herself to open her eyes. Surely the sight of Morgan's ghostly, fervent face would break the spell.

Deft fingers caressed the soft triangle where her thighs joined, then gently probed farther, finding the pulsing bud. Devon's hands clenched; she let her legs part and then gasped when firm lips scorched her swelling breasts. Morgan's mouth teased each nipple in turn, gently sucking until Devon felt the heat build and explode deep in her belly as he touched her with magical perception.

She was gasping helplessly when his mouth left her breasts and moved lower, his hands spreading her thighs. Her mind recoiled from what was happening, but her body greedily welcomed his audacity.

Over and over again, Morgan brought her to the fever pitch of desire and sent her plummeting over the edge, shuddering with the searing waves of ecstasy. By the time he moved silently upward, planting burning kisses on her belly and breasts, Devon was weak and shivering. Surrendering, she encircled Morgan's back with her arms, surprised to feel how muscular he seemed. Slowly, smiling contentedly, she opened her eyes.

"Bon soir, petite chatte." Raveneau's silver gaze glinted in the moonlight; white teeth flashed when he smiled.

Utterly stupefied, Devon opened her mouth to speak, but no words would come out. Raveneau solved the problem by covering her parted lips with his own. He turned her easily on her side, pressing her naked body intimately to his hard, warm manhood.

When Raveneau's mouth left hers to explore the curve of her throat, she managed to gasp, "What . . . how . . . you must be mad!"

"Au contraire," he whispered huskily against her ear. His teeth nibbled slowly, gently, at Devon's shoulder, sending goose bumps down her entire arm. "You are glad that it is I who holds you now, rather than Morgan, aren't you?"

Devon searched for his mouth, but he drew back. "Say it."

"Yes. Yes, I'm glad it's you! Glad! Very—" His mouth closed over hers, crushing it pleasurably, demanding a response that she joyfully gave.

Chapter Seventeen

———◆———

October 25-27, 1781

A rosy glow filtered through the draperies and fell upon the canopy bed where Devon lay in André's arms. She opened her eyes slowly. His face was just inches away, but she fought the impulse to touch the wicked scar on his jaw with her lips.

Her body was tender, almost bruised, after a night of passion that seemed unreal. They had devoured each other with a hunger that had remained unsatisfied for hours. Devon blushed, remembering the brazen things she had done and had allowed, even urged, André to do.

Yet she was content. Her emotions defied logic, but somehow it seemed right that she had spent the night struggling happily in André's arms rather than shrinking from Morgan's touch.

But what had happened? What of her marriage to Morgan? Where was he? How could he have allowed Raveneau to usurp his rights as her husband? Could he have drunk too much in his nervousness and passed out?

Muscles flexed against her back as Raveneau stretched handsome brown arms. Devon watched his face tenderly as he yawned and his eyes slowly opened. She gave him a smile, but he didn't return it.

"Good morning," she whispered.

"Is it?"

Devon went cold as she recognized the enigmatic mask he wore. Abruptly, he pulled free of her and swung his long legs over the side of the bed.

"I suppose you are wondering what has become of dear Mervin," he remarked, crossing naked to the washstand.

Devon fought the flame of desire that kindled at the sight of his magnificent body. "I have wondered, yes."

"The wedding was a farce. The parson was a cooper who occasionally acts in plays. His talent is limited, as you may have noticed. As for Morgan—he was persuaded to cooperate for a price." Coolly, he lathered his face and neck and took out his razor. "Your erstwhile fiancé has borne out my suspicions about the reality of love. For all his supposed desire to make you his wife, it would seem that he desired money more."

Devon convulsively reached for the quilts that had been pushed away hours ago. "But . . . why?" she choked.

Raveneau flicked a glance over one broad shoulder as he shaved. "If you imagine that my motive was jealousy or—God forbid!—love, then you may as well revise your thinking. Let us call it an experiment. You both failed—though, of course, the outcome was as I suspected."

Despair, anger, humiliation, burned in Devon's heart. "You devil! How dare you tamper with other people's lives, just to prove your own bitter opinions of love! Maybe I wasn't physically attracted to Morgan, but at least he cared about me and wanted to marry me!"

"True. However, you ran a poor second to one hundred pounds sterling." Raveneau splashed water over his face and neck, then blotted it with a towel.

He returned leisurely to the bed and ripped back the quilts with one swift movement. "And your love for Malcolm, it seems, ran a poor second to your carnal appetites. *N'est-ce pas,* mademoiselle?"

"His name is Mor—" Devon's sobbing protest was lost as Raveneau reached out to pull her roughly to her knees, his hard mouth capturing her own.

After breakfast, Raveneau left the tavern and, to Devon's horror, locked the door to his bedchamber, imprisoning her there. Furious and frustrated, Devon spent the long hours napping and reading the three old copies of the *Virginia Gazette* that lay on the table. Raveneau returned after dark, accompanied by two serving girls carrying steaming, covered dishes.

In spite of everything that he had done, Devon could not repress the thrill that ran through her when he appeared. It did no good to tell herself that she hated him; hate or love, she was caught in a spell of fiery splendor.

Raveneau silently stripped off a fawn jacket and buff waistcoat, watching as the supper was laid out and the wine poured. When the girls were finished, he gave them each a shilling, then reached for his wine. As soon as the door had closed, Devon was on her feet, sapphire eyes flashing. All day long she had rehearsed the things she would say to him, and the speech had swelled to a veritable tirade.

"I have a few things to say to you, Captain Raveneau!"

He glanced up with exaggerated weariness. "Save it, Devon. I am hungry and my patience is minimal. You may eat or sulk, as you choose, but do not scream at me. I will have you put in the stable with the horses."

Devon stiffened from head to toe, seething. Finally she gave in to her own hunger pangs and sat down across from him. "Someday you'll be sorry for the overbearing way you have treated me," she hissed.

"Please! You'll frighten away my appetite!"

Furious, Devon turned her attention to the meal laid out before them. She hadn't eaten since breakfast, and the array of tantalizing aromatic dishes caused her stomach to growl audibly. They ate without exchanging another word, Devon taking every care to pretend he did not exist.

When the last bites of apple tapioca had been eaten, Raveneau lit a thin cigar and sat back in his chair. "Well?"

Meeting his cool, half-amused gaze, Devon felt her temper gather steam and jumped to her feet. *"Well!?* Is that all you can say? You act as if I am slightly mad to take offense after you have rearranged my entire life. I have a perfect right to be angry and to despise you!"

"Absolutely." A hint of a smile flickered at the corner of his mouth and fanned the flame of Devon's outrage.

"Look at you! So smug and confident—and odious! Do I amuse you? Am I your plaything?"

"I do not choose to give the reasons for what I have done. I know that you are relieved to have escaped marriage to Morgan, so this pose of the mistreated victim does little besides bore me."

Devon longed to pummel him, to scratch his face and tear his hair. "I hate you!" she shouted, near tears. "How dare you presume to know what I want or how I feel? Do you suppose that I am such an imbecile that I cannot manage my own life?"

"Not an imbecile, but a female. As for the other— Do you wish that yesterday had ended differently, with Morgan in your bed?" Raveneau perceived her involuntary shudder. "Do you yearn to be sharing this evening's supper with him, as his wife?"

"That is not the point! You don't want me! What am I supposed to do now? Beg Mr. Hay to hire me as a serving girl?"

Raveneau rose soundlessly and crossed to where

she leaned weakly against a bedpost, choking back sobs. He reached out to catch her trembling chin and turned it up; their faces were inches apart. Devon shivered at the angry set of his scarred jaw and the icy silver gleam in his eyes.

"You are wrong, *petite chatte*. I want you very much."

Two days later, Devon accompanied Raveneau when he returned to Yorktown.

She was confused, resentful of him and of herself for responding so helplessly to his touch. They rarely spoke, but at night Raveneau came to bed and reached for her urgently. At first Devon would attempt to lie coldly in his arms, but soon she would be twisting passionately, meeting his kisses with demanding, fiery lips. They slipped outside of time, leaving behind the coolness that existed during the day. Raveneau's hostility would temper to hot-blooded tenderness; Devon could hear the French words of love that he whispered huskily into the flame-gold cloud of her hair. But when morning came, she could not believe that this heartless, withdrawn devil could have possibly said such things.

Never had he seemed so enigmatic, so much a stranger. Devon's secret heart, beating under the mask of her pride, was thrilled to accompany Raveneau. She knew that he couldn't really hate her, or he would have gladly married her off to Morgan. For all his cruel, unfeeling demeanor, he wanted her, and it had to be more than a physical attraction.

At night it was impossible to resist him, but during the day she pretended to despise him. He made it easy, acting so abominably that she felt constantly angry. They never laughed together any more. In fact, Raveneau didn't laugh at all.

They arrived outside Yorktown in midafternoon. The sky was overcast, the air bitingly cold, intensified by a stiff wind that reddened Devon's cheeks and tore any remaining leaves from the trees. October was nearly gone, giving them a preview of the weeks ahead, the bleak limbo between autumn and winter.

Devon sat wearily on her horse while Raveneau made repeated stops to inquire after his crew. She remained stoically silent, determined not to complain or give him the satisfaction of knowing she was miserably uncomfortable.

Eventually they drew up before a huge white house located east of Yorktown, within sight of the water. Raveneau dismounted and handed his horse over to a boy before seeming to recall Devon.

"This house has recently been converted into an inn," he said. "I understand Mrs. Strivingham's husband was killed in the battle at Guilford Court House. Apparently the remaining members of my crew are here, awaiting my arrival, and I'm told that Minter rode in last night, accompanied by Isaac and Azalea."

The prospect of seeing Azalea brought a brilliant smile to Devon's face. Warmth and affection! How she needed a friend . . .

Mrs. Strivingham, a plump, nervous, suspicious-looking woman, gave Raveneau and Devon separate rooms as soon as she determined that they were not married. Devon was relieved to be spared the ordeal of explaining, and Raveneau seemed not to care.

The inn still felt like a home. The parlor had been converted into a genteel taproom and the dining room was crowded with extra chairs, but there remained a profusion of family knickknacks wherever one looked.

Most of the *Black Eagle*'s crew had returned to the privateer, but Mr. Lane, Wheaton, and Treasel had stayed behind to await Raveneau, and they had been joined last night by Minter. The reunion now was a noisy one, aided by frosty jugs of ale.

Everyone seemed surprised to see Devon, but all were happy to know she would be accompanying the ship, except for a disgusted-looking Mr. Lane. Devon gave Minter a kiss and greeted Isaac cheerfully, but reserved her real enthusiasm for Azalea. The two girls hugged, regarded each other, then hugged again. Leaving Isaac to fraternize with the men, they went up to Devon's chamber and chatted while she unpacked and washed away the grime of the road.

"You look wonderful!" Devon exclaimed. "Married life must agree with you. How are your parents?"

"Devon, you goose, it has only been a week since you've seen them! Of course they are fine, and as a bride of two days, I am naturally in heaven. But what I want to know is—what has happened with *you?*"

Cringing, Devon told her everything. The false wedding and the past three days were painfully difficult to explain, but Azalea urged her on.

"Have you been sleeping with André?" she demanded.

Devon hesitated, then nodded. "He tricked me, you see. I thought it was Morgan until I opened my eyes—"

"Oh, Lord, what a fabulous surprise! I would give anything to open *my* eyes some evening and find André on top of *me!*"

"Azalea! You don't mean that!"

"Not really, though a part of me does. I love Isaac, but truth is truth, and to my mind, André in bed is a dream come true. Don't tell me you don't think so!"

"Azalea! The words that come out of your mouth—"

"Well?"

"All right—yes. I love the nights. I've never felt this way in my life or known such excitement was possible."

Azalea nodded triumphantly, dropping into a bow-back chair. "And André? What's he up to? Is he going to make an honest woman of you?"

"No. Are you joking? You said yourself he would never pin himself down." Devon's voice rose bitterly. "He behaves as if I am some curse. He won't tell me

225

why he botched my wedding to Morgan. He just uses me at night and behaves as though I'm a leper during the day. As for the future—I'm as much in the dark as you are."

Exhausted after the trip, Devon lay down on her pencil-post bed and immediately fell asleep. When she awoke, the room was dark. Her stomach protested hungrily, and she slipped into the newly washed sea-green frock and went downstairs.

Supper had already been served. The dining-room table was now covered with cards and coins, ringed by laughing men. Halsey Minter sat beside Isaac Smith, who seemed to be winning and was very pleased about it. There was no sign of Raveneau—or Azalea.

"Azalea went up to look for you a few minutes ago," Minter said. "Strange you didn't see her."

"Where is André?" Devon asked in a small voice.

"He went up after supper to look at the charts Mr. Lane brought."

Filled with dread, Devon hesitated on the stairs but finally forced her legs to move upward. Azalea wouldn't—would she?

Meanwhile, Raveneau and Azalea stood a few feet inside the door to his bedchamber. He poured a glass of claret and handed it to her.

"It's difficult to tell one door from the next," she said. "Mrs. Strivingham really must light the hallway. I hope I didn't disturb you."

"Not at all. You say you were looking for Devon's chamber?"

"Yes. Mmmm . . . this wine is wonderful!"

"Hers is the next one, toward the stairs."

"Oh." Azalea didn't move, but stared longingly at Raveneau over her wine glass.

"You have beautiful eyes, *chérie*. I had almost for-gotten."

Azalea swayed a bit, faint with desire for him. He

was so near, staring at her with the seductive silver eyes she knew only too well. His shirt was open; she yearned to touch the warm, muscular brown chest and run her fingertips through the soft mat of black hair.

"Oh, André . . . I feel so odd."

"Really?" He smiled slightly, one brow arching.

"I . . . will you tell me how you feel about Devon? I do wonder, for her sake—"

A cloud passed over Raveneau's face. Abruptly, he took the wine glass from Azalea and drew her into his arms, her lush curves melting into his taut, lean body. She thought she would collapse; her heart raced frighteningly, loudly. Raveneau looked like Satan himself as he pulled her head back and crushed her lips with his own. It was a burning, demanding, angry kiss, and it left her breathless and trembling.

"André. Oh, André. Please—" It had been so long. He pulled her gown open and her breasts spilled out like ripe, round melons. Then his raven head bent and his lips and tongue captured one swollen, dark rose nipple. "Oh . . ." She began to weep convulsively, can't. No." Shaking, she tried to push him away and feeling the heat grow, achingly, in her loins. "No. I stumbled backward against his bed.

Raveneau's face was tense, menacing. "What the hell is wrong with you?"

Sobbing, Azalea fumbled to adjust her bodice over her lush, quivering breasts. "I mustn't. I thought I could, but I cannot betray Isaac. I must be growing up. It would be wrong. And . . . André, we'd both be betraying Devon!"

"For Christ's sake, what are you babbling about? What does Devon have to do with us?"

In the hallway, Devon leaned weakly against the doorframe. The door was ajar only a crack, but it had been enough for her to hear and see all. Feeling soiled and despicable and sneaky, she walked blindly back to the haven of her own bedchamber, tears rolling down her face.

Azalea was regaining her composure, meeting Raveneau's steely gaze as she refastened her gown. "Devon has a great deal to do with this. You would never have wanted me if I hadn't mentioned her name, so you needn't tell me you don't care. You may not be able to admit your feelings to her or even to me, but the day will come when you must face them yourself." She rose and put a hand up to his dark, chiseled face. "For your sake as well as Devon's, try to overcome your stubborn pride. Darling André, I wish you only the best."

Chapter Eighteen

October 28, 1781

"I'M in love with André," Devon said softly. She lay in bed, wide awake and curled into a tense ball of pain. It was long after midnight, and moonlight streamed in, turning the white sheets and spread to pale blue.

Only love could cause her such deep, paralyzing pain. Only love could make her abandon all pride to be near him and suffer his moodiness. Love forced her to return his kisses in the darkness and lit her up with a golden glow when he came to her. Raveneau was the center of her existence, and the reason was nothing so trivial as physical attraction. *I love him,* her heart said, and sent a fresh stream of hot, acid tears.

The door opened. Without a word, Raveneau set the candle on a table and sat down on the bed, bending to pull off his boots.

Devon lunged. She pulled his gleaming hair and pummeled his wide back ferociously. Raveneau put out an arm, shaking her off as though she were an overplayful kitten. *"Dieu!* What has gotten into *you?"* He peered closer in the shadows and saw the fury in her great sapphire eyes. A twinge of guilt in his gut suggested the reason.

"Get away from me." Devon's voice was poisonously even. "If you touch me, I will kill you."

Raveneau blinked. "I believe you would try at any rate. Women! You're all lunatics. Is it jealousy that's eating at you?"

"Leave my room!" she shrilled.

"Now, Devon, be reasonable—"

She threw herself at him again, clawing at his chest and face until he caught her wrists and pulled her to him. He kissed her, and for one dangerous moment Devon felt herself soften in response. Then she summoned every ounce of strength and bit his tongue, savagely. An astonished Raveneau released her and she slapped him full across the face with all her might. "Son of a bitch! Bastard! Get out of my room!"

His own eyes now flashed silver. He returned her slap, just hard enough to knock a bit of steam out of her, and stalked toward the door. Devon tumbled backward on the bed, but managed to scramble up. Before he reached the door, she seized the pitcher from her washstand and flung it after him. Raveneau deftly sidestepped, and it crashed loudly against the wall.

"I ought to put you over my knee, you murderous little bitch!" He paused, listening with satisfaction to the sudden patter of footsteps downstairs. "I have a feeling that Mrs. Strivingham may be just angry enough to save me the trouble."

"Get out!" Devon screamed. She picked up the washstand basin and brandished it at him, but Raveneau ducked out the doorway before she could throw it. He slammed the door shut behind him.

The privateersmen assembled and breakfasted at dawn. Hearing the commotion, Azalea slipped on her dressing gown and padded out to the hall. Raveneau was at Devon's door, knocking, and Azalea paused, watching curiously. "We are departing," he said tonelessly to the closed door. "I trust you are ready."

Raveneau turned away and saw Azalea. *"Au revoir,*

Madame Smith," he murmured, meeting her as she came forward.

Azalea could see the tension in his jaw, the odd, frosty pain in his gray eyes. She had been right last night, she thought. Somehow André had changed. "How are you today?" she asked gently.

"I am choking on the morality forced down my throat, that's how the hell I am! Any more questions, virtuous lady?"

Azalea stepped backward, her doe eyes wide. "Goodness!" she whispered.

At that moment Devon's door opened and the younger girl appeared, looking pale and worn. She saw Raveneau standing with Azalea, and a sizzling fire lit her blue eyes. She did not speak, but started toward the stairway, shoulders squared.

"Wait, Devon!" Azalea called, and hurried after her. Raveneau brushed by both of them and descended the stairs.

"Please! I—" Azalea began. Then their eyes met straight-on and Azalea's heart wrenched. "Oh. I'm sorry. Oh, Devon."

Devon could not resist the stricken expression on Azalea's face. After all, Azalea had never hidden her feelings for André or her views on physical love. And Devon *had* heard Azalea stop André. She was really only angry at him, and it suddenly seemed foolish to turn away from the only person of whose love she could be certain. The two girls embraced fervently.

"I—I'm so sorry," Azalea faltered. "I could never intentionally hurt you!"

"I know. It's all right. I'm not angry."

"And . . . André?"

Devon drew back, her delicate face hardening. "He doesn't matter." Seeing Treasel looking up expectantly from the entryway, she said hurriedly, "I must go, though God only knows why. I wish I had another choice."

Azalea almost invited Devon to return with her and

Isaac, but then she said, "I have a feeling that your fate lies with him, Devon. Take care. I love you."

"I love you, too. Thank you—and good fortune to you and Isaac."

They hugged again, and Azalea watched her friend quickly descend the stairs and draw up the hood of her pelisse. "Good fortune to you, too, Devon!" she called as Raveneau opened the front door, letting in a blast of frosty mist to greet the band of privateers-men.

The *Black Eagle* felt like an old friend. Devon was happy to see it, and somehow she felt that the privateer returned her affection. The crewmen cheered when they sighted Raveneau's party on the shore. They were as eager to set sail after weeks away from the ocean as their captain. He boarded and greeted his men, a brilliant smile transforming his dangerous-looking face. He walked about and surveyed his privateer, stroking the sleek wood, the mahogany masts, the gleaming brass fittings. He had returned to his private kingdom.

Halsey Minter calmly took Devon's arm and led her toward the hatch. "You must be yearning for a bit of rest," he suggested.

Devon sighed tensely. "It is hard to say just what I yearn for right now."

"Well, I'll get you settled in and then you can think it over. Perhaps a hot meal might help."

"Perhaps." The familiar gangway warmed her heart. It was good to be back.

Minter opened the door to the captain's cabin and carried her things inside. Devon stopped short. "Wait. Just wait! You can't mean to put me here? Have you spoken to Captain Raveneau today?"

Blushing, Minter said, "Yes. In fact, he made a special point of telling me that these would be your quarters."

"Oh! That overbearing, uncivilized—"

Devon broke off at the sight of Raveneau filling the doorway with his forbidding presence. Minter glanced nervously from one to the other, but his dilemma was solved when his captain said, "That will be all, Minter. I would like a bath, a mug of cold ale, and the best beefsteak on board in half an hour."

Minter nodded and dashed out gratefully, pulling the door shut.

"You arrogant tyrant! What is the meaning of this?" Devon demanded. "If you imagine that I will share your bed *now,* either you are a fool or you believe that I am—and I assure you that the latter is not the case!"

"Devon, my spoiled child-bitch, you flatter yourself. You are more than free to retire to the crew's quarters at any time. Or you may sleep here on the floor." He sat down on the bed and proceeded to pull off his boots. "Or you may jump overboard. Or you may leave the boat and go to Yorktown. I really don't care." Unbuttoning his shirt, he glanced up and added, *"Or* you can stop pouting like a child and allow yourself to enjoy the warmth of my bed. We both know you want to."

Devon's heart was pounding, but she managed to curl her lip disdainfully. "Your conceit is unparalleled, Captain. I would sooner sleep with a snake!"

Raveneau put his dark head back and shouted with laughter. "Mademoiselle, that is without a doubt the most ridiculous pronouncement you have made yet!"

Raveneau paid no further attention to Devon during their first day at sea. He appeared in the cabin only long enough to remove something from his desk or bittacle, or to bolt down a portion of the meal Minter had laid out for him.

Devon lay down on a pile of blankets on the hard cabin floor early that evening. However, sleep was as elusive as it had been the night before at the inn. Moonlight streamed through the transom, lazy waves slapped the hull, and Raveneau was shouting impatiently on deck. Finally she jumped up irritably and stalked over to the neatly made bed on which Raveneau had ended her girlhood only a few weeks before. The tick was cool and deep; the soft pillows retained his arousing scent.

Devon stretched elaborately, yawning, and snuggled down.

An hour later, she was still awake. Something was amiss. There were muted voices above, mingling with a flurry of footsteps. Devon quickly slipped out of bed and drew on a pair of breeches over her bedgown, tucking the cambric garment into the waistband.

The gangway was eerily quiet, its polished lanterns bobbing, sending dancing orbs of light along the bulkheads. Devon padded toward the hatch and ascended to the gun deck. The gun crews were in position, standing by their cannon. Devon flattened herself against the dark curve of the mainmast.

On the quarter-deck, André Raveneau tensed, peering into the pale mist that hung from the night sky like a curtain. Minter stood beside him, the captain's heavy peacoat in his hands.

"Do you see anything, sir?" Minter inquired hesitantly.

"No, damn it, but I don't need to. It's too late to switch flags. They've seen us and are in pursuit."

Minter helped Raveneau into the coat. "Sir, I cannot even *hear* anything!"

"Look, Minter, the damned ship is *there* and I don't wish to argue the point!"

The two men stood together uneasily. When Raveneau moved at last, rubbing the back of his neck, Minter said, "Well, I'll leave you alone, then, sir. If there is—"

"No, wait." Raveneau glanced down with studied detachment, but Minter recognized the silver flame in his eyes. "Ah . . . I've been wondering about Devon. Do you think she is well?"

Minter was hard pressed to hide his astonishment. What could *this* mean? "As a matter of fact, Captain, I don't think Devon is well."

"What do you mean?"

"I think she is hurting."

Raveneau wished he had never begun this conversation. "Oh? What ails her?"

"If you'll pardon me for saying so—you, sir. You've hurt her deeply and I think it's a terrible thing. Devon's young and eager, and if you don't stop you'll kill all that fresh sweetness. Glare at me if you like, Captain, but I'm determined to speak. I say that you should treat Devon properly or let her go to someone who will!" Minter drew himself up to his full height. "Good night, sir. Call if you need me. I am going below."

The ship bustled with quiet activity. All hands had been called on deck and excitement charged the air. Across the deck, Devon heard one lusty-looking seaman chortle, "Aye, it's been too long! We all need a bloody good fight!"

Devon crept behind a heavy coil of rope in an out-of-the-way corner. She waited, listening, determined not to miss the action this time. Part of her welcomed the prospect of reckless danger, a dramatic distraction for her aching heart.

Time passed slowly, then all at once there was a great deal of noise. On the quarter-deck, Raveneau shouted, "Lane! See to the boarding nets! Now!" He turned to Wheaton, white teeth flashing in a face that could have been the devil's own. "Ha! Do you see her? The monster is a first-rate frigate! Perfect. She thinks to snap us up like a fish for dinner!" He laughed harshly. "I love surprises, don't you, Wheaton?"

The old man grinned in response, feeling Raveneau's fire. A night to remember, by God! If anyone could do it, this Frenchie was the man!

Raveneau snapped orders like gunshots. The *Black*

Eagle paced herself gracefully, moving to leeward as she sailed. Raveneau watched the approaching enemy with sharp silver eyes that seemed to cut through the night fog. When the *Black Eagle* was exactly two ship-lengths ahead, he gave the order to shiver the sails, and instantly the sheets of white canvas were laid flat against the masts, spilling the wind.

The *Black Eagle* swerved abruptly to starboard, directly in the path of the British frigate. The two ships collided, wood splintered, and the *Black Eagle* shuddered violently.

The frigate found her bowsprit and jib gear hopelessly tangled in the privateer's foremast and in the shrouds which ran from the masthead to the *Black Eagle*'s sides. It was impossible for the British to board over their own bowsprit and through the nets which Raveneau had ordered put up.

The *Black Eagle* fired her starboard guns, raking the length of the frigate's decks. The British armed their swivel guns and fought back, but sharp-shooting riflemen aboard the privateer were able to pick off the gun crews.

The privateer's crew was amazingly well trained. Even in her heart-stopping fear Devon noticed the expert, unwasted movements of the men. They seemed to enjoy themselves, whooping when a particularly fine shot found its mark.

No one noticed Devon. Even Raveneau, springing across the deck, shouting staccato orders, failed to see her. Treasel appeared with Minter by his side and combed the deck for wounded men. When they approached the hatch carrying the first casualty, Devon took one look at the young seaman's bloody leg and shook off her panic. "Minter! Let me help!"

There was no time for surprise at her presence, or for scolding. "Stay low and scout around for the worst hurt," Treasel ordered.

Devon lost herself in the pandemonium. Between searches for wounded men, she helped to hand stinkpots up to the main tree on the mast, where they were lit and hurled down to the enemy's decks. She unpacked rifles from the arms chest and passed them out to men with empty hands. All around, shots passed her in the night.

Then Mr. Lane began to scream hysterically that there was no more ammunition. Devon, crouching beside an injured gunner's mate with Minter, cried, "Oh, Minter, did you hear? Does this mean we're beaten?"

"Captain Raveneau'd never allow it," the gunner's mate answered, gritting his teeth against the pain of his shattered shoulder.

"All hands collect every crowbar, bayonet, any metal!" Raveneau bellowed. "Pack those gun muzzles —*now!*"

Devon leaped to her feet to join in and collided head-on with Raveneau as he strode toward her. Rough hands caught her forearms and steely eyes cut through the darkness.

"—*Mon Dieu!* You lunatic! What the hell are you up to now?"

Devon tried to shake free. Her bedgown, so hastily stuffed into the breeches, was streaked with powder and spattered with blood. Her face was smudged, framed by tangled curls and highlighted by glowing, sapphire-blue eyes. "Captain, if you want to save your ship, kindly unhand me so that we both can join in the effort!"

Astounded, he let her go, watching as she dashed across the deck toward the hatch where crowbars were being passed up from the hold.

Then one of the enemy succeeded in hitting the man who had been hurling the stinkpots from the platform above. He toppled forward and fell to the deck only a few feet away from Devon. Horrified, she nevertheless saw what needed to be done. She instantly started for the mast and clambered up the ratlines. A ball whistled by a short distance away, but she kept on going until she reached the platform.

There were only three stinkpots left beside a tarnished, flickering lantern.

"Devon!" a familiar voice thundered. "I could strangle you! Lie down and don't move!"

But Devon lit the stinkpot, held it over her head, and threw it toward the frigate with every ounce of her strength. "Leave me alone!" she called down to the furious Raveneau.

A string of evil-sounding French words met her; then, as Devon lit the second stinkpot, she saw him start up the ratlines.

"If you must come, bring some more of these!" she shouted.

In moments, Raveneau was on the platform, dropping his armload of stinkpots before pulling Devon flat against the planks. "For Christ's sake, *imbecile*, will you stay *down?!*"

Splintery wood scraped her cheek and she felt Raveneau's hand on her neck like a steel band. "Unhand me!" she ground out, eyes flashing. "I can fight just like the rest of your crew. I want to help!" Pinned to the platform, she could see nothing but the corner of the lantern and Raveneau's dark, cut-stone visage. Abruptly, he released her and reached for a stinkpot. Devon scrambled up to grab the lantern and bring it over to light the noxious missile. By the time Raveneau had thrown the last one, all the crowbars and other sundry weapons had been thrust into the cannon.

"We are ready, Captain!" shouted Mr. Lane.

"Mon Dieu—fire!" was Raveneau's reply. He held Devon down again, but the two of them peered over the edge of the platform, watching as the metal exploded from the cannon, sweeping the frigate's decks clear, making hash of anyone who stood in the way. Even the men on the *Black Eagle* seemed stunned by their success. They stood staring, mouths agape, then turned in unison to seek out their captain.

"Nothin' for it," declared a burly boatswain's mate. " 'E's bloody charmed!"

"Devil's fortune," muttered another in disbelief.

Grasping Devon's elbow, Raveneau thrust her forward. "Go on!" The ratlines burned her bare feet, but she descended as nimbly as a cat, landing on the deck only an instant before Raveneau.

Wheaton shouted, loud enough to be heard over the rumbling voices, "Men! I give you the finest captain on any sea!"

Devon, dazed and ebullient all at once, looked up into Raveneau's chiseled face. He regarded his worshipful men with a flickering smile, and his eyes crinkled at the corners before he glanced down and saw Devon, dirty and bloody and brave.

As Raveneau's arms caught her up and locked her body against his own, she felt her heart swell and ache with bittersweet love.

Chapter Nineteen

October 29-November 4, 1781

DAWN was breaking by the time Raveneau finished his work. Despite his urging, Devon had not been able to bring herself to leave him. The two ships had been separated and most of the *Black Eagle*'s huge crew transferred to the frigate. The captain and top officers had been hustled on board the privateer and locked in the gloomy brig. The frigate had carried no cargo, but such a fine warship was prize enough.

The cook appeared with breakfast, and before taking Devon below, Raveneau drank a mug of strong, rich coffee, sharing it with the tattered, flame-haired waif at his side. Then he held her close as they descended to the berth deck.

"Your feet!" Raveneau exclaimed, noticing her shoeless state for the first time as he helped her climb through the hatch. Her tiny feet were filthy, badly cut, and spattered with the blood of dozens of men.

Devon looked down, surprised. "Do you know that I'd forgotten? Hmmm. Do you suppose we shall ever be clean again?"

Raveneau rubbed his eyes with long, blackened fingers and smiled. "Perhaps if we endeavor to help each other, a memorable bath might be effected."

Devon saw the wicked gleam in his eyes and laughed with uninhibited joy.

The rest of their week at sea was tranquil. Raveneau, after taking such a magnificent prize, was more relaxed than Devon had ever seen him. She asked only once where they were bound. Raveneau mysteriously declined to answer and she was not particularly curious. She almost wished they could stay at sea forever. She and Raveneau spent long, luxurious hours in bed together. Devon learned to respond to a man's caress with such heightened sensation that it approached pain. Total ecstasy. Sweet, sweet love. And in the night, André held her close while he slept, her face burrowed in the warm, brown expanse of his chest, her delicate legs entwined with his long, muscular ones. Happiness threatened to burst her heart.

It was true that he never spoke of love or what lay ahead for them, but Devon couldn't let that upset her contentment. She was beginning to believe that tomorrow would take care of itself if she made the most of today.

On the seventh morning, Devon woke and reached for André, only to find him gone. She sat up in bed. Only the barest smoky-pink glow tinted the sky; André had not risen so early in all their days at sea. She had lacked appetite for days, but now a sickening vise of nausea squeezed inside her. Somehow she knew that the idyll had ended.

Woodenly, Devon rose. Her cheeks were pale when she looked in Raveneau's shaving mirror. She put on her sea-green gown and sat down in the red wing chair to brush her curls with special care.

Finally satisfied, she left the cabin and made her way to the open deck above. The privateer was still quiet; snores rumbled down the gangway from the crew's quarters. The captain was on the quarter-deck, leaning on the rail, watching the sun rise over the ocean. The sight of André could still stop her heart,

Devon thought, as surely as when she had been a child, colliding with him on New London's waterfront.

She went up to him, smiling when he turned, his eyes registering only momentary surprise. *"Bon matin, petite chatte,"* he said in a low voice. He took off his peacoat and put it around her, then pulled her against his body. They kissed, leisurely. Devon tried to keep the flame from igniting, but it was no use, and the fire of happy desire burned away her discontent.

"I am surprised to see you up so early," he murmured, kissing her ear and sending shivers down her back.

"I woke to find you gone," Devon admitted as she leaned back to study his face. He was in good spirits; his next words came as no surprise.

"We are nearly there."

"Where?"

"My home." He smiled at her widening blue eyes and shrugged. "Well, as near a home on land as I can claim. It is an island."

"André, won't you tell me what your plans are? You have kept me docile these past days—using quite underhanded tactics, I might add—but it can't go on forever. I am not part of your cargo. I have feelings and opinions."

Raveneau gazed down at her earnest face, memorizing it with the coral-hued sea as its backdrop. Her blazing blue eyes with their sooty lashes were so expressive, and he had come to realize how strongly his own heart responded to the emotions mirrored in them. Lovely red-gold cloud of curls, scent of hyacinths, delicate nose and willful, kissable mouth, pert, rose-tipped breasts.

"You are telling *me* that you have opinions?" He laughed gently. "Sweet Devon, I know that better than anyone. Do you imagine that I thought to transform you with my lovemaking?" He framed her face with his sun-browned hands and bent to kiss her.

"You are sounding like a typical Frenchman!"

"I see! You prefer me as a wicked pirate?" He raised an eyebrow and grinned devilishly, drawing the laughter he wanted.

"You are in a fine mood today, Captain."

"True. I am. It is always a pleasure for me to come home."

"Which is?" Devon nudged him with an elbow.

"All right! You needn't use physical force. My home is a tiny island east of Virginia, nearly one-third of the way to Bermuda, but for personal reasons I cannot divulge more than that. It is seldom encountered by other ships, since it is not located on any commonly used trade routes. My father came here over forty years ago and claimed it; it has been ours ever since. When he died in late 1775, it became mine."

"Please, do tell me the entire story. I really am curious."

"No doubt!" His mouth quirked in the way she loved. "There is not much to tell. My father was a French nobleman, but he loved the sea. My mother quarreled with him but found it difficult to resist him when he returned to France, for all her protestations of hatred. Three times he took me with him to this island where he had built his home. It took ten years to complete; he had to import a huge crew of workmen and all the building materials."

Devon was thinking of his mother—suffering as Deborah had, unable to compete with so alluring a mistress as the sea. She watched Raveneau as he looked out at the indigo-blue waves, and her heart ached unbearably.

"At any rate, I've kept the island and staffed the house, and now I come back whenever time permits ... though that is not often."

"And when you *are* home?" Devon managed to get out.

"I can read your thoughts, my dear. You are right.

When I am home I enjoy it for a short while, then I long for the sea. I love my ship the best . . . it is impossible to explain."

Devon tried to swallow the lump in her throat. "I understand."

She prayed for an end to the conversation, leaning into his chest with its familiar warmth and scent and hard planes. Safety . . . contentment . . . for how long?

At midmorning, when the *Black Eagle* reached Secret Island, as Devon had silently dubbed it, the truth came out.

"You'll stay here, Devon, until I can return," André said. "As you know, the frigate has been taken ahead, so I can only stay long enough to complete repairs on the *Black Eagle*. Winters are severe at sea . . . you'll be safe here until spring."

Wheaton and his boatswain's mate were at the wheel, Lane was examining the charts, while the rigging was alive with men. It wouldn't be long now.

Devon stood near the bow with Raveneau, fighting tears, away from most of the chaos. *Safe!* That was the word he had used. Didn't he know that he was the source of all her safety? He must be aware that I love the sea, too, she thought. But to say these things aloud would sound like pleading, and she couldn't bear that.

"Fine!" Devon heard her voice, brittle and cheerful, from a distance. "When spring comes, we'll find a real solution."

Raveneau looked down at her sharply, scrutinizing her profile as she pretended to study the sea. Their minds and hearts suddenly were farther apart than ever.

The island was incredible. Almost against her will, Devon warmed to it, to the lush jungle that crowded twisted pathways, to the wild, isolated beaches, but most of all to the huge, almost vulgarly ornate house that Raveneau's father had built.

House! Devon thought. "Castle" would more accurately describe it. Set on a hill in the center of the island, it was built square with sculptured turrets. Inside, the house was a marvel of lofty proportions, marble panels and carving, tapestries, wood, glass, and mirrors. The gilt furniture was ornamented with nymphs, shells, and sphinxes. Raveneau, during the tour he gave her of the house, pointed out many fine pieces which had been part of captured cargo.

It seemed like the ultimate fantasy—a secret island belonging to the most dashing pirate-patriot, complete with a castle which could have been lifted from a sumptuous fairy tale. Devon wandered speechlessly through the rooms.

As they mounted the white marble stairway that would lead them to the bedchambers, Raveneau observed Devon. Her reaction to the house was surprising; somehow he had hoped that she would mock it and insist that she preferred the warm, paneled cabin they had shared on the *Black Eagle*. The awe-struck expression she wore hurt and disillusioned him. Cynicism came easily—hadn't he told himself all along that all women were alike?

The bedchamber which Raveneau announced would be hers left Devon utterly spellbound. Just standing on the thick rose carpet decorated with swirling pale green vines made her feel like a princess. The large windows opened to a breathtaking view of lush greenery, rocky cliffs, ribbonlike beaches, crashing white waves and an expanse of blue ocean.

A towering, intricately carved canopy bed dominated the room. It was hung with rose, green, and gold tapestry and covered with a counterpane of luxurious rose velour. Near the marble fireplace there was an intimate seating group that consisted of a long chaise, two gilt chairs, a curved sofa, and three ottomans.

"Oh, André . . ." Devon's voice sounded far away,

a sigh of pure pleasure. She turned dreamily to find him leaning against the doorframe, glaring. "I never imagined such a place could truly exist! In my mind I used to make up—" The expression on his face made her stop.

"I am so pleased that you approve, mademoiselle," Raveneau replied coldly. He slowly crossed the room to gaze moodily out a window. "You aren't curious about this chamber? Its former occupants? The star boarder was my father's mistress, who lived on this island for twenty years. What a woman! She turned my cool, adventurous father into a besotted idiot. She played with him like a cat with a mouse. Everyone could see her for what she was but *mon cher papa*. It was Véronique who persuaded him to build this outrageous palace. She nagged him night and day for more money—the marble stairs were her major victory. She refused—" Raveneau broke off. He stared out at the ocean and pressed a fist to his brow. "At any rate, sweet Devon, it would seem that you and this house were meant for each other. However, it would be a mistake for you to imagine that it is a gift. As the owner, I shall determine your method of payment."

Devon's sapphire eyes were stricken and confused as she watched him turn and walk toward her. The playful lover she had known at sea was dead, replaced by a man who moved like a stalking panther, his harsh face more dangerous-looking than she had ever seen it before. When they were standing face to face, Raveneau reached out to capture her bare arms with painfully powerful hands. His mouth covered Devon's, searing and cruel, lighting a fire in her loins but scorching her heart.

Her brain cried silently against the scene being played out, but Devon was lost to the fierce chemistry that exploded whenever he touched her. The savagery of his attack somehow seemed to heighten her own fever pitch. She clung dazedly to his broad shoulders and pressed herself closer, hungering for him.

In minutes they were naked, twisting together on the priceless velour counterpane; bronzed, muscular length and peach-soft, frenzied fragility. There was nothing gentle or tender in the way they treated each other. Their kisses were bruising, and each devoured the other's body without regard to past shyness or the white-gold sunlight that flooded the bed. At last they met, joining feverishly, moving together until the end came in a burst of silver fire.

"M'sieur Raveneau?"

Through a dense fog Devon heard the tapping. She lay with André, their sleeping bodies tightly fitted together. Silk sheets. With an effort, she opened her eyes and saw him watching her from only inches away. For a long minute they remained thus, measuring each other.

"We . . . slept?" she whispered.

Raveneau smiled, slightly taunting. "How could we not?"

Devon felt a sudden, humiliated blush begin in her breasts and rush upward, heating her face. André had taken her over and over again with a ruthless fervor that she had matched. Every muscle in her body ached. How could I have behaved so . . . wantonly? she wondered.

It was puzzling—the difference between this fierce, caustic Raveneau and the relaxed, tender lover she had grown to trust on the *Black Eagle*. Did this island work some sort of dangerous magic on him? Underneath the confusing tangle of her thoughts crouched the most fearful question of all. After last night, was there any possibility that André could learn to love her? At this moment, even his respect seemed beyond her grasp.

The tapping began again. *"Attendez!"* Raveneau shouted, getting out of bed to search for his breeches.

They trailed across the rug beside the chaise, at the other side of the room. Devon watched the play of muscles over his golden-brown body as he stalked over and pulled them on. Then, to her horrified embarrassment, he threw open the door and waved a stranger into the bedchamber.

"A thousand pardons, m'sieur!" the man exclaimed, instantly averting his eyes from the bed. "I did not know—"

"Like hell," Raveneau muttered. He made a sweeping motion with his hand, mocking them both. "Bernard Souchet, allow me to present Mademoiselle Devon Lindsay, who will be occupying this room for the next few months. Devon, this is the gentleman who manages the house. He is the voice of authority in my absence."

Souchet appeared to be around forty-five years of age, of less than medium height with a thickening waist. He wore a white wig with side curls and a splendid green brocade coat over a gold satin waistcoat. He cleared his throat nervously and said, without looking at Devon, "I am honored to make your acquaintance, Mademoiselle Lindsay. It will be a pleasure to have you here."

Sick with embarrassment, Devon looked over the covers and replied, "Thank you, Mr. Souchet."

"I would not have bothered you, sir, but since you have been in the house for more than six hours, I thought perhaps you might have need of my assistance in some way. The cook has been wondering . . ."

"Yes. Feed the crew. Let them come to the house to eat and get out a few bottles of rum. Mademoiselle Lindsay and I would like a hot bath and a chilled bottle of champagne. We will eat here in two hours, and you may have a table and chairs brought in. See that the fire is lit."

"As you wish, m'sieur." Souchet bowed and began to back out.

Raveneau added, "Incidentally, I will be using this

chamber during my stay. Ask my steward to bring my things here."

Souchet opened his mouth as if to protest. Then he nodded, and left.

Chapter Twenty

———◆———

November 9, 1781

FIVE days slipped away until the day the *Black Eagle* was scheduled to sail.

André and Devon had spoken little, but had clung together violently, all their pent-up emotions exploding in turbulent, often desperate lovemaking. Out of bed, Raveneau remained icily cold, and Devon's confusion and humiliation grew.

The last day, Raveneau awoke first and stared at the bed which had belonged to Véronique, the scheming bitch who had made a fool of his father. When he turned to look at Devon, knowing it was the last time they would awaken together, he found it more difficult than usual to believe her a scheming bitch as well. Frothy curls, the color of the sunrise, trailed across his chest. Her face nestled in the hollow of his shoulder. Deceptive innocence! he reminded himself, gazing at her soft, parted lips, tilted nose, and thick lashes. One bare breast peeped enticingly from the covers.

A voice in the corner of his brain declared, "You will miss her!" Raveneau silenced it by turning his hard body toward the supple warmth of hers, embracing her roughly, kissing her awake. For a moment she was limp, then stiffened in the token resistance he had come to expect. When he pushed her deep into the silk pillows and let her feel the strength of his desire, her slender arms came up to grip his back, nails cutting into sun-browned muscles as she feverishly answered his kiss.

Devon watched Raveneau the entire day, and it was impossible for him not to notice. She joked and laughed, but her sapphire eyes swam with sorrow, and though he doubted its authenticity, he still could not muster his usual coolness.

Just a few more hours, Raveneau told himself. By evening, his existence would be simple once more; he would know exactly who he was and how he should react at sea. And in port he would go to luscious, uncomplicated Isabelle, who would welcome him with open arms.

As Devon smiled at him across the breakfast table, Raveneau silently cursed Noah Jackson for having found her. Until that September day, he had never wavered or wondered in all his adult life. He was escaping not a moment too soon. One more day might find him mooning in her wake just as his usually sane father had with Véronique.

Minter was there to see to Raveneau's belongings. Everything he needed would be returned to his cabin without the slightest effort on his part. Mr. Lane was completely in charge on board the *Black Eagle,* full of himself and his responsibility.

Picking up his coffee cup, Raveneau moved to look out the huge windows, appraising the efficient action on the island and his ship, then turned to Devon. She wore the white muslin gown she had been "married" in. Her luxuriant hair was freshly washed and worn loose, inviting his touch. She sat on the edge of the gilt chair and looked up at him, her expression poignant with hope and longing. Something inside Raveneau crumbled and he said, "I would enjoy a long walk today. Would you care to join me? We might steal some wine and food from the kitchen and have our noon meal on the far beach."

Devon swallowed visibly, fighting the urge to shriek with glee and throw herself into his arms. Her joy showed itself in a heart-melting smile. "Oh . . . I think that is a magnificent idea!"

"Well, then, get up!" He smiled back, sending a hot shiver through her breast, and put out a tanned hand to assist her. Devon thought she would collapse with happiness when he slipped an arm around her, leading her off toward the stairs and one last bright adventure.

It was only a few hours away from the misunderstandings that divided their hearts, but this was a day that Devon would contemplate often in the months to come.

Raveneau held her hand as they walked, explaining the island's vegetation and rock formations and even allowing her a few lighthearted reminiscences of their colorful past. On the beach, at the opposite end of the island from the *Black Eagle,* Devon lay back against his chest as she sipped wine and recalled the times she had stared after him as a child.

"Are you serious?" Raveneau exclaimed, wishing he could believe she was as guileless as she seemed.

"Of course I am!" Devon laughed, remembering that he had forgotten their first kiss in Nick's carriage. "I thought that you were wonderfully dangerous. Totally disreputable."

"And now?" His arm closed tightly around her back, turning her body.

"My opinion has not altered."

"Nor mine of you, *petite chatte.* The first time I saw you, I knew you would bring nothing but trouble."

He reached up to slip his fingers into her hair and bring her face closer. They kissed, their lips scarcely touching, yet a searing flame shot through Devon's body and found its mark.

"I have never known a female like you," Raveneau whispered, watching her face.

"Really?" Devon was horrified to feel tears scald her eyes and hastily moved from his gaze, back to the sheltering shoulder. "I suppose I must seem unbearably drab, but then one must make do."

"Please! No plays for flattery. I hope we are beyond that."

Gulping back tears, Devon sat up and announced, "I am famished!"

They ate slowly, chatting about the war, General Washington, the French fleet, and the island again. The future was a taboo subject. Devon watched André, not tasting her food but memorizing every chiseled line of his face, the special silver-gray of his eyes, the magic brilliance of his sudden smiles, the contours of his bronzed, powerful body. In a plain linen shirt, biscuit breeches, and knee boots, he was more attractive than anyone she had ever seen in formal garb.

After pouring the last of the wine into Devon's glass, Raveneau slipped out a pocket watch and glanced at it. "It is getting late."

"Yes. Of course." She wanted to cry, to have him hold her while she poured out every hidden feeling. There were so many things that needed to be said. But Devon knew they would have to remain locked in her heart, at least through the winter.

Together, they replaced plates, bowls, napkins, glasses, and cutlery in the wicker basket that the cook had supplied. Then Raveneau sat back on his heels and looked hard at Devon's flushed face. He struggled with a powerful desire to let his heart go, but, as always, he remembered the lesson of his father and Véronique in time to save himself.

"Should we start back?" Devon asked, knotting the end of her sash with nervous fingers.

"Ah . . . no. No, we have a bit of time." His hand reached to capture her own, and suddenly they were kneeling face to face, his arms encircling her waist. "Devon, I—"

Raveneau groped for words, but, finding none, he pulled Devon against him more roughly than he had intended and covered her soft, wine-sweet lips with his mouth. Both of them were hungry now in a different, more urgent way. Eyes locked, they undressed each other in the sandy sunlight and touched slowly, savoring every caress. Raveneau's lips scorched her shoulders and tender breasts as she closed her eyes and moaned aloud.

Finally, he lay back in the sand and pulled Devon over his narrow hips, filling her eager body with his hard, pulsing shaft of desire. As she rode him, her head thrown back in the salt breeze, his flaming silver eyes committed the picture she made to memory.

After returning a disheveled Devon to the house, Raveneau went aboard the *Black Eagle,* promising that he would send Minter to fetch her when they were ready to sail.

In less than half an hour, the steward was at her door. Devon had hurriedly changed her gown and washed away most of the sand that had caked her entire body. When Minter knocked, she had just begun to brush her tangled curls.

"Minter? Come in."

He stood in the doorway and gave her a sad smile. "I'm sorry."

"I am, too." She walked to the window and stared out at the ocean, her rival.

"I know that you can't be looking forward to winter here alone, but if it is any consolation, I will do what I can to steer the captain's heart in the right direction during your separation."

Devon's stomach was knotted and each breath an effort. "Thank you. You know, I feel so helpless! Part of me wants to tell him off; he has no right to treat me as he does, and I shouldn't allow it. But,

Minter . . ." Her face crumpled and she pressed a hand convulsively to her mouth. "I am such a coward these days. I am frightened that anything I might say or do would tip the balance against me. At least now I can cling to the hope that spring will bring us together, but if I ever truly lost him I believe I would die. This love is torment!"

"Now, it must have its good points! Please—I hate to see you cry! Do cling to that hope. I have a feeling here"—he pointed to his chest—"that all will be well. Captain Raveneau is not an ordinary man; he rebels against domesticity like a wild animal. He is suspicious. He has never needed anyone before, that I know of. It has always been the other way around."

"It would seem that his childhood was not very loving," Devon allowed, comforted by Minter's logic.

"There, you see? And you must realize that so many years of damage cannot be undone overnight." The question was, he brooded silently, was it possible for the captain to *ever* love Devon as she deserved to be loved?

After a brief sigh, Minter forced his widest grin. "I knew you would be lonely, so I asked Captain Raveneau if I might select a maid for you among the serving girls—one who might also provide some agreeable companionship. I found a girl you should adore. Her name is Elsa, and she will be waiting when you return from the beach."

"Oh, thank you! How shall I manage without you?" She touched his tousled red hair affectionately. "You have been a wonderful friend . . . I will miss you."

"And I will miss you." He was blushing like a schoolboy. "You may trust me to continue as your friend in the months to come. I shall watch over the captain for you as best I can."

Devon kissed his cheek and accepted his handkerchief to wipe away her tears. "Well, I know we should go. A long delay on my part will only anger André, and I don't want that. Not today."

*   *   *

Devon's heart began to pound the moment she glimpsed Raveneau coming up the tree-choked path from the beach to meet them. He was so magnificent —tall, broad-shouldered, striding with powerful grace, the hard muscles in his thighs visible under his breeches as he neared. Rapier-sharp silver eyes met Devon's, revealing none of his feelings.

Minter mumbled a hasty farewell and left them alone. In the distance, a chorus of deep voices could be heard from the privateer, along with clattering footsteps on the decks and squeaking groans from the yardarms.

"Is there anything you require?" Raveneau asked, distantly polite. "I have instructed Souchet to see to your every need; you are to be treated as a member of my family, with every courtesy. I have told him to give you total access to the entire house and also to the storerooms. I want you to choose anything you see that strikes your fancy, especially fabric for gowns. Make as many as you like. The serving girls will help.

"Enjoy the island, but have a care. The cliffs are treacherous. Also—" He broke off as he realized Devon's shoulders were shaking. Almost apprehensively, he enfolded her in his strong embrace, feeling wet warmth soak through the linen shirt he wore. She wept silently against his broad chest, her heart splintering.

"Devon—"

Had his voice caught? She lifted her tear-stained face in wonder.

"I—" A muscle moved along the scar on his jaw.

"Oh, m'sieur! *Padonnez-moi!*" Souchet exclaimed, standing behind them on the path. "I was only going to the beach to bid you a last farewell. Please excuse my interruption."

Raveneau sighed harshly. "No, that's all right, Souchet. We were just going down ourselves." He put out a hand to smooth Devon's damp cheeks, then shifted it to her waist as they started toward the beach.

Souchet followed along, even hovering nearby as Raveneau pressed a last, searing kiss on Devon's trembling mouth.

"Take care, *petite chatte*," he said. "I shall return in the spring, and, as you said, we shall then endeavor to find a workable solution to your future."

Moments later, the boatswain's pipe shrilled and the *Black Eagle* began to get underway. The anchor was lifted and the sails were set amidst the flurry of activity that usually charged Devon with excitement.

This time, watching with Souchet from the windswept shore, she felt as though she might die.

Chapter Twenty-one

———◆———

December, 1781

IF not for Elsa, Devon's talkative German maid, she might not have survived the next months with her sanity intact. Each morning Elsa woke her with a steaming cup of chocolate and a constant, shining-white smile. Devon would feel the sadness lift as Elsa opened the drapes to let in sunshine or, occasionally, pale gray light, chattering cheerfully until she was able to draw a smile from her mistress.

After Raveneau's departure, Devon became self-absorbed for the first time in weeks, and it didn't take her long to suspect that something was amiss physically. How is it that I never thought of this before? she wondered. Was I so lost in my adventurous dream world that I believed myself immune to the realities of life? Still, she kept silent, hoping crazily that it was a mistake. By the end of November, she had missed her time for the third month in a row. She faced the fact that a child was growing within her body, and it was Elsa to whom she turned for advice and support.

"I don't know . . ." the flaxen-haired maid murmured, pursing her rosy lips. Devon sat on a chair before her, her hair crackling as Elsa brushed it. "You have gone through a great deal since September. What happened to your mother could be enough to stop your menses. I knew a girl once whose husband was killed in a carriage accident. Her flow stopped that same day and hasn't begun since, as far as I know. That was more than five years ago!"

Devon sighed heavily. Elsa was only a few years older than she—twenty-five, perhaps—but her maturity was reassuring. She talked and gossiped too much, but when the subject was serious, she would offer a strong, reasonable-sounding opinion.

"Elsa, I wish I could believe that were the case, but there are other signs that just haven't gone away."

"*Ja?*"

"I have been sleepy for weeks. My appetite hasn't been good. I cry easily and feel so sad. I've never been like that. At first I thought I just missed André, but too much time has passed and these feelings persist. That soup we had for dinner yesterday was perfectly prepared, yet all I could think of was oil and grease. I don't like wine any more—"

"And you haven't bled since the end of August," Elsa concluded, her tone less optimistic. She had been pregnant three times and delivered two babies successfully; the catalogue of symptoms was all too familiar. "When do you think the child was begun?"

Devon blushed. "It must have been in mid-September, while we were sailing from New London to Yorktown. There was only that one time, until last month. It must have been September. I always flow at the end of each month, but I've been too preoccupied to notice. André and I were so close at the end of October—I probably thought I wished it away."

Elsa bit her lip. "If it is so, you must not worry, Fräulein. Hermann and I will help you. You aren't alone. And now, even when I am away during the night, you will have your baby warm inside."

Elsa clucked over Devon like a mother hen, fortifying her with cheerful thoughts about the miracle of birth and the rewards of motherhood. André Raveneau was an adventurer who appeared to care for nothing but his sharp-hulled privateer, and she thought it would be cruel to offer Devon hope where he was concerned. Still, Elsa felt sure that he would care for the mother and child—he had brought Devon to his island, hadn't he?

The two women agreed to keep Devon's pregnancy a secret from the other residents of the house. This was Elsa's idea, and she argued hard to convince Devon. She argued that Souchet would make Devon's life unpleasant, that she might be gossiped about by other servants, and that it was important that the early months of pregnancy be tranquil and serene. Privately, Elsa worried about letting the news out until Raveneau's reaction was known, but she refrained from sharing this concern with Devon.

Devon urged Elsa to confide in her husband at least, for she knew how close the couple were. Hermann Kass was a dark-haired German giant of a man who labored in the bowels of the house as a carpenter, repairing the furniture already in use and the pieces that came to the storerooms. Hermann was as quiet as his wife was talkative, but Elsa decided to keep Devon's secret to herself for the present.

The taciturn Souchet appeared glad to leave Devon alone as long as she made no trouble. When André Raveneau had left, the little Frenchman worried that the titian-haired coquette might attempt to usurp the entire household, as Véronique had, but just the opposite was true. Devon kept to her room, leaving it only to scan the library shelves or to walk outside with her attentive maid.

Better Elsa than me, Souchet thought acidly, watching one December afternoon as the two women disappeared through the front door.

Outside in the balmy sunshine, Elsa asked, "How do you feel today? I don't want you to overdo—"

"No, no. I'm fine, really. It is a lovely day; I keep

expecting to wake one morning and find the island covered with snow!"

"If you did, you would be dreaming, Fräulein. The winters are pleasant here, aside from an occasional storm or a north wind."

"Good. My baby and I shall be able to enjoy the outdoors until the day I deliver."

"Walking is fine, Fräulein, but you must be very careful now. I lost a baby myself after three months."

As they wandered away from the house toward the far side of the island, Devon considered Elsa's advice. So . . . a bit of imprudent exercise might put an end to her complicated problem. She tested the thought and found that it chilled her brow with cold sweat. I'm sorry, my baby, she thought. I didn't mean it. I love you and want you.

After a half mile, they paused to rest on a bed of lush, perfumed grass and made plans to begin Devon's new wardrobe as well as the tiny gowns for her baby the next day. Aloud, Devon impishly envisioned herself waddling along in a few months, clad in lavish gowns of gold brocade or crimson satin. "Perhaps the baby might look well in royal purple velvet," she teased, and Elsa giggled in response.

"I am full of energy today," Devon announced at length. "Couldn't we please go on to the beach? I have always heard that salt wind is good for women with child."

Elsa looked at her in surprise, then saw the twinkle in her mistress's blue eyes. It was so heartening to see Devon in good spirits that she could not refuse. "We will go on if you promise to tell me when you tire."

Devon held up her hand, palm out, and vowed with mock solemnity, "I promise!"

When they reached the cliff, Devon recognized the location instantly. Below them lay the secluded beach where she and Raveneau had spent their last afternoon. Heart swelling, she dropped gently to the ground and stared meditatively at the few feet of sand on which they had made love with such urgent tenderness. This baby growing in her belly was one half Raveneau's, but Devon refused to think about what that could mean. It was easier to concentrate on each new morning, on loving her baby and enjoying Elsa's companionship. Devon disciplined her heart, building a wall between romantic love and mother love. As for the future . . . to brood about it would have driven her insane, so, for the baby's sake, she strove to remain calm and cheerful, looking ahead only to the day she would give birth.

"Do you know," Elsa was muttering, tapping a pink finger against her nose, "I believe this is the place where that woman died."

Devon blinked, coming back from her reverie. "I beg your pardon?"

"*Ja*, I'm quite certain. That woman—you know, the first *Meister* Raveneau's mistress. Véronique."

"Did you say that she died? Here? But how?"

"Do you mean he didn't tell you? Hmmm!" Elsa settled her firm bulk on the ground, relishing the chance to reveal all she knew. "Of course, I have been here only seven years, so most of this has been told to me by the other servants. Cook has been on the island since the house was finished some thirty years ago." Elsa's voice dropped as she added with a wink, "She knows *everything!*"

"Will you please get on with it?" Devon demanded, smiling in exasperation.

"You have heard of the old *Meister*'s . . . ah . . . lady? It is said that he built this house for her."

"Yes, I know all about that."

"Well, as I understand it, after a few years she gave birth to a child, which old Herr Raveneau accepted as his own. According to Cook, when the little girl was about five, the old *Meister* somehow learned the truth—that another man was the father. That night he and Véronique had a terrible argument. Cook says she could hear them through two floors, down in the kitchen. Then it was quiet." Elsa paused for dramatic effect. "The next morning the lady—Véronique—was missing. They found her there—" She pointed to the beach below. "Her neck was broken."

Devon gasped, "Oh, my God!" She stared down at the beach. She and Raveneau had made love on the spot where Véronique's dead body had lain. Shuddering with revulsion, she met Elsa's sky-blue eyes. "What happened after that?"

Elsa pursed her lips, concentrating. "I do remember that old Herr Raveneau denied killing the lady. Cook says he was quite distraught; shut himself away for days and refused food. He was certain that it must have been an accident—that she had been upset after their quarrel and had gone out for some air. You know—a misstep in the darkness."

"Quite a misstep!"

Elsa nodded skeptically. "Cook told me that the old *Meister* ordered his mistress's child removed from the island at once. I gather he had her sent back to that Véronique's relations in France. He went to sea soon after and was away for two years."

"No one knows who the real father was?"

"No one on the island except for Véronique and perhaps the old Herr Raveneau."

"Wouldn't the servants have known if Véronique had been unfaithful to André's father?"

Elsa rolled her eyes. "There were plenty of ships in and out in those days, before the war. When the old *Meister* was away, I hear that the lady was quite fond of her play, and no doubt those horny seamen were happy to oblige."

The bitch! Devon thought furiously. No wonder Raveneau despised her memory so bitterly. "André's poor father! If he possessed even a fraction of his son's pride, he must have been shattered by the entire ordeal."

"I think that is true. He died only a year after I arrived here. He always seemed old and joyless to me, but I do recall hearing the older servants remark on how greatly he had changed since his youth. Cook must have told Hermann and me two dozen times that the younger Raveneau is the image of his father thirty years before, when the house was first built."

Christmas week came, bringing melancholy feelings for Devon. It was impossible not to remember other years, years of her early childhood. When her father was alive, Christmas had been overwhelmingly festive. They had lived in their fine big house then, and Jamie had joined Devon in her high spirits. The house had been festooned with garlands of pine, while rich, dense snow had covered New London and the surrounding woods like a white blanket. Happy people had skimmed over the curving streets in sleighs; great quantities of syllabub and hot mulled cider had been consumed. Devon and Jamie had spent long hours in the kitchen, watching as Deborah created all manner of pies and confections, inhaling the wonderful aromas. And on Christmas Eve, their father had lit the yule log, a moment of speechless entrancement for the two small children.

In retrospect, Devon thought that the gifts on Christmas morning had been of the least importance, though at that time anticipation had ruled the children's lives. Tears filled her eyes as she remembered the gorgeous meal that had followed the presents—a golden, fragrant bird, spicy meat pies, sweet potatoes, hot rolls —her father saying the blessing, and her own inevitable poke in Jamie's ribs when he had grown long-winded . . .

On the island, Christmas was only an illusion. Warm, moist breezes blew; there were no evergreens from which to fashion garlands. Cook prepared a wonderful feast on Christmas Day, complete with flaming plum pudding, and Devon decided to eat below with the servants. She watched the children, including Elsa's two blond toddlers, Rudolph and Winifreda, as they pulled the wrapping from their modest gifts—toys handmade by Hermann, each one unique.

Afterward, Devon returned to her room, lay down on the plush velour counterpane, and wept tears that burned her eyes and throat like acid. She grieved for all she had lost and all the dreams that might never be fulfilled.

Chapter Twenty-two

January, 1782

THE new year renewed Devon's spirit. Day by day, she felt better. Her appetite returned, and she had more energy than ever before. Her hair shone, a blend of sun and flame, her cheeks glowed with color, and the constant urge to cry disappeared. Elsa was a perfect companion. She listened cheerfully to Devon's conversation about the baby, and the two women spent long, contented hours creating a wardrobe for the mother and her child. Six other serving girls were enlisted to help. They weren't told the reason, Elsa leaving them to assume that Captain Raveneau's latest mistress desired elegant gowns, most of them cut with high waists and billowing skirts. Elsa whispered that Marie Antoinette wore nothing else.

The baby's things were sewn by Devon and Elsa alone, and hidden away.

Bernard Souchet cast the only shadow in Devon's life. His rudeness grew in proportion to her radiance. From time to time she would fret about his attitude, but Elsa supplied quick and effective diversions and Devon would put Souchet out of her mind.

January fourteenth was like many other days before, until late afternoon. Elsa urged Devon to lie down and rest, for the baby's sake, while she gathered up their sewing and put it away in the back of the wardrobe. They were both at peace; Devon smiled dreamily, one hand on the still-hidden, hard curve of her abdomen.

Suddenly Devon's eyes opened wide. She lifted her head and whispered, "Elsa!" urgently. The German maid rushed to her side, but her expression of fear disappeared when Devon breathed, "I felt him. Elsa, he moved! Oh! There it is again!" Her sapphire eyes filled with tears of joy. "My baby!"

They hugged, and Elsa remained on the side of the bed for several minutes, chatting happily with her excited mistress until a noise outside roused her. Voices?

Casually, Elsa stood up and walked over to the window. Figures moved under the trees below. There were several men, at least one woman in a fine gown, and what appeared to be a child. In the distance Elsa saw a schooner anchored off the beach. Then Bernard Souchet appeared. Arms outstretched, he ran down the front steps and the woman ran forward to embrace him. Elsa narrowed her eyes. Sable hair tumbled in curls down the woman's back. An incredibly wasp waist and round, prominent breasts were apparent even under the bronze silk gown.

Eugénie! Elsa thought, anger and wariness mixing. What was she doing here again?

"What is it, Elsa? Has a ship come in?" Devon sat up on the bed, suddenly anxious. "It's not—"

"No, no, it's not the *Black Eagle*. Ah . . ."

"Elsa! If you know who it is, I insist that you tell me. I don't like the look on your face."

Elsa had no choice. Wincing, she perched on the edge of the bed and concentrated on not meeting Devon's eyes. "Someone has come," she began lamely. "Her name is Eugénie . . . Richoux, I believe. Yes, Richoux."

"And?"

"She . . . ah . . . has been here before. Six years ago, after the old Herr Raveneau died, his son came at once from America. As I recall, Fräulein Richoux arrived soon after he did. She was some friend of the family or of Souchet. I don't remember, exactly, though I do know that she and Souchet became friends."

"I suppose that she had an affair with André," Devon said in a hard voice.

Elsa flushed. "I think so. But no sooner had she begun to hang on his arm, smiling like a cat with a canary, than he had to leave. Suddenly. I must say, it was a pleasure to see her lose that smug look. I suspect she thought he'd marry her so she could stay and be the queen here on the island."

"What did she do then?"

"Oh, she sulked and pouted for a week or two, then left herself in a big hurry. That morning I helped to pack her trunk, and I remember that she was smiling in a way that gave me goose flesh. I had a feeling that we hadn't seen the last of her."

Devon lay back on the bed, pensive. "Sea travel has been too dangerous for the past six years. She is French? I'll wager that she heard the news about Yorktown. People think that Cornwallis's surrender unofficially ended the war."

Elsa sighed. "I do not like this."

"What do you suppose she is up to? I can't believe she would try to win André over a second time."

"She has had six years to think of a new plan," Elsa muttered.

"Well, it's all silly. I know André Raveneau very well, and he is not about to marry this Eugénie Richoux, plan or no plan. I may not win him, either, but I certainly have a better chance than she does!" Devon patted her abdomen for emphasis.

The hall door had been left ajar, and now it moved. To Devon and Elsa's utter astonishment, a little girl appeared. "Hello!" Her accent was an odd mix of

British and French. "My name is Louisa Richoux. Who are you?"

Spellbound, Devon sat up on the edge of the bed and held out her arms in a gesture of welcome. Elsa stared, gaping, as the little girl walked happily to meet her new friend.

"I am Devon Lindsay. It is a pleasure to meet you, Louisa." Smiling, she took the child's hand. "How old are you?"

"Five."

Elsa made a strangled noise, which Devon took to be a reminder of her presence. "Oh, dear. I've forgotten Elsa! Louisa, this is Elsa Kass, my dear friend."

"I am her maid," Elsa clarified.

Devon was looking at Louisa. The child was beautiful. Her head was covered with gleaming gingery curls that fell in cheerful profusion past her shoulders. Warm, long-lashed brown eyes dominated a charming face that also boasted a turned-up nose and engaging dimples. Her smile was irresistible.

"Where have you come from?" Devon asked.

"England. Mama has wanted to visit this island for a long time, but it was too dangerous to come in a boat." She pronounced her words with matter-of-fact assurance. "Someone might have shooted a cannon at us."

"You were wise indeed to wait. Have you always lived in England?"

"Mmmmm." Louisa was looking admiringly around the luxurious room. "Sometimes we visit France. That's where my mama's *grand-mère* lives. She's very old!"

"Don't you have a father?"

"I think so. Mama says I will have one soon."

Devon's eyebrows went up. Meeting Elsa's narrowed gaze from across the room, she felt her smile become flimsy. Elsa held up a hand, its five fingers splayed, and nodded vigorously at the child.

"Do you know your father's name?" Devon asked weakly.

"Papa, I suppose. He fights wars and kills people."

"Oh." She nodded mechanically.

Louisa leaned against Devon's knees and stroked the velour counterpane dreamily. "This is almost as soft as my cat," she murmured. "Do you have any little girls?"

"No . . . not yet."

"You're nice. I like you."

"I like you, too. Very much."

Another voice brought both their heads up. "Very cozy!" Eugénie Richoux's accent was trained to British precision; it held only a whisper of French to betray her origins. Sleek sable-black hair was piled in a fashionable mass atop her head, but a handful of long coils were left to trail down her back. Her face was a perfect ivory oval; gold-flecked hazel eyes slanted up slightly at the corners, emphasized by winged brows. Her nose was thin, its tip curving down somewhat, and her mouth tapered like a cupid's bow. She wore an elegant gown of bronze silk, and its severe quality seemed only to accentuate the high, round breasts and incredibly tiny waist.

Devon managed to swallow a loud groan, but before she could speak, Louisa broke the tension. "Mama, this is Devon Lindsay! She's wonderful!" Halfway across the thick rose and green carpet, she looked back at Devon. "This is my mother!"

Bracing herself, Devon went forward and offered her hand. Eugénie barely touched it, her own fingers dry and cold. "My name is Eugénie Richoux. André and I are very old and dear friends."

Devon summoned a sweet smile. "In that case, I hope we shall be friends as well. He will be desolate to learn he has missed you. He will be at sea for several more months."

A winged eyebrow lifted frostily. "I understood the figure to be *three* months. Possibly less."

"Possibly." Devon smiled. "Probably more, knowing André."

271

"We shall wait," Eugénie said venomously.

"Oh, lovely! Your husband won't be missing you?"

"I am not married," was the icy reply.

Devon decided not to press the issue. "Oh. Well . . . I am certain that you both must be exhausted. I'll let you go to your rooms." She dropped a warm smile on Louisa, who beamed in return. "You have a lovely child, Miss Richoux."

"Please, do call me Eugénie. And thank you. I feel that Louisa is *very* special. Do you think André will agree?"

"I vow, Papa, I have never felt such frustration in my life!"

Bernard Souchet put down the teapot and rushed to pat Eugénie's shoulder. "Shh, *ma chère*. You must keep your voice down—someone will hear! All this fretting will do you no good. You must stay calm."

"Papa, I cannot help it. I have been here two weeks and have tried every trick I know to drive the slut away, but she only smiles. She sits in the bedchamber that should be *mine,* and I cannot pry Louisa away from her. How do you think that makes me look? My own child is a traitor! I have done everything except *announce* that André is Louisa's father, but she only smiles more as my hints grow more obvious."

Souchet pressed the teacup into her gesturing hands. "She is worried. I know it, *ma petite*. It is only a matter of wearing her down. Every time she looks at Louisa, she must think that even our disreputable privateersman could not resist such a daughter. I'm sure the slut will leave before André returns—her pride won't let her stay to face his rejection."

"I hope you are right, Papa," said Eugénie. "You had such confidence in this outrageous plan when I left six years ago. I hope for your sake that I have not wasted my time. I could have married a real duke if I hadn't been burdened with Louisa!"

"*Chérie! Ma fille!* You must trust me, and you must

have confidence in yourself. I have sensed a change in Raveneau; his heart is weakening."

"For this red-haired bitch!" Eugénie spat, slamming down her cup and saucer.

"Shh! Do you doubt your ability to persuade her to leave? We must find a way. There is plenty of time—two or three months, at least. And Raveneau will return, find you and Louisa in her place, and the game will be over. You shall be mistress of this palace and we will be together, always."

Eugénie tapped a lacquered nail against her teeth. "Papa, do you suppose there might be a rejected beau who would come here and woo her back? Or perhaps an anxious parent who could be persuaded to come after her?"

Souchet's angular face lit up. *"Ma chère,* you may have the answer. Do you think you could get her to confide in you?"

Wrinkling her nose, Eugénie sighed. "I would rather get the information by holding a knife to that German maid's throat, but that would no doubt be imprudent." She smiled archly at her father's expression. "A jest, Papa."

She kissed Souchet's cheek with cool lips and left the library. It was late afternoon, almost dusk. A cold wind swept the island, left over from the morning's rain, and Eugénie knew that Devon would be upstairs.

As she lifted her hand to knock, she saw that Devon's bedroom door was ajar; soft voices came from within. Eugénie gently pushed the door until she could see the bed on which Devon and Louisa reclined. Candles had been lit on either side, bathing the woman and child in a pink-gold luster. Devon lay on the near side, her head turned toward Louisa, her arm cradling the little girl's head.

Eugénie could not make out their whispered conversation. It seemed as if Devon were telling Louisa a story. Burnished-rose hair spread across the pillows in a cloud of curls; Eugénie could see the soft flush in Devon's cheeks and somehow understood what Raveneau saw in the girl. It was a quality she herself could never imitate. There was only one solution: he could not be allowed to compare them.

As she started to move back into the hallway to knock, her eyes slid over Devon's coral velvet gown. Her heart seemed to freeze. The line of Devon's abdomen could only mean one thing. How had she hidden it so long? Perhaps she was only gaining weight? Eugénie stepped back and put her head against the cool wall, trying to think. No, Devon had to be pregnant. She couldn't have become fat in her belly while staying so slender everywhere else. Damn! She was pregnant with Raveneau's bastard! Could he know? No. If he knew, why would she take such pains to conceal her condition? All those new empire-waisted gowns!

Flooded with resolve, Eugénie gritted her teeth and knocked at the door. "Excuse me—"

"Mama!" Louisa cried. "Come in!" When Eugénie peeked in, the little girl exclaimed, "Devon has been telling me about America! She lived in a town where all the privateers stayed. When she was a little girl like me, she used to watch them unload things like diamonds and gold—"

"Now, Louisa, I said wonderful cargoes, but as for diamonds . . ." Devon smiled uneasily as she sat up.

"How interesting, Louisa." Eugénie's eyes shifted to Devon, striving for a friendly look. "Where in America did you grow up?"

"In New London—Connecticut."

"Oh, yes. I have heard André speak of the place often." When she saw her rival's eyes narrow defensively, Eugénie decided not to mention his name again. "I hope the two of you don't mind this interruption."

"No, no," Devon assured her.

"Sit down, Mama!"

Eugénie smiled, perching at the foot of the bed. "I am getting lonely. I long for someone to talk to, another woman who would understand my feelings. If you don't mind?"

Devon searched her face, wanting to trust her. She hated the constant tension of the past two weeks. Could the other woman be weary of feuding as well? Perhaps she was willing to accept Devon's presence, to live and let live . . . "No, I don't mind," Devon said. "We are all isolated here. It would be wonderful if we could talk."

"Ah! I agree. It is time that we behave like adults. Perhaps if we got to know each other better . . ."

Devon's skin prickled with suspicion, but when the conversation continued innocently for another quarter hour with no mention of Raveneau, she began to relax. Eugénie had always longed to visit America, she said. She asked questions about Connecticut, and slowly, insidiously, the questions led up through Devon's early years to her first love. A childhood sweetheart! How sweet and romantic! Bursting with interest, Eugénie drew Devon out. But Devon backed away when the narrative crept close to her time with Raveneau, and Eugénie made a hasty retreat.

"No, no! Don't say anything that makes you uncomfortable. I suppose it must have ended sadly—young love so often does. I had a similar experience myself, but believe me, it's better that you found out you weren't suited when you did, rather than rushing into a hasty marriage."

"Yes, that's very true," Devon agreed.

"But the poor boy's heart must have been broken. What do you suppose became of him? Has he found a nice girl to comfort him?"

"I couldn't say," Devon replied carefully. "I imagine he must have gone home, unless he stayed with the army, which I doubt. His parents own a drug shop, and frankly, I think he belonged there all along."

"I'm sure you are right. So all's well that ends well!" Eugénie leaned forward to pat Devon's hand solicitously. "My gracious! Look, it is nearly dark. I think, Louisa, that you and I should hurry to our chambers and freshen up before supper."

Louisa kissed Devon's cheek, then scrambled off the bed to take her mother's outstretched hand.

"*Bon soir,*" Eugénie said affectedly. "I am so glad we had this little chat."

"Yes. I am glad, too." Devon watched them leave the room, then stared at the closed door. Uneasily, she whispered, "I hope I won't regret it later!"

That evening Eugénie and Souchet retreated to a corner of the grand salon after supper, brandies in hand, sitting close together on a priceless tapestry chaise. In rapid French, she repeated all that Devon had told her about Morgan.

"She walked into our trap as innocently as a rabbit!" Eugénie said, gleefully derisive. "She even told me that her sweetheart's parents own a drug shop in New London. How many can there be?"

Souchet chuckled. "Who should we send?"

"I have been considering this, and I think it should be someone who works here. Someone who has a great deal to lose should he betray us—preferably a man you know to be trustworthy and loyal."

"Hermann Kass," Souchet replied. "He is quiet and obedient. His wife is the Lindsay girl's maid, but Hermann steers clear of her meddling ways. If I gave him a sealed letter and ordered him to deliver it unopened, he would do so without a question or a moment of curiosity."

"Your trust is fine, Papa, but I think you should make him understand that his family will suffer should he betray us."

"Yes. His wife and children are his life."

"Lovely." Eugénie beamed. "Now, if our good fortune continues, dear, reliable Hermann will find Morgan without any problems and the wronged lover will fly to Devon's rescue—before André returns!"

"*Salut!*" Souchet whispered with enthusiasm, and father and daughter touched glasses to toast their scheme.

April, 1782

Chapter Twenty-three

April, 1782

WORRIED, Elsa watched her napping mistress. The winter had not been a happy one. For some reason, Souchet had joined forces with Eugénie in an effort to make Devon's life miserable. They both were either frosty or sarcastic, their rudeness increasing as Devon's condition became more and more evident.

Elsa wished Hermann were here so that she could discuss the problem with him, but he had been away for two months and had refused to tell her what business separated them or where he was going.

Devon stirred and sat up, revealing the half-moon of her velvet-draped belly. She displayed it proudly now, walking through the house with her back straight and a peaceful smile on her face—until either Eugénie or Souchet would appear. Somehow their behavior seemed to attack her baby as well as herself, and this bothered her the most.

Elsa saw the way Devon's nose pinched below her delicate brows and sighed. *"Liebling,* I implore you. For the baby's sake, you must be tranquil."

"I know you are right. I do try to keep my mind on the baby, but it is difficult not to worry about the other circumstances of my life. The day will come when I must leave this island—"

"Save your worry for that day."

"André will return in a few weeks. Oh, how ill I feel whenever I think of it. I will be huge and ugly, and there will be beautiful Eugénie and another child for him to deal with—one who is already heartbreakingly lovable. I cannot imagine how he will react. I dread it."

"You must not think—"

"I know Eugénie has laid her plans as carefully as the siege at Yorktown. *I* have no strategy!"

"Of course you don't! Have you considered the idea that André Raveneau may not care to be the object of her schemes? He is an intelligent man, after all."

"I hope you are right, Elsa, but she can be quite convincing." Devon thought back with agitation to the heart-to-heart talk she had had with Eugénie at the end of January. That had been her last overture of friendship, and now Devon could only wonder what the woman had been up to.

"I know that you are feeling helpless. But worrying won't help. You must be tranquil, for your baby," Elsa soothed.

"I am tired of being 'tranquil' and quiet and allowing Eugénie and Souchet to walk all over me."

"Fräulein, I wish that you wouldn't get angry—"

"Well, Elsa, I *am* angry and I rather enjoy it. I feel like my old self! I am done cowering in my room, hiding from unpleasantness."

With that, Devon stood up, squared her shoulders, and started for the door.

"What are you going to do?" fretted Elsa.

"I crave a chat with Souchet," she smiled. "Don't worry. Why don't you go and see to your children and meet me back here later."

Purposefully, she strode down the hall, descended the staircase, and opened the library door without knocking. Bernard Souchet was a virtual fixture in this huge, book-filled room and today was no exception. He stood beside the heavy, carved mahogany desk, apparently searching for a paper, and the look of surprise on his face almost made Devon laugh.

"Good afternoon, M'sieur Souchet," she said. "I have come to choose a few books, but I do not mind if you remain."

He blinked, but recovered rapidly. "What did you have in mind, mademoiselle? I will be pleased to advise you."

She bristled at his condescending tone. "I assure you, I am perfectly capable of reading titles. Now, if you will excuse me . . . "

Souchet fumed as he watched her examine the bookshelves. He couldn't just stand here like some sort of lackey! He edged his way across the room to where she stood, and hovered like a suspicious shopkeeper. Devon glanced up once, slanting the coolest look she could muster in his direction. When Souchet saw the volume of Shakespeare's *Sonnets* she had chosen, he pounced like a desperate cat.

"Mademoiselle, if you please." He tried to remove the book from her hands. "I cannot allow you to take this particular volume. Mademoiselle Richoux has requested that I save it for her. She will be along at any moment to fetch it."

"That is a shame. M'sieur Souchet, do let go!" She forceably yanked the book from him and left him standing empty-handed, his eyes burning with indignation. "In case you have forgotten, Captain Raveneau gave you clear instructions to treat me courteously, as you would a family member, and further told you that I was to have complete access to this house! I do not intend to be bullied for another moment by you or by anyone else!" Holding fast to Shakespeare's *Sonnets,* she strode to the door and turned to add, "You may tell Eugénie that she is welcome to this book just as soon as *I* am finished."

Once in the hallway, Devon felt dizzy with anger and triumph, but she took several deep breaths and started up the stairs. Eugénie materialized at the top, her mouth open at a sharp angle, ready to speak, but Devon glanced at her coldly and brushed past.

It was time for the story she read to Louisa each afternoon, and she found the little girl waiting impatiently on the edge of Devon's bed. Sitting down beside her, Devon put a hand out to stroke the child's gingerly curls and suddenly felt a powerful yearning for Raveneau. She let the feeling soak in as she closed her eyes and saw his harsh, splendid face. If he were only here, holding her, kissing away her tears with a mouth that scorched her flesh, whispering huskily against her ear . . .

"Devon!" Louisa implored. "Here! I've brought the book."

Opening her eyes, Devon faced the reality sharing this bed in Raveneau's place. A sweet, bewildered little girl who needed a father . . . and an innocent baby not yet born.

One sunny morning, still early in April, a bold little sloop skimmed over the horizon and headed straight for the island. Elsa, her children, Louisa, and Devon watched from one of the turrets, beaming with pleasure as the craft approached. Mild, perfumed breezes blew up from the trees.

Devon and Elsa decided to take the children down to the beach when it became clear that the sloop was anchoring in the cove. "It will probably be another of André's mistresses," Devon remarked with wry humor. "Perhaps an entire boatload!"

Elsa let out a snort of laughter.

Suddenly Devon gasped in astonishment. A woman had appeared at the rail, and she was waving and screaming something unintelligible. "It's Azalea!" Devon explained as a jolly boat was lowered. "She is Halsey Minter's sister."

"Who?"

"Minter! André's steward."

"Hmmm." Elsa narrowed her eyes at the boat. "She has been here before, I think."

Devon laughed, glad that she was able to. "Now that you mention it, I suppose I was right about the visitor being one of André's mistresses! He may very well have brought her here a few years ago. But now she is married . . . to the fair-haired man beside her in the boat. She is no threat, Elsa, but in truth a dear friend!"

As the jolly boat skidded onto the beach, Devon was there to embrace an excited Azalea. She gave Isaac a hug and somehow managed to introduce the hopping children, while Azalea talked without a moment's pause. Arm in arm, the two women started up the path to the house, and as soon as they had put some distance between themselves and the others, Azalea demanded, "What is *this!?* I am speechless, Devon!"

"You could have fooled me!"

"Don't tease! It must be André's child—?"

"Yes. Yes, of course it is! The only other man who ever tempted me was the Blue Jay, but I resisted, and of course I was already pregnant when I met him."

Azalea coughed nervously. "Devon, are you all right? I'll bet you are frantic! André—"

"André doesn't know. I wasn't aware myself until the *Black Eagle* left. And I am fine. Blooming, as they say. I have my share of worries, but I am trying to focus my attention on the baby." Devon's smile was eloquent. "But wait! You breeze in here as though we lived just around the corner! What has brought you and Isaac all this way?"

Azalea put her off until they were able to retreat to Devon's bedchamber. Eugénie and Souchet were standing in the entryway, but Devon made casual introductions and led her friend up the stairs. Elsa was promising to find something for Isaac to eat and drink, and he smiled indulgently at his wife, waving to her as she bustled off with Devon.

It was obvious that Azalea had been here before. She didn't bat an eye when Devon opened the door to her bedchamber, but went right on chattering.

"André brought you here, didn't he?" Devon accused with mock outrage.

"Oh, yes. After we first met—you know, when he rescued me from that British warship. I can't say I am particularly thrilled to return."

Devon settled down beside her on the sofa. "Do you know, I was so overwhelmed when we first arrived . . . it seemed like a castle out of a fairy tale. But all the gold and velvet and beautiful paintings in the world can't begin to substitute for love. This house has begun to seem almost evil—"

There was a gleam in Azalea's doe eyes. "You know what they say about André . . ."

"Oh, stop. Besides, he doesn't like this house at all. I think he avoids it."

"That's right, I remember now. Something about his father and a mistress."

Devon thought about asking Azalea what she knew about Véronique's death, but before she could speak, her friend exclaimed, "I am dying to know who that stunning woman downstairs is! A new housekeeper?"

"I wish that she were." Briefly, Devon related the events of the winter, including her suspicions about Louisa and her uneasiness concerning Eugénie and Souchet. Finally, they turned the conversation back to the reason for Azalea and Isaac's sea voyage.

"Isaac's grandfather died a year or so ago, in England," Azalea said. "But because of the war, nothing has been done about his estate. My father-in-law is the sole heir. He received another letter last month from the executor, urging him to come and hinting at a surprisingly large estate. So he asked if Isaac could do this errand. Isaac is his father's heir, of course."

Devon knew what a windfall could mean to their farm and she hugged Azalea excitedly. "Oh, how wonderful for you! Such an adventure—sailing to England—and a chance to fulfill your dreams for the farm when you return."

"And, best of all, I am happier with Isaac than I ever thought I could be."

"You've given up pining for André?"

"As a matter of fact, I believe I have!"

Devon let out an exaggerated sigh. "Whew! There's *one* rival I can cross off the list!"

They giggled and chatted about the war, the Minters, Devon's pregnancy, her sewing projects, and Elsa. Finally, as their stomachs began to cry for luncheon, they leaned back against the sofa and looked at each other.

"It is so good to be with you." Devon smiled warmly. "You have cheered me greatly."

"Good. I could ask nothing more. I only wish we could remain longer than one day."

"I am glad for that much. And . . . André will be here very soon. The suspense will be over."

Azalea dropped her eyes, plucking nervously at her muslin skirt. "Devon, hasn't it occurred to you that I might have word from the *Black Eagle?*"

"Yes. It has."

"The ship was in South Carolina last month, and Halsey managed to visit the farm for a few hours on the way back. He had some news for you."

"Yes?"

"Well, the *Black Eagle* was to sail to the Indies next, hoping to take a good prize, then return to New London. Do you know, they have taken four ships this winter! At any rate, there have been terrible stories circulating, about one of the largest British prison ships anchored off Long Island. Beatings, starvation . . ."

"Yes?"

"Halsey told me that Raveneau means to attack it when they get back to New London. It's a very dangerous proposition, and it will also delay their return to the Island by a fortnight or more. Halsey said you should not look for them until May . . . or later."

"André could be killed," Devon whispered hollowly.

"Well, you know he takes those risks every day."

"Not the same . . ." Blankly, she looked into Azalea's wary eyes. "Tell me the truth. Did André come with Minter to the farm?"

"Actually . . . yes. He wanted to see Mama and Pa."

"He knew you would be coming to see me?"

Azalea could only nod reluctantly.

"He sent no letter? No message at all?"

For a brief moment Azalea considered lying, but Devon's gaze was too penetrating. Azalea dropped her eyes and muttered, "No . . . nothing."

Raveneau sat down on the Queen Anne four-poster to pull on his boots and Isabelle was behind him in an instant, her soft, pale arms wrapped around his chest. He could feel the pressure of taut breasts against his back, but continued to dress.

"André!" she implored, her voice like velvet. "Why do you rush away from me? Did I disappoint you?"

Groaning, Raveneau turned to face her and tried to resist her golden-haired charms. "Isabelle, I have other matters to attend to." She was rubbing her breasts against him, smiling wickedly into his flinty eyes. "You know that you did not disappoint me. Stop that! I must go."

"One more kiss, André. Please. I have missed you so. I have been so hungry and I am not yet satisfied."

She nibbled at his stubborn mouth until he relented and opened it to her kiss. Her passion was almost cloying, yet it was impossible not to respond. Dark hands cupped teasing breasts, while slender arms slithered around a muscular back to draw Raveneau slowly down into the musky sheets. Isabelle's fingers moved swiftly, with practiced skill, over his buttons, then caressed the hard, powerful body beyond.

An hour later, Raveneau emerged from the small house to find that dusk was upon the town of New London. He thought of all he had meant to do this day and cursed his own weakness. What he hated most was a nagging prod of guilt in the recesses of his mind. There was absolutely no reason for it! That cursed Minter had put it into his mind. Raveneau started to walk toward the Beach, inspiring caution and fear from the passersby who encountered his stormy-looking eyes.

It was impossible to dismiss the argument he and Minter had had that morning. Minter, his damned steward, daring to offer advice! It was intolerable, and part of him still wished he had tossed the boy into the Thames and told him never to show his face again.

A gloomy Minter had watched him dress that morning while assembling the breakfast dishes to return them to the galley. Finally he said, "Excuse me, sir, but I think it is wrong for you to go to that woman."

How the hell had he known? And Raveneau had given himself away by retorting, "When I want your advice, I'll ask for it."

"I am Devon's friend, as well as your steward," Minter had replied, offended.

"Devon!" Raveneau had shouted irritably. "Are we married? Did I miss something? And even if we were, that chit is hundreds of miles away."

"I suppose I am rather old-fashioned, sir. I believe in commitments and trust when two people are in love."

"Damn! You sound exactly like your *maman!*" Raveneau had blazed. "And all that is beside the point. I sure as hell am not in love with your *merveilleuse* Devon!"

"If you say so, sir."

"Minter, you have been with me for more than six

287

years. What is the reason for this sudden attack of morals?"

"Sir, to be honest, I believe that you love Devon Lindsay very much, and I know that she loves you. I think you would rest easier tonight if you could admit this and remain faithful to her. If you sleep with another woman, it will tarnish what Devon has given to you as her gift of love."

"Arrêtez!" Raveneau had roared. "This gift of love, as you so charmingly term it, may well have come to me secondhand, and as for *trust!* You are a fool, Minter. Women are useful in many ways, but I trust no one but myself, and I am never disillusioned. The women who seem most vulnerable and innocent are the worst kind. If you relinquish even a portion of yourself to such a female, you are destined to be hurt."

"Captain, I hesitate to say this . . . but I feel that *you* are the fool in this case."

Stalking now through the cool spring twilight, Raveneau seethed at the memory. The insolent pup! He had enough problems. His mind had no business straying from the plan to attack the prison ship. It had to succeed; failure might well cost him his life.

Turning the corner of Union Street, Raveneau experienced an unsettling feeling. As he walked, he stared hard at the cobblestones and burned buildings and houses, trying to remember, trying to put both Devon and Minter out of his mind.

Yet . . . this ash-pink light lent itself to remembered visions, and there had been many nights disturbed by vivid dreams these past months. Dreams of silky, flame-gold hair coiled around his neck, of brilliant sapphire eyes that drew him in no matter how he resisted, of enchanting, mischievous laughter.

A man on horseback trotted by and Raveneau stepped aside. Alert again, he looked around at the houses and shops; the horse's hooves had touched off another spark of memory.

What could it be? Frustrated, he concentrated harder. He walked on, following the curve of the lane that led toward the Beach, his eyes drinking in the scene as he struggled to call forth the face that tugged at his mind. A girl—young, guileless, candid. Fifteen? Sixteen? Red hair . . . auburn? Self-conscious.

Ah, yes! The girl he had met at Nicholson's house and accompanied back to the Bank. A carriage ride along this same route in the midst of just such a sunset. She had been a minx! Raveneau recalled that she had spoken of reading *Joseph Andrews,* or perhaps *Tom Jones.* He squinted now, trying to conjure up a clear image of her face, but remembered instead the dried leaf caught in her tousled curls, the budding breasts outlined by a faded blue gown, and the most captivating manner and smile. It had been wrong of him to kiss so young a girl, but her nearness in the carriage had been bewitching. Those deep blue eyes, dusky cheeks, and lips that intoxicated with their sweetness . . .

Raveneau froze in the middle of Church Street. People and horses passed on either side, but he stared into the dipping coral sun in dazed disbelief.

"Devon. *Devon.*"

"Say what?" an old man inquired helpfully.

Raveneau clenched his fists, unaware of the voice or of the confusion that swirled around him as people hurried home at the end of the working day. It seemed inconceivable that he could have failed to remember Devon when they had met on the *Black Eagle.* Had the hectic tension of the day been to blame? The fact that she had worn breeches? Over and over, he recalled how she had been that day and the heady innocence of her kiss. *Mon Dieu! La petite chatte* even slapped me! Smiling, he put a hand to his jaw.

Suddenly Raveneau was seized by a violent desire to consume an indecent quantity of cognac. Dusk was deepening to indigo night as he quickened his step along John Street, anxious to feel the reassuring sway of the *Black Eagle* under his legs.

Everyone told Devon that the oppressively warm weather was highly unusual, especially for April. Unusual or not, she wasn't sure if she could stand another day. Her back had begun to ache and the baby seemed restless, often waking her repeatedly through the night with a series of acrobatics.

"Just another month," she whispered aloud. She lay on her bed, fully dressed. Uneaten food and clean dishes were neatly arranged on the table.

Hermann Kass had returned from his travels, closed-mouthed and suffering with a fatigued cough. Elsa had spent the day with him, and a young maid named Jeannette had taken over her duties. The girl was nice enough, but so obsequious that Devon felt uncomfortable and had dismissed her when supper was served. It was barely seven o'clock, but Devon felt drained and let her eyes close.

The dream was disturbingly vivid. In it, she was standing on the beach where Véronique had died and she and Raveneau had made love. A delicate white skiff emerged out of the starless night, and she watched it approach until it came up onto the beach. The Blue Jay stepped out, garbed in his usual cape and mask, sending a burst of joy through Devon. When she attempted an embrace, however, Jay held her off, whispering, "Later."

"Have you brought me a message?"

"No, I have come to take you away. When you leave this island, your troubles will be over."

Mesmerized by the intensity of his gaze, Devon allowed Jay to take her hand. Slowly, they moved toward the boat, but before she could step in, she woke up. A warm breeze billowed the edges of the brocade draperies and cooled the tears on Devon's cheeks. Lying in the darkness, she put her hands on her awkwardly round belly. The baby had begun to kick again and she tried to sooth it and herself with a rhythmic massage, while her mind drifted back to the Blue Jay. His appeal was potent even in a dream, and she wondered what it meant. What had become of Jay? Did he ever think of her?

Sighing, she closed her eyes and allowed her thoughts to turn to Raveneau. Where was he tonight? Had he attacked the prison ship yet? Perhaps he was already dead.

Devon struggled up from the bed and went to the dumbwaiter in the hallway, opening the door to see if the stand was there so that she could clear the dishes from the table. The contraption was at the bottom of the shaft, level with the kitchen, and Devon was pulling the rope to raise it when she heard a shrill, all-too-familiar voice rising up the dark well from the library or dining room.

"Mais, Papa, ce n'est pas beaucoup de temps jusqu'à l'arrivée d'André!"

"Oui, je le sais, chérie." Souchet's voice dropped. There were footsteps, a strangled sob, and the conversation continued in whispers. Devon recognized only one other phrase—*"avant la naissance de ce bâtard-là!"*

Devon closed the door and put her warm cheek against it. Was it true? Was Souchet Eugénie's father? If so, what were they after, and how did her unborn child fit in?

Devon bolted from the hallway like a prisoner escaping from a cage—she had to get away from this house. A balmy breeze sifted over the island and the perfume of flowers rose out of the trees. Devon folded her arms over her belly and began to walk, her thoughts chaotic. Breathing hard, she headed straight for the secluded beach at the other end of the island, but when she was about to emerge from the concealment of the overgrown, vine-draped trees, she stopped short.

On the cliff, the black silhouette of a man stood

out against the inky-blue, star-strewn sky. There was
no mistaking the full coat, the stockinged calves, or
the outline of side curls on his wig.

Souchet! To keep from gasping aloud, Devon
pressed a hand to her mouth. What on earth was he
doing *here,* of all places? She had thought to escape
from him and Eugénie, to ponder what she had over-
heard and to attempt to unravel the tangled questions
in her head, but now she was more confused than
ever.

"Véronique . . ." Souchet implored in French.
"What am I to do? I have *tried* to direct Eugénie,
but it is difficult. If only you were here!" Tears glittered in the starlight as he shook a fist at the moon.
"It was your own fault, Véronique. I loved you! I
watched you and Eugénie for five years, waiting for
you to tell *him.* You promised me!"

Caught in the emotion of his tirade, Souchet stumbled slightly and turned as he tried to regain his balance. His wild eyes fell on Devon, who stood rooted
to the ground, pale and wide-eyed with shock. Her
French was not perfect, but after nearly six months
of living with a largely French staff, she had absorbed
enough to translate Souchet's rantings.

"You followed me!" he shouted.

"No—no—I just came here for a walk. Truly—"

"You heard? Do you speak French?" He came
nearer, staring. "I can see that you do. I am sure that
talkative maid of yours has related the tale of Véronique's death."

Devon could only nod. She saw the fire dim in his
eyes; suddenly he dropped to his knees on the thick,
wild grass. "She should have been *mine,*" he choked,
emotions squelched for twenty-five years finally pouring out.

"Véronique?" Devon's fear abated. Souchet seemed
too distraught to harm her and she bent to hear his
answer.

"*Oui.* Yes. Véronique. I was only eighteen years

old when I came here. I was the butler then. The first time the master went to sea, she invited me to her room—the one where you stay. My passion for Véronique ruled my life. When *he* was at home, I used to think of killing him. I couldn't eat or sleep. Once, while he was away for two months, Véronique became *enceinte*. He was at sea when the child was born as well, so we were able to juggle the birthdate a bit. He was a fool . . . but of course, she was bewitching . . ." His sigh echoed mournfully on the night breeze. "She could not bring herself to break off with Raveneau, though we spent five long years making plans. Eugénie grew older, and by the time she was Louisa's age, I was in agony each time I saw her on the master's knee or heard her call him papa. Finally, I told him that Eugénie was not his child, and when he sent for Véronique, she promised me again that this time she would break off with him. We could all hear them fighting, throwing things, and after a few hours—she said she waited until he was asleep—we met and slipped outside to walk."

The tortured voice trailed away and Souchet looked up to meet Devon's intent gaze as if he had just noticed her. "What are you doing here?" he asked, dazed.

"But . . . was it you? Did you kill her?"

Souchet ignited like a torch, leaping to his feet. "She brought it on herself! She told me that they *made up!* I . . . just couldn't take any more." He lapsed back into French, raving about spending over half his life as the faithful servant, keeping all his emotions hidden. "After Véronique . . . our daughter was my only reason for living." A vein stood out on Souchet's forehead as his voice rose. "If it were not for you and that bastard in your belly . . . You probably think you can tell M'sieur Raveneau that Eugénie is Véronique's daughter and that he will turn from her to you." He paused to draw a ragged breath.

Devon didn't wait to find out what he would say or

do next. She turned and lifted her skirts to run. She felt damp fingers grasp at her arm. Utterly terrified, more for her innocent baby than for herself, Devon scrambled and stumbled in the night-shrouded underbrush. Somewhere behind, she could hear Souchet coming, and each time her foot caught in a hole or tripped over a rock, she thought he would be upon her. Then, on the winding path leading up the hill to the house, a snarl of vines twisted Devon's skirts and she fell backward, onto rocks and branches. The sound of Souchet's labored breathing, nearing by the moment, forced her to pull herself up. Her belly seemed like dead weight and she felt a long, wrenching cramp when she started back up the hill. No time for worry now. Later . . .

Somehow she staggered across the grass to the rear door. A cramp tore through her insides again; her legs were wet. Devon began to sob, crumpling on the landing of the servants' stairs. "Elsa! Elsa!" she screamed.

A blond, plaited head appeared, blurring as Devon blinked and lost consciousness.

Chapter Twenty-four

———◆———

May 7, 1782

THIS day marked a fortnight of life for Mouette Deborah, who was about the same size as the porcelain doll Louisa had brought with her from England. During the first days following her premature birth on the servants' stairs, everyone had waited sadly for her to die, except Devon. She had been groggy and weak as a kitten herself, but she had insisted that Mouette stay in her bed. All through the day and night she had held the swaddled infant close to her body, warming her and loving her. Devon had known that Mouette was meant to live.

And she did. Mother and daughter stayed in the servants' quarters, sharing a room and a lowpost bed that was made up daily with fresh linens. Cook was in heaven and never questioned Devon's refusal to return to the lavish bedchamber two floors above. Once it was evident that Mouette was going to survive, Cook was transformed into a solicitous *grand-mère*, who delighted in every moment she could spend with the tiny raven-haired charmer. The rest of the staff was nearly as doting. Devon let the children gather around the bed when she changed Mouette's diaper or gown, and they cooed and giggled at the baby's wide-eyed, uncoordinated antics.

Devon was completely well now. She had dressed four days after giving birth, and except for her refusal to leave the servants' quarters, she had been engaged in a busy mother's routine ever since. Elsa no longer waited on her; their relationship was that of affectionate friends who helped each other. Mouette had only her mother for a nurse, and if anyone else rocked her or changed her diaper, it was because Devon allowed it.

This day in early May found Devon alone with Mouette in her room, primrose muslin bodice unfastened to allow the baby her noon meal. Devon put out her free hand and ran it lightly over the feathery jet hair covering Mouette's perfectly sculpted head. Even at birth it had been just this round, though the rest of her had not been so pretty. For three days she had been unable to coordinate her mouth to nurse; as soon as she managed to get a drop of milk, she would jerk with excitement in another direction.

How far she's come in only two weeks! Devon smiled. Mouette sucked greedily, and had a pink, healthy appearance to prove it. Astonishingly long lashes lay against cheeks that were curved and rosy; a miniature hand rested trustingly on the creamy swell of Devon's breast.

A timid knock sounded at the door.

"Who is it?"

"Me," a child's voice declared after a moment's pause.

"Oh, Louisa! Come in. I missed you yesterday."

The little girl opened the door but stopped after one or two steps.

"Don't be shy, Louisa. This is how babies take nourishment. When Mouette was growing inside me, my breasts were making milk to feed her. She won't need any other food for several months! Isn't it lovely how God planned every detail?"

Devon's relaxed manner put Louisa at ease. "My cat had babies one time," she revealed, coming closer to perch on a ladder-back chair beside the bed. "She had milk inside her, too."

"Yes, that's right. Most animals are the same. What is your cat's name?"

"Duke," Louisa replied innocently. "But I had to give her to my friend Sarah before we went on the ship."

"That's a shame. No doubt you miss her."

Louisa nodded.

"Tell me, how did you happen to choose Duke's name?"

"I named her after Mama's best friend. His name was Duke, and I think Mama wanted it to be her name, too, but I told her Eugénie is lots prettier."

Devon's smile was crooked. "Tell me, sweetheart, how is your mother? I know she must have been very sad about M'sieur Souchet. I hope she's feeling better."

Louisa's hazel-gold eyes clouded. "I told her that he's in heaven, way up on top of the clouds, but she still cries—every hour almost! She tells me to go away."

Mouette had dozed off and Devon gently lifted her to burp, trying to decide what to say to Louisa. She hadn't learned of Souchet's death herself until Mouette was four days old and out of danger. Elsa had blurted out the story then: it seemed that Louisa had risen early the morning after Mouette's birth, and finding Devon's room empty, had gone to look for her outside. Halfway down the hill behind the house, she had discovered the cold, chalky body of Bernard Souchet, sprawled with arms reaching forward. Thinking him asleep, the child had shaken his shoulders until fear had replaced confusion; then she had run to the house, screaming and sobbing. Hermann had heard her and gone back to Souchet. There wasn't a mark on the body, not even a bump to the head. Everyone had agreed the man's heart must have simply stopped.

In spite of her sublime contentment, Devon had dreamed more than once of darkness and terror and raspy, labored breathing that pursued her maniacally. She felt no pity for Bernard Souchet; it was a blessing that he hadn't lived, for certainly total madness would have claimed him soon. During the four days when she had thought him still alive, she had worried that he might again attempt to kill her, and Mouette too, but the news of his death did not entirely dispel her concern. Eugénie, in her own way, was just as dangerous.

Mouette's eyes opened drowsily as she emitted a resonant belch, and Louisa giggled.

"She's cute! I wish I had a baby sister or brother."

"You'll have to come back more often, sweetheart. You can help me dress her and rock her. Would you like that?"

Louisa nodded vigorously, her eyes luminous. "I'd *love* it!"

"Good. I don't see nearly enough of you these days."

"Devon . . . doesn't Mouette have a papa, either? Is she going to get one like me?"

Louisa's vulnerable, hopeful expression made Devon's heart turn over. At least Mouette had one parent who loved her enough to insure a secure childhood, but this little ginger-haired girl was starved for affection. And Raveneau was not a piece of pie that she, Devon, and Eugénie could divide among themselves and their daughters.

"Well, Mouette does have a papa, but he had to go away."

"Will he come back and take care of Mouette?"

"I don't think so, Louisa. I will have to love her twice as much."

There was another knock at the door. "Fräulein, there is a young man here to see you." Elsa's tone was heavy with meaning, and for a moment Devon shivered with panic, thinking that Raveneau had returned.

Gulping, she lay Mouette along her lap and fumbled at the hooks on her gown.

"F—fine! Send in this mysterious visitor!"

A long, heart-pounding minute passed. Devon smoothed her loosely upswept hair, gathered the napping Mouette back into her arms, and smiled nervously at Louisa. What irony! she thought. He will meet both daughters at the same time!

The door opened slowly. Morgan Gadwin stepped in, twisting a tricorn hat in his hands.

"Hello, Devon," he said.

Her mouth opened, but no sound came out. Louisa looked back and forth curiously. "Who are you?"

"Uh . . . Louisa, this is an old friend of mine from New London. He . . . we—"

"Are you Morgan?" the little girl pursued. "Devon told Mama and me a long story about you."

This news seemed to bolster Morgan's courage. "Yes, I'm Morgan. I hope it was a nice story." His eyes met Devon's.

"Louisa!" she exclaimed, "Would you mind leaving us alone for a little while? I think I smell cookies baking, and if you ask nicely, Cook is sure to give you one."

The little girl took the hint, said goodbye, and left.

"What are you doing here?" Devon burst out.

Morgan shambled over and took Louisa's chair. "I had second thoughts. And I heard you were unhappy. That was all I needed to know to make me want another chance." His eyes kept flicking curiously to Mouette. "Who is that?"

"My daughter. Mouette."

Morgan's long face registered shock, bewilderment, and finally comprehension. "You don't mean . . . you . . . this . . . *his* baby?"

Devon nodded.

"B—but that's impossible! Why, it was October barely over six months ago—that we were in Williams-

burg! You were going to marry *me!* You thought you
had! I . . . you must be joking!"

"No, I'm quite serious. Mouette was already begun
when we reached Williamsburg, but of course I didn't
know. If I had, I would never have spoken of marriage
to you."

She felt sorry for Morgan. She knew him well enough
to understand how much self-respect he had doubtless
lost in Williamsburg, but this was the crowning blow.
He sat there, clutching the seat of his chair with white-
knuckled hands, and his face clearly showed his hatred
for Raveneau.

"I . . . Devon . . . I simply cannot believe this! Did
he *rape* you?"

"No." A split-second memory flashed in her mind:
Raveneau murmuring that he should not take advantage of her, then her own voice, imploring, "I want you
to! I demand it!" In happier times since, they had
laughed about that night, but now her mouth could
manage only a sad, crooked parody of a smile. "No, he
is not to blame. Not at all."

Morgan's face burned with chagrin as he thought of
all the times she had pushed him away—apparently
even after she was no longer a virgin!

"I am sorry that you came so far to be disappointed."

"I don't understand—at all. Are you . . . married to
him?"

"No. He left the island before I was aware I carried
Mouette."

"And when he returns?"

"I . . . do not expect to continue my relationship
with André. He is a hard man; I doubt that he knows
how to love. My concern is for Mouette, and I can de-
pend on no one to nurture her but myself. Even if
André did agree to marry me, I could not bear to go
through life knowing that he longed for freedom. I
have responsibilities to my baby; I cannot go on chasing and clinging to André." She couldn't discuss Louisa

and Eugénie with Morgan, and in any event, she was reasonably certain that she would feel the same even if Louisa didn't exist. The pain of involvement with Raveneau was too intense; it wouldn't mix with motherhood.

"I realize that this must be hard for you to accept—my involvement with another man outside marriage, and my baby—but, Morgan, you must face the fact that a great deal has happened since we were children making plans above the Thames. We are both older and have learned some painful truths. I am a woman now, and cruel though it sounds, my love for you simply did not mature. I still love you, Morgan, but not as a husband or a lover."

He nodded bleakly. A dozen different emotions churned inside him. Devon seemed almost a stranger to him; she was an adult, while he still felt clumsy and cowardly. Before he had gone to war, he had absorbed spirit and courage from her, but his time in the army had brought him face to face with his true spineless self.

Morgan had prolonged recovery from his case of camp fever to avoid the battle at Yorktown, though such malingering had made him despise himself. Other symptoms of weakness had appeared, from overindulgence in spirits to backing down before André Raveneau. Raveneau had witnessed Morgan's weaknesses—including the girl Morgan had had in his room—and Morgan hated him for it. In Morgan's mind, he became the victim and Raveneau the ultimate villain. When Hermann Kass had appeared at the drug shop, offering money and advice, he had seemed a messenger from God. Morgan thirsted for revenge and redemption, and despite Devon's speech and her baby, he could see that his dual aims were still within reach.

"Devon . . . as hard as it is to understand," said Morgan, "I think I do. And maybe you are right. I have been living in the past and I can see now that those times are gone." He licked his lips, searching for

the right words. "I can't make you love me—that way
—but we do care for each other. I love you and always will, but I can accept it if it is only spiritual."

Devon laid Mouette down on the quilt beside her.
If he could truly offer her platonic love, she knew she
would accept it happily. At this point in her life,
friends were precious; their affection kept her from
freezing inside.

"Thank you, Morgan."

He saw her sapphire eyes glisten with tears and
seized the advantage. "I mean it. Truly. Devon, if I
were in trouble, wouldn't you help me?"

"Of course!"

"Well, I want to help you. I have a ketch. It's not
much compared with that privateer, but I got it for
you. I wanted to show you that our old dreams weren't
so idle, and I want to take you away from here.
And—" His hesitation went undetected by Devon.
"And Mouette, of course. Let me take you back to
New London, and later, if your feelings should, ah,
grow, we could be married."

"New London! Oh, no, Morgan, I don't think—"

"Devon, Devon! It's not as bad as you think. I want
you to discover it for yourself, but you must trust me.
My parents are alive and you love *them,* don't you? I
admit, the town is still sad, but we all have to begin
again, don't we? And compared with this island—"

Devon begged him to let her think. "If I *do* say yes,
I just want to be certain you remember what you've
said. You won't pressure me about marriage, because I
don't think—"

"I know, I know!" His pale face had more color now.
"Just remember that you would be a woman alone . . .
and if we did marry, you would have me to take care
of you. Mou—ah—"

"Mouette."

"Yes. She would have a father. You could hold your
head up in town."

Devon felt that she could take care of herself and

Mouette at least as well as any man, especially Morgan, but after an hour of solitary thought, she was forced to admit to herself that he was right about society. And for Mouette's sake . . .

She watched her baby sleep. Tiny, pale blue veins were visible under translucent eyelids, and for all the feminine beauty of Mouette's profile, Devon could see Raveneau as well, especially in the way her infant's lips tightened with determination. Devon knew what Cook would say that expression meant—gas, or worse—but she knew better.

Devon's heart might have won the battle, for she loved Raveneau more than she hated him, but Louisa was an innocent child, and Devon couldn't forget the look of utter longing on her face. After all, she thought, I'll be sparing Mouette and myself a greater amount of pain later on. It will be easier for everyone, including André, if I leave now. I need some peace and tranquility.

Morgan was jubilant when she told him her decision. He even forced himself to pick up Mouette.

"What does Mouette mean?" he asked conversationally.

Devon paused for a moment before replying, "Sea gull." André would not help shape his daughter's life, she thought, but the essence of his spirit would always be present in her name.

Chapter Twenty-five

———◆———

May 16, 1782

MOUETTE gurgled happily from her pillow-throne, smiling with each sway and lurch of the ketch. They had been at sea two days now, and within an hour of their departure from the island, the baby had produced her first real smile. Devon had worried that Mouette might be seasick, but soon realized that this was an impossibility, given her parentage. There were times when she felt so sick at heart that only Mouette's happy cooing could alleviate the pain.

Devon lay sideways across the bunk, forming a barrier in case Mouette should topple from her pillow. This cabin was a far cry from Raveneau's on board the *Black Eagle*, but then the entire craft paled in comparison. It was obvious that Morgan had acquired the ketch for the sole purpose of "rescuing" her, and Devon wondered where he had gotten the money.

During the week that had elapsed between his arrival on the island and their departure together, it had become increasingly evident that Morgan did not need her love. His eyes had glowed at the revenge he thought he was taking against Raveneau, which he seemed to believe would restore his own self-respect and wipe out past humiliations. He had urged Devon to make haste for their departure, but Devon, suspecting that Eugénie was coaching him, had refused to be pushed out of the house until she was certain that Mouette was strong enough.

It had taken nearly the full week for Devon to compose a letter to Raveneau. In simple terms, she had admitted the baby's birth but left him a suspicion by not declaring him the father. She explained her feelings about the futility of their relationship and the importance of a secure home for her baby. The written words had sounded cold, but certainly there was no other way. The break had to be unquestioned.

Devon had also written what she had learned about Souchet and Véronique, telling André that his father had not killed her after all. An entire page had been devoted to Louisa, who needed her papa so much, begging Raveneau to give her a chance, knowing that once he saw her smile and held her in his arms, he would be as captivated as Devon had been.

She had rewritten the letter over and over, striving for an impersonal tone. When she had finally signed her name at the bottom and sealed the sheets of parchment, bitter tears had burned her cheeks.

Saying goodbye had been horrible. Elsa and Cook had wept openly, but worst of all had been little Louisa. Devon had held her on her lap, embracing her for several minutes as they both wept. "Your papa will be here very soon, sweetheart," she had said, "and I have a feeling that you and he will be great friends."

In the kitchen, all the servants had clustered around to say farewell and wish Devon and Mouette happiness; then Elsa had carried Mouette, Louisa clinging to Devon's hand, as they had gone upstairs. On the landing where she had given birth, Devon had stopped and taken something out of her reticule, pressing it into Elsa's hands.

"Please, promise me that you will deliver this to André when he arrives. Guard it carefully and put it into his hand when you find him alone."

Morgan had been conversing with Eugénie in the entryway, their heads close together. The woman wore a beautiful gown of pink velvet over an ivory satin petticoat trimmed with layers of ruching. More ivory satin fashioned a sash around Eugénie's wasp waist and was fluted on the neckline to accentuate her stunning bosom. When she looked up at Devon, her hazel-gold eyes were fiery with triumph.

"Goodbye," had been all Devon could manage.

"Goodbye."

After one last hug for Louisa, Devon had taken Mouette from Elsa, and Morgan had gone forward to open the door.

Morgan had insisted that Devon have a servant who could see to clothes and baths and other services for her and Mouette. Quiet little Jeannette had been eager to fill this position, and now, as mother and daughter lay together on the narrow bunk, the young maid was preparing a tray for Devon's noon meal.

When the cabin door opened, Devon looked up, expecting to find Jeannette but discovering Morgan instead. It seemed to Devon that Morgan's arms and legs were longer and thinner than ever. He had sprouted to a respectable height, but his shoulders hadn't grown since adolescence, and his limbs seemed to move independently of the rest of his body.

"Hello, Morgan. It's nice to see you."

"You are all right? I've been busy—"

"We're fine." In truth, his infrequent appearances made her nervous. The only conversation that she wished to have with him concerned New London, but he had an irritating habit of smirking secretively and refusing to give her any news at all.

Mouette tried one of her winning smiles on Morgan, but he looked away uneasily.

"For a man who speaks of becoming this child's father, you certainly don't act very enthusiastic!" Devon sat up and reached for Mouette. "Here—why don't you hold her?"

"No. I'd really rather not. My shirt is soiled."

Devon shrugged and kissed her baby's round cheek. Morgan took a seat next to the fold-down table, opened his mouth as if to speak, then closed it. Devon watched his eyes shift over the floor, saw the gleam that came into them, and knew where his thoughts were. So! He had made another visit to look at Raveneau's mistress and child and taste the full sweetness of his revenge.

Devon was more certain than ever that she could never share her future with Morgan. Somehow, together, she and Mouette would find a way to survive. She would never become like Deborah—her child would come first and she would never let Mouette forget how much she was loved.

"Morgan . . ." Devon murmured uneasily. "I feel—"

"Excusez-moi, mam'selle," Jeannette interrupted, pushing open the door with her hip. As the girl crossed the cabin to deposit the tray on the table, she dropped her eyes and smiled shyly at Morgan. *"Bonjour, Capitaine."*

"Captain!" Devon echoed, eyes wide with mock awe.

Morgan ignored her gibe. "Hello, Jeannette. I trust you are well today?"

Devon stared as he assumed a gruff pose, lowering his voice to amusing depths. Jeannette, however, was not amused. Her blush darkened as she nervously clasped and unclasped her hands and, rendered speechless, nodded in response to his question.

One of Devon's delicate eyebrows curved up. An interesting scene! It would seem that Jeannette might be the solution to all her future problems with Morgan!

The silence was broken by a scuffling on the deck above, followed by the appearance of Morgan's unsavory-looking first mate.

"Cap'n! A ship is bearin' down fast, due south!"

Devon let Morgan rush out, then made a quick decision. She was dressed much differently than in the old days on the *Black Eagle*. Her gown of cream silk was striped in a vivid blue, a shade softer than the sapphire of her eyes. The neckline dipped to reveal the curve of her breasts, and her shoulders were more ivory than in the past.

Yet, despite her more mature femininity and her maternal practicality, her blood heated up at the prospect of a clash at sea. Morgan wouldn't have the faintest idea what to do!

"Jeannette, I want you to stay right here in this cabin, with Mouette. Please sit down." When the girl obeyed, Devon put the baby in her arms. "Don't move until someone comes and tells you otherwise. *Comprends-tu?*"

"*Oui, mam'selle.*"

Devon started for the door, pausing to glance back briefly at the frightened-looking maid. As the ship dipped to the starboard side, Mouette crowed gleefully, and Devon smiled as she turned into the narrow, stinking gangway. In moments she was hoisting her skirts with one hand and pulling herself through the hatch. On the tiny quarter-deck, Morgan stood out like a third mast, clutching the rail.

Devon looked around. Behind them, like a dark, white-winged avenging angel, was the *Black Eagle*. The figurehead loomed over them, noble and demonic at once, black wings arched. For a moment Devon was paralyzed. What was Raveneau *doing?*

Devon swung around. The men, such as they were, scrambled about crazily. Morgan was totally unstrung.

Devon forced herself to think only of the present. Coolly, she lifted her silk gown and petticoats and walked to the larboard rail. The *Black Eagle* sliced through the scalloped blue waves like a sword; it was barely two ship-lengths behind now, and Devon recognized familiar figures in the rigging.

Turning her head, she saw Morgan choking and

shouting at the red-faced, drunken boatswain at the wheel. They could not outrun the *Black Eagle,* nor was there any question of fighting. The pitiful ketch had no armament—her men had nothing but their knives and possibly a pistol or two.

Devon stood silently at the rail and watched as the *Black Eagle* drew alongside. Although she remained frosty and expressionless on the outside, her heart beat frantically and chills ran down her spine when she saw Raveneau. He stood on the *Black Eagle's* quarter-deck, starboard side, leaning forward confidently, hands on the rail to brace his lean, powerful body.

Their eyes met, glittering; neither showed the slightest expression.

Devon's stomach knotted and she felt a wild desire to weep. Oh, it was unfair that he should affect her so! She had forgotten this strange twinge between her thighs, but it returned now, convulsively, prompted merely by the sight of him from afar. He was harsh and splendid, clad in knee boots, buff breeches that skimmed his hard thighs, and a plain shirt that showed half of his broad, dark chest.

She stood there, frozen, as the *Black Eagle* grappled the smaller ketch, and two dozen well-trained privateersmen swarmed over the side and lined the deck, weapons poised.

Morgan trembled with impotent rage. He cowered against the stern rail when Raveneau, his rapier flashing in the sun, landed with easy grace on the deck. Realizing that Morgan would not meet him, Raveneau arched a dark, cynical eyebrow and walked as far as the mainmast.

"Capitaine!" he shouted mockingly in French. "The *Black Eagle* demands that you surrender!"

Devon turned, hands clasping the rail behind her back. Though she did not think he looked in her direction, Raveneau was well aware of the lovely picture she made, breasts swelling against the bodice of a fashionable gown. Almost casually, he moved in her direction, and without meeting her gaze, he reached out with a bronzed hand to grip her arm.

"I have no desire for your sad-looking crew or ship, *Capitaine,*" Raveneau continued. "I will take this female and leave you to your business."

"I refuse to abandon her to such a savage!" Morgan shouted shakily.

"Ah, I see!" Raveneau was grinning now, and Devon's bones had long since melted. "Do you challenge me? Where is your rapier, *Capitaine?*" He slanted his own weapon toward Morgan.

"But . . . I—"

"Morgan, don't be a fool! Jeannette will comfort you, and I certainly won't hold you responsible!" Devon cried. "You did your best, and I will always remember that. Let me go with Captain Raveneau."

Morgan bowed in silent surrender, while Raveneau whispered, "A most inspiring speech, *petite chatte.* It would seem that you've convinced him!"

Still gripping her arm, he turned to leave the ketch, but Devon stopped after two steps, eyes blazing and nostrils flaring. "If you please, I will not go anywhere without my daughter!" She pulled her arm free and headed toward the hatch.

Raveneau watched her, noting the stubborn set of her shoulders and head. She had changed, there was no doubt, and his instincts told him that the sparks would fly between them with more frenzy than ever.

The instant her silk-slippered feet touched the deck of the *Black Eagle,* Devon's divided heart grew together again. Mouette lay snuggled in her arms, Raveneau stood beside them, and returning to this ship was like coming home.

She narrowed blue eyes at Raveneau. "You are a villainous pirate."

"Your flattery is music to my ears." He frowned at Wheaton and all the others who stood beaming and gawking at Devon. "Which of you knows how to hold a baby?"

Devon tightened her grip on the sleeping bundle. "I will not leave Mouette."

"Oh! *Mouette!*" Raveneau's tone suggested to Devon that he believed the worst about the pregnancy.

"Where is Minter? I might entrust her to him—for a few minutes."

"Minter is busy, and in case you've forgotten, you are my prisoner, mademoiselle."

Treasel darted forward. "I know a bit about babes," he offered. Devon had no choice. Grudgingly, she put Mouette in his arms and let Raveneau pull her down the hatch to his cabin.

The moment he closed the door, Devon exploded like a well-loaded cannon. "You arrogant, swaggering, vile—*man!* I cannot believe that you—"

"How dare you leave that island without even showing me the courtesy of a personal explanation?" Raveneau interrupted coldly.

"Courtesy! Ha, ha! That is certainly not one of *your* virtues!"

"I do not run from confrontation like a cowardly rabbit, nor do I seek help from rodents who are even more cowardly. Did you imagine that I would eat your child for breakfast in my rage?"

His voice was deadly calm. They faced each other, standing a dozen feet apart, eyes locked in combat.

"I see! Tell me, Captain, what do you think about my daughter? Do you suppose that she was already hidden in my belly when Noah brought me to the *Black Eagle?* Perhaps you suspect that *he* was her father?"

Raveneau leaned back against the door. "The notion has occurred to me."

"Oooh . . . you make me furious!"

"Please, don't strike me," Raveneau taunted.

Devon strode over to him, burning with outrage. "You are a fool! You don't know me at all!"

"Dear Devon, it has been my experience that the moment a man believes he understands a woman, that is when he is usually the furthest from the truth."

"Fool!" she repeated vehemently. "Do you actually think I am like Véronique? Have I been *acting* all these months? And you are an even greater fool if you think that my pregnancy was more than one-third over when we were together last! My belly was as flat the day we said goodbye on the beach as it was the night you took my maidenhood in this very cabin!" She was screaming now, and didn't care.

Raveneau stared, his eyes sharpened silver, and brown hands reached out to catch her forearms. "Do you hear what you are saying? Even we fools know how much time elapses between conception and birth. Are you asking me to believe you over simple mathematics?"

"Yes!" Tears sparkled in her eyes. Her softly elegant coiffure had begun to tumble down, and she looked more like the minx Raveneau was used to. His stare seemed to penetrate to her very soul.

"D'accord," he whispered. "I believe you."

They moved together slowly until their mouths touched in a wondering, salty kiss. Devon felt faint as his fingers slipped into her hair and warm lips grazed the line of her cheekbone and brow. Suddenly she began to weep in earnest.

"What is it?"

"You don't remember me!" she burbled, her hurt exposed at last.

"What madness is this? Remember you! Do you imagine that I am holding a stranger?"

"No! I mean *really* remember—the first time we met."

Raveneau savored the scene. Deliberately, he played at bewilderment, narrowing his eyes at the bulkhead, rubbing a knuckle over the scar on his jaw. Devon's tears stopped. Hands on hips, she fumed.

"Hmmm," he mused. "I gather you do not refer to our introduction last September . . . so you must have in mind that afternoon in October of 1780. You came into Nicholson's library, wearing a blue dress and a leaf in your hair—and later you seduced me in the carriage."

"Seduced you! *I* seduced *you?* How dare—"

Devon stopped short at the sight of his face. She had never seen his eyes flash quite so mischievously, or so lovingly. "You make a jest of my feelings."

"I have missed you. I like to see all your facets; you are as priceless as the most brilliant diamond. Very nearly a miracle—a beautiful, brave, intelligent, witty female who is totally without guile."

Devon could scarcely believe her ears. "Are you serious?"

"Absolutely." He stared at her, gently running his hands over her hips, waist, breasts, arms, shoulders, and neck. When they reached her delicate face, deft fingers slid into rose-gold hair and he bent to kiss her with a stirring tenderness that she hadn't thought him capable of. "Devon, I love you."

"I . . . but . . . have you been drinking?"

Raveneau threw back his head and shouted with laughter before swinging her up into his arms. Several minutes passed as they lay across the familiar bed, kissing and touching with hungry elation. Devon's lovely silk gown was nearly removed before she remembered a small detail.

"André . . . I don't think I should. It has been only three weeks since Mouette was born . . . I'm still tender. Perhaps in a few days?"

She looked terribly disappointed herself, and Raveneau mustered all his understanding while trying to subdue the more obvious proof of his desire. "We have waited this long, I do not mind a few more days. It is enough—almost!—to hold you in my arms and

taste your mouth, inhale the scent of your hair . . ."
They kissed again, tongues teasing playfully, and
Raveneau tried to endure.

"I can't believe that you really remember . . ."
Devon murmured.

"That again!" he laughed.

"André—about my leaving the island—" Devon
shifted upward, resting her cheek against the hard
muscles of his arm and meeting his molten gaze. "I
went with Morgan because I felt that Louisa needed
you more than we did. I love that child, and it hurts
me that you've turned away from her. Please—"

"Devon, Louisa is fine. The matter is settled."

"The 'matter'! You call the heart of a little girl a
'matter'?"

"Do you want to fight again, or will you trust me
as I trust you?"

She swallowed a painful sigh. "All right. I will trust
you."

"You say those words as if I forced them out with
torture." Raveneau's face grew harsh again as he slid
his arm free and swung his legs over the side of the
bed. Neither spoke while he buttoned his shirt and
reached for his boots.

There was a knock at the door. Raveneau shot an
icy look at Devon, then got up to open it, leaving her
to grapple with her twisted, unfastened gown.

"Bonjour, ma citrouille!" he exclaimed.

Devon looked up in curious surprise, just in time to
hear a well-loved giggle.

"I told you a hundred times—don't call me a pump-
kin!" Little arms reached out and Raveneau hoisted
the little girl into his arms.

"You just couldn't wait, could you?" he teased,
turning toward the bed. "Didn't I tell you that I would
come and get you *later?*"

"Devon!" squealed Louisa. She threw herself out of
André's arms and dove into Devon's embrace. Over

the child's shoulder Devon could see Raveneau, one black brow arched grimly.

"Louisa, what a surprise!" she said. "You are a lucky girl, getting to sail on the *Black Eagle* with your papa!"

"I know! It's really fun! And you were right about my papa. He's wonderful!"

"Of course he is."

"Would you like to meet him? Wait—" She scrambled off the bed. "I'll be right back."

Devon was still staring in shock, afraid to look at Raveneau's face, when Louisa reappeared in the doorway, clutching the hand of a flustered Halsey Minter.

"I cannot believe it," Devon breathed. "Why didn't I see it before?" She was alone in the cabin; Raveneau had accompanied Minter to discuss "a few minor matters."

When Halsey Minter had come in, taken a chair at Raveneau's invitation, and scooped Louisa into his lap, the sight of their two faces side by side had been incredible. Louisa's ginger hair was a shade less fiery than her father's, but her eyes, face shape, and expressions were identical.

Minter was a smitten man. He and Louisa had seemed to be off in a private world of their own, whispering jokes, hugging, even tickling each other from time to time. He had met Devon's eyes and given her a boyish smile that had lit up the cabin.

Raveneau returned now, lingering in the doorway to observe Devon's pensive profile. It was an amazing day; all the emotions that he had buried for years had come to the surface . . . and Raveneau's relief was immeasurable. Crossing the cabin, he sat down beside Devon and she nestled against him. A slim arm attempted to reach around his muscle-ridged back as she smiled up, touching his sleek hair with her other hand.

One side of Raveneau's mouth twitched. "Are you glad to see me, perhaps?"

"Ecstatic. Am I too forward? Overpowering?"

He grinned lazily. "Overpowering . . . yes, that's the word. I surrender."

He bent to kiss her, but Devon put her hand over his lips. "Wait. I wonder how Mouette is."

"Sleeping. Treasel has promised to bring her in as soon as she awakens."

"She'll be hungry soon."

"Hungry? What do you suppose we can feed her?"

Devon giggled. "I carry her meals wherever I go! Oh, my, are you blushing? It's hard to tell under that swarthy complexion, but I actually do believe—"

Slate-gray eyes narrowed. "You try my patience, *petite chatte.*"

"I know." She beamed. "And see how you have distracted me! I have been consumed with curiosity about Minter and Louisa! Please, tell me how—when —everything."

Raveneau smiled as she snuggled her head against his shoulder, and idly caressed her titian cloud of hair as he spoke.

"When we arrived at the island late the night before last, Eugénie was in prime form. I was surprised and annoyed to see her, but after I found you gone and read your letter, I became quite disagreeable. Ah, 'savage' was the word Eugénie used, as I recall . . ." He smothered a grin. "When she produced Louisa and rattled off her story, I was certain, in my gut, that she was lying, but no matter what I said or did, she wouldn't admit it. Minter won the day. He came down after unpacking my things and saw and heard enough to know what the situation was. Louisa had fallen asleep in the salon, but as soon as he got a look at her, he came to me and exposed Eugénie."

"Hurry up!"

"Well, between Minter and Eugénie, I pieced the story together. It seems that six years ago, on the is-

land, Eugénie was certain she had me snagged, but
when I suddenly escaped her trap, she and Souchet
—her *cher père,* as now I know—concocted this
scheme. They rushed out to find someone to make her
pregnant. To avoid her, I had moved onto the privateer the last few nights before we sailed, and Minter
was left to collect my clothing from the house. He
was only sixteen then, and easily seduced by a viper
like Eugénie. I assume that she recruited more volun-
teers during the next weeks until she was positive of
the child, but it would seem that Minter had begin-
ner's luck!"

"But *why* would she do such a thing?"

"Pour moi, chérie!" Raveneau's exclamation was
heavy with sarcasm. "She returned to France, then
England, gave birth, and bided her time until the opportunity presented itself to introduce me to my
'child.' She tried to tell me the other night that she
had been pregnant when I left, but didn't know it
herself until she was back in Europe. Ironically, that
is true, but of course, I was not the father."

"And now that her plan has failed?"

"Minter and I convinced her to give him a turn as
a parent. As much as I hated to, I gave her some
money to tide her over, and will arrange for a Europe-
bound ship to stop for her. Of course, she made a
great show of maternal tragedy, but she agreed to see
how things work out these next months. I would wager
this privateer that Eugénie finds a wealthy husband
and we never hear from her again—and that Minter
and Louisa live happily ever after!"

"What will Minter do? He can't stay here!"

"He isn't certain. After we are in port, he plans to
take Louisa to Virginia for a visit with her grandpar-
ents, and I suppose that he'll reach a decision about
the future then."

"Oh, André, won't Azalea be thrilled when she returns! She'll adore Louisa!"

"Everyone does." His mouth drifted along Devon's

318

chin, then over her throat until she shuddered in reaction.

"Excuse me—Captain?" Treasel stood in the doorway with Mouette.

"Mouette!" Devon cried. Raveneau stood up and accepted the tiny infant almost warily. Devon bit back a grin at the sight of his bemused face. "She's not going to break! Come over here. She must be famished."

Mouette looked smaller than ever in Raveneau's arms, and she wriggled about, uneasy with the way he held her so stiffly. When they reached the bed, Devon prompted, "André, cuddle her a little! Hold her against your chest and smile at her!"

He sat down and regarded the baby with more than a trace of suspicion. "When I think about it, Devon, your story is remarkably similar to Eugénie's. Why have I swallowed it so agreeably?"

"Because you trust me."

"Oh, yes. Of course."

Mouette was clad in a long gown of layered ivory batiste embroidered with green leaves and an occasional blue flower. A soft, knitted bonnet, tied coquettishly under the chin, covered most of her feathery black hair.

"Well? Isn't she beautiful?"

Mouette opened her eyes wide at the sound of her mother's voice, but focused them on Raveneau. They were a clear shade of blue-gray, as though the parents' eyes had been mixed to an exact blend. Raveneau slowly extended a long, tanned finger and touched a lock of black hair, then the curve of Mouette's cheek and nose. When it brushed her mouth, she seized it and began to suck.

"What the devil is she doing?"

Devon laughed. "She's hungry. Perhaps you'd better hand her over."

"Look! She raised her eyebrow at me! How can she do that?"

"Her father's daughter," Devon explained sagely.

He stared as she unfastened her bodice and fit Mouette into the curve of her arm. The baby began to nurse. The swell of emotion in his chest was alarming, totally unlike anything he had ever felt before. On top of his declaration of love and trust for Devon, this helpless, entrancing infant was nearly more than he could cope with in one day.

The tiny hand was curved in a fist of pleasure, fluttering on the side of Devon's breast. To his horror, Raveneau felt a tear sting his eyes. "It is difficult to comprehend—my *daughter,*" he whispered.

Devon glanced up at the husky note in his voice. Her heart thudded wildly when she saw the telltale glint in his silver eyes, but she only smiled. "Mouette is a miracle of love. She was born so early . . . but I was certain that she would be charmed—like you."

Standing up abruptly, Raveneau announced, "I think I need a drink. Will you join me?"

"Only a drop."

He splashed cognac into two snifters and returned to the bed. Handing one to Devon, he then pulled up the wing chair and sat down. "To us, *petite chatte.*" He lifted his glass a fraction and cast an eye at Mouette. "I know she would join us were she not so greedy."

Devon smiled and took a sip of cognac, closing her eyes briefly against the almost unbearable surge of joy that flushed her cheeks.

While her eyes were closed, Louisa appeared in the doorway and waved to Raveneau, then vanished. "Ah . . . when Mouette is finished," he said, "I thought we might take her for a stroll on deck—show her around a bit."

"She would love it!" Devon approved, switching the baby to the other side. "Just a few more minutes."

While they waited, Raveneau made idle conversation about the British merchant ship they had taken the day before, after leaving the island. Most of the crew had gone with it back to New London, which accounted for the small show of force when they had boarded Morgan's ketch.

Then he rose, cigar clenched between strong white teeth as he retucked his shirt more neatly into the buff breeches. "You might like to rearrange your hair."

Slightly surprised, Devon gave Mouette to her father and fastened her bodice again, then went to the shaving stand. She did look rather disheveled, but certainly happy! Her eyes had never sparkled so, nor had her cheeks looked so lovely while flushed. She quickly pulled the remaining pins from her strawberry-blond curls and let them tumble down her back. A few smoothing flicks with the comb and she turned to smile at Raveneau, who was shrugging into an amber coat, switching Mouette from arm to arm.

"I'm ready!"

His eyes were soft. "You look exactly like the girl I met in Nicholson's library." Arching an eyebrow at her bosom, he added, "With a few minor improvements."

"Minor!" Devon laughed. Raveneau caught her hand, held it tightly, and together the trio went into the gangway. As they reached the open hatch, Devon could hear the rumble of voices from the brig below. "How many prisoners are there?"

"A dozen, perhaps. Actually, I think they're rather enjoying this. Our food is much better than what they have been eating the last few months."

He took Mouette up first, then leaned down to help Devon, causing her to think of all the times she had climbed through the hatch without so much as a glance from him.

"I cannot believe this is the same devil who once threatened to toss me overboard!" she whispered with amusement.

Raveneau smiled ironically. "Neither can I."

She looked around then and found the remaining two dozen crewmen assembled on deck. Each man had combed his hair and slipped a new eelskin over his queue. Their faces were clean; flat-brimmed hats were clutched nervously over their bellies, and several sported bright, freshly washed neckerchiefs.

"What are all of you doing?" Devon asked, unused to seeing them so sober-looking. None answered, though Wheaton's sea-blue eyes twinkled in a broad wink.

Minter came up through the hatch. Someone handed up a beautifully gowned Louisa, and then another man appeared. He was tall, with a nose like a rudder, but his smile was infectious.

"Devon Lindsay," Minter said, smiling, "may I present Captain Silas Longheart."

"How do you do, Captain?" Her eyes rested curiously on his gold-trimmed blue uniform and the red sash that crossed his chest.

"The pleasure is mine, I assure you, Miss Lindsay!"

"Captain Longheart joined us yesterday," Raveneau said casually, studying Mouette's tiny head on his shoulder.

"I don't understand!" Devon said.

Some of the men had begun to grin. She was a fetching little chit after all! Just the one for their captain.

"Devon," cautioned Raveneau, struggling to repress laughter, "please do not make a scene—especially on the occasion of our wedding."

She caught his sleeve for balance, choking audibly. "Oh . . . oh . . . *cruel!* You couldn't warn me? I—"

"You are not pleased by my surprise? You wish me to send Captain Longheart back to the brig?"

"André! No! Oh, you have me in such a state. I don't know what I'm saying!"

"*Petite chatte,* as long as you can say 'I do,' I will be satisfied."

Captain Longheart was grinning toothily. "I say!" he hooted. "Let's get on with it, then!"

The sun was just beginning to slide downward, streaking the sky and ocean with a soft apricot glow. A gentle, warm breeze caressed the *Black Eagle* and wrapped itself around André, Devon, and Mouette as they became a family in name as well as in spirit.

When the ceremony was over, Wheaton and Treasel volunteered to watch Mouette for a little while, promising to keep her safe. Raveneau wrapped an arm around his bride, marveling, "I never would have believed I could feel so incredibly pleased about being someone's *husband!* Never!"

Minter, Louisa, and Captain Longheart were persuaded to join the Raveneaus in the cabin to share a glass of champagne and sign the ship's log.

Inside the cozy, lantern-lit cabin, the cook brought champagne, and after the first toast and a sizzling round of kisses for the bride, the log book was produced. There were few entries in it; it would seem that the captain was not a man much concerned with records. Devon signed with a flourish, followed by Raveneau and the English captain.

She gazed at the inscriptions dreamily. There it was, in black ink . . . "Wedded this sixteenth day of May, 1782." Raveneau's hand was confident, the unembellished signature of a man who didn't need to impress others. *André Geai Raveneau.*

Devon looked up. "I never knew your second name! What does Geai mean?"

Minter flinched, but Raveneau flashed a casual smile. "Who knows? What does André mean?"

"But I never heard this name before." She glanced at Minter, who threw up his hands and shrugged excessively.

Captain Longheart laughed. "I don't know a bloody word of French, madam!"

Louisa had been staring at the bubbles in her tiny portion of champagne, but now she looked up. "Uncle André, if you are from France, why don't you know that *geai* means jay?"

Devon whirled on Raveneau, murder in her eyes. "You! *You!* How could you? You made a fool of me! Azalea, Minter"—she spared a fiery glare for Halsey —"all of you must have been laughing up your sleeves while I mooned over the Blue Jay!"

"Mooned?" Raveneau echoed. "Really?"

"Don't tease me! I could kill you right now!" Her nostrils flared; bright spots of color showed on her cheeks.

"I *say!*" ejaculated Captain Longheart. "I'm not anxious to return to that brig, but I do suddenly feel in the way!"

Raveneau caught Devon's arm and pulled her against the length of his body. "My wife is fine now, Captain. She apologizes for creating a scene, don't you, Devon? I know that you will hold the rest of your threats and insults and physical violence for when we are alone. *N'est-ce pas?*"

Conversation resumed, more champagne was opened, and Louisa eventually drifted off to sleep in her father's lap. Devon pouted, sitting next to Halsey on the bed, avoiding Raveneau's flinty gaze. When good nights were exchanged at last and the newlyweds were alone, Raveneau returned to his wing chair and stared at his wife.

Silence was thick in the air before Devon finally burst out, "You deceived me! You have been laughing at my foolish infatuation with the Blue Jay—all of you! How can you look at me like that, as if I am in the wrong?"

"You are, my dear," he said evenly. "This is our wedding night. I thought we had agreed to put past understandings in their proper place."

Suddenly, seeing her childish behavior in this new light, she felt wretched. Chin trembling, she went to Raveneau, waiting until his arms opened to her, then wrapped her in comforting strength.

"Devon, I love you."

"I love you!" Turning her face into his hard, warm chest, she let the tears come. "I should have known. The Blue Jay had to be you. I've never wanted anyone else in my entire life . . . and I never will."

Chapter Twenty-six

May 23, 1782

SHORTLY before noon on Mouette Raveneau's one-month birthday, the *Black Eagle* sailed into the harbor of New London. The weather was dazzling; cool and crisp. The sun was a ball of gold fire against a brilliant blue sky, transforming the water into a wide ribbon of glittering sapphires.

They had dropped a very happy Halsey and Louisa Minter at their Virginia farm, but Devon missed Halsey now. He had always known just what to say to her, his manner a perfect blend of compassion and common sense.

Devon had passed the morning on deck, pacing in agitation as the privateer skimmed along Fisher's Island Sound in sight of the Connecticut coastline. The view was wrenchingly familiar: the village of Stonington, Mason's Island, and the smaller islands below it, Noank, Groton Long Point, and Mumford's Cove. Beyond Pine Island, Devon could see the Thames, and she recognized White Beach and the lighthouse on the far side. Benedict Arnold's British fleet had landed there . . . could it have been less than nine months ago? Her stomach was in knots, her palms were icy. She hadn't slept at all the night before, plagued by

nerves and a fear that the nightmare would return.
Raveneau had brought her cognac and listened for
hours as she relived her childhood and adolescence,
and finally the last day she had spent in New London.
Coming back to face the consequences of that day
took all the courage she had, and still it was not
enough. If not for Raveneau . . .

Devon had turned away from her first view of the
Thames and had run for the cabin, nearly falling
through the hatch in her desperation.

Raveneau was shaving, a wide towel wrapped and
knotted around his waist. He had propped two plump
pillows on his desk so that Mouette lay at a slant,
gurgling and smiling at her father's performance.

Devon flung herself on the bed. "I want to stay
right here. I'm very tired. Let me just sleep today."

Raveneau put down his razor, sighing as he flexed
his shoulders and sent muscles playing down his
tawny back. "Devon. Are you going to make me suffer through an entire day of this? I understand how
you feel, but I don't have the patience to cajole and
coax you until you finally give up and do what you
know damn well you must. Why not spare us both
these exhausting dramatics and show me your mettle
instead?" His dark, chiseled face betrayed no hint of
sympathy, but this was the result of a lifetime of hiding his feelings. "I am certain you can manage,
Devon, and you must believe, this time, that I know
you best."

She was shaken by the sharpness of his voice, so
cool that it lost nearly all of its accent. Tears pooled
in her eyes, but Raveneau's expression did not soften.
He gave her one last rapier-sharp look, lifted a black
brow almost imperceptibly, then returned to his
shaving-stand.

"You don't understand," she whimpered after a
long minute. "I have been through so much . . . "

Raveneau didn't answer, didn't miss a stroke with
his razor. Devon's chin quivered and tears spilled onto

her cheeks, while Mouette continued to coo and swing her hand at a sunbeam. Not until he had finished shaving and had rinsed and dried his face and neck did Raveneau turn back to his wife. She saw him through her tears, looming over her, his lean, muscular body taut with anger. She cringed.

He caught her arms roughly and pulled her to him. "Don't you ever shrink from me again! Dry your eyes and get dressed, Devon. You only hurt yourself with this self-pity, and I will not allow it. You have suffered much, but you have also survived much and your blessings are many. You are not alone, as you were a year ago, before all this madness began. You have a husband and a daughter who love and need you, and you owe it to all three of us to face the past and put it to rest. All the tears in the world can't bring back the dead or wash away your fears and grief. I want you to put up your chin and tell yourself you are strong. And if you begin to weaken, hold on to me. That's what I am here for."

One arm encircled her slim back, while his other hand caught her chin, holding it as he covered her wet, trembling lips with his hard mouth. It was a potent kiss that burned a path to her heart and fired her with his strength. "You can lean on me, Devon, but I'll be damned if I'll carry you and do your walking. *Comprends-tu?*"

Her cheeks were flushed. In spite of Raveneau's stern manner, she felt the ridge of desire concealed by his towel—a reminder of his celibate frustration. No words would come, so she nodded, again and again.

They stood together on the deck as the *Black Eagle* docked. "Now, let's go ashore," Raveneau said gently, after all was made secure. He handed his baby daughter to Devon, and assisted her down the gangplank.

The Beach, once her playground, was nearly destroyed. Most of the storehouses were burned to the ground, the Customs House was a charred shell, and the courthouse and other buildings which had comprised the Parade were gone. The once-crowded waterfront looked forlorn; there were huge gaps between the ships.

Raveneau's arm hugged her waist. "At least the war is as good as over, and the triumph of freedom is certain. All of this can be restored, Devon."

Devon looked around the Bank as she walked. André had already told her that this was the most damaged area, and there was nothing else to say now. She looked beautiful; her head was erect, her back straight. She wore an elegant gown of cream-colored muslin striped in soft peach, its long-waisted boned bodice and square neckline flattering the high curve of her breasts. A wide-brimmed straw hat was tied around her throat with peach silk ribbons, a few apricot curls falling loose down her back, and she carried a sunshade of peach silk.

"There it is." Devon stopped and whispered the words.

Raveneau rearranged a squirming Mouette and looked at the burned building where Devon and her mother had lived and worked. The top was entirely destroyed, but part of the ground floor survived, and enough of the hanging sign remained for him to make out the words: "Linen and Pewter Shop."

"Devon, I think we should go to Nicholson's house. You may find that he survived the battle, and his wife's company should be reassuring for you. No doubt she can answer most of your questions."

They set out then, retracing in reverse the route they had followed in the carriage so long ago. Devon pointed out every home or shop that held meaning for her. They passed Gadwin's Drug Shop, but she had no wish to see Morgan's parents yet.

There was the gambrel-roofed schoolhouse where

Nathan Hale had awakened her mind long years ago. It sat away from the footpath, surrounded by a stone wall, and Devon touched the stones musingly.

"Do you know I turned nineteen last month?" she asked. "I'd forgotten . . . it was two weeks before Mouette was born."

"What made you think of it now?"

"Because I had had my twelfth birthday shortly before Master Hale went to war. He gave me *Common Sense* as a gift, and I was absolutely thrilled by the gesture. He always encouraged me to study, but after he left, there was never a schoolmaster who had a moment to spare for a female."

"I cannot believe you let that stop you!"

Seeing the gleam in his eye, Devon smiled. "Master Hale laid a good foundation. The rest I could do on my own, with the help of Nick's library."

They were approaching the handsome dark blue Nicholson home. It had survived the fire perfectly, looking exactly the same as when Devon was growing up.

"Don't panic," Raveneau said. "There is bound to be at least one familiar face here, *n'est-ce pas?* Look, Mouette is scowling, too!"

Raveneau went forward to lift the familiar brass knocker. Just the sight of him warmed Devon's blood and made her feel more secure. He had never looked more irresistibly disreputable, clad in a frock coat of soft dove-gray velvet that only served to emphasize the steel-flint of his eyes and jet-black sweep of hair queued at his neck. The lean brown line of his jaw showed above a white shirt and cravat, while a waist-coat of slate silk fitted neatly against his tapering chest and narrow waist. Finally, slate breeches and gleaming black knee boots completed the picture of danger-ous, masculine elegance.

Devon allowed herself a sigh. She had waited these past days for him to ask eagerly if she was able to make love yet, but after the first day he hadn't said a word. His eyes had let her know what he wanted, but it was obvious now that he expected her to come to him.

Dreamily, she shivered.

"You certainly look pleased for someone who is suffering," he murmured sarcastically, and Devon met his knowing eyes with a guilty blush.

"I—I—"

"I am glad to hear it." White teeth flashed in a wicked grin.

The door swung open then, revealing a tall Negro butler Devon had never seen before.

"Is your mistress at home?" Raveneau inquired.

"Yes, sir," replied the butler, his voice deep and melodious. "Who is calling?"

"André Raveneau—and family."

The butler turned to hurry up to the second floor. Devon's heart was beating like a wild drum when Raveneau took her arm and drew her into the stair-hall. She gazed around, curiously dazed. The cream walls had been repainted pale green, and there was a new tall-case clock beside the parlor door. Uneasily, Devon peeked around the corner. Most of the furniture was different, one entire wall was papered in a pastel French pattern, and a huge painting hung over the mantel that she had never—

"Oh, God! Oh, my God!"

Instinctively, Raveneau reached for Mouette before Devon went completely mad and dropped her. *"Mon Dieu!* What is the matter with you?"

She was pointing at something in the next room, so he stepped forward to look. On the far wall there was a giant portrait of a fair, delicate, pretty woman.

"That is my mother!" Devon gasped.

Raveneau blinked at the painting. "Perhaps it was done as a memorial."

Devon made a face. "That sounds insane. A portrait that size of my mother—in Temperance's parlor? I might believe it were it anyone but *my* mother, but—"

"But you see, Devon, it is *my* parlor now!" a voice interrupted from the top of the stairs. Two startled faces looked up, and Raveneau braced Devon with his free arm when her knees started to buckle.

"M—Mama?" she choked.

"Dear, didn't Morgan tell you? He said he was going to fetch you."

Deborah came down the steps like a queen, nearly unrecognizable as the drab, pinched woman who had worked night and day in the Linen and Pewter Shop. Devon gaped. Her mother wore a gown of deep rose moire, striped with pale green and white satin, over a pale green petticoat. Emeralds glittered against her white throat; her blond hair was powdered and dressed into an elaborate coiffure. Smiling, she embraced her daughter.

"Come into the parlor, dear, and sit down. You've had a shock." As she led her in, Deborah glanced back quizzically at Raveneau and Mouette. "I don't believe we have met . . . ?"

He grinned raffishly and took a brocade wing chair across from the sofa where they seated themselves. "André Raveneau, madame. This is my daughter, Mouette."

"Oh . . . ?"

Devon managed a crooked smile. "André is my husband, Mama, and Mouette is our daughter."

"Oh?" A pale brow arched as she counted the months perplexedly.

"Mouette was quite premature."

"I see." She didn't, obviously, but managed a smile all the same. "It would seem that we have both done surprising things these past months!"

"I'm *very* happy, Mama."

"Good. I am also. I have some other news that I have been anxious to share. This may be hard for you to comprehend, but I am going to become a mother again in October!"

It took nearly an hour of conversation to unravel

their separate stories and put mother and daughter at ease. Deborah relaxed enough to hold her grand-daughter and gaze into her beguiling little face; then she explained to Devon what had brought her to this house and her position as Nick's wife.

"You shouldn't have worried so about me. I have always been a survivor, even at my most miserable moments. When that redcoat shouted from downstairs and the one who held me looked up, I reached for the candlestick and hit the beast over the head. Since the front of the shop was already in flames, I climbed out the back window, onto a tree, and escaped that way. After it was all over and I hadn't seen you at all, I came here and found that Nick had been in the battle at Fort Griswold. Temperance . . ." Brow furrowed, Deborah stared at her fingers, which worked nerv-ously at Mouette's lace gown. "Temperance apparently feared the worst and panicked. Mary found her in her bed . . . she had taken poison. And, of course, we all shared her belief that Nick was dead. I stayed here, in one of the other bedchambers, and it was midnight be-fore the message came from Groton Bank. He had been wounded and was unconscious for hours—they had taken him for dead. But, thank God, he recov-ered."

The rest of the story was obvious. Devon looked at her mother, so radiantly different from the woman she had known, and wondered if she had loved Nick before the battle. Had unrequited love contributed to her bitterness?

"Tell me," Deborah was saying, "what do you do, M'sieur Raveneau? How did you and Devon meet and fall in love so suddenly? When Morgan came home after Yorktown, he said he had seen Devon and that she was provided for, but that was all he would re-veal."

"Madame, I am the captain of a privateer, the *Black Eagle*. After the battle here, Devon was quite distraught, and I agreed to take her in search of

M'sieur Gadwin. In the meantime . . ." His voice trailed off suggestively.

Deborah's face tightened. "A sea captain. The *Black Eagle*—of course. Oh, *Devon.*"

"Mama! Don't look that way. I am not like you. I love the sea, and I love the *Black Eagle!* I am happy!"

"For now, perhaps."

"Madame, if it will reassure you at all, let me say that my first allegiance is to my wife and my child."

"The sea makes a bewitching mistress, m'sieur."

Raveneau's eyes sharpened, but before he could respond, Zedidiah Nicholson appeared in the doorway. He was as dynamic and wonderful as Devon remembered him, only now his smile seemed wider and more complete. She threw herself into the arms of her old friend, chattering excitedly as she told him the news of her marriage and child. Nick beamed. He wrapped Devon in a bear hug, embraced Raveneau, and insisted on holding Mouette. They all sat down again, coupled on facing sofas, and stories were repeated for Nick's benefit. This time Devon was more candid, admitting that all had not been perfect between her and Raveneau, that Mouette had been born on the island out of wedlock. Raveneau hastened to explain that he had not known of his daughter's existence, but admitted that love and commitment had not come easily to him.

Nick laughed and called for wine. He was remembering the only other time he had seen these two together, on the day of their first meeting. The sparks had flown even then. Was love simply a matter of destiny? Grinning, he slipped an arm around Deborah and chuckled when she blushed. Toasts were proposed —to the new marriages, to Mouette, to the Nicholson baby, who would be born in the fall.

Finally, the conversation turned from personal topics. Devon quizzed her mother and stepfather about the battle and its aftermath. Nick reported that 85 men had been killed and 35 wounded at Fort Griswold. The 30 prisoners had been returned in less than two months, thanks to Nathaniel Shaw's negotiations, but 4 of them died in the meantime. He told bitterly of the death of Colonel Ledyard, commanding officer of the fort, who had been run through with his own sword after he presented it in surrender. Devon chimed in with her heated account of the hours she had spent in the tree over the Burial Ground, watching the traitor who had led the redcoats. Nick informed her that Benedict Arnold had left for England the previous December, though rumor had it that the British thought him less than a hero and society ostracized him and his wife.

Nearly 150 buildings had been burned in New London alone. Nathaniel Shaw's wife, Lucretia, had contracted a fever while nursing sick prisoners and died five months ago. The most shocking piece of news was that Shaw himself had been killed in a hunting accident only a few weeks before, leaving the war-ravaged New London without the leader who had helped the town through its most perilous years.

After two hours of animated conversation, the group quieted. Devon took Mouette and opened her bodice so that the baby could nurse. Nick and Raveneau smoked cigars and talked of General Washington, now at his headquarters at Newburgh, New York, wondering if any more fighting would precede the peace treaty.

As Mouette dozed off, Devon refastened her gown and became conscious of a certain electricity traveling from Raveneau's body to hers. When she looked over at him, his scarred jaw tightened and silver eyes slanted briefly in her direction, sending a delicious fiery thrill down her spine.

"Nick, Mama . . . might we impose and ask you to watch Mouette for a while? I am so anxious to explore New London. I was so overwrought when we came here, and now I feel that I can enjoy seeing familiar places."

"Certainly!" Nick boomed. "We'll be happy to have the little babe all to ourselves, won't we, Debby?"

"Of course. I know you must be wanting to visit the Gadwins and your other friends. Your old friend Mary still works for us, and she should be back for supper. She'll be beside herself with excitement to find you home. And when she sees Mouette!" Deborah smiled at the thought.

Raveneau let Devon lead him out of the house without a question. Her hand was warm and tense in his, her cheeks flushed. The wide-brimmed hat and sunshade were left behind and her hair slipped free of the pins, abundant rose-gold curls gleaming in the late afternoon sun.

Devon felt as nervous as a virgin, blushing more hotly each time she met his flinty, knowing eyes. His very nearness undid her, pulling her like a tantalizing magnet, scattering reason, upsetting the rhythm of her heart, lighting a fire of quicksilver in her blood.

They walked quickly away from the heart of New London. Devon led the way, tugging at Raveneau's hand, urging him to meet the frantic pace she set. He did not make it easy for her, though at least he spared her the torturous ordeal of mock conversation. Later they would talk. Still, his eyes were on her, aware of the effect he had on her, his chiseled mouth quirked slightly with ironic amusement.

His hand was tightening around hers, strong bronzed fingers sending fresh currents of passion over her. She lifted her gown with her free hand as they crossed the Post Hill Road and set out over Little Owl Meadow, past the sawmill. Deep green grass rose up like a river and Devon waded onward, along the edge of Perry's Pond. Finally they reached a thick, sprawling orchard and Raveneau stopped. He pulled Devon around to face him, piercing her with his silver-blade eyes.

"No one ever comes here," she whispered brazenly.

"Madame, what are you saying?"

When his hands touched her sides, they seemed to burn away her gown, scorching the soft flesh where her breasts blossomed. Devon's knees gave way and she swayed against his tall, hard-muscled body. "Please . . ."

He lifted her up and kissed her with a savage tenderness that betrayed his own need. Devon was swallowing hot, aching tears, trembling in his arms. Now it was André who led, half carrying her deep into the orchard where apple blossoms still clung to the trees and the grass was as thick as a feather bed.

Pure love and fiery passion met and blended like snow and sunlight. This was a perfect union, for Devon was free to give herself without shame or anxiety, and André at last expressed his love for her with an eloquence that words could never match. For once, nothing tainted their moments of wild fury, and André was able to reveal the depth of his tenderness.

When at last they were spent, the sun was beginning to set above the trees. Devon turned on her side and pressed her face into the dark mat of hair that covered André's chest. He caressed her tangled curls and the softness of her back, kissing an ear, shoulder, bruised mouth.

Slowly, leisurely, their hands and lips explored until Raveneau hooked her leg over his waist, joining their bodies once more. They moved almost lazily, hips grazing and sliding apart, teasing, savoring each wondrous sensation. They smiled and kissed as they climbed the peak together, then fell in an excruciating blaze of slow motion. Devon put a hand on his buttocks, keeping him joined to her, and closed her eyes as he laughed and kissed her at the same time.

"Are you cold, *petite chatte?*"

"I've never been warmer, but I don't think I will be able to walk," she groaned.

"*Quel dommage.*" Raveneau made a face of mock sympathy.

"Mouette will be hungry . . ."

"Mmm . . . not half as hungry as I have been."

Desire kindled anew as he slipped a hand into her hair and pulled her against his mouth. It was a long, deep kiss, but Devon started in surprise as she felt him stiffen inside her.

"André! I don't believe it! Impossible!"

"My appetite and capacity are both legendary," he murmured, flashing a devilish grin. "Ah, Devon, it has been so long! You'll never know how I have craved this. My restraint has truly been proof of my love for you."

"I still cannot believe it. You love me!" She laughed with delight.

"I do. Yes. Today, when you were dragging me off to ravish me, I knew it more certainly than ever before. There isn't a woman alive who could compare with you." He chuckled as she nibbled hard on his ear. "You are guileless down to your bones, and it's not just youth. I know you will never change."

"*Ravish* you!" she giggled. "Honestly!"

He arched a black brow. "I would say that the word is entirely appropriate!" His hands moved to hold her still. "This is a beautiful place. Would you like to live in this area? Mystic, or Stonington, or perhaps Newport?"

"But what about your island?"

"Devil take that island. I never want to see the place again. I've arranged to free Captain Longheart and his ship—*sans* cargo, of course—on the condition that he picks up Eugénie en route. Also, I wrote a letter this morning asking Cook, Hermann, and Elsa to come staff our new home. I see no reason to leave any more than a handful of servants on the island, and those only to keep the place from rotting away."

"Oh, André, do you mean it? How wonderful! I cannot absorb such news! Elsa! Cook! A house of our own!"

"I thought we might leave Mouette with your

339

mother for a few days and take a short honeymoon along the coast, looking for the ideal spot. I'd like a large place with sunny rooms and a great library, a few dozen acres with woods, and a stable for horses. What do you think?"

"I am numb."

"I only need to be near a good harbor. The privateering business will end with the war, and I want to lay the groundwork for the China trade. I don't plan to sail on every voyage, now that I have other responsibilities, but I'll admit the excitement of it is already in my blood."

Devon stiffened. She could feel the pain of separation even now; the long months alone at home with Mouette, waiting and watching, while Raveneau tasted adventure and explored new oceans and lands.

"Why do you draw away from me?" he whispered, kissing her hair.

Devon pulled free and reached for her chemise, yanking it over her head. "I am cold. We must be getting back. Mouette—"

"Devon, look at me." When she resisted, he gripped her small chin and turned it angrily. "Faithless tears! I never want to see them again. *Mon Dieu!* Do you think so little of me? Do you imagine I could ever leave you behind? I need you, *petite chatte,* and I need our daughter as well. You have already proved to me your seaworthiness. In fact, you have been a true asset to my crew. If you will say yes, I would be honored to count you as one of my officers from this day forward."

She wept and laughed at the same time, while Raveneau dressed. She was still fumbling happily with her own fastenings when he pulled on his boots and stood up.

"Silly chit," he admonished. "Never doubt me again."

With deft expertise, he hooked her gown and watched as she put on her silk slippers. Devon beamed when Raveneau smoothed back her flame-gold curls, purposely neglecting to remove the crumpled leaf that peeked from one side.

"Our daughter awaits," he said sternly, but his lips twitched in a loving smile. Devon stood on tiptoe to kiss her husband, then took his arm and lifted her rumpled skirts as they walked off through the twilight toward New London.

About the Author

Twenty-six-year-old Cynthia Challed Wright interrupted her college education in 1972 to marry her high-school sweetheart, Richard, and follow where the Navy took him. Their daughter, Jennifer, was born in 1973, after which Cynthia decided to redirect her old writing hobby into the creation of a book. She never did return to college, but, to her endless pleasure, she now has the career she dreamed of since childhood.

Cynthia was raised in Sioux City, Iowa, but during the writing of this novel lived in New London, Connecticut. The Wrights currently live in Bremmerton, Washington, where Richard is an officer on a nuclear submarine. Cynthia enjoys antiques, photography, and traveling, but most of all, her husband and her daughter.

Caroline, her first attempt at a full-length novel, was written during spare moments while raising her daughter. Most of Cynthia's family and friends tried to dissuade her from submitting the manuscript to publishers, but, encouraged by Richard, she put it in the mail. Initially it was rejected, but on a spring day she received a phone call from a publishing house that *was* interested. *Caroline* was published in 1977, followed by *Touch the Sun* a year later. Due to the success of these books and an enormous amount of requests from enthusiastic readers, she wrote *Silver Storm*. Cynthia is currently working on her fourth novel.

The bestselling romantic suspense of

Rona Randall

"Rona Randall draws her readers on enticingly ... serving up just what they long for in the way of thrills and chills." —*Publishers Weekly*·

14   NE-8